WHISPERER RISING

CORPSE WHISPERER
THE SERIES

H.R. BOLDWOOD

OLIVERHEBERBOOKS

DISCLAIMER

This work of fiction includes information about various locations in the city of Cincinnati. While the locations exist, in some instances, the author has taken literary license in regard to their layouts and features.

Whisperer Rising is dedicated to Allie Nighthawk fans across the world. You are the air she breathes.

1

—————

VINNY AND HIS
FREAKING DUCT TAPE

Mayor Capshaw made a fine-looking corpse. Everyone said so. After a wake attended by every fat cat in Cincinnati, he was laid to rest at Rose Hill Cemetery, presumably until the Rapture.

But not two weeks later, things changed.

"Hey, be careful!" I yelled. "You scratch that casket, you buy it."

The caretaker scowled as he shifted the backhoe into reverse to make way for the Weller Concrete rep, who slid the hydraulic lift trailer into position and pulled the mayor's vault from its resting place. When the rep finished, he broke the vault's seal with a crowbar and removed the roughly five-hundred-pound lid with the mechanical lift.

At the time of his death, the mayor was under investigation for misappropriation of 300K in city funds. So when a confidential informant insisted that he had been murdered, the DA decided to raise him and get to the bottom of things. Since a raised corpse can't lie, it was perfect timing in a macabre way.

The district attorney's rep and Vinnie Abruzzi, my twenty-one-year-old 'senior' field investigator, hovered beside me, mouths agape, gawking down at the Sunset Bronze Presidential-model coffin. The DA looked a little green around the gills. It wasn't surprising. Exhumations take some getting used to. But Vinny's wide-eyed wonderment materialized every time he watched me use my supernatural skills.

We were professionals, damn it. He needed to look like he'd been in this situation a time or two.

"What are you, a potted plant?" I asked, smacking his shoulder. "Unlock that casket. Let's see what we've got to work with."

Vinnie eyed me through a thatch of gel-infused hair. "No offense, boss, but once the coffin's like, out of the ground, isn't it your baby?"

What a set of balls, this kid.

"Listen up," I snapped. "Today, you're my *assistant*. Now unlock the freaking casket."

"Sure, but the assistant thing, that's temporary, right?"

Vinny's antics frequently made my eye twitch, but he'd come through in the clutch on some big cases. With a steady influx of biters shambling through the city, I had promoted him to fieldwork and taught him the art of zombie remediation—otherwise known as zombie hunting or zombie extermination. Until the ACLU stuck their big fat faces in and said that rotters, having been people once, deserved more respect.

Freaking ACLU.

There are only a handful of corpse whisperers, like me, who can raise the dead—a talent law enforcement appreciates when forensic evidence sucks, or a case grows cold. That's when I wake the deceased, get the necessary information, and lay them back to rest. No muss, no fuss. But I do have rules.

Rule number one: Any corpse I raise must be put down. I won't let them shuffle around until they decompose into puddles of zushi, aka zombie chum. Besides, letting them wander increases the chance they will bite a human, thereby creating another rotter that needs to be put down.

I waved off the DA's rep and the exhumation guys. "You might want to back off in case things go sideways."

I didn't have to ask the guys to move more than once. They took cover behind the newly renovated Kapinski Mausoleum and popped their heads out like meerkats to watch me do my thing. But the DA's rep, Susie Something-or-other, refused to budge. She said she wanted to 'make sure things progressed legally and respectfully.'

Suit yourself, sister.

Vinny swiped specks of concrete dust from the top of the coffin with his sleeve and inserted a universal casket key into the access hole. He gave it a three-quarters twist, and the latch popped.

"Ready, Gel Boy?" I asked.

The Brylcreemed bobblehead nodded.

"Remember, this is the mayor we're raising," I said. "For God's sake, keep your gun holstered. It's broad daylight. We don't need another Elysian Fields fiasco."

Susie Something-or-other frowned. "What happened at Elysian Fields?"

"Nothing," I mumbled.

Vinny's face blazed.

I lifted the casket lid, and the stink of death rose to meet us. Deep in his perpetual rest, the mayor looked peaceful and content, as if he might open his eyes at any moment and be confused by our presence. The dead usually are when I meet them. It was a shame to wake him, but he needed to fill us in on some facts before I returned him to his eternal dirt nap.

"Tie him down," I said.

"Yeah, about that." Vinny balked. "I kind of forgot the ratchet straps at the house."

"Hand to God, kid, you're giving me a blood rush."

We'd started using straps to secure corpses in case they woke up with an attitude. Safety first—that's my motto.

Vinny put his hands on his hips and sighed. "I took the straps out of Nonnie's trunk last week when I went to the car wash. But it's okay. I found a roll of duct tape in her console."

"Duct tape..."

"Yeah. See?" He wound double strips of two-inch tape around the mayor's chest and thighs. "This'll hold."

"It damn well better, MacGyver."

I knelt beside the casket, gathered my thoughts, laid my hands over the deceased mayor, and called on the higher power who gave me this strange and incredible ability. "Eugene Capshaw, in the name of God, I command you to rise."

He moaned, low and long, but refused to open his eyes. Having been dead for two weeks, upon awakening, he would technically be in what I call the flesh-eater stage of undeath. He'd be highly unpredictable, have seventy-five percent of his premortem reflexes, and eat exclusively human or animal flesh and brains. In other words, Cincinnati's worst nightmare.

It was my job to make sure that didn't happen.

Tendrils of brilliant light arced from my fingertips into his body, illuminating his bones and internal organs. The ground beneath me grew hot.

I leaned in close to his ear and whispered a single command. "Awaken."

The mayor shuddered violently and rocked against the sides of his coffin. The soft *ping* of popping adhesive caught my ear. His neck muscles corded as he stretched his lips into an unnaturally wide grin and opened his mouth. The stench of decay grew even stronger. Capshaw's eyes snapped open, over-bright and feverish-looking. Eyes that had no way of making sense of the world around him.

"Mr. Mayor, don't be afraid. My name is Allie Nighthawk. My friends and I have some questions for you."

He bolted upright, bursting through the tape that bound his chest, then swiveled to face me. His cervical vertebrae ground and scraped against each other, creating a hideous nails-on-a-chalkboard sound. Of all the funky things Capshaw could have done next, he twitched.

God, I hate when they twitch.

After uttering a string of curse words, I commenced a silent countdown: *Four, three, two, one...*

The mayor obliterated the tape across his thighs by vaulting from his casket, clocking me in the jaw with his knee, and bulldozing me onto my back. Then he and his massive abs of flab stampeded, flattening me in the dirt.

Stunned, I watched Susie Something-or-other streak toward the cemetery gates like a surface-to-air missile, hurdling headstones and sprinkler heads faster than Lolo Jones. The guys hiding behind the Kapinski Mausoleum scattered as the mayor tore past them. I darted my eyes to Vinny, who had pulled his gun and brought it to bear on the mayor.

"Don't shoot," I shrieked. "Tackle that corpse!"

I hoped Vinny's training would return to him as he sprinted through the tombstones, chasing our runaway rotter. But mostly, I hoped he was faster than an old dead guy and would run his fat ass down. Trapping a mobile meatbag is harder than it looks.

To decommission a zombie, you aim for its brain. That's the only thing that works. But for situations like this, where we need the biter capable of speech, if you can't run it down, you shoot for the torso or legs. If history was any predictor, Vinny had a twenty, maybe twenty-five-percent chance of even hitting the mayor's corpse. And if he did, there was no telling what body part. Worst of all, he'd strafe half the headstones in between.

Peripheral damage. Dollar signs raced through my mind.

I scrambled to my feet, rubbed my aching jaw, and trotted after Vinny. I hadn't gotten far when the distant bellow of my name stopped me in my tracks. A man carrying a briefcase waved at me as he crested the nearest rise, yelling something like peas and Cheez-Its, or cheese and grits. He stumbled to a stop a few tombstones away from me, then bent over, dropped his briefcase, and put his hands on his knees.

"Allie...Nighthawk," he gasped between breaths. "Owner of...American..."

For shit's sake. I'd have been there all day. "American Corpse Management Executives, Inc. Yeah, that's me."

"Really? Who names their...company...ACME, Inc.?"

"I'm busy right now—"

"Cease and desist," he yelled. After straightening up, he huffed and puffed and pulled a piece of paper from the brief-case at his feet. "I have...an injunction. You are hereby ordered...not to raise Mayor Capshaw."

"I have an order, too, pal. The DA's office wants to chat with him."

"His wife objects to...the exhumation. That's her right."

"What? He didn't have any family."

"Probably forgot he was...married. Happens every day. Consider yourself served," he said, thrusting the paper into my hands.

A gunshot popped in the distance.

Damn it, Vinny.

"You're a little late, guy," I said, tossing the paper in the air and massaging my temples, hoping to stave off the headache setting in.

The process server eyed the mayor's empty casket, the pile of shredded duct tape, and the mound of dirt and whistled. "That's something you don't see every day." After wiping sweat from his face, he snatched up his briefcase and started back the way he came, slowly picking his way through the tombstones and flower vases.

I hoped the little turd would trip over one of them.

I CHASED Vinny across the cemetery and reflected that corpse whispering is a wretched way to earn a paycheck. But it's my sole talent in life. It's like I won the suckiest lottery on Earth. Cheap shots about my company's acronym didn't make it easier.

Not so long ago, I'd returned to my hometown, Cincinnati, broke and alone. In what seemed like no time, I accumulated a kinetically-challenged bulldog named Headbutt (the best zombie hunter on earth), a loudmouthed African Grey feather duster named Kulu, an equally loud but loveable blue-haired neighbor, Nonnie Nussbaum, and Vinny, my fledgling intern.

We'd banded together to form ACME, Inc., a company dedicated to managing problematic corpses that refused to stay put. I usually subcontract with the Cincinnati Police Department, but ACME is a private venture. It takes a lot of work to keep this hot mess afloat. Money is tighter than a duck's ass. Unless Nonnie fixes dinner, I live on chicken-flavored dog biscuits and Doritos. The liver-flavored rejects go to Headbutt and Kulu.

Another shot rang out, closer this time. Vinny's screams pierced the air.

I pulled Hawkeye, my new custom 9mm semi-auto, and sprinted toward the commotion, ready for the worst but praying I could subdue the mayor without firing. My heart nearly exploded as I crested a rise and saw Vinny on the ground, pinned beneath the city's late great mayor. Vinny's gun lay several feet away, out of reach. His hands were on the mayor's shoulders, pushing against him, but the mayor had leverage and a good seventy pounds on the kid.

Capshaw's mossy teeth clacked like a wind-up toy. I leveled Hawkeye and put a round in his shoulder. He flinched and glanced at me briefly, but driven by his need to feed, he quickly returned to Vinny's neck. I pulled the trigger again, this time blasting the top of the mayor's head to smithereens.

Well, shit. Capshaw won't be chatting with anyone now.

Vinny rolled the politician's corpse off his chest, then used his sleeves to wipe bone fragments and zushi from his face. He scrambled to his feet and groaned. "Sorry, boss. After I cornered him against the hedges, he rushed me. I tried to wing him but missed, and he tackled me, the big flabby bastard."

"No shit. Cap's going to be furious."

I yanked out my phone with a grunt and decided to leave Cap's call for last. My first call was to advise the caretaker's office that Mayor Capshaw must be reinterred ASAP. Like the ASAPer, the better, given the mess that had just transpired.

A rushed reinterment would be easier said than done. The seal on the mayor's vault was broken when his body was exhumed. The caretaker agreed to recover the mayor's remains, minus most of his skull, then request expedited service from Weller Concrete and, most importantly, to bill the City of Cincinnati.

I sure as hell wasn't paying for this clusterfuck.

One problem down.

Even as I dialed Captain Philip Dorsey at Cincinnati's 51st Precinct, I envisioned the big winding vein on the side of his head turning purple and threatening to blow. I was hoping that Susie Something-or-other had already contacted Cap. If she had, that would have given him a few moments to digest the situation and calm down.

Silly me.

"Damn it, Nighthawk! What the hell—"

"Vinny had him cornered, sir, but—"

"I should have known this was his mess."

Gel Boy blushed as Cap's rant bleated through my phone.

I winced at my next words before they even tumbled from

my mouth. "We'll get our answers another way. I'll see to it myself."

"What a fucking PR disaster. Do you need Rico over there?"

Oh, hell no.

"No, sir. We've got things covered here."

Rico De Palma, my CPD Paranormal Crimes Unit partner, was a great cop, my ride-or-die partner, and a sworn friend who would laugh his ass off at what had just happened. I hoped my assurance would end Cap's tirade, but he hadn't finished dressing me down.

"Didn't you get my messages to abort the raising? I left three of them. I had to send that damn briefcase-carrying suit down there to—"

"No, sir. I...had my hands full."

"Don't interrupt me when I'm yelling at you. It's almost noon. Be in my office at 1:30. The mayor's widow and her attorney want to chat. And next time, check your fucking messages."

"Something isn't right, Cap. The mayor wasn't married, was he? And even if he were, we wouldn't have gotten an exhumation order without contacting the family."

"Thanks for clarifying that, Nighthawk."

The line went dead. Cap can be a sarcastic son of a bitch.

The day's damage done and my ration of shit received, I sent Vinny back to ACME, Inc. Central, my kitchen table, to reconnoiter with Nonnie, the office manager, and brainstorm— if his brain decided to join him.

The only saving grace in all of this was that Jade Chen, the Channel 10 news reporter who stayed on my scent like a Bluetick hound, was on her honeymoon. With any luck, this would be a big news day, and Vinny's escapade wouldn't make us the headline of the day. I wasn't in any rush to face Rico's ridicule either, so I decided to take a drive, shake this mess off, and decompress.

After a series of unintentional twists and turns, I found myself in Cincinnati's oldest neighborhood, at the corner of Tusculum and Sachem Avenues, staring at the gorgeous Victorian-era Painted Ladies. The classic bones and brilliant colors of those homes took me back to a time that was hard to remember but even harder to forget.

I parked at the curb, closed my eyes, and recalled a similar Painted Lady in New Orleans that, for a time, had been my home. And I pictured its owner, the woman whose unparalleled power and infinite grace had never failed me. Believers in The Crescent City knew her as the formidable Hoodoo Queen, Madame Olufemi Okoye. Those closer to her called her Mama Femi.

When she and I conversed in her beloved Creole, I called her *Manman*.

2

THE PAINTED LADY

Everyone in St. Bernard Parish knew Mama's house. Her two-story Victorian, with its wrap-around porch and basketweave sidewalk, sprawled at the foot of Rue de Triumph. We slept in the converted attic space. Mama's tiny bedroom, sectioned off by hand-stitched quilts, was sandwiched between twin dormers—girls on one side, boys on the other. The second floor functioned as a great room. Mama Femi's Restaurant, the best eatery in New Orleans, occupied the entire first floor.

The haint-blue ceiling of the old girl's portico clashed with the brilliant reds and yellows of her clapboard paneling and gingerbread eaves. But choosing a more compatible color for the porch was out of the question. Mama believed that spirits, fearful of water, would see the blue as a river and leave us be.

Nobody understood spirits better than Mama.

Most locals dropped in for dinner or to buy potted herbs from the old Creole woman who fixed the best food this side of the Mississippi. But other folks, conjurers and rootworkers who dabbled in magick sought Mama's more mystical greenhouse offerings.

A sign that read *Kindness and Charity Abound Here* hung

above the entrance to the restaurant. True enough, that sign. The poor and hungry were never turned away. The sight of children in need especially wounded Mama. Over the years, she'd taken in four misfits and strays: Toussaint, Cai, Johnse, and me. By Mama's decree, we all worked shifts in the restaurant after school and in the evenings, washing dishes, mopping floors, chopping vegetables, bussing and waiting tables, and anything else that needed doing. The restaurant served from 5:00 p.m. to 10:00 p.m., six days a week. (Sundays, according to Mama, belonged to God.) A part-time roster of townies rotated in to give us time for homework—the school's and hers. Downtime was a gift.

"Idle hands and all," Mama had said.

Maybe so. But all my life, I've found trouble faster than most people find excuses.

And sometimes, trouble finds me.

***

"Take a seat, Ms. Nighthawk." Principal Durbin ushered me into her office and closed the door behind me with a crisp bang.

I knew that bang. Nothing good ever came from that bang.

The Palladian windows behind her desk looked like my best shot of escape. But it wouldn't be pretty—we were on the third floor. A concrete apron adjacent to the school parking lot sprawled below.

Sucky odds, I mused. I'll probably die, but maybe not. If I land just right—

"Ms. Nighthawk, I asked you to sit."

Trapped like a fly in the principal's web, I plopped into one of two ratty visitor chairs. Air farted from its faded red cushion. Rather than meet Mrs. Durbin's withering gaze, I focused on her engraved desk plaque:

Eloise Durbin, Principal, Crescent City Academy
Molding Young Minds Since 1982

God help me, I thought. I'm about to have my mind molded.

Mama Femi, who had arrived earlier, occupied the chair opposite mine. She had yet to speak. Seventy years old and more round than tall, she made a fierce ally or a dangerous enemy, depending on which side of her good nature you fell. She'd cut me a lot of slack since she'd taken me in, but the daggers in her eyes told me I'd stepped into a steaming pile of shit.

My mother, who shared my talent for raising the dead, died when I was eleven. She and Mama Femi had been inseparable friends for most of their lives. When my dad couldn't handle me anymore, Mama, with her knowledge of the veil between life and death, was the natural choice to be my guardian.

Principal Durbin settled in behind her desk and reviewed my large...who am I kidding, impressively large file. The clock ticked as she held Mama and me in suspense. I picked the stuffing out of my chair cushion through a tear in the corner of the upholstery. Random white puffs accumulated on the floor around me.

The principal leaned forward and peered over the top of my file. "This is your third fight this semester, Ms. Nighthawk. You broke Michael Dever's nose."

"He called me a freak."

"You're sixteen. You should be developing non-conflict resolution strategies at your age."

"What about him?" I snapped. "He verbally assaulted me."

"Mr. Dever is my responsibility. We're talking about you now, and I can't ignore the two previous physical altercations for which you have already been disciplined. This behavior has become a pattern."

Heat rose in my cheeks. "Brian Shoemaker deserved to get

knocked on his as—on his rear end. He hung a sketch of Ann Pettigrew on the bulletin board titled *Fat Annie's Fanny*. It made her cry. And Sherri Whittaker is lucky that all I did was pull her hair after she called me a voodoo-loving-ho-bitch."

"You left her with a two-inch-bald patch, Allie."

"Those kids are bullies."

Mama Femi, hands clasped in her lap, shot me a warning glance and sat forward to speak. Her soft voice and Haitian accent lent substance to her comments.

"Principal Durbin, Allie was only fourteen when her father placed her in my care. Raising her has been hard on him. He struggles to meet her...unique needs. Her father and I wish nothing more than to ease the suffering from her mother's loss and to set her on the straight and narrow pat'."

'Unique needs' was Mama's sanitized way of referring to the demands of a child who could raise the dead. She knew better than to spout the words 'corpse whisperer' and have them become part of my school record. But word got around. Mama had taken in another whisperer before me named Toussaint. He had battled his way through Cresent City Academy, too, but he never bothered to hide his necromancing ways. So by the time I arrived, my legacy was carved in stone.

And as for Mama wanting me to walk the straight and narrow path, she would have been better off wishing for unicorns to fly out of my ass. In our zombie-infested world, paths were never linear—especially for people like me.

Mrs. Durbin settled back in her chair and continued leafing through my file.

"Wit' all due respect," Mama said, "my Allie reacted badly without considering the consequences. But she did not do so in a vacuum. She despises bullies. As do I."

"Mr. Dever's behavior will be addressed. But that is not why we are here today. Ms. Okoye, you've read the school counselor's reports on Allie. She has unresolved anger management issues. And despite the counselor's guidance, she has yet to accept responsibility for cultivating safe and healthy conflict resolution skills."

Mama nodded. "Agreed. And so, we will focus on t'ese—"

Principal Durbin raised her hand. "The safety of our students is our utmost priority—without exception. Ms. Nighthawk, I'm sorry, but this is your third offense. You are hereby suspended for ten days, with a recommendation for expulsion. Your case will be forwarded to the superintendent for consideration. A formal hearing will be set within the next ten days. You will be notified of the date and time of the hearing. You and your guardian, Ms. Okoye, or any other designees of your choice, are entitled to attend." The principal slid from behind her desk and showed us to the door. "I am truly sorry. Word to the wise, Ms. Okoye. If you offer to pay Mr. Dever's associated medical expenses, you may avoid a potential civil suit brought by the boy's parents for damages."

Mama's back stiffened. "As it should be. Allie knows better than to harm any livin' soul."

My stomach bottomed out.

Mama was on the hook for something I'd done, and she didn't have a dime to spare. The four of us kids never went without, but we ate leftovers from the restaurant and wore thrift store clothes. She would struggle to come up with that kind of money.

The mouthy bitch who lives in the back of my brain called me a thoughtless punk.

I hated that she was right.

IT WAS FAR TOO SOON, but I sucked it up and apologized anyway—in Creole yet. "*Mwen ye dezole, Manman.*"

Mama ignored me as she took the long way home, silently

navigating her second-hand mini-van through the late after-noon traffic. Her eyes focused straight ahead. Her breaths were measured and deep, the cadence almost yogic. Maybe she was trying to calm down so she wouldn't kill me, or perhaps she was trying to figure out how to conjure up enough dead presi-dents to pay that loser's medical bills.

I used the drive time to isolate my feelings—an exercise the guidance counselors had taught me.

It didn't take long. Bitter, angry and alone popped right out.

My so-called gift was a matter of genetics, like blue eyes or buckteeth. I never asked for it and never wanted it. Worse, it forced me into an inescapable destiny I would never have chosen for myself. It was the thing that separated me from everyone else—the thing that made me *different*. Kids at school didn't see me as some nerdy, gifted kid who played piano like Mozart or painted frescoes like Raphael. Those kids saw me as a freak. A mutant. Something to be feared.

Maybe they were right.

Not that it mattered.

They would never accept me, regardless of how many stupid parties I attended. Or how many inane extracurricular groups I joined. Or how many times I swallowed my pride when they whispered about me behind my back, just loud enough for me to hear.

Screw that game.

Mama pulled the minivan into our driveway and turned off the engine. It knocked and shimmied several times before a cloud of black smoke belched from the exhaust pipe.

"You need a tune-up," I muttered, checking my watch and feeling another pang of guilt. It was 3:30 on a Friday after-noon. Mama should have been home prepping for the dinner crowd, not getting reamed for my lack of conflict resolution skills.

What a load of crap. I had a shit ton of skills. I just chose not to use them sometimes, which explained a lot, although I doubted Mama would find that a mitigating circumstance.

I raced upstairs, dumped my backpack on my bed, sprinted to the kitchen, and tied on an apron. Thankfully, twenty-year-old Toussaint Le Clerc, with his hair pulled back in a man bun, had taken charge of cooking while Mama and I battled Principal Durbin. The Creole pot roast was already in the oven, the catfish had been cleaned, and the gumbo was a rich, muddy brown. A symphony of delicious smells wafted up my nose.

According to Mama, Toussaint had been a twelve-year-old hellion when he came to live with her. Of the four of us fosters, only he and I shared the power to raise the dead. I asked once how two young whisperers, rare as we were, found their way to her in this big world. Mama had smiled and called it her biggest blessing.

Toussaint side-eyed me as he chopped a mound of okra. Mama must have told him why she had to pick me up at school. I scowled and reached across him for a paring knife. He stopped chopping, pulled a thread-bare kitchen towel from his shoulder, and swatted it at my behind. What happened next was beyond my control, not to mention out of character. It happened so quickly that I couldn't take it back. It was the most mortifying moment of my life.

I giggled.

I never giggle, damn it. When I like a guy, I flirt. Not well, but in my own vaguely indeterminate style. Giggling is for girly girls. And I never flirted with Toussaint. Sure, he was 6'4", hot and ripped, with emerald eyes and sun-kissed waves of brown hair that hung below his shoulders. Every female over twelve forgot to breathe when he walked by. But Mama raised us like brother and sister. I'd never been physically attracted to him... until recently.

I'd begun seeing Toussaint in a new, disquieting light. I found myself staring at him, mentally cataloging his features—

wondering what his lips tasted like and how they would feel touching mine—even more distracting, what it would be like to have his powerful arms wrapped around me.

My face grew warm, and my heart began to pound. I opened my eyes and realized that I'd been parked on Sachem Avenue and daydreaming for the better part of an hour.

Bittersweet daydreams that had left me unsettled.

Over the years, I'd tried to bury thoughts of Toussaint. Memories of him from when we were close, then closer still, and later when we were sworn enemies always left me torn and heartsick.

"He's dead now," I murmured as I pulled into traffic and headed toward Cap's office. "He can't hurt me anymore."

I told myself it didn't matter that I was the one who killed him—killed him in such a way that he could never rise again.

Dead was dead. And that's all that mattered.

3

NOSE FARTS AND GLOBAL EGGPLANT

Thanks to my daydreams and Cincinnati's maze of construction barrels, I arrived at the 51st Precinct right on time, which is to say, ten minutes late—more like fifteen... ish. I hoped that with any luck, the mayor's mystery wife would arrive even later than me.

I'd never had that kind of luck, but it didn't hurt to hope.

After brake-skidding my Lowrider to a stop and parking on the sidewalk, I blew through the precinct doors and blazed across the bullpen faster than a knife fight in a phone booth. The detectives snickered openly and pointed me toward the conference room.

Watching me screw up was their favorite pastime and usually led to a betting pool. I'd been known to take a piece of that action from time to time. Why not? Nobody knew the inside line better than me.

"Don't even think about it," I yelled to Wycowski, the oldest of the gumshoes, who was pointing through the window at my illegally parked Harley. God knew what prank that bunch of overgrown toddlers might cook up.

A passing glance at Rico's desk confirmed he wasn't there.

That was a bad sign. So much for hoping I could slip into the meeting behind him. Any dream of not being last to arrive at Cap's party faded as I rounded the conference room door and saw an officious-looking suit seated on the far side of the table, glowering at me over the top of his horn-rimmed glasses. A twenty-something woman, chest bursting out of her little black Armani dress, sat to his right, ugly-crying her false lashes onto her cheek and smearing her Fuck Me Red lipstick with a tissue. Every bit of the femme fatale from a 40's noir flick.

Puh-leeze.

Someday, I thought, fixing her in a steely glare, I will eat you for lunch, you two-bit, money-grubbing hose bag. But it won't be today, damn it.

I slid into the open chair beside Rico, who played it close to the vest by silently side-eyeing me.

Cap's greeting was less dubious. "Nighthawk, was I in any way unclear about the start time of this meeting?"

"No, sir. Traffic...construction cones..."

Cap closed his eyes and sighed. Who could blame him? That excuse had sounded lame even to me. No doubt we would revisit my tardiness later, but he was on a roll.

"As I was saying when you finally graced us with your presence, Mayor Capshaw's widow, Cricket—"

Cricket Capshaw?

My nose farted, producing an involuntary snort that morphed into a cough when Rico kicked me beneath the table.

A stone-faced Cap continued, "Mrs. Capshaw and her attorney, Eric Burklander of Faust, Schill and Phibbs, are here to discuss this morning's events at Rosehill Cemetery."

While driving in, I'd wondered what she'd been told about the raising. That question was quickly answered.

The grieving widow leaped from her chair and shoved a crimson-shellacked talon at me. "You defiled my husband's grave and blew half his head off! You, you...Cadaver Diver! I'll have the city's ass, the cemetery's ass, the concrete company's ass, your ass, and the underwear that covers it before this is over!"

There may have been some truth in her rant, but the term Cadaver Diver was downright hurtful. Rico's ex-lover, a reporter named Jade Chen, who hated me worse than anal fissures, had cursed me with that moniker a while back, oddly, at the same cemetery. I'd had a few media handles over the years, but Cadaver Diver's the one that stuck.

Go figure.

Rude as she was, at least the gold-digging shrew had shown her hand. I was about to ask for her marriage certificate when Cap slid a copy across the table. Cricket Elizabeth Handley and Eugene Martin Capshaw had been married by Shelby Pickens, a minister of the Church of the… Purple Kush, in Newport, Kentucky, six months earlier.

"Oh, for fuck's sake, you miserable skank." I flung the certificate at the crying Cricket and issued my second snort of the meeting. "What kind of bullshit is this? The Church of the Purple Kush?"

Mrs. Capshaw, as hard as that title was for me to swallow, collapsed into sobs and melted back into her chair. Rico gawked at me in disbelief.

Cap's entire head turned magenta. "Nighthawk, enough!"

I'd prompted many shades of agita from Cap over the years but never full-head magenta. The pulsating-vein-on-the-side-of-his-head kind, sure, but this global eggplant thing had me teetering at the edge of dangerous and unprecedented ground.

Attorney Burklander handed Cricket a tissue, cradled her into his shoulder, then turned to me and blew his stack. "We had an injunction! Do you even know what that is? It's—"

"You were too late!" I snapped. "We had already risen the mayor when your process server showed up."

"No, *we*, lady. *You*." Burklander took off his glasses and folded them into his breast pocket with a smirk. "*You* rose the mayor in direct violation of our injunction order. And *you* will receive a certified copy of our lawsuit in the mail. You will also be scheduled for deposition. Word to the wise, Ms. Nighthawk, we're suing for joint and several liability." He pried Cricket from his chest and snapped his briefcase closed. "I suggest you obtain separate representation."

"Wait, please." Cap rose to his feet. "Detective De Palma, escort Ms. Nighthawk out of the room and close the door behind you, so counsel and I can chat."

"I'm sorry, Captain," Burklander said as he stood and helped Cricket from her chair. "There's no point in further discussion. The city will be served a copy of the complaint. Good day."

As the human cricket turned to leave, her Gucci tote toppled, dumping an appointment card onto the floor.

I covered it with my boot, slid it toward me, then picked it up and handed it back to her. "Here," I mumbled. "You wouldn't want to miss your four o'clock on Tuesday at the...Giggling Goat Day Spa for," I squinted at the handwriting, "goat yoga and a mud bath."

"It's holistic," she huffed.

The grieving widow and her bulldog attorney paraded out of the conference room, smirking. Cricket's stiletto heels clacked across the precinct's worn black and white checkerboard linoleum floor and echoed down the hallway. None of us dared speak until the clacking disappeared.

Cap put his head in his hands and glared at me through splayed fingers.

"What?" I said. "I did what you asked me to do. I raised the mayor."

"I didn't ask you to call her a miserable skank."

"Consider that a freebie."

Rico pushed back from the conference table. "Everything

about that woman stinks. For starters, no one even knew the mayor was married. She came out of left field when we exhumed the body, which means her injunction order was already in the works. And then, the process server just happened to arrive a few minutes too late? No. Not buying it."

"Church of The Purple Kush, my ass," I huffed.

"Burklander's just grandstanding," Cap said. "Trying to drive up the settlement value by lobbing threats. You two dig into this woman's background. I want to know when she takes a shit and where she takes it. Check out that Minister, Shelby Pickens, while you're at it, and that phony-baloney marriage certificate."

Rico and I turned to leave. In fact, I was at his heels, pushing him toward the door, hoping to escape before Cap raised the issues that I was sure would follow.

"Nighthawk, before you leave..."

Please don't ask.

"You told me Vinny cornered the mayor, right?"

Damn it. "Yes."

"That means Vinny was chasing him. Did Vinny fire his gun?"

Double damn it. "He did."

"It's not that you don't excel at racking up damages on your own, but when Vinny's involved, the number always seems to escalate. What did he shoot this time?"

"The, ah...The Kapinski Mausoleum," I muttered.

Cap's magenta complexion, which had slowly been returning to normal, faded to fish-belly white. "No. No, he did not."

"Just a teensy-weensy, tiny graze, sir, on one of its pillars. Hardly took off any cement at all. Easily fixed."

"I already paid to fix that mausoleum once, to the tune of $13K from your backhoe incident in the Cephus McCoy case."

"I'll have Vinny get over there with some spackle and white paint and fix it before anyone notices."

"Any other damages?"

"No, sir."

Truthfully, I had no clue. But I wanted to get the fuck out of there, so I said what he wanted to hear and headed for the door again.

"Nighthawk?"

Triple damn it all to hell.

"I hope your liability insurance is current. Burklander wasn't kidding. It would be best if you got your own attorney. With so many parties involved in this suit, they'll all be looking to dump on you—including the city. Remember, you're still a subcontractor."

My subcontractor status had been the bane of my existence since I started working with CPD. Sure, when the meatbags show up, everyone wants the Corpse Whisperer to mow them down with a 9mm or melt them into blackened zushi with a flamethrower, but nobody wants to ante up. My motto is: If you have to break some eggs to make an omelet, zombie hunting requires a ton more eggs in the form of ammo. And ammo eggs costs money. Stick a crowbar in it, people. Isn't it enough that I *save* the world every stinking day? Should I have to pay for it too?

Ridiculous.

Rico was already behind his computer by the time I reached his desk. The look on my face must have given my mood away.

"Which conversation was it?" he asked. "The damage report from this morning, or whether your liability insurance is paid up."

"Both."

"Sucks to be you," Rico said, pointing to his laptop screen. "I ran Cricket Elizabeth Handley's background. Looks like our widow's been arrested for prostitution, check kiting, blackmail and theft."

"Color me shocked."

"That doesn't mean she murdered him."

"It doesn't mean she didn't."

Rico shrugged. "It also doesn't mean she and the mayor weren't married. He wouldn't be the first old goat to fall for a hot hooker with larceny on her mind. I'll request a certified copy of their marriage license from probate."

"Good start," I said, handing him his phone. "Let's call Doc Blanchard and have him pull up the mayor's COD from his death cert."

Doc Blanchard, the city's Medical Examiner, and I have a love-hate relationship—mostly hate on his part. A couple of raisings went south in his morgue, and he's never let me live it down. I don't know why he's still pissed. He got a new cold storage system out of one of the episodes. The other just required a deep clean of his walk-in cooler by Splatz, the biohazard remediation company I have on retainer.

Rico dialed and put my least favorite ME on speakerphone. "Hey, Doc. De Palma here. Can you—"

"Damn, De Palma, that was some Donnybrook at the cemetery this morning."

"Wasn't it, though?"

"Nighthawk isn't looking to raise anybody I have on ice, is she?"

"No. You're safe."

I smacked Rico's arm, but he kept talking.

"Can you check your records and give me the COD on Mayor Capshaw?"

"No problemo. Only take a minute."

"Perfect." Rico turned to me and mouthed, "Only take a minute," earning him a second smack.

Within seconds, Doc was back on the line. "Natural causes for the win. Looks like your garden variety heart attack, with a few other co-morbidities thrown in. Eugene wasn't exactly the picture of health."

Rico frowned. "No kidding. Did you do an autopsy?"

"Didn't need to. His attending signed off. A Dr. Richard Blasnick."

"Thanks, Doc."

"You bet."

"I'm still not buying this," I said as Rico disconnected.

"Me neither. It's too neat, and that chick's as hinky as a three-dollar bill." He swiveled back to his laptop. "Time to request that marriage license and confirm the minister's credentials with the Secretary of State."

"You go right ahead. I'm outta here."

"Where're you going?"

"I have personal business to attend to. Besides, as Cap likes to remind me, I'm a subcontractor and my work for the day is done."

Rico glanced around to make sure no one was watching and gave me a quick kiss on the lips. "Dinner, your house, six o'clock. Nonnie's cooking?"

"Well, it sure won't be me." I brushed against him and winked as I walked away. "Bring your toothbrush."

Oh, crap. Did I forget to mention that Rico and I are a thing?

4

I'D RATHER HAVE NAPALM

I went full throttle on my way home, breathing the fresh spring air and smiling at the night ahead. Rico and I, after dinner—alone. All night. Sans jammies.

We'd come a long way in a year and a half.

The two of us had formed an unlikely partnership when he roped me into helping him find a missing child. Oil and water had a better shot of gelling than we'd had. Imagine some smug, Oakley-wearing cop banging on your door, demanding your help, then telling you that the entire precinct had drawn straws to see who got stuck working with you.

What a putz.

But day by day and case by case, we settled into a kickass team. Rico had seen me at my best and worst, strongest and weakest, and had never blinked. That's saying something. A little of me goes a long way. There'd always been a spark between us, but he'd been seeing that prissy, pain-in-the-ass reporter, Jade Chen, and I'd been dating an FBI agent named Sean Ferris. The nicest, bravest guy in the world, who wormed his way into my heart just long enough to make me care about him before Toussaint put a bullet in his brain. But the worst part, the part that kept me awake at night, was that in our last moments together, I'd accused Ferris of lying to me.

Guilt will gobble you up and spit out your bones if you let it. I wallowed in it like a dog in mud for a while. And still, Rico didn't blink. When I was ready, I kicked guilt's mangy ass to the curb and moved on with the man who'd saved me more times, and in more ways, than I could count.

Ferris would have approved.

I veered onto Pitty Pat Lane and began to Nonnie-proof my arrival. No matter how many times I replaced the Lowrider's pipes or muffler, the *vroom vroom* of its engine irritated the crap out of her. Nonnie's house sits next to mine. She'd been complaining about my Lowrider since I moved back home. In deference to her sensitive ears, I throttled down. Then once I hit the driveway, I shifted into neutral, key-killed the engine, and cruised to a quiet stop.

The woman does my laundry, cooks my meals, keeps the books for ACME, and bakes the best rugelach in the city. It doesn't kill me to throw her a bone once in a while.

The first thing that hit me when I stepped through the kitchen door was the heavenly smell of fresh-baked bread. The second thing was Headbutt, my eighty-pound bulldog who dove between my legs to go outside and pee on my other neighbor's newly replaced wisteria vine. The Winstels—our mortal enemies. Fuck them and their stupid stinky vine.

I held the door open and tossed Headbutt's rubber ball outside, not because he would chase it (he wouldn't) but because the *throwing of the ball* ritual had become our thing. The ball rolled to a stop. He considered it briefly before turning to me, then back to the ball, and finally shooting me a defiant look before trotting back into the house—leaving me to fetch the ball. The dog's a badass with an attitude problem, and he can take out biters like the Thursday night trash. We're so much alike, it's scary.

Nonnie was seated at the kitchen table with Kulu, my slutty African Grey, perched on her shoulder. Kulu's birdie-bastard love-children, Hyrum and Gertie, roosted on the slats of Nonnie's ladderback chair. They'd flapped and screeched themselves into a frenzy the moment I opened the door and didn't stop until Nonnie handed them each a dog biscuit.

How we had ended up with three biscuit-begging, loud-mouthed peckerheads squatting in our house defied explanation. Initially, Nonnie had tried to float the theory of the immaculate birdception. I didn't know shit about birds, but I knew a big fat lie when I heard one.

Plonked in the middle of the table was a black metal rack holding four ACME file folders labeled: New Cases, Pending Invoices, Bills, and Payments. Without looking, I knew the only folder with anything in it was the bill folder. And as usual, it was overflowing.

A plate of homemade cannoli lured me to the kitchen counter. I swiped one and said, "Rico's coming to dinner tonight, okay?"

"Mr. Rico!" Nonnie's eyes sparkled. "Good. We have plenties. Dallas be here too."

Everyone crawls out of the woodwork when Nonnie cooks. Someday, when Nonnie gets tired of keeping my house and managing my business, she will run off with Rico and feed him rugelach until he blows up and bursts. Those two love each other more than they love me...but in totally and completely different ways.

Dallas Monroe was Nonnie's current main squeeze. Current being the operative word. For a blue-haired biddy with cankles, Nonnie Nussbaum got around. Patient as the day is long, seventy-year-old Dallas made the perfect match for her and her feathered flock.

He owned The Blue Note Lounge on Liberty Street, and when I'd returned to town with nothing but moths in my pockets, he hired me as a combination bartender/ bouncer. The Blue Note was a nice place, with a good crop of regulars. Rico and I stopped there occasionally to wind down after a long hard day.

I hung my jacket on the hook beside the kitchen door and told Nonnie I was going to take a shower and change my clothes before Rico arrived. Unable to resist the call of the cannoli, I reached for the plate a second time.

Nonnie smacked my hand, then swiveled in her chair, and eyeballed me from top to bottom. "Good. No zushi today. Regular basket is fine."

There's a gradation scale when it comes to sorting my laundry. There's everyday dirty, to needs peroxide, to options that sound like they fell off a Waffle House menu: splattered, covered, chunked, and for-the-love-of-God, burn it. Nonnie, who does the sorting, set me up with a fully-contained biohazard basket for the extra juicy stuff.

That kind of love is hard to come by.

VINNY HADN'T CALLED me since I'd ~~bitched him ou~~ constructively criticized him at the cemetery, but I knew he'd be home for dinner. Mostly because he worked for me and couldn't help but be broke, but also because he lived with me. Watching over him was part of a promise I'd made to his dying father Leo.

Rico showed up at 5:30 on the dot, carrying a large bouquet of flowers—musky-smelling, intoxicatingly sweet, almost... sultry. I thought they might be for Nonnie, but after he walked in and kissed her cheek, he turned and handed them to me.

Seriously, dude?

Rico had never given me flowers, and for good reason. I'm not a flowers and candy kind of chick. Small arms ammo, you bet. Flamethrowers, absolutely. God only knows what I'd do for the odd canister of Napalm. But the smell of heavily perfumed flowers repulses me.

"Wow," I said, dutifully admiring the bouquet. "What did I do to deserve these?"

"Call it an impulse buy. A vendor was hawking them at the corner of Madison and Brotherton on my way here, and I thought, why not?"

Because I'd rather have napalm.

I handed them to Nonnie. "Let's put these in a pretty vase and set them in the living room, in front of the picture window."

Nonnie snorted. "Like you have pretty vase." The only gardener I knew examined the star-shaped white blossoms and cocked her head toward Rico. "This Sambac Jasmine. Doesn't grows in Cincinnati. Too colds outside. Very hard to find heres."

Vinny blew through the kitchen door like a hurricane and dropped his Big Gulp coffee mug in the sink.

"Oh, look," I deadpanned. "The reason for my shitty day is home."

Vinny pretended he hadn't heard me. "Man, I'm starved. Manicotti night, right?" Three steps later, and said, "That's not manicotti I'm smelling. What is that?"

"Flowers," Nonnie said, pushing him back out the door toward her house, and telling him to bring back a vase. Not five minutes later, he charged through the door for the second time, handed the vase to Nonnie, and plopped into his seat at the table.

"Let's eat."

Nonnie put the flowers in the vase and ruffled Vinny's hair on her way to the living room. "We waits for Dallas. Then we eat."

Rico chuckled. "Heard you had quite the day at the cemetery, Vinny."

"Yeah. I won't forget the ratchet straps again any time soon."

The kid's face was blazing. Good, I thought. A little humility never hurt anyone.

"That reminds me," I said, sticking my finger in his face. "First thing tomorrow, head back to Rose Hill and touch up that graze mark your bullet left on the Kapinski Mausoleum."

Nonnie fluttered out of the living room, primping, at the sound of a rap on the kitchen door.

Rico, who'd barely gotten past the threshold, welcomed his old friend Dallas inside. "Perfect timing, my man. How are you? It's been a while."

"I'm right as rain, buddy. Wow, is that manicotti and... flowers I smell? Interesting combination," Dallas said, wriggling his nose. "Sorry, I'm late, and I can't stay long. Had to leave the bar in Tiffany's hands until I get back."

"At least she's a great bouncer," I said.

Six-foot-tall Tiffany "Stretch" Swarovski was a half Polish, half Latina, half Niuean former hooker/WWE star I met in jail—a true story—the details aren't important. Tiffany retired recently from wrestling after a back injury and returned to town, looking for a different job. Goodhearted Dallas hired her on as a barback. Not exactly her skill-set, but that was the kind of guy Dallas was.

Dinner conversation was light. It's hard to talk when you're stuffing in double helpings of manicotti, fresh-baked bread, salad, and cannoli. In between bites, Dallas filled us in on plans to add a beach volleyball court at the bar to draw a younger crowd. Nonnie yacked about planting flowers in the mulch bed, and an unusually silent Vinny inhaled his food like a Hoover.

"Thanks for the eats, Nonnie. Gotta grab a shower," he said, sliding out of his chair, headed for the hallway. "I got a date tonight."

Dallas told him to bring his lady friend by the bar—code for 'I'll give you free drinks.'

Rico, the kiss ass, yanked me from my chair to help him wash dishes, so Nonnie could walk her beau outside and smooch him goodnight. When she came back in all moony-eyed, I told her that Rico and I had the kitchen under control and to call it a night. I emphasized it with a gentle shove out the door and said I'd see her in the morning.

The countdown to my night with Rico had commenced. It wasn't until I closed the door behind her that I realized the flowers were still in the living room. I'd intended to send them home with her as both a thank you and a way to get rid of them. A perfect twofer.

After we finished the dishes and put them away, Rico poured us a couple of drinks—my usual Jack Daniel's slushie and his, a Johnny Walker, neat. I let Headbutt out the door for his nightly constitutional and cheered silently as he once again defiled the Winstel's vine. When he trotted back in, I flipped him a chicken flavored treat, patted him on the head, and told him he was a good boy.

Kulu and the baby birdies, who snag more treats than Headbutt, screeched until I tossed them each a liver biscuit, because there are only so many chicken-flavored treats to go around, and frankly, because the flappy bastards are next to useless. Once they finished shrieking their objections, I told them lights out and covered their cage.

Rico and I had assumed our positions on the couch when Vinny tore down the hallway and headed toward the kitchen door. I stopped him and asked whose car he would be using, even though I already knew he'd be taking Nonnie's Pinto wagon. The geriatric menace had to borrow her own car from Vinny when she wanted to go out. And I was fine with that. The city was safer without Nonnie behind the wheel.

Rico arched a brow. "So, who is this mystery woman, Vinny?"

"She's hot. That's all I know. I just met her today at Brassholes."

"The shooting range? How romantic," I said, crossing the living room and reaching for the vase.

Vinny put up his hands. "That's okay. I just met this chick. I wouldn't want to freak her out by bringing her flowers."

Damn. I can't give the things away.

My heart skipped a beat when Vinny closed the door behind him.

Rico pulled me onto his lap and kissed me long and hard. When we came up for air, he took a breath and murmured, "Those flowers really are pungent, aren't they?"

"They smell almost as sweet as you," I said, trying to walk back my ingratitude. "You've never bought me flowers before. Why today?"

He traced my lip with his finger and shrugged. "Something told me you needed them."

After we finished our drinks and necked a little longer, he carried me off to bed. There was no place else either of us wanted to be. The night was warm. My window was open. A soft spring breeze ruffled the curtains and wafted over us. The breeze picked up, and soon, lightning lit the horizon. Thunder rumbled, far away at first, then closer. Rico's rhythmic snores reached my ears.

Despite the peaceful end of the evening, I tossed and turned. Images and conversations from long ago hijacked my thoughts. Surely, my curbside daydream from earlier in the day had been prompted by the sight of the beautiful Victorian manses. But since then, more snippets of my years with Mama in her Painted Lady had scrabbled to the surface.

5

BROKEN PEOPLE,
BROKEN MEMORIES

A maelstrom of memories surfaced within me, still-shots and videos of the smallest, cutest kid in the world. I was seventeen the last time I saw Johnse Renfro, and the memory would always cut like a knife.

Johnse had burst through the screen door in his socks and slid across the hardwood, stopping only when he grabbed hold of the kitchen archway. Dirty shoes stayed on the porch, per Mama. No one who wanted to survive the day tracked mud across Mama's floors.

Johnse, with his buck teeth and wicked stutter, was puny for ten. He chattered like a magpie as he skipped to the counter and snagged a carrot. I ruffled the curly blonde mop on his head because he'd come to expect it. A strip of medical tape bound the bridge of his wire-rimmed glasses. I grinned at the shy kid who stuck to me like gum on the bottom of my shoe.

Johnse giggled, wrapped me from behind in a bear hug, and chirped, "What's up, A-Allie?"

After planting a kiss on top of his head, I gave his butt a playful swat. "Make sure all the tables have napkins and silverware—and check the candles under the chafing dishes, please."

"On it!" he said, tearing out of the kitchen like a munchkin on fire. I stared after him, thinking that Johnse was the best of us. Pure and sweet—an outcast bullied because he was small and stuttered—and because he was different, like me.

I whispered, "I love you, you little shit." But he wasn't there to hear it. He would never hear me say it again.

THUNDER CRACKED as I wiped a tear from the corner of my eye. Damn it, there was a reason I had buried his memory. With everything that was expected of me, raising the dead and putting them back to rest, I'd developed a tolerance to pain. But what happened to Johnse left scars that would never heal.

After several bouts of pillow punching and counting imaginary sheep, I finally gave up trying to stop the memory in midstream. Go ahead and wallow in it, I thought bitterly. It's no less than you deserve.

MAMA HAD CHECKED Johnse's bed around midnight and found him missing. I'd been out all night searching for him. It was early morning, and the grass was wet with dew. There was a glint on the ground ahead. When I moved closer, I discovered a crumpled strip of medical tape and a lens from a pair of glasses. The frames lay nearby, down an embankment, broken and twisted. A body sprawled face down beside them. It was broken and twisted, too. The grass was red. So, very red. I climbed into the ditch, knelt, and reached for the body to turn it over—to see who it is. But something inside tried to stop me.

"You don't want to do that," it taunted. "You'll be sorry."

It was too late. My heart was already broken—I knew, without knowing who it was. I scooped his cold, frail body into my arms, cradled it against me, and screamed. Tears slipped down my face, and I began to sob. "Oh, Johnse. This is all my fault."

For God's sake! Enough already, I mumbled, looking at the clock through a haze of tearsIt was two in the morning. Rico lay beside me, sound asleep, drool slipping from the corner of his mouth. We were still new to sleeping together, but he always seemed so peaceful. Like his conscience was clear, and he didn't have a care in the world.

You can count the nights I've slept well on one hand. Too many ghosts, of one kind or another, come back to haunt me. In some cosmic way, that seemed appropriate for someone who raised the dead for a living. I'd be pissed at me, too, if I were them.

I climbed out of bed and padded to the kitchen for a glass of water. Sitting at the table in the dark, I poured a shot of Jack and tossed it back, hoping Johnse's face would fade away. The best nighttime-crappy-dreams-stink-so-I-need-to-pass-out medicine in the world, unless you thought you drank too much. I didn't think that. I knew I drank too much—another side effect of my glorious, soul-sucking gift.

One more should do it, I thought, sipping a second shot, letting it slip down my throat and settle in my stomach. Yep. That ought to do it, all right.

I climbed back into bed, kissed Rico's cheek, and curled up beside him, hoping my ghosts would let me be. Even with two shots down my gullet, I didn't like the odds. Because sad as it was, Johnse's story hadn't ended there.

Within a week of putting Johnse in the ground, the lines on Mama's face had deepened. She wouldn't speak and refused to eat. Her hands trembled, and she stared, unblinking, into the distance, tears streaming down her face. She was broken. And I was the reason why.

I ran from the house, crying, with the screen door slamming behind me. Mama will get angry. I thought. But then I remembered her fugue and thought even anger would be better than her silence.

All I had was guilt.

I sprinted to Torres Park, not because that's where Johnse was murdered, but because it was where we had pretended to be pirates and dug for fossils in the creek. My lungs burned. My legs ached. But I didn't slow until I ducked under the no-tres-passing chain. There was a full-blood moon. It was peaceful. Best of all, I was alone.

Lying on a picnic table, I watched the night sky and traced the constellations with my finger. *So many stars. Johnse would have loved this.*

"Why did you run away?"

I sat up with a start and realized that Toussaint had followed me.

"Go away."

He sat on the table beside me, wearing a sad smile. "Come home," he said, wrapping his arm around my shoulders. "No one should grieve alone, *Ti Kras Zwazo*."

Little Bird. Mama had nicknamed me the day I'd arrived at her doorstep.

I shooed Toussaint away with a flick of my hand. "I'm fine. Mama needs you. Go home."

"Mama needs us both. But right now, you need me."

"Really." The word came out more harshly than I intended. "And why is that?"

"Because Mama fights her own battle right now. Let me help you."

Toussaint scooted closer, tucked me into his body, and waited for me to open up.

It's exhausting, shutting out the world, not to mention totally futile.

"I don't deserve help," I cried, pushing against him." Johnse is dead because of me!"

Toussaint frowned but held tight. "How so?"

"Mama asked me to keep an eye on him because the other kids picked on him. He was small and such an easy target. Johnse needed me, and I wasn't there to protect him. Now he's dead."

My tears fell despite my resolve. And once they started, they came in rivers.

Toussaint rocked me in his arms and hushed me. "Guilt is an ugly thing, Allie. You could not have prevented Johnse's death any more than you could stop the tide. Evil killed Johnse. You protected him in life. Release him in death. He loved you and would have it no other way."

"What about justice?" I asked, swiping the tears from my cheeks. "Whoever killed him needs to pay."

Toussaint's tone turned grim. "Leave the vengeance to me, Little Bird."

One by one, my muscles relaxed until I melted into him like a second skin. I felt his touch and smelled his scent. He kissed my forehead in a gesture of comfort. I raised my lips to his and kissed him long and hard. He yielded but then gently pulled away.

"No, no, no. You are too young for this. Too young for me." He pushed me away, grabbed my hand, and yanked me to my feet. "Time to go home now. Come."

I stood him toe-to-toe and searched his face. "Tell me you don't feel the same, and I'll stop. But don't say I'm too young for you. Our gift sets us apart from everyone else. I've never been young a day in my life, and neither have you. We are the same, you and me."

He fidgeted and glanced away.

"I love you," I murmured, wrapping myself around him.

"And you love me, too. I see it in your eyes. That's why you looked away, isn't it?"

He hesitated, then held me in his arms and kissed me tenderly. Every nerve ending in my body ignited. "This thing you wish for," he said, "I want, too. But once it's done, it cannot be undone. You understand this?"

"There is no one for me but you," I whispered, brushing my finger along his jawline. "We were made for each other."

Toussaint took me there under the light of a billion stars. My guilt, sorrow, and pain washed away in a fiery wave that, until that moment, I had never known existed. We finished, entwined on the grass, and drifted to sleep, inhaling the intoxicating scent of spring's freshly bloomed jasmine.

The jasmine! I thought, sitting up with a start.

The fragrance of Rico's bouquet had brought back that memory. After all this time, I marveled, I finally understand why the scent sickens me.

Rico was already in the shower, so I let myself dive headfirst into that memory. Ten years had passed since Toussaint and I fell in love. It felt like yesterday, yet it seemed like a lifetime ago.

Toussaint was a different person then—and so was I. He hadn't gone to the dark side yet, and I was too young to realize that there was no one more blind than a woman in love. Nobody could have told me what Toussaint would become. I wouldn't have believed them. I had no concept of how painful it would be when we were forced to go our separate ways. But even then, I knew we wouldn't be over until one of us was dead.

You can overlook a lot of things in your mate—like leaving the toilet seat up or letting milk sit on the counter, but you can't ignore them morphing into a soulless, rotter-raising monster.

I mean, how do *you* spell irreconcilable differences?

The sounds of Nonnie banging around in the kitchen and the mixed aroma of jasmine and frying bacon drifted down the hallway. I realized that I no longer minded the smell of the jasmine. As random as that memory of my night with Toussaint had been, maybe it held some therapeutic value.

After a quick breakfast, I turned down Rico's offer of a ride to work, opting instead to take my Lowrider. We were too new as a couple, and the guys in the office were such toddlers that them seeing me getting out of his Mustang at the butt crack of dawn might give them the vapors.

I knocked softly on Vinny's door and stuck my head into his room to remind him to patch the Kapinski mausoleum, but he wasn't there. Judging by his perfectly made bed (courtesy of Nonnie), he hadn't come home all night.

Exhausted from my midnight stroll down memory lane, I didn't have the energy to get upset about it. Vinny was twenty-one now, and even blind squirrels find acorns once in a while. But if Gel-boy didn't get his raggedy ass over to the cemetery to fix the damage he'd caused, that one-night stand might be his last.

6

THE ERRANDS OF A
CORPSE WHISPERER

By the time I moseyed into the precinct, Rico was engrossed in his computer screen. As I passed his desk, he shot me a distracted wave and mumbled something about Purple Kush.

Oh yeah, I thought, stifling a yawn, the mayor's murder. I need to get on that. But after more coffee—like an IV full of coffee. The breakroom was a quiet place to wait until Rico was ready to share what he'd found online. But more importantly, the breakroom was out of Cap's line of sight. After yesterday's dust-up with the Widow Capshaw, that seemed like a wise choice.

I slumped into a chair, plonked my head on the table, and prayed I wouldn't snore. I needn't have worried. Unwelcome memories of Toussaint raced through my mind like monkeys on meth.

Why am I so preoccupied with him? I wondered. The bastard was dead and gone. I should have been relieved, not reliving the past. No one wants to be reminded of the biggest mistake of their life. And why was I suddenly fixated on

Johnse's death? Maybe I had some of those...what did they call them? Unresolved issues.

I didn't believe in psycho-babble mumbo-jumbo, but tossing back shooters at two in the morning wasn't cutting it, either. Something had to give. Keeping my head down and slogging forward seemed the best way past whatever I was dealing with. Since I wasn't going to get a nap, I poured Rico a coffee and wandered back to his desk to check on him.

An image of the Church of the Purple Kush filled Rico's laptop screen. He gave me a virtual tour of their website, rudimentary as it was—a picture of The Reverend Shelby Pickens preaching from the pulpit to a full house, a donations page (complete with a PayPal link and every other payment method known to man), and a list of contact numbers but not much else.

"I tried to call the reverend," Rico said, taking his coffee from me. "But no one answered. Let's see what the widow's been up to."

While he pulled up Cricket Capshaw's Facebook page, I collapsed into his visitor's chair and speed-dialed Vinny. Straight to stinking voicemail. That knucklehead had a way of irritating the crap out of me, but he didn't usually do it by ducking my calls. I couldn't wait to wrap my hands around his scrawny neck. Bored waiting for Rico to resurface from social media land, I started scrolling on my phone.

"Look, it's the happy couple," Rico said, distracting me with Instagram pictures of Cricket and the mayor's wedding.

A glance was all I could handle. Just looking at that woman's face made my blood pressure rise.

"Glad to see you're on top of this," Cap said as he walked by, carrying a stack of weekly crime reports. "Have you requested the subpoenas for the mayor's life insurance policy and his will yet?"

Rico shook his head. "That's next on the agenda."

"And what about you?" Cap said, nodding to me. "Have you retained counsel yet? You need somebody in your corner for those depositions. They get ugly."

Cap lost me at counsel. Attorneys cost money, and I had none. "Not yet. But I will." After he walked away, I added, "As soon as hell freezes over."

Rico leaned back in his chair and sighed. "We need to check out that church in Newport, but it's going to take me a while to get these subpoenas moving. And I want to call the Secretary of State's office to expedite my request for a copy of the minister's license."

Sitting and waiting has never been my style, so I told Rico I had an errand to run and would circle back in a bit. After hopping on my bike, I headed to Rose Hill Cemetery, hoping to get a bead on Vinny.

"Strike one," I mumbled, pulling into the cemetery's parking lot. Nonnie's Pinto was nowhere to be found. Figuring Vinny could have already come and gone while I was at the precinct, I jogged back to inspect the crypt. The scratch was still there, mocking me. That freaking Kapinski Mausoleum would be the death of me yet.

I tried Vinny a second time, and that call went to voicemail, too. Wondering if he might have gone home, I tried Nonnie. She hadn't seen him and wanted to know where her car was. My answer, "Probably with Vinny," didn't sit well. Nonnie wanted to go to lunch with Lucia Falconi, one of her non-driving, fossilized friends.

Lucia was a chiseler who stashed her money in socks. I knew this because once, when she and Nonnie convinced me to break into Templeman's Funeral Home to raise Lucia's deceased son, she'd had the nerve to haggle over my fee and then paid me from her Bingo sock. We got busted breaking in and were hauled to the station.

We would all have mug shots now if it hadn't been for Rico's schmoozing. It wasn't my finest hour, and if I live to be one hundred, Rico will never let it go. With that in mind, I told Nonnie that Lucia could suck on some lead paint chips. The line went dead.

Rushing back to the precinct was pointless, so I strolled to Mayor Capshaw's plot. No harm in making sure his grave had been restored to its pre-clusterfuck status. I plopped on a memorial bench a few yards away from his marker and made my assessment: The grave had been filled in, and the headstone was back in place. I scored it a win. It's not like I was going to dig him up to make sure his vault was sealed. And if it wasn't, that was on the Weller Concrete rep, anyway.

A thought occurred to me as I wandered back to my bike, so I made a call to an attorney named Tim Andrews, aka Opie, because of his red hair and freckles. I'd used him on a tax issue once—and also when I was arrested for gross abuse of a corpse. A long, ridiculous story. Opie and I got along like anchovies and ice cream, but he was affordable when he agreed to work pro bono. It had been a while since we'd last spoken. I called, hoping time had left him kinder memories of me. Apparently, we needed more time.

"Damn it. I knew I should have changed my number."

"Don't be like that, Opie. I haven't needed you in months."

"It's Tim. And I work for the DA's office now. I can't represent you. You know that, right?"

"You're all I can afford."

"That's because I never charged you. What is it this time?"

"It's...complicated."

"When isn't it, Nighthawk?"

It took some convincing, but Opie agreed to meet me at The Blue Note at five o'clock to discuss the matter in greater detail.

Naturally, I said I was buying. We both knew that was a crock of shit, but when I told him Rico would be there, he caved. He liked Rico. Everybody liked Rico.

I glanced at my watch and was surprised to see it was after eleven. With any luck, Rico was finished shuffling his paperwork. I took off down the road, figuring that if I played my cards right, he might buy me lunch on our way to The Church of the Purple Kush.

7

TAKE ME TO CHURCH

The drive-through at Wendy's wasn't my first choice, but Rico, itching to make headway on the mayor's case, hadn't wanted to stop anywhere.

"Explain this again," I said, balancing a cheeseburger on my lap. "Why are we checking this church out? You requested the marriage certificate and the minister's credentials online. What do you expect to find?"

Rico shrugged. "I want to interview the guy—see how hinky he is—eyeball him face-to-face. And I want to see his reaction when I ask about the mayor's wedding. See if it sets off any alarm bells."

As we shoveled in our food and crossed the bridge into Kentucky, my thoughts wandered back to Vinny.

"Gel-Boy's been MIA since dinner last night," I said, munching a French fry. "I hope this new girl of his isn't an axe murderer."

Rico nearly choked on his spicy chicken sandwich. "He's a twenty-one-year-old horndog, babe. Knowing him, he's shacked up with her somewhere."

There was likely more to the story than that, but I had to

agree. Vinny getting laid was at least story-adjacent. He was a goofball but a good-looking goofball. And when he cranked up the charm, he drew hot chicks like nectar draws bees.

Rico pulled to the curb and parked in front of a gothic-revival-style church on York Street in Newport's historic district. The outside of the building seemed normal enough. Its stone exterior was weathered but clean and free of graffiti. A peaked slate roof gave way to a single spire that jutted from its middle. Two bushy, broad plants bordered a low wooden sign, emblazoned with *The Church of the Purple Kush*, anchored in a mulch bed on the front lawn. The plants were short, distinctly shorter than any pot plants I'd seen, but two-to-one, they were a cannabis strain of one kind or another.

Twin red doors marked entrances to the rectory and the church. The church was locked, so we entered the rectory and were greeted by a short, stout, gray-haired lady whose glasses hung from a chain around her neck. Her eyes were kind, if a little bloodshot, and her far-off smile, as sweet as molasses. Either she was high or...no, wait. She was high.

"Welcome! Welcome!" she said, ushering us into a small anteroom/office in a cove off of the vestibule. A funny, familiar stank filled the air, and my eye spied an empty roach clip in the ashtray on her windowsill. She cracked a casement window behind her desk and doused the air with Renuzit. "We seldom get walk-ins, but praise God! We're pleased as punch you came by. What brings you in today?"

Rico held her gaze as he flashed his perfect smile, reached across the desk, and gently took her hand. There he goes, I thought, quashing an eye roll. My flirty partner had a seductive way with the blue-haired set. He'd perfected it over time with Nonnie.

"We're pleased to be here too, Mrs..."

"Ms. Ms. Amelia Hinkley. But you can call me Amy."

"Amy, I'm Detective Rico De Palma from the Cincinnati

police department. And this is my partner, Allie Nighthawk. We'd like to speak to Reverend Pickens."

Amy's dilated pupils swallowed her eyes. "Detective, is it? I hope there's no trouble," she said, fidgeting with the chain around her neck.

Rico handed her his card with a wink. "No trouble, ma'am. Just a few questions. We won't take much of his time."

"Certainly," she said, sliding out from behind the desk. "Let me get him for you."

When Amy disappeared into the vestibule, I shook my head and whispered, "Have you no shame, man? You're in a House of God."

Rico eyeballed me. "A little flirting never hurt anyone. It got us what we wanted, didn't it?"

A short, skinny dude in his seventies stuck his head in the office and boomed, "Hi, folks! I'm Reverend Shelby Pickens, pastor of The Church of the Purple Kush." He planted himself in the doorway like a statue. "How can I help our law enforcement brethren today?"

Rico introduced us and got down to business. "We need to confirm a few facts about a wedding you officiated last November for Cincinnati's Mayor Eugene Capshaw and Cricket Elizabeth Handley. According to Mrs. Capshaw, they were married here at the church. Is that correct?"

Pickens smiled. "Absolutely. Lovely couple. Why do you ask?"

"You may have heard the mayor passed away a while back. We're gathering some background information for a related investigation."

"Sad, wasn't it?" Pickens said, nodding. "We'll help in any way we can. Why don't I take you on a tour and show you where the ceremony took place? Did you know this building is nearly two hundred years old, Detective? It's survived floods, tornadoes, and even an exceedingly rare earthquake. We couldn't imagine a better home for our congregation than this sturdy old church."

"A tour." Rico's taut smile was more of a grimace. "Why not? But first, can we get copies of the Capshaw's marriage license? Oh, and your minister's license, please?"

Amy pulled the documents, ran the copies at Pickens' request, and handed them to Rico. We'd officially gotten what we came for, and Rico didn't look enthused about the tour, but I'd been chomping at the bit for a look-see since we arrived. Clearly, the reverend only offered the tour in a show of transparency, but we weren't there for the kush. Well, Rico wasn't, anyway. Short of finding a random dead body or some unlikely tidbit relative to the mayor's murder, for the time being, the reverend was in the clear.

We followed Pickens into the hallway and through a door that opened to the church. The nave was spacious, with cathedral ceilings, padded wooden pews, and an intricate mosaic-tiled floor. Par for the course as churches go, I thought, until I looked toward the altar. After shoving my eyeballs back in their sockets, I had to stop myself from yanking out my camera and snapping pics.

What had likely served as a communion rail for a prior congregation held rows and rows of cannabis plants. Track-based grow lights shone down on the kush, illuminating it in all its glory. Prominently perched on the altar was a huge planter with a gold plaque that read, "God's Gift." Rico glanced, mouth agape, from the altar to the reverend and back again.

Pickens smiled proudly. "The Church of the Purple Kush distributes cannabis sacramentally, much like other religions distribute communion wafers. Kentucky's Religious Freedom Restoration Act protects the religious free exercise of all individuals and entities. This crop of lovely plants sustains our entire flock."

Rico stared wide-eyed at the jungle.

"Well," Pickens mumbled after an awkward silence. "It's a very big flock."

"What's God's Gift?" I asked.

"Excellent question, Ms. Nighthawk! God's Gift is an Indica-dominant hybrid strain, 90% Indica, 10% Sativa. It provides a relaxing, full-body high with a dreamy, meditative mental state. It's perfect for our services. Here, let me show you." He jogged to the altar, opened the tabernacle, and pulled out a silver tray mounded with spliffs. "Please, help yourselves," he said, presenting us with the tray.

Rico waved him off. "No thanks, Reverend. I think we're finished here. Thanks for your cooperation and the tour." As he started down the center aisle toward the main entrance, I plucked two joints off the tray, then glanced at Pickens with hopeful eyes. He winked and nodded, so I took a few more—eight, to be exact. I figured, why not? People use gummies, right? This was just a paper-rolled gummy that could be my new nighttime-shitty-dreams-stink-so-I need-to-pass-out medicine. Moral dilemma resolved.

Needless to say, the ability to rationalize is one of my better qualities.

8

A GIGANTIC, STAR-SUCKING HOOVER

After idling in bridge traffic for almost an hour and stopping at the precinct so I could pick up my bike and drop it off at home, Rico and I barely made my five o'clock meeting with Opie. Dallas waved us into The Blue Note from behind the bar and motioned Tiffany "Stretch" Swarovski to bring us menus. Stretch might have looked like a waitress with a towel draped across her shoulder and a pencil tucked behind her ear, but that's where the similarity ended.

Stretch teetered over to us on a pair of leopard-skin stilettos, smacked our menus down on the bar, and tapped them with one of her sparkly, purple talons.

"Well, come on—order. I ain't got all day. I'm cookin' burgers. Say what you want and be done with it."

The fire in her eyes could have burned down Tokyo. Stretch had grit, and she knew every wrestling hold in the book, but she'd never struck me as the customer-service type.

I leaned across the bar and whispered, "I thought Dallas hired you as a barback."

"So did I!" she barked. "Cleaning, and stocking and shit.

Now he's got me waiting tables and cooking. Stick a damn broom up my ass; I'll sweep the fuckin' floor too."

Dallas eyed her over the top of his glasses. "I may be seventy, missy, but my ears work fine. Dial it back, please."

Tiffany harrumphed but took our orders and then stomped toward the kitchen, possibly to spit in our food. When Dallas finished serving a couple at the other end of the bar, he mixed our usuals and took a minute to hang with us. I sipped my Jack Daniel's slushie and asked if Vinny had come in the night before.

"He sure did. Brought in that new gal of his—sweet as can be and as shiny as a new penny. Talk your ear off, though."

"Did he say where they were headed when they left?"

Dallas snorted. "Princess Tiffany got a migraine and went home early. I didn't have time for chit-chat. Why?"

"Nothing important. If you see him, tell him to check in with me."

Opie, who'd slipped into the bar unnoticed, strolled beside me and nodded to the group. "Long time no see, Dallas."

"Well, I'll be!" My favorite bartender clapped Opie on the back. "Good to see you, son. What brings you in?"

"Nighthawk dug herself another legal hole. But since I'm here, how about some boilermakers for me and my friends— one for you, too."

Boilermakers! Those were a blast from the past. I glanced at Harry Delk's favorite stool and silently wished he would put in an appearance. But I knew better. My old partner wasn't around these days—in spirit or in the flesh. I missed that crusty old dinosaur. He'd taught me a lot about having a partner—and being one, too.

Opie shot the breeze with Rico for a bit before he settled into the stool next to mine and asked, "Who'd you piss off this time so bad they want to sue you?"

"Mayor Capshaw's money-grubbing widow."

Rico leaned across me and added, "Nighthawk called her a miserable skank."

"Well, she deserved it!"

"Of course she did," Opie said, tossing a bar nut in his mouth, "Is there anyone who *doesn't* piss you off, Nighthawk?"

That was a fair question. I refused to answer on the grounds it might incriminate me. After filling my ex-attorney in on the facts surrounding the mayor's raising, I mentioned that Cap thought I should have my own attorney.

"He's right about that," Opie said. "I can't represent you since I'm with the DAs office now. I'll try to find you somebody cheap. Let me know when you receive a copy of the complaint. You've only got twenty-eight days to respond."

Dallas arrived with the tray of boilermakers, putting an end to the legal portion of our evening. Opie dropped a shot of Jameson into his Guinness and raised his glass high. "To Harry Delk, a damn fine cop and an even better man."

We followed suit with a toast, "To Harry!" and then downed our drinks in unison.

I stared at his empty stool and lost myself in memories of the time we'd spent working together. That was much easier than dwelling on than his death.

The sound of Vinny's voice pulled me from my reverie. He'd snuck up on the opposite side of Rico and was introducing him to the shiny new penny. Dallas's comparison had been right on. The girl was tall and thin, with delicate features and cat-like green eyes. Her blond hair was spun into one of those casual updos that, no matter how I tried, looked like roadkill on my head. She wore strappy leather sandals that twisted around her calves and a white t-shirt gathered in a knot at her midriff. Her Boho skirt swished gently around her legs as she left Vinny's side and strolled toward me, wearing an enigmatic smile.

When she reached my stool, she took my hands and said, "Hi, you must be Allie. I'm Phoebe."

Fire radiated from her palms into mine, and I froze, thinking the only other person who exuded that kind of heat was me, and only when I raised the dead.

She giggled and whispered, "You feel it, too, don't you? I knew you would the minute I laid eyes on you. I'm psychic."

Dear God, I thought, hoping I hadn't rolled my eyes too loud.

The odds of this chick being a bonafide psychic were nil. Prescience was a gift that, like mine, didn't grow on trees. The only true seer I'd ever known was Mama, and I lived in the world of the supernatural. This girl was either a flake or a con artist.

My money was on con artist.

Somehow, someway, she'd induced heat into her hands to make me think we had some metaphysical connection. The question was, why? The odds of a pretty girl conning Vinny were better than good but thinking she could get over on me was a mistake.

Gel-Boy's eyes flew wide when he spun to look for his girl and found her beside me. He covered the space between us in a heartbeat.

"Nighthawk," he said, wrapping his arm around Scammy-McScammer-Chick, "This is Phoebe Todd, my date from the other night."

"We've met." The flat tone in my voice would have been hard for anyone other than Vinny to miss.

"She's something, isn't she" he said, pride gleaming in his eyes like he'd given birth to her. "I mean, look at her."

"She's something, all right," I said, gliding Phoebe around me and foisting her on Opie. "Tim, this is Vinny's girlfriend, Phoebe. Maybe you two can chat for a bit. I need a minute with Vinny. We won't be long."

I grabbed Vinny's arm and nearly dislocated his shoulder,

yanking him out of earshot of the others. "Where the hell have you been?"

"With Phoebe," he said, rubbing his arm. "Jesus, what the hell did I do?"

"Not a damn thing. But you were supposed to patch the graze mark on the Kapinski Mausoleum. You know, the one your bullet made when you fired at the meatbag mayor."

"Oh, yeah. I'll do it first thing tomorrow. Listen, you have to talk to Phoebe. She's psychic—"

"So she said."

"She is, I swear to God. She said there's like a disturbance in the force or something."

"That's from Star Wars, Vinny."

"Look," he said, leaning close and lowering his voice, "whatever it is, it's huge, and she wants to speak with you about it."

This ought to be good. "Fine. I'll talk to her. But you fix that mausoleum tomorrow before Cap blows a gasket, capiche?"

Vinny agreed, shoved a handful of nuts into his mouth, and motioned me toward his girlfriend, the Oracle of Delphi.

I swiveled toward Opie, thanked him for entertaining Phoebe, and then whisked her to a quiet area across the bar. God only knew what she was about to say, but if it came back to bite me later, privacy would ensure plausible deniability.

"So, Phoebe," I said, attempting a straight face, "how long have you been a psychic?"

"Oh, I was born this way. It's a gift from my mother's side. Vinny said you got your gift from your mother, too."

"My gift?"

"Yeah, you know," she murmured behind her hand, 'the whole raising the dead thing."

"Oh, that one." *That big-mouthed bonehead.*

"Guess we have lots in common, you and me."

"Could be. Vinny said you wanted to talk to me about something."

"I do," she said, lowering her voice and glancing from side to side. "I can't say for sure what's coming 'cause I don't know... exactly, but it's huge, and it's got to do with you. Yeah, and it's dark. Really dark. Like an uprising of the dead kind of stuff. Oh, and a blue McDonald's Filet-O-Fish box."

"A fish box..."

Phoebe giggled. "Sometimes, I'm dead on, and sometimes, I don't even hit the map. On average, I run about sixty/forty."

She paused for a response, but she'd lost me at the fish box.

"My accuracy ratio," she continued. "Sixty percent of my visions come to pass, and the rest don't. It's a Where's Waldo kind of deal, where you have to wade through a bunch of fake Waldos to find the real one. And that Filet-O-Fish box—I might have just been hungry."

I'd been so caught up in her bullshit that I hadn't noticed Vinny and Rico standing alongside me, listening.

"It's true, Nighthawk," Vinny said. "I've seen her in action. She's the real deal."

A stone-faced Rico, gaze fixed in the distance, knew better than to open his mouth.

Swallowing my anger, I plastered a smile across my face, and said, "Nice to meet you, Phoenix. And thanks for sharing your...vision."

"Excuse us, *Phoebe*," Vinny said, correcting me with a glare. "We'll be right back." This time, it was Vinny pulling me aside for a chat. "Jesus, at least get her name right. I vetted her, Nighthawk. She's telling the truth."

"Oh, really? And where did you inquire? Psychics R Us?"

"Seriously? I—"

"It's okay, Vinny." Phoebe walked over and put her hand on his arm. "I'm used to people not believing me. I just hoped that, given what Allie does for a living, she might be more flexible than most."

Rico hooted and tried to cover it with a coughing fit.

"Vinny," I snapped, "speaking of what I do for a living, we need to discuss Rule Number Five later."

"Five? The one about not telling neighbors what you do for a—"

"I said later."

"C'mon, baby, let's have a drink," Phoebe said, guiding Vinny back toward the other side of the bar. After a few steps, she stopped and spun on her heel. "Wanna know why you don't sleep well, Allie?"

Holy shit... "Excuse me?"

"Bad memories are haunting you big time. Your aura is pitch black—there's jet black, then indigo black, and then there's you. You're like a big black hole, sucking in light like a... a gigantic, star-sucking Hoover."

"She gets that a lot," Rico mumbled.

Between our professional relationship and our romance, Rico and I had been spending an awful lot of time together. Maybe my sarcasm was rubbing off on him. I'd circle back to his ill-conceived wisecrack later—after I figured out how grifter girl had known about my memories.

9

INTROSPECTION STINKS

The rocky introduction between Phoebe and me had put a damper on the evening. After another round of drinks and an early dinner, Rico and I scooted out of The Blue Note by eight o'clock. Silence reigned on our ride home, while Rico navigated the rain-slicked streets in his Mustang and I stared out the window, fuming in his passenger seat.

Anger management isn't my strongest skill. There's only so much fury I can swallow before I blow like Vesuvius, and on that night, I felt an extinction-level event coming on. Holding things in is never healthy.

"Ugh." I smacked the dashboard. "The nerve of that hustler, Phoenix, Felicity, whoever."

"Phoebe," Rico corrected, throwing me a side-eye. "Are you sure she's a hustler?"

I glared a hole through his head.

"Well, you're a corpse whisperer. Why can't she be a psychic?"

"For God's sake, forget I brought it up," I said, turning back to the window.

Undeterred, Rico went in for round two.

"What was that shit about you being haunted by your memories?"

"Hello—she's a scammer. Maybe she wanted to sound mystical or something."

"Or...maybe she's psychic."

"Really? You, who thought my power was bullshit when we met, are totally buying her as a psychic?"

Rico reached across and took my hand. "Well, she wasn't wrong. You aren't sleeping well. You're up and down all night. When I got up this morning and noticed the empty Jack bottle in the garbage..."

Oh no, he did not. "Rico, for the love of God, stop while you're ahead."

"Fine," he muttered, dropping my hand. "Message received."

Great. I'd squashed his feelings like a bug, and now I hated myself for it.

It scared me that this chick had a front-row seat to my subconscious. Busting me about my memories was too random to have been a lucky guess. The worst thing about it was that I'd been asking myself the same question: Why didn't I believe her? Why couldn't I at least consider the possibility that she was clairvoyant?

Maybe because if she were the real deal, the only thing more frightening than her vision would be why she was so tuned into me.

The thought made my flesh creep.

Rico let the engine run when he pulled into my driveway. "I'm going to head home tonight. See you tomorrow," he said, waiting for me to climb out. He didn't sound angry; he sounded exhausted—exhausted from trying to figure out when to push things with me and when to leave them be.

I had never opened up about the memories that twisted me into the nutjob I am. Vulnerability, feelings, and emotions, none of that shit was hardcoded into me. And Rico paid the price.

"I'm sorry," I murmured, brushing his stubbled cheek with my hand. "I shouldn't have snapped at you."

For those keeping score, apologizing is another thing I suck at. Those two little words almost never pass my lips.

I waited in the driveway and waved when he reached the street. He didn't wave back. The newbie girlfriend in me wanted to chase after him and scream that I was an idiot. But the emotionally stunted part of me (the vastly larger part) figured a night of space might do us both some good.

None of my flaws were news to Rico. He'd seen me at my best, my worst, and everything in between. Why he hadn't dropped me like a hot glob of zushi was anyone's guess.

HEADBUTT, sprawled across the return air vent, was waiting patiently for me in the kitchen. He waggled and barked, indignant that his evening treats were almost late. The birds' cages were covered, which meant Nonnie had stopped by. A magical smell led me to my oven, where a still-warm casserole awaited. Not a night went by that she didn't leave me dinner. My dirty laundry that had been heaped on the hall floor had been replaced by neatly folded, clean clothes stacked on my bed. Life was good, and Nonnie was magic.

After hanging my shoulder holster on the back of a kitchen chair and opening my mail, I flipped Headbutt his treat. An angry, "What the fuck!" flew out from beneath Kulu's cage cover. Hyrum and Gertie joined the protest by screeching in unison and flapping themselves into a tizzy. I gave them each a biscuit, called them good little peckerheads, then told them to shut the fuck up and re-covered their cages.

When Headbutt pawed the kitchen door to go outside, I

flicked the porch light switch. It didn't come on. When I opened the cabinet to grab a new bulb, he stood stock-still in front of the door, ears pricked, a low growl humming in his throat. He sniffed wildly, then howled and lunged against the door, snarling.

My mouth went dry.

Edging to the kitchen chair, I drew Hawkeye from my holster and whispered, "What you smelling, buddy?"

The door shook and banged against its frame. Something had rammed it from the outside. Headbutt slammed against the door, whining, and gnashing his teeth. The door banged a second time.

"Headbutt, go. Now!" I yelled, pointing through the hallway toward my bedroom. The last thing I wanted was for him to be anywhere near that door when I opened it. But the best rotter hound in the world wasn't eager to let me ace him out of a night's work. "You listen to me," I said, bending down and kissing his muzzle. "No heroics. You stay here and wait for me to call you. Capiche?" He licked my face, and his sad brown eyes held mine a bit longer than usual. He'd understood.

I flung back the door, and that bulldog shot past me like an eighty-pound cannonball.

"Headbutt, no!" I screamed, chasing him into the darkness. Nonnie's yard light flicked on. I watched that disobedient dog run the length of my backyard without stopping until he reached the tool shed. It had been a while since he'd run that far. He lay down with his feet splayed in front of the doorway to the shanty, wheezing like an old fart. "I'll take it from here," I whispered, swiftly rolling him aside. "Thanks for the assist. Now, get on that porch before I sick Nonnie on you." He clambered to his feet and wobbled away. "And no more treats!" I yelled, snapping my focus to the shed. The door hung half-open—no banging and clanging or moaning and groaning coming from inside. The night had grown quiet. Too quiet.

Rotters aren't known for stealthiness, and they don't play hide-and-seek with food sources. That deadhead should have been barreling at me, wearing a napkin and holding a fork. Something was wrong. But Headbutt's nose never lied. I brought Hawkeye to bear, edged through the doorway, and sliced the pie from left to right. Even with Nonnie's yard light on, the inside of the shack was dark as pitch. I crept forward and yanked back a tarp to examine the body-shaped lump beneath it, revealing a fifty-pound bag of peat moss.

"Seriously, Nonnie?" I muttered, kicking the bag. "Why do we need peat moss?"

"Is for Winstel's vine."

"Jesus!" I screamed, tripping over the bag and falling on my face. I rolled to my feet with a grunt and raised Hawkeye.

"Don't shoots!" Nonnie screamed, holding her Zumba-smacking skillet high above her head. "Is me!"

"I could have killed you!" I yelled, lowering my weapon. "Never sneak up on someone with a gun—especially me." My kills at Brasshole's tactical training course usually included at least one cardboard civilian.

Nonnie sighed in relief and lowered her skillet. "Where zumba?"

"I'm not sure there was one," I said. "Something about this was...off."

"But Headbutt smelled zumbas. He is never wrong."

"I know. Maybe someone wanted us to think the intruder was a biter. C'mon," I said, shooing her out of the shed. "I'll check inside my house, then walk you home and check yours. But who or whatever it was is likely gone. Thanks for turning on your yard light. You probably scared him away."

"Thanks for not shootings me," she said, taking my arm and tottering toward my house, lugging her ten-pound cast iron skillet beside her.

Our would-be invader left no sign of his presence and was officially in the wind. A gentle rain fell as Headbutt and I walked Nonnie home, checked her house, and ensured she was locked in for the night.

When my rotter-wrangler and I arrived back home, after checking my own locks, I gave him another treat along with an apology for making up that no-more-treats crap. As thunder rolled in the distance, I pulled out a glass for a double-shot to calm my nerves and remembered that I had drained the last of the Jack the night before, which reminded me that I had snapped at Rico.

Once again, sleep might be a challenge.

Down but not out, I lit one of the reverend's spliffs and soon after decided he had been right. God's Gift delivered a full-body high with a dreamy, meditative mental state. Just what the doctor ordered.

Out of an abundance of caution, I hung Hawkeye on my bedpost, then changed into my jammies and climbed under the covers, making room for Headbutt to join me. He circled a few times, snuggled down, and we lay there together, listening to the night sounds. Lightly medicated or not, every familiar creak of the house sounded different...unnerving. I told myself that I was being an idiot. Although rare, biter break-ins happen, especially to people in my profession. It had been months since the last incident at my house. I'd gotten lulled into a false sense of security, and under the circumstances, it would be natural to feel violated. My safe space didn't feel as safe as it had just hours earlier.

Little Allie, the voice in the back of my brain told me to stop spouting psycho-babble words from *Cosmo* (i.e., violated) and call the feeling what it really was. Fear.

Fear in a corpse whisperer is a dangerous thing. It could get me and the people I work with killed. My partners pay a hefty price, I thought, as images of Rico and Harry cycled through my mind in a continuous loop.

Maybe it was my case of the jitters or the rambling of my too-tired brain, but when I closed my eyes, I spiraled down an obsidian hole, where at the bottom, I stumbled upon the worst memory of my life. The memory that, on sleepless nights like this, I always see.

10

"I'LL TAKE SHITTY MEMORIES
AND ZUSHI FOR $500"

When cops dig into a case, they can lose all sense of time. So, when Harry didn't show up at The Blue Note that night, it wasn't unusual. I was working at the bar part-time in those days, and I called him around nine to make sure he was okay.

Harry said he'd brought home the case file we'd been working on and that he'd identified the killer, but he refused to go into detail over the phone. Although he still had some 'i's to dot and 't's to cross, given his findings, Harry believed our circle of trust had grown smaller. We agreed to meet in the bar parking lot at 2:30, closing time, to form a new circle—a circle of two.

But closing time had come and gone. He should have been there waiting for me. Something felt wrong—the kind of wrong that ached in your bones. I dialed his number, and the call went straight to voicemail.

Harry needs you, Little Allie screamed.

My hands burned like ice as I kicked the Harley into gear and tore up the road, cursing myself for forgetting to wear gloves in the bitter January cold.

I'd been to Harry's house once before, but his exact address escaped me. The street signs blurred as I whizzed by, but one intersection looked familiar. I turned the corner, cut my engine, and coasted to a stop in front of his driveway. An unnatural silence draped his house. My gut churned. Something was horribly wrong.

A light was on inside. His curtains were drawn. It didn't matter that nothing seemed out of place as I crept to his porch through the darkness. That false sense of security could get me killed. The voice in the back of my brain was screaming for me to leave. But no matter how ugly it might be, I could never turn my back on Harry and walk away.

When I grabbed the knob, the door to his house popped open. I crossed the threshold, gun drawn, and whispered his name. No response, so I shouted, "Harry!"

A small, "Help me," bleated from of the darkness.

Harry's bird.

Moving deeper into the house, I cleared the rooms one at time. Even with the light from my cell phone, trusting my eyes was risky. Shadows from the streetlight danced across the walls. So I used all of my senses, feeling the rooms, trying to absorb their energy. Smelling normal everyday things like the sweet scent of bird millet and freshly cooked marinara. But there was also the pong of gunpowder and oil.

Please, God. Let Harry have been cleaning his .38.

When I rounded the corner into his kitchen, a sickening metallic odor hit my nose. I slipped and fell, landing in something sticky. Pulling myself up along the wall, I staggered to my feet, and with the flick of a switch, I saw Harry, crumpled on the floor. Half his head was missing. Some of his gray matter had clung to the crevices of acoustic-tile ceiling, the rest was...

MY EYES SNAPPED open in the darkness. The memory of Harry's mutilated corpse had receded into whatever fucked-up corner of my brain it called home and had been replaced by the reek of decay.

Headbutt was no longer lying beside me, but his frantic growls and snarls let me know he was alive. Teeth clacked in my left ear. *Crap, my gun's on that bedpost. How many of them are there?* I whirled off the bed to my right. The biter lunged after me, but something stopped it cold. Unless I missed my guess, it was my zombie-hunting, four-legged cannonball.

A chorus of grunts and growls filled the air as Headbutt shook that rotter like a rag doll and brought it to its knees. I scrambled back across the bed and flipped on the light, then pulled Hawkeye from his holster and squeezed off a round. Booyah! Nailed it right between the eyeballs.

The deadhead dropped like a rock.

Headbutt and I and most everything else in my bedroom were bathed in zushi. The only way we could clear the house was to move from room to room, tracking bloody biter bits through the entire first floor and the second-floor dormer.

Call it an occupational hazard, but damn, I hate when that happens.

I also hate when I miss something. None of my doors or windows had been compromised. That didn't make sense. Rotters aren't the B&E type; they're opportunistic. If you wandered by one late at night in a dark, secluded area, you were a prime target. The takeaway: A deadhead didn't wander into my house by chance.

When I retraced my route and still didn't find an entry point, I remembered the one place I hadn't checked—the basement. Sure enough, one of the casement windows had been removed, not broken, or smashed—removed. My biter buddy hadn't possessed that kind of dexterity. He'd had help of the living kind.

With Toussaint gone, the list of obvious suspects was small, as in non-existent. The list of not-so-obvious suspects was also empty. We had a player to be named later, which didn't sit well with me. Neither did the mess slathered from one end of my house to the other.

I picked up my phone, looked at the time, and thought, what the hell. I pay him more than enough.

"Jimmy, it's Nighthawk." I held the phone away from my ear and waited for him to stop yelling. "Who cares if it's 6:00 a.m.? It's a Code One, dude. My house is covered in zushi. I need it done today." I yawned and nodded. "Yeah, finished today. You got the key. I'll tell Nonnie you're coming. Over and out."

Splatz is the best biohazard remediation service around, even if Jimmy sometimes forgets that I put him on the map. He grouses about turnaround expectations, and yet, he never fails to meet them.

The light in Nonnie's kitchen was on, so I called to let her know what had happened and not to be worried if she saw the Splatz team going in and out. After she finished hyperventilating, I told her to work at her house so she wouldn't accidentally clobber one of Jimmy's guys with her skillet.

Rico called as I was getting dressed. I figured he wanted to apologize, so I answered with an expectant voice, ready to forgive and forget. But that was the last thing on his mind.

"Turn on the TV, Nighthawk, Channel 10. There're deadheads on the streets."

"So? There's always a few—"

"More than a few. And they're congregating. Cap wants you at the station pronto."

11

DESTINY'S A BITCH

I showered, scrubbed, and dressed in a record-breaking fifteen minutes. More importantly, I reloaded and holstered Hawkeye, crammed extra mags into my pockets, added a Ka-Bar knife to my belt sheath, slapped on my Glock 26 ankle gun, and slid a blade into my boot. On biter calls, you either go big or go home dead.

Screaming down I-71 on my bike, I couldn't shake the feeling that something was dangerously wrong and that the increased number of rotters was just one piece of a bigger puzzle. Because, whether I liked it or not, there was something off with me, too.

My prickly memories and daydreams about Mama, Johnse, and Toussaint were entirely out of character. And I'd buried the experience of finding Harry's body so deep I didn't think it would ever resurface. I had been so scattered since the biter attack that I hadn't had time to ponder why my past was haunting me. Now that I had a moment, I still couldn't figure it out, but Mama might know. I made a mental note to call her.

. . .

For the first time, Phoebe's premonition gnawed at my gut. She'd seen something 'dark' and 'huge' that involved me and an uprising of the undead. The convergence of these oddities was uncanny, but it still didn't make me a believer.

I've never had qualms about what I do for a living. This gift came from God, and He'd given it to me for a reason. If Phoebe's vision was on the nose, then maybe she was delivering a warning. Then again, there was the Filet-O-Fish box, so maybe she was full of shit.

Exiting south on Erie, I noticed a few rotters shambling down the street. Seeing deadheads in the daytime was unusual, especially out in the open. More concerning was that these stragglers seemed to stack up at street corners, almost as if they were meeting.

Biters aren't social butterflies. They don't chat or go for walks and take in the flowers together. If they didn't bump into each other, there'd be no interaction between them at all. So why didn't they keep shambling on their merry ways?

Rico was right. They weren't randomly converging; they were congregating.

Patrol officers herded people off the sidewalks to their homes, cars, or the few shops that were open and began roping off the streets with police tape. What would come next usually happened in the dead of night, out of the public eye, when civilians were tucked safely into bed. And that was a good thing because watching biters get taken out with headshots is disconcerting to the average person. Hell, it wasn't pleasant to do, either, but somebody had to step up. More often than not, it was me. A simple thank you, health insurance, and 60K a year would have been sufficient.

A rotter, not thirty feet away, spotted me as I pulled into the parking lot of the precinct. I turned off my bike and removed my helmet, keeping the biter in my line of sight. The damn thing rushed me. That deadhead had wheels, too—it had to be a freshie. I pulled Hawkeye, brought him to bear, and fired a single round, air conditioning its brain. Another biter rounded the corner of the precinct as I jogged toward the entrance.

Rico pushed the double glass doors open from inside. After I slipped past him, he slammed them closed behind me. "Best go condition one," he said, peering through the doors and scanning the lot.

"You know me. I'm always cocked and locked."

There wasn't a single cop in the bullpen. Even at an early hour, the guys were in and out. The emptiness was mildly disconcerting. I jumped at the sound of a slamming door.

Cap had exited the armory, dressed head to toe in tactical gear, and was headed our way with an armload of suits. He tossed me a vest and said, "This was the smallest one I could find."

"Where is everybody?" I asked, tossing the suit aside.

"Working the streets, where we'll be as soon as you and Rico suit up."

Tac gear? You've got to be kidding. "Oh, come on. How many biters are we talking about?"

"I didn't get a head count," Cap barked from behind his visor.

"All right, in round numbers, then," I snapped. "Ten? Twenty?"

Rico and Cap stared at each other in silence.

"For God's sake," I said, throwing up my hands. "What's the sitrep? I just got off the expressway, and there weren't any flying down the high-speed lane."

Rico strapped on his Kevlar and filled me in as best he could. "Biter reports started coming in about 5:00 a.m. Calls are flooding our phone lines. The choppers are up," he said, glancing to the sky through the doors. "At first, there didn't seem to be a pattern to their movements. I mean, with rotters, when *is* there a pattern, right? But copter reports confirm they're moving in from every direction."

"Okay," I said. "So, theoretically, where's ground zero?"

"It's here, Nighthawk. At the 51st."

Movement caught my eye through the door. Wycowski, the oldest detective in the squad, was tearing across the parking lot with three freshies nipping at his heels. He had his 9mm in hand, but instead of firing, he focused on sprinting away from them. Turning around to fire would have slowed him down, and he wasn't the fastest cop to start with. He was right. Running was his best play.

"Open the door," Wycowski screamed through the glass. "Open the fucking door. *Now!*"

Cap and I moved into position and covered Rico as he opened the door far enough to let Wycowski dive through. The old fart made it to the glass and got everything inside except the bottom half of his right leg. He shrieked as one of the deadheads dropped to the ground, sunk its teeth into his calf, and ripped off a chunk of meat. Rico reached down and pulled Wycowski through the opening by his belt but then stumbled over the detective's outstretched body and fell.

There had only been three rotters chasing Wycowski. Within seconds, that number doubled. More rotters arrived, piling against the glass, trying to push through the doorway. Cap and I aimed through the opening, squeezing off round after round.

"10-22," Cap screamed into his throat mic. "Repeat, 10-22. Officer down! Officer down, 51st precinct!"

I'd shoved extra mags into my pockets. With any luck, Cap had done the same. But the situation required some strategy— we couldn't simply blast through the glass at the deadheads. Those doors were the only thing keeping them at bay. If we'd been outside, we might have been able to shoot our way clear.

As it was, we were sitting ducks, hoping the glass would hold against the force of the multiplying biters.

Wycowski hobbled past me, gasping, Glock in hand, and collapsed on the floor. Rico scrambled to his feet and leveraged his body against the glass door, pushing the biters back out. When the doors finally engaged, he cranked over the mortise locks—a smart move that didn't make much difference. The biters banged their heads against the glass, over and over, spraying decomp across the glass. They pounded their heads in unison against the doors, shaking them loose from their frames.

Sweet Jesus, I thought, the damn things are problem-solving.

Tiny fractures spidered across the glass. The three of us inched backward, shoulder to shoulder, and leveled our guns at the doors. Sirens blared in the distance.

How long 'til they get here?

A massive crack shot across the glass, and the biters pushed inside. Rico tucked and rolled away, then sprinted behind one of the desks for cover.

"Headshots only," I shouted above the din. "Make 'em count."

"Got it!" Wyco said, pulling himself to a seated position and leaning against the wall. He gave me a thumbs up, then slapped in a fresh mag, racked his slide, and rejoined the fight.

Our semi-autos could take out a lot of biters, but once the mags ran out, we'd be toast.

Hawkeye's magazine held ten plus one in the pipe, which meant that every eleven shots, I'd have to pause to change mags. The same with my ankle gun. Being unprotected and out in the open made the reloading process dangerous.

Without taking my eyes from the horde, I stepped behind a desk, patted my pocket, and fished out a fresh mag. A rotter wandered in through what was left of the door and lumbered forward, shuffling through the pack, swiveling its head from right to left as if searching for something. The bastard was moldered and stunk of decomp, a corpsicle, most likely.

I ejected my old mag and slapped in a new one, producing an audible 'click'. The rotter swiveled its head in my direction and stopped when our eyes locked. Its gaze mesmerized me. Everything else in the room, the blood and guts, the noise and confusion, all faded into a dark, empty void.

The deadhead smirked and spoke to me telepathically. "Destiny's a bitch, *Ti Kras Zwazo*. And she wants her pound of flesh, now."

My blood curdled.

Only two people knew my Creole nickname. And one of them was dead.

A haze fell over me. Thoughts scattered; vision blurred. I was fully awake and aware but not inside the precinct anymore. I was outside, shambling up an unnamed road.

My reflection in a street-side store window was barely recognizable. Rotting skin bubbled and draped from my bones. Tendons and muscles bulged through the rot, glistening in the sunlight. A hunger burned inside me unlike any I'd ever felt before.

I didn't love. I didn't want. I didn't feel.

I needed to feed—like the others.

I led the horde as we shuffled through the streets, killing and consuming the flesh and brains of every living creature we found. I sank my teeth into a man's neck as he ran from me. He screamed, wrenched his body from my mouth, and spun toward me with an incredulous look in his eyes.

"Nighthawk!" he screamed. "Allie, wake up. It's Rico. Talk to me, baby."

The haze lifted, and I was back in the precinct, lying in Rico's arms.

What the hell?

"It's all right," Rico murmured, stroking my hair. "It's over now. You're safe."

I searched his face, desperate for a sign that I hadn't bitten his neck and condemned him to life as a soulless, shuffling monster. His smile swam before me, and that was enough.

Then, the world went black.

12

TOO MUCH TO PROCESS

I awoke to find Rico asleep in the chair beside me, with his feet propped up on the side rail of my hospital bed. Elephants were tap-dancing inside my skull. Running my fingers across the back of my head, I discovered a massive goose egg.

The wall clock might have read 2:15, but the numbers were blurred. I looked away, thinking that it didn't matter anyway because I had no idea whether it was a.m. or p.m. An IV, inserted into my arm, delivered two bags of clear fluids, and strategically-placed electrodes transmitted my vitals to a beeping monitor that assured me I was still alive.

Rico stirred, then sat up with a yawn, and glanced over at me. "Well, there she is! How you feeling?"

"Like I've got the mother of all hangovers."

He threw off his blanket, climbed out of the chair, and stood beside my bed.

"They ran a CT scan. You don't have any skull fractures, but the doctor says you have a concussion. Looks like you need a fresh one of these," he said, repositioning a half-melted icebag at the base of my skull.

"Care to fill me in on what happened?" I asked.

"What's the last thing you remember?"

"The biters breaking the glass."

I suck at lying, and no one has ever accused me of sugar-coating the truth. I may not have known exactly how I came to be in this room, but I remembered everything that led up to it—including the telepathic message from a long-dead Toussaint. I didn't have the energy to confront that slice of reality yet. Dealing with that would have to wait until I was alone. For now, Rico could do the talking.

"The short version is you stopped shooting," he said, unable to meet my gaze. "One minute you were sending a shit ton of lead downrange, and the next, you weren't."

"Why?" I asked, rubbing my hands across my face. "Why did I stop shooting?"

"I was hoping you'd tell me. A biter zeroed in on you, and you didn't even blink. You just stood there, waiting to...get bitten."

I stared at Rico like he'd lost his mind.

"It's true," he said. "It was going for your neck, Nighthawk. I put it in my sights, but I ran out of ammo, so I shoved you out of the way and tackled the damn thing. You fell when I shoved you, and you slammed your head into a desk. Sorry about that. Oh," he said, flashing my Ka-Bar knife. "I pulled this out of your sheath and took the bastard down."

"Really?" I chuckled but winced from the pain. "I don't think I've ever seen you use a knife on a rotter."

"Well, it won't happen again if I can help it." He wrinkled his nose and put the knife back in my belt sheath with my clothes in the closet. "That was way too up close and personal for me."

Holy shit! I bolted upright, instantly regretting it. "How's Wycowski?"

"Scared shitless. Hoping you can do something for him, like you did for Jade."

"Jesus," I said, feeling the weight of the world on my shoulders.

After I killed Toussaint, we had found the antidote for the most recent Z-virus strain and forwarded it to the FDA for testing and development. But it wasn't available on the market yet.

"Look," I said, "I can't promise it'll work because we don't know which strain of the virus is in his bloodstream, but there's still a vial of Jade's old medicine in the hall closet on the shelf above the sheets. Grab it and tell him to take it—"

"At the full moon. Yeah. I remember."

A sharp reminder that he and Jade Chen had a history. Rico had hated me hard when his former girlfriend was bitten. He'd blamed me, saying that if I'd given her the information she'd needed to write her zombie expose piece, she wouldn't have had to put herself in danger. He'd been so angry that he'd almost requested a transfer. She would have died if not for Mama's tonic. I'd long since taught her how to make the medicine herself.

What a difference the last year had made in our lives.

"That tonic is all we've got, "I said. "I'll call Dr. Sheridan at the European CDC to let him know about Wycowski. His doctor needs to send Sheridan the lab reports and a supply of Wyco's blood for testing potential antidotes. We'll go from there. If the tonic we have works, I can make it for Wyco myself. If not, I'll get with Mama and see what other magick she has up her sleeve." I made a note to call Jimmy at Splatz to have the zushi residue from my house collected and sent to the ECDC, too. Both these biters seemed to demonstrate cognitive ability.

A winded Nonnie waddled into the room, carrying an over-loaded shopping bag. She plopped it on the floor beside Rico, then launched herself across the bed, hugging me. "Thank goodness Mr. Rico let me know you here. What happened?"

I glared at my loose-lipped partner, who shrugged in response.

"It's just a bump on my head, Nonnie. I'll be fine."

She trundled back to the bag and pulled out a plate of rugelach and a half-gallon of milk, her homeopathic cure for everything from a lousy day to the death of a loved one. "Eats. You need to eats for strength."

"Thanks. Maybe later," I said, feeling queasy. "Help yourself, dude," I said, fluttering a hand at Rico.

Nonnie settled into the recliner while Rico scouted out a smaller folding chair and pulled it alongside the bed. He flipped on the TV and watched *The Maltese Falcon* while munching on Nonnie's pastry and drinking milk from a plastic cup. I'd started dozing off when the doctor paid a visit.

"Ms. Nighthawk, I'm Dr. Cleary. How are you feeling?"

"I've got a wicked headache," I said, fingering the knot on my skull. "And I'm bit woozy. Nothing some Tylenol won't fix."

"More than likely, but we're going to keep you for observation—to rule out brain swelling or a slow bleed. We'll send you home in the morning."

"I don't think so," I said, swinging my legs over the side of the bed. Everything blurred, and the room began to swim. "Maybe a few hours' rest wouldn't kill me," I muttered, lying back.

THE NEXT TIME I opened my eyes, everyone was gone. My headache had dulled to a steady thud. The room was warm and comfortable, and I was glad to have some time to myself. To remember and process everything that had happened. Easier said than done.

Where to begin?

Impossible as it seemed, the biter's telepathic message could only have been sent by Toussaint. But I'd killed the man —watched him get sucked into an industrial fan blade and chopped into an unrecognizable bucket of zushi. His brain had been liquified. There wasn't a necromancer on earth who could have brought him back from the dead.

That left only one other possibility: Somehow, his soul had crossed the void. In all of my battles with Toussaint, that eventuality had never occurred to me, and I had no idea how to deal with it. The spirit world was Mama's domain. I would need her guidance more than ever.

Toussaint's telepathic message had been ridiculously campy. He'd always been a theatrical son-of-a-bitch, and I couldn't imagine a more dramatic way for him to announce his return. Hopefully, with Mama's help, he and I would simply play another game of cat and mouse.

There was, however, the matter of my vision. Watching myself lead a throng of biters on a deadly rampage across the city had been unnerving. But there, safe and sound in the hospital, I saw it for the empty, ugly threat it was. If bitten, I would never allow myself to turn, and Toussaint knew it.

A mind-bending thought struck me. Toussaint the Spirit— Toussaint 2.0—had not only crossed the veil to haunt me, he had manipulated my thoughts by forcing my daydreams and memories to surface.

Had he nudged Rico into buying that jasmine bouquet, knowing the smell would remind me of the worst night of my life—the night I'd fallen in love with an evil man whom I was destined to kill?

My God, I thought with a shiver, how do I fight a demon who's capable of thought control?

13

CAN IT, SID!

Vinny picked me up from the hospital at 1:00 p.m. the next day. Doctors always take forever to set you free. I'd been packed, dressed, and ready to go since dawn. It was nice to think that my medical stability had something to do with it, but the nurses' petition to release me probably carried the day. After all, there was only so much whining and bitching a person could handle.

I'd reached my limit by midnight.

My discharge instructions included taking Tylenol, using ice packs, resting, and avoiding driving, as well as making major decisions, and operating heavy equipment for the next twenty-four to forty-eight hours, which loosely translated to: Until I drove myself or Nonnie up the wall.

"How're you feeling?" Vinny asked as I stepped out of the wheelchair at the hospital's entrance and ducked into Nonnie's Pinto.

"I'll be fine. But I want you to go to Home Depot and buy four Ring cameras, one for each side of the house, and install them."

"You want a system that sends out an alarm?"

"God, no. Cameras are enough, but I want the 4K pro model with high-res."

All I could picture was Nonnie forgetting the alarm code and having the police show up at my house three times a day. The neighbors, what the hell, the entire HOA already hated me — and not without cause. They'd seen some wild shit go down at my place over the years. The arrival of the freaking Splatz truck in my driveway was like a flashing neon sign.

The last thing I needed was another petition to oust me from the neighborhood. The situation called for simple, covert surveillance that would allow me to identify and dispatch deadheads with the least amount of zushi possible.

Nonnie had bowls of chicken and rice soup waiting for Vinny and me at the house. After she watched me eat, she led me down the hallway to my bedroom where she'd left a vase of fresh roses, straight from her garden, on my bedside table. She had turned down the bed, fluffed my pillows, and drawn the blinds. When I climbed into bed, she scrambled in beside me, took my hand, and said a short prayer.

"Nonnie," I begged, "please get out of my bed."

"Bah! Fine." She hopped to the floor with a sigh and tucked me back in. "I leavings anyway. Lucia and I go bra shoppings."

There's a visual.

"Your phone here on table if you needs it."

Getting out from under Nonnie's thumb sounded great until I realized she'd have the Pinto, which meant Vinny would have to pick up the cameras another day. I asked her to have him stop by before she left.

Vinny didn't seem fazed by the news. In fact, he responded so quickly that I wondered if he'd set me up.

"Those cameras should have been up after the last invasion. I'll take your Lowrider. The rack on the back is plenty big."

I blinked a few times. "You'll what?"

"Take your bike."

"The hell you will!"

"Christ, Nighthawk, I know how to ride."

"The bike isn't even here," I said, feeling victorious. "It's still at the precinct."

"No it's not. Rico took me there to pick it up last night."

Damn it.

"I'll be back with your cameras in an hour. I promise."

"Okay," I blurted, making one of those major decisions I wasn't supposed to make. "But if you wreck the bike, I'll dock you every penny it takes to fix it."

With Nonnie and Vinnie out of my hair, the house was quiet. I decided to call Jimmy at Splatz before my nap and ask him to send some zushi residue from my biter cleanup to Dr. Sheridan at the ECDC for testing. Headbutt curled up beside me, and we dozed for all of five minutes before the droning of heavy equipment shook the fillings in my teeth.

As I scrambled out of bed to investigate "Take This Job and Shove It" blared from my phone.

"Hey, Cap," I said, covering my ear to block the din.

"How you feeling, Nighthawk?"

"Better. I'll be back tomorrow."

"If you're up to it, fine, but don't overdo it. Rico's working the mayor's case."

Vinny's fuck up, I thought, trying not to picture him on my Lowrider.

"Listen," Cap said, "City Council's asking who or what prompted the attack at the 51st."

"And?"

"And now I'm asking you."

The wheels had certainly come off this conversation. How could I tell him Toussaint had come back as a demon? My fearless leader would send me back to the hospital for another CT scan.

"I'm not sure," I yelled over the background noise. "But I'll get with the European CDC tomorrow. It's a big world. Maybe they've run across this behavior before."

Fat chance, Little Allie snapped.

"One more thing, Nighthawk." Cap paused. "We've known each other a while, now, and in all that time, I never saw you freeze—until yesterday. What happened?"

Oh, for the love of God, let it go. "I blanked, okay? When I figure out why, you'll be the second to know. See you tomorrow, huh?"

He let it drop, said a quick goodbye, and told me to get some rest, as if that hadn't been my plan to start with. But the heavy equipment sounded even closer. I jumped out of bed, looked out the window, and found the source of the commotion. The Winstel's house.

A bulldozer was digging a massive hole in their yard. Those turdballs could dig down to China for all I cared, but they'd knocked down my fence and the crappy pee-soaked Wysteria vine they'd sued to have me replace. Stepping into my fuzzy slippers, I headed for the door, bent on ~~knocking some sense into them~~, ~~threatening legal action~~, having a reasonable discussion about our property line. Oddly, the construction commotion stopped cold.

I threw back the door and found a woman with a microphone hovering on my porch. She and the cameraman behind her both wore Channel 5 press badges. In the past, Jade Chen, from Channel 10, had always gotten my biter-related scoops because Rico had been schtupping her. Apparently, their breakup had signaled open season on Allie Nighthawk.

Freaking awesome.

The woman gaped at me with a deer-in-the-headlights stare.

"Excuse me, Ms.... Derringer," I said, eyeing her badge and pushing past her. "I'm on my way out."

"Ms. Nighthawk." It hadn't been a question or even a

sentence. It was more of a stall tactic. She sucked in a breath, stood tall, and asked, "Is it true you recently sustained a biter invasion at your home?"

I shot her a menacing eye. "Where would you get an idea like that?"

"An anonymous tip."

"Well, they're wrong," I said, shooing her off my porch. "Bye-bye, now."

She held out her phone with a smile. "We have video."

"Let me see that," I said, snatching it from her.

The video, posted with yesterday's date, showed Jimmy and his crew in my driveway at the butt crack of dawn. Clearly, from the angle, the video came from the Winstel's security camera— the greedy bastards.

I flashed a deadly grin. "Who did you say the tip came from?"

"It was anonymous. But we have our sources."

Beads of sweat dotted her upper lip.

"Do you pay your tipsters?"

"Normally, no. But biter news is big stuff."

I knew it. "No comment," I said, forcing them off the porch.

The woman jabbed her mic at me. "Are you sure, Ms. Nighthawk?"

"Well, okay. Maybe just this once." I leaned into the microphone and waved the cameraman closer. "Get in tight for a good shot, now. Ready? Here you go. Get off my property, Ms. Derringer, or I will give the next biter who visits me your name and address. Yes, you festering newshound, I, too, have sources."

That did the trick.

I was accustomed to being the scourge of the neighborhood. Why wouldn't they hate me? I was the pied piper of pusbags, leading the horde toward their homes on Pitty Pat Lane. But this was the second time the Winstels had profited from my exploits. Jade shared with me once that checkbook journalism is generally frowned upon, but when it came to biter business, all bets were off.

Now, my chat with the Winstels would have two topics of conversation.

Somewhere between my porch and the side of my house, it occurred to me that their security camera might have caught more than the Splatz team. It might have also captured the person who removed my basement window to let the biter in.

I jogged into the side yard, coming face to face with Sid and Evelyn Winstel, who had stopped excavating their hole long enough to eavesdrop on my conversation with Channel 5.

"What?' barked Sid as Evelyn leapt behind him, cradling some kind of hairball with legs to her chest.

"You tell me," I said. "You're in my yard."

"We're...ah, installing an inground pool. So, if you hear any construction..."

"Yeah. About that," I said, pointing to what was left of my split-rail fence. "Your bulldozer knocked my fence down."

Sid shrugged. "It was in our yard."

"Not hardly. Nighthawks have lived in this house since it was built. That fence has always been there."

"Then it's always been in our yard. We had the lot surveyed."

My ass. "Then, I'm sure you won't mind providing me a report copy."

Sid cleared his throat. "We aren't legally required to."

"But since we're such good neighbors, you will, right? Oh, one other thing. Let's watch your security video from two nights ago—the night before you saw the Splatz truck in my driveway and called a tip into Channel 5." I peered around Sid and waved at Evelyn. "That's the second time you two have made money off me."

"Just give it to her," Evelyn whispered, peering out from behind her hubby.

"The law's on our side," Sid murmured back. "She doesn't have a leg to stand on."

I spread my arms and shrugged. "Maybe, maybe not. All I want is a copy of your survey so we can deal with this peaceably and to view your security footage of my house. That's fair, isn't it?"

Sid jutted his chin. "No. You don't get your way this time. What do you think of that, Ms. Zombie Hunter?"

"I think," I said, stepping closer, "If you don't cooperate, the next time a biter breaks into my house in the middle of the night, I'll bring it over here and tuck it into bed with you."

"For God's sake, Sid!" Evelyn's eyeballs nearly exploded from their sockets. "Show her the video!"

Sid pulled out his phone and opened the video with a sigh. "Here," he said, shoving his phone at me. "I assume this is what you're looking for."

The video was dark and grainy, but the camera showed a blonde guy, maybe six feet tall with a broad, crooked nose, chiseling my basement window out of the foundation. He left and returned a few minutes later with a biter in tow, motioning it toward the opening. Amazingly, the rotter cooperated and followed his instructions without trying to eat him. Wowza. Cognitive ability in a deadhead—if that wasn't fuel for the perfect nightmare.

"It's exactly what I'm looking for," I said, selecting "Share" and emailing it to myself as he ripped the phone out of my hands.

"Thanks, Evelyn," I said, starting back toward my house. "I appreciate it."

"Wait!" She called, stopping me mid-step. Evelyn held her four-legged hairball over her head, like it was Simba from *The Lion King*. "Meet Princess, our new Schnoodle."

A schnoodle?

I gave Evelyn a wooden smile, wondering when Headbutt would eat the thing for lunch. A few steps later, I paused and called over my shoulder, "Yo, Sid! I still want a copy of that survey."

"When pigs fly, Nighthawk!"

"Can it, Sid!" Evelyn bellowed, slamming their back door behind them.

Who knows? I thought. Maybe in another lifetime, in a universe far, far away, Evelyn and I could have been friends.

Pfft! Who the hell was I kidding?

Sometimes, it's like I've never even met me.

14

NONNIE'S ITALIAN-YIDDISH EPIC

True to my word, I returned to the 51st the following morning at the crack of eleven. Rest is important after a concussion, and since my plans for yesterday's quiet afternoon took a turn for the disastrous, sleeping late made sense. I told Cap it was by doctor's orders, and I will stick to that story until the day I die.

Rico, hunched over his keyboard, barely acknowledged my arrival.

"How's Wycowski?' I asked.

"Oh, the tonic was where you said it would be. I ran it to the hospital, and his doc dosed him up. Wyco's holding his own. Blood draws will tell them more."

I remembered that I still needed to check with Mama about other options, then pulled a visitor's chair alongside Rico's desk, and made a nuisance of myself. "So, how's the mayor's case coming? Have you solved his murder yet?"

My partner grunted, without taking his eyes off the screen. "We aren't even sure he was murdered. All we have is a CI's tip saying that he was."

"So you've gotten nowhere?"

"Affirmative." He swallowed a gulp of coffee, put the cup on his desk, and rubbed his face. "I'm halfway serious. His COD was myocardial infarction, with a shit-ton of medical complications, all certified by his attending. There was no autopsy, and no tox screen. The marriage license and officiant registration I picked up at The Church of the Purple Kush look legit, but I'm still waiting on copies from the Secretary of State's office to verify that."

"And?"

"I'm coordinating with The Ohio Special Investigations Unit to get hold of his credit card bills, phone statements, and bank records. Until I get those, there's nothing left to investigate."

True enough, I thought, plopping my feet on the corner of his garbage can. "Sounds like you've done all you can for now. Got any other ideas?"

Rico rested his elbows on the desk and steepled his fingers beneath his chin. "Too bad the mayor went rogue when you raised him. It would have been nice if he could have told us whether or not he was murdered. Short of digging his ass back up again for hair and tissue samples, I got nothing."

The thought of going another round with the widow made me wince. "Mrs. Cray-Cray Hinky Bitch will never sign off on that."

"No shit. But if we can solve the embezzlement case, maybe we'll figure out who's behind the murder."

"Two birds, one stone. I like it. When did the subpoenas go out?"

"Like I said, OSIU is lead on the funds case. I just requested subpoenas two days ago for the mayor's life insurance policy and his will. It's not like I don't have fifteen other cases to work. This is just one—"

"Okay, Okay!" I said, scrambling away from his desk. "Work your cases. I have some crap of my own to take care of. We'll talk later." No one was watching, so I blew him a kiss. He didn't exactly catch it in his hand, throw it down, and stomp on it, but he didn't blow it back, either. The shithead. Clearly, I didn't have a clear understanding of the playbook on romance, but if you asked me, the damn thing was written in Klingon anyway.

While scouting out an empty desk, my gaze landed on Wycowski's. I'd have gotten flogged if I'd have sat at his desk, so I chose one a couple of rows over.

The first item on my agenda was to call Dr. Sheridan at the ECDC in Stockholm. It was a little after 5:00 p.m. there. No matter the time of day, I'd yet to call and not reach a live person. Dr. Sheridan, the world's foremost expert on the Z-virus, was my third contact with the European center in the last year and a half. His predecessors, Drs. Latka and Christian, had both fallen at the hands of Toussaint. I didn't know Larry Sheridan well, but if the past was any predictor, we'd rely heavily on each other before this case was over.

"Ilse!" I said when the department's secretary answered. "It's been a while, hasn't it?" Ilsa was the constant that remained after the deaths of Latka and Christian. She and I had bonded over our shared loss and formed a friendship by working closely together. Once we got past our usual chitchat, she connected me with Dr. Sheridan in the lab.

"Doc, Allie here. Just wondering if you're seeing a global spike in biter attacks."

I was almost disappointed when he said that the numbers had remained steady over the past few months. That meant the horde attack in Cincinnati was an anomaly. After a brief conversation about his family and his beloved Husky Moon, it was time for me to get off the line. "Keep your eyes open, Doc, and let me know if anything changes, okay? Oh, two sets of forensic tissue samples are headed your way for testing. One is from Christ Hospital, and the other is from Splatz, a biohazard clean-up company. The samples were taken from rotters that seemed to have some cognitive ability. They weren't interested in eating their handlers, either." I nodded at his soft gasp, then added, "Yes, that is concerning, isn't it?"

Sheridan said he'd continue to cross-reference and match Z-virus strains from his necropsies and agreed to keep me informed. When we hung up, I moved on to the second item on my to-do list—calling Mama.

I needed to know how to battle a demon. If she didn't ask, I wouldn't volunteer that I was talking about Toussaint, but knowing her, she was already aware of his return. She also might have some tips on niggling the tonic if the virus in Wycowski differed from the strain Jade contracted. When Mama didn't answer, I left a message on her landline, asking her to call. It was past noon, and she was likely hard at work on meal prep at the restaurant.

The last chore on my list was rousting Vinny to make sure he would get my cameras installed. When he didn't answer his phone, I called the house. Nonnie said she'd sent him on an errand, but he should be back soon, and she promised to get him cracking on the installations when he returned.

With my chore list completed, I rose to grab Rico, angling for a free lunch. But I ran into Cap instead, and the little vein on the side of his head was throbbing again. There was no way around him in the aisle. I was trapped.

He folded his arms across his chest and glowered at me. "Rico's working on his backlog. Hit the streets—check all the biter nests and get me some intel. I need to know who orchestrated that attack and why."

He didn't wait for my response before walking away, and I was grateful. It ruled out my accidentally spouting some stupid word like demon that would make his purple vein get even bigger. I let Rico know my marching orders and said I'd circle back later.

THERE WAS no shortage of dark and dingy places for rotters to hide in the city. The most promising targets were abandoned buildings, alleyways, and areas beneath railroad trestles and overpasses. It would take days to check each location systematically.

After an hour and a half of playing come-out-come-out-wherever-you-are with minimal results, I got pissed. Where the heck was Vinny when I needed him? Sure, this was CPD business as opposed to ACME's, but I was paying him to be my field operative. Ipso facto, he should be in the field with me. He knew the streets as well as I did, and he'd chased through each one of them looking for biters, just like I had. Together, we could cut the search time in half, but Nonnie had him out running some stupid errand.

And I was hangry, damn it.

It was three o'clock, and I hadn't had lunch. The biter population in the locations I checked wasn't abnormally high—just a few here and there, which was typical. I put them down quietly and called for a bus to take them away before the public freaked out. That news might keep Cap's vein from exploding. It might have been the hunger, but against my better judgment, I stopped at the worst (and closest) bar in the city for lunch. Hopefully, the visit would generate some intel.

Enzo's Bar was held together by tightly grouped mortar-filled bullet holes. The tiny dive was tucked between popular places where up-and-comers eat and drink. Only down-and-outers risked ptomaine at Enzo's.

The ancient street door opened with a familiar squeal, drawing stares from the regulars hunched over their drinks.

The Amazonian blonde behind the bar glanced up and pointed at me. "Arlene Nightbird, I never forget a face!"

Maybe so, lady, but you suck at names. I stepped inside,

plopped onto a stool, and plastered a smile across my face. "Hi, Ronnie. How's it going?"

"Can't complain. Besides, nobody would listen if I did. How's that hunky De Palma doing?"

"He's great. Got held up doing some paperwork. I was in the neighborhood and thought I'd drop in for one of your cheese-burgers."

"How about a little Fireball on the side, eh?" She brayed and drilled my shoulder with one of her man-sized meat hooks.

Bionic Ronnie was tall enough to swat planes from the sky. She had a tattoo on her bicep of a flaming skull with blazing spark plugs in its eyes. Below it were inked the words, "The hard run fast."

Ronnie and I had a minor misunderstanding when we met, and she broke a bottle of Fireball over my head. I smelled like a cinnamon Renuzit for a week. We've since called a truce, but the chick and her big, honking donkey laugh grated on my last nerve. It didn't sit well with me that Rico flirted shamelessly with her, either. Charm was his superpower, and the cheesy bastard used it to keep his female informants on the hook, not to mention every other woman on the planet.

Ronnie wiped the bar top with her towel. "What else can I get you today?"

"A Coke Zero and a little info, maybe." Who knew how helpful she'd be, given that Rico wasn't the one asking? I crossed my fingers, pulled out my phone, and played the video of the blonde guy from the Winstel's security video. "Ever seen this dude before?"

She watched the grainy video, then grabbed her cheaters from her pocket, and viewed it again. "Nope. Can't say that I have. Eww! Look at the nasty old biter. How can you do that for a living, girl?"

Says the bimbo who serves these booze hounds. "What can I say, Ronnie? It pays the bills."

"I feel ya, sister. If he happens to show up, I'll call Rico. I got his number."

I didn't bother to offer my number. If she did see the guy, she'd be thrilled to tell Rico all about it. That was good enough in my book. And not that I would have told her, but the cheeseburger that day tasted as yummy as I remembered it. After leaving a decent tip, given our history, I stepped outside and thought about trying Vinny again, but Nonnie called instead.

"Oh, Miss Allie! Miss Allie!" she warbled hysterically.

That warble was the harbinger of doom.

"What's wrong, Nonnie?"

"Vinny is terrible troubles! He needs you and Mr. Rico, now!"

"Where is he?" I asked, jogging toward my Lowrider. "What's happening?"

"Lucia Falconi, she say he in ababandeds building at 12th and Clay Street. He needs you now! Hurrys! Please hurrys!"

I started my bike with Nonnie still on the line. "Is Lucia *with* Vinny? How would—Why would—What the hell is going on?"

After cobbling together the most confusing Italian-Yiddish epic ever told, I disconnected from Nonnie and used the bike's Bluetooth to shout an S.O.S. to Rico. Damned if this kid of Leo's wouldn't be the death of me yet. I throttled up, tore down the street, and sent a message out into the universe, "*Hang on, Vinny! We're coming!*"

15

SHUFFLING SAM

"Whoa, take a breath; slow down," Rico said in his just-the-facts-ma'am tone. "What's wrong?"

I sighed in exasperation and blew past a car dawdling in the high-speed lane. "Just meet me at 12th and Clay, pronto! I'll explain along the way."

"Heading out the door now," he said, jangling his keys into the phone. "Read me in."

"Remember Lucia Falcone?"

"Nonnie's friend, right? Little Granny Goodwitch from the old country, with the money socks."

"Yeah, that's her. Lucia asked Nonnie if Vinny could help her convince some old fart to repay a small loan she'd made to him."

"Uh-huh."

"Supposedly, the guy only needed a few bucks until his Social Security check showed up, but he never paid her back. Now he's trying to gaslight her, saying he never borrowed the money."

Rico's voice dropped an octave. "Uh-huh."

I throttled down, veered onto Reading Road, and continued

the saga. "So, Vinny picked Lucia up in the Pinto and drove to some business on Republic Street, eh...Troy Brothers' Tire. She waited in the car while he went inside and had a word with the dude. Twenty minutes later, Vinny, the dude, and two other guys came back out. One of the guys had a gun in Vinny's back, and Vinny's face was busted up. Lucia slouched in the passenger seat, rolled the window down, and heard the guy say they had a rotter picked out special just for him, courtesy of their boss. They shoved Vinny into the back of a black caddy and took off, so Lucia followed them. Not that it's paramount, but Lucia doesn't *have* a driver's license. She called Nonnie, screaming that they were at 12th and Clay."

"They kidnapped Vinny? Christ, Nighthawk! Lead with that next time, huh? Let me call this in. 1 David 4, vicinity of 12th and Clay. Suspected kidnapping. Suspect armed with a hand-gun, unknown caliber. Possible zombie involvement, uncon-firmed and unknown quantity. All available units requested. Routine. Repeat routine."

Smart. A routine call meant no lights or sirens. No need to push them into a shootout.

"Wait, there's more!" I yelled. "The guy's no ordinary schmuck. Lucia lied. This isn't about some small loan. Miss My-Bingo-Money-Is-In-My-Socks is a freaking bookie—and this skel is into her for 50K! He's some big wheel in the Giordano crime family."

"Shut the front door! That blue-haired hobbit's a bookie? Giordano...They aren't local. Why is that name familiar?"

"That's the outfit Leo worked for! I'm almost there; three minutes out."

"Son of a bitch!" Rico said, radioing dispatch. "1 David 4 ETA five minutes 12th and Clay. Nighthawk ETA three minutes, 12th and Clay. Routine. Repeat, routine."

The late Leo Abruzzi was Vinny's father. More importantly, he'd been an accountant for the Giordano Crime Family and had turned state's evidence against them. Toussaint, who formed an alliance with the Giordanos, was more than happy to provide them with a rotter to ensure Leo's silence.

That was before Mama developed the tonic that kept bite victims from turning into deadheads. The best defense in those days was a drug that simply slowed the virus. Once Leo was attacked, it was only a matter of time before he died. The guy knew he was toast, yet he testified anyway. Gutsy move. I didn't know him long, but I got to know him well. Leo even asked that when the time came, I would be the one who took him down. I swore to him on his deathbed that I'd watch over Vinny.

And I'd kill to keep that promise.

After parking my Harley curbside a half-block south on Clay, I sprinted toward 12th, pressed against the buildings, and double-timed it past Nonnie's Pinto to the southeast corner of the intersection. A wild-eyed Lucia made eye contact with me, then leaned out of the driver's side window, and bellowed at me like a wounded elk. I put my finger to my lips, signaling her to keep it down, then positioned myself beside the corner building and motioned for her to join me.

Lucia, being Lucia, shook me off. I shot her an angry stare and stabbed my finger at the ground beside me, mouthing the words "it's safer here." She rolled her eyes, threw up her hands, and clambered out of the Pinto, muttering some old-world snark, then moseyed toward me at the speed of a sloth.

One by one, the cruisers began to arrive, sans lights and sirens per Rico's routine call instruction, parking well to the west of the intersection to avoid drawing attention.

By the time Lucia, the human snail, reached my side, she was bent over and gasping. "They takest him inside...here," she huffed, leaning against the fourplex we were hunkered beside. "First floor. This side... I sees them through window."

While Rico trotted up quietly behind her, I shot her the

stink eye. "Thanks for the tip, Baba Yaga. You're in big, big trouble."

"*Ah! Il malocchio!*" she jeered, spitting three times and waggling the Italian horned hand at me.

Rico reached out from behind and lowered her hand with a whisper, "Later, ladies."

"Ahh!" Lucia whirled with a gasp and whacked him upside of his head with her moon-sized pocketbook.

He batted it away with a grunt and cast her a malevolent side-eye. "What have you got in there—the freaking Yellow Pages? See that unit over there?" he whispered, pointing to a black and white down the street. "Go—now!"

Raising his fist to signal the street unis to freeze, we conducted some last-minute recon. Crawling on all fours behind a hedgerow, Rico crept to the corner of the apartment's picture window and glanced inside. After several seconds, he backed out from behind the bushes and whispered, "Vinny's in there, tied to a chair, along with three armed skels and a rotter chained to a radiator. We could use a smoke grenade...or a flash bang...or the big red door key."

"Really—the battering ram?" I said, creeping into the bushes to surveil the situation for myself.

Rico crawled in behind me and whispered, "Things are stable for now. The biter's chained up, and the guns are holstered. Cap will want to weigh in on our tactical plan before we move."

Ugh. Plans require discussing, formulating, and evaluating—all the damn 'ings.' Plan is the four-letter word I hate most in the English language. I'm an act-now, think-later kind of chick. If I relied on plans to save the day, I'd have lost half the people I've rescued over the years. Besides, stable situations can go south in a heartbeat.

Peering through the window, I saw a guy walk over to the biter, pick up the heavy-gauge chain that secured it, and laugh, dangling the padlock key from his finger. Vinny yelled and kicked furiously, scooting his chair as far away as he could. Our stable sitrep was now a hair's breadth from unstable and creeping dangerously close to too late. I darted a glance at Rico, who signaled me to hold while he waved the unis around the back of the building. For shit's sake, I thought. How much longer can we wait?

When the guy shoved the key into the padlock and shouted, "Sic 'em, meatbag!" the answer to that question clarified. "Sorry, excrement circumstances," I muttered, popping up and shooting the rotter twice through the glass. While leaping inside through what was left of the picture window, my foot got tangled in the Venetian blinds, causing me to faceplant onto the hardwood floor. The goons drew their guns.

Rico and his Glock covered me from the bushes, taking out the bogeys one, two, three, painting the walls a blood-spatter red. But the rotter was still in play, dragging itself across the floor and snapping its gnarly teeth at Vinny, who had tipped over his chair and was frantically scooting away.

"Jesus, Nighthawk!" he screamed, "What happened to shoot for the head?"

To my eternal embarrassment, the Eveready rotter, face down on the floor, had one of the two bullets I fired lodged in its ass. My other shot hadn't fared any better. The biter's bullet-severed pinky finger, continuing its attack, insistently inching toward my boot.

Rico climbed inside the apartment through the obliterated window and gingerly picked his way through the gore, shaking his head.

A silent groan hummed inside me. I would never hear the end of this.

"Uh, uh, uh," Rico said, raising his Glock and training it on one of the skels. "Toss it."

The sole surviving perp, slouched against the wall with a

bullet wound in his left bicep, dropped his gun and kicked it across the floor. Rico handcuffed him, then radioed for a bus and the coroner.

I raised Hawk to finish off the rotter, but Rico, the planner, had a different idea.

"Don't put it down yet, Nighthawk. Just keep it controlled."

Controlled, he says. Nothing like doing things the hard way. I holstered Hawk and blocked in the deadhead with the sofa and chairs. My makeshift corral wouldn't hold for long. I hoped that whatever Rico had in mind, he'd do it quickly.

Vinny breathed a sigh of relief as I untied him. He lay on his back, sucking in air and eyeballing the rotter, while I dusted glass shards and zushi bits out of my hair.

"I can't believe it," Gel-Boy huffed. "After all the bitching you do about shooting for the head, you hit the damn thing's pinky."

And so, the shit ration began.

I skewered him with a stink eye. "Like you could do better, Mr. I-Blast-Every-Tombstone-I-See. Gimme a break. I was shooting through a window on the fly—and to save your ass, no less." Since the best defense is deflection, I turned my attention to the skel. "What's the Giordano family doing in Cincinnati?"

The goon grimaced. "The who? I have no idea to whom you are referring."

Rico rifled through the perp's pockets and found his I.D. "Talk—don't talk, Mr....Ed Lasky. It's all the same to me. You're as good as dead once Giordano hears you're in custody. He'll send a biter after you, just like he did with Leo Abruzzi."

The mobster chuckled. "Is that a fact?"

"Yeah, it is. But I have a better idea. How about you tell me what I want to know, or I turn this meatbag loose on you now?"

"You can't do that. You're a cop."

Rico's voice dropped. "Watch me. There's nobody here but

us chickens. Who's to say what happened, huh?" He glanced at Vinny. "What do you say?"

"Go for it, dude."

Rico pointed to the door. "Nighthawk, take Vinny outside, then come back in and let the rotter loose."

I locked eyes with Rico, trying to read him, but all I saw was anger.

"I'm serious," he added. "And thank the unis for the assist. Problem solved. They can leave now."

I helped Vinny to his feet, led him out the door to the waiting officers, and, despite my reservations, gave them the all-clear. Things were about to take an ugly turn that could hurt Rico more than he realized. But I had seen that look in his eyes before. He was determined. So, I did as he had asked, came back inside, pulled the furniture barricade apart, and waited for fate to take its course.

"Now, leave," Rico said, looking at me.

"The hell I will."

"Suit yourself," he said with a shrug. He pulled Lasky to his feet and threw him on the sofa, inches away from the rotter. I drew Hawkeye and concealed him at my side, committed to stopping the insane plan Rico had set into motion. The biter stared at the goon, but curiously, didn't attack.

Lasky laughed. "Sit down, Sam." He looked at the deadhead and patted the sofa beside him. "Take a load off."

The rotter, totally docile, sat beside Lasky and stared into the distance.

"Crazy, ain't it?" Lasky said, with a cough and another grimace. "That rotter ain't gonna hurt me. Gio had 'em programmed not to attack his guys. You, on the other hand..." Lasky smiled apologetically and shrugged. "Sic her, Sam!"

The biter barreled at me from the sofa while Lasky dove head-first into Rico's gut.

I raised Hawkeye and squeezed the trigger, giving the

meatbag a 9mm migraine. Lasky got TKO'd by Rico's right fist to his jaw.

Splatter from the meatbag layered the already blood-stained walls. Shuffling Sam had been less than three feet from me when I fired. I was drenched in zushi blowback.

Nasty as hell, but worth every speck.

We had gotten confirmation of Giordano's presence in the city and his involvement with biters—and Rico hadn't had to sell his soul to get it. I'd take that as a win.

16

LET IT GO! LET IT GO!

I was hoping to calm down before making it into the precinct for the debriefing.

Newsflash: I didn't.

After riding Rico's bumper into the lot, I skidded to a stop and was on him before he even got out of his car.

"What's with you?' I asked, leaning into the driver's side window of the Mustang. "Turning a deadhead loose on that goon! You want to spend the rest of your life in prison?"

Rico shoved his door open, pushing me back. "It's no more than the bastards did to Wycowski," he said, climbing out of his seat and heading for the entrance. "Thirty years on the force and the guy's wondering if he's going to have to take a bullet to the brain to keep from turning rotter. And that fucker Lasky laughed about it. He's lucky you were there to stop me."

"Exactly," I said, grabbing his arm and forcing him to look at me. "That isn't you. That's me, the irrational one; you're calm, cool, and collected."

"Let it go," he growled. "I've known Wyco since I was a kid. My dad was a cop, remember? How do I tell a guy I've known my entire life that he's as good as dead?"

"Why would you think that? Jade's medicine worked. She's still living and breathing and making life difficult, right? Why would Wycowski's outcome be different?"

"You said they might not have the same strains."

"They probably don't," I said, avoiding his gaze. "But that tonic is a good start. I called Mama and left a message. She hasn't gotten back to me yet. But I'll call her again just as soon as we get out of the debriefing, okay?"

He nodded, so I knew he'd heard me, but it was his turn to avoid my eyes. We walked into the 51st in awkward silence. His rage seemed to have played out, but I had to wonder if the man I thought I knew—even loved—would have allowed that rotter to attack Lasky. Vengeance was a flaw I had never witnessed in Rico; it didn't suit him.

Cap's secretary told us he was finishing up a budget meeting, but Lucia and Vinny were waiting for us in interrogation room one. The last time Lucia had chatted with Rico, after we'd broken into Templeman's Funeral Home, she'd fallen head-over-heels for my partner's irresistible smile. He was far less charming today when he walked through the door and glared at her.

Rico flipped a chair around backwards, straddled it, and then plopped down so hard that the back of the chair rammed into the table. "Start from the beginning, Mrs. Falconi."

Lucia smiled sweetly. "Is me, Mr. Rico. Nonnie's friend, Lucia, from Templeman's, remember?"

"How could I forget. It's been a long day, Mrs. Falconi. Are you a bookie?"

"Is not so simple—"

"Yes, it is. Answer the question."

Lucia paused and twisted her gnarled hands in her lap. "Yes."

"Did someone welch on a bet with you? Is that who you sent Vinny to see?"

Vinny leaned forward with a wince, pulling an ice pack off his jaw as he tried to jump in, but Rico shut him down by putting a hand in his face.

Lucia glanced around the room with tear-filled eyes. "I... I..."

Rico's voice boomed. "Mrs. Falconi, answer the question!"

"I don't care no mores," she said, starting to weep. "He can keep his monies. I old womans who just wants to go home. Please, please takes me home."

Vinny threw up his arms and groaned. "Mrs. Falconi, tell them who—"

Rico pointed at Vinny to shut him up, then softened his tone. "Who owes you money, Lucia? And how much?"

Thirty minutes later, with the real story in the bag, Rico and I were summoned to Cap's office for our debriefing.

"Get out of town!" Cap gaped at me over the top of his readers. "That gray-haired, gum-grinding midget is a bookie?"

"Yep."

Cap squinted at the file. "Lucia Falconi. That's who we're talking about?"

I snorted. "Truth really is stranger than fiction."

Rico rubbed his face and sighed. "Lucia told Nonnie that she'd loaned some old coot a little money, and he wasn't paying her back. So, she asked Nonnie if Vinny could persuade the old fart to pay up. Vinny went there to—"

"Strong arm some geezer?" Cap finished Rico's sentence with a frown.

"More or less, sir. Only when Vinny agreed to help her, Lucia took him to some place on Republic Street named Troy Brothers' Tire. She stayed in the car while Vinny went inside and got blindsided by the truth. The 'old coot' who owed her money was Dominic Giordano, the head of the Giordano Crime Family! Three hoods from inside the tire company took Vinny to the apartment at 12th and Clay. And, well, you know the rest."

"Most of it," Cap said, turning to me. "Nighthawk, according to dashcam video, you shot out the picture window of an apartment, then leapt inside through the remaining shards of glass. Care to share why you went lone wolf with a cadre of officers on site?"

Jesus, when he put it like that, he made me sound like Catwoman on crack.

"Rico and I crept below the window, peered inside, and saw Vinny tied to a chair, with three bogeys guarding him. The perp we have in custody unchained a biter and sicced it on Vinny. So, it was a case of, what do you call them—excrement circumstances."

Rico kicked my chair. "Exigent...not excrement. We've covered this before. You need to get that straight."

"Among other things," Cap said, glaring at me over his cheaters. "Nighthawk, De Palma was the lead on this operation. You are never the lead. You are a subcontractor, working under the supervision of CPD. And in this case, under the direct supervision of Detective De Palma." Cap swiveled his chair toward Rico. "Did you deem this to be a case of exigent circumstances?"

Rico dropped his eyes and paused before muttering, "Yes, sir."

"You're sure? Because you hesitated before answering."

"Just recalling the sequence of events, Cap."

"If the circumstances were exigent, then why didn't *you* shoot through the window and leap inside?"

"Because Nighthawk's reflexes were faster than mine."

Now that was a damn fine answer.

Cap frowned as he reviewed the incident report. "Detective,

when you entered the window behind Nighthawk, why did you find it necessary to kill the other two suspects?"

"They had their guns drawn and pointed at her, Cap."

"Our perp, a Mr. Ed Lasky, says you threatened to turn the biter loose on him. Is that true, Detective?"

Here it comes...

"Absolutely not, sir."

"Nighthawk," Cap said, his eyes never leaving Rico, "Did Detective De Palma threaten to turn a biter loose on Mr. Lasky?"

Shit, shit, shit. "No, sir." *I'm going to hell, I'm going to hell, I'm going to hell...*

"And if I were to ask Vincent Abruzzi, he would say the same?"

He'd better. "Of course, sir."

Cap leaned back in his chair and studied Rico. "Okay then," he finally said. "Write it up."

I blasted out of my chair like a Patriot missile and waited while Rico casually lumbered to his feet like he'd just awakened from a nap.

"Nighthawk," Cap said. "I'd like a word with you. Alone."

"Sure." I plopped back into the chair, mainly because my knees buckled.

Cap excused my partner with a nod. "She'll be along shortly."

When Rico closed the door behind him, Cap took a deep breath and asked, "Is Rico okay?"

"Sure," I said, squirming as if I were tied to an ant hill. "I mean, he's concerned about Wycowski, but everyone is. He's holding up fine."

"He doesn't seem overly stressed to you?"

I know I am. "No. Same amount of stress as usual, sir. You know Rico. He's...intense."

"Yeah, I guess you're right," he muttered, running his hands across his bald head.

To change the topic, I posed a question that had been nagging me about Lucia's ridiculous mess. "Of all the bookies in the world, why would a Jersey mobster like Giordano, known to traffic in biters, choose a penny-ante bookie with ties to me to take his bet—and then renege on it? Ten grand is peanuts to him."

"Good point." Cap paused and stared thoughtfully out the window. "Leo was involved with the Giordanos, wasn't he? Maybe Dominic Giordano is gunning for you."

Or a certain demon is using Giordano to get to me.

A text notification pinged on my phone. I glanced at the screen, hoping for good news. The message was from the European CDC, and as usual, my hopes were instantly dashed.

17

NOTHING GOLD CAN STAY

— Robert Frost

I could have lied and told Cap that the text was from Nonnie, or some Nigerian prince needing money, but that was beyond ridiculous. Even that prince knew I was the last person he could turn to for money. Besides, the latest biter attack had put Cap under a microscope. He'd need to come up with some quick answers, so I kept him in the loop by sharing the latest turd in the punchbowl.

"Dr. Sheridan told me earlier that he hadn't seen an uptick in global biter attacks. But there's a one-day reporting lag. Today's update shows a..." I glanced at my phone screen, "Small but demonstrable increase in attacks in Europe and North America. As always, they'll continue to necropsy the deadheads and take tissue samples for analysis. He'll let me know if the virus has mutated again."

Cap frowned. "You think we're looking at a new strain?"

I'd come to that conclusion after watching the Winstel's video of the meatbag breaking into my house, but with everything happening, I hadn't had time to share my thoughts with Cap.

He handled bad news better than anyone else I knew. He'd simply take a breath, regroup, and charge up whatever mountain stood in his way. Maybe it was the light that day, but the stubble on his cheeks looked grayer, and the lines in his face appeared more defined.

Cap's shoulders sagged when I nodded to confirm my suspicions about a new strain, so I softened the update by telling him we wouldn't know for sure until Dr. Sheridan's test results came in. The delay was a false glimmer of hope, but Cap looked so worn that I figured a white lie might give him some peace. I left his office wondering how much stress his heart could handle.

After a quick trip to the coffee machine, I found Vinny and Lucia parked beside Rico's desk. Vinny slumped in his chair, his head tilted back while he held an icepack to his blackened eyes and bloodied nose. For the first time ever, Ms. Money Socks Lucia looked suitably humble, like she wasn't trying to get over on someone. Rico, sitting ramrod straight, barked questions like a drill sergeant.

"Mrs. Falconi, how do you know Dominic Giordano?"

Lucia's voice trembled. "He owes me moneys from bet. But as I says, he can keeps it. I finish with him."

"No," Rico said, shaking his head. "Recouping that bet is the reason you took Vinny to Republic Street today. I want to know how and when you met Dominic Giordano."

"In old country," she mumbled, looking everywhere except in Rico's eyes. "*Mia famigghia*, Nonnie *famigghia*, Giordano *famigghia*, we *cumpari*...ah..." she shrugged and covered her mouth with her hand. "We friends."

"Friends as in let's go eat pasta and drink some wine, or friends as in let's go do some shady shit?"

"Second one," Lucia snapped, with a hint of annoyance.

Rico darted his eyes toward Vinny. "Did the goons mention any names we can trace?"

"Just Lasky, the guy Rico brought in, and some guy named McCain. No,...Cain. That's it."

"Did they mention Nighthawk?"

Vinny pulled the ice pack from his face, revealing a split, swollen lip. "I heard her name once or twice, but the guy who spoke English and was doing most of the talking got shut down with a slap upside his head. From then on, they spoke Sicilian. Most of the Sicilian I know comes from Nonnie. I couldn't follow what they were saying."

"Did they say anything about arranging the mass biter attack?"

"Not that I heard."

I asked a question of my own. "Did they know your name, Vinny?"

He put his hand to his jaw and winced. "Yeah, after I introduced myself like a dipstick. The Abruzzi *famigghia* goes way back. Talk about adding fuel to the fire. It didn't take them long to figure out who my dad was. They called somebody pronto. I don't know who, but after they hung up, things got dicey."

The next question I asked tugged at my heart. "Did they tell you what they did to your dad?"

Vinny's eyes grew cold. "Yeah. I told 'em to untie me and say that shit again. Said I'd kick their bitch asses all the way back to Palermo."

"Good man," Rico said, with a hint of a smile.

I almost swallowed the question perched on the tip of my tongue, but with everything that had been happening to me, I had to ask. "Did any of them mention Toussaint?"

He frowned. "No. Why would they? He's dead."

Rico stared at me like I'd lost my mind.

My phone rang, bringing my part of Vinny's interview to an end. The call was from Mama's restaurant. Five o'clock was a busy time for Mama to chat. I moved to the breakroom to speak to her privately, wondering if she'd finally brought in some help and was slowing down to enjoy her old age.

Ten minutes later, I would have traded my soul for that call to have never come in.

"Bonswa, Manman!" My eyes welled at the thought of hearing her voice. I missed her more than I knew. *"Mwen te manke ou anpil."*

"Allie, it's Luna...Luna Michon."

One of Mama's waitresses and an old flame of Vinny's from our time in New Orleans. Sweet girl, but the last person I expected to be calling.

"Luna, hi...how's Mama?"

"Umm, that's why I'm calling." Her voice trembled. "I have some bad news. Mama's been acting strangely, talking to people who aren't there and seeing spirits and such. A few days ago, she collapsed at the restaurant after salting the doorways and praying over the customers. The squad took her to the hospital. She told the doctors she's been fighting demons—

Sweet Jesus. "How long has this been going on?"

"A couple of weeks. I'm sorry—"

"Two weeks! I should be there! Why didn't you call me?"

"I wanted to, Allie, but Mama forbade me. She said you were fighting a battle of your own, and you needed to stay focused."

I wondered how Mama had known about my issues. But then, how had Mama ever known anything? "You let me handle Mama," I said. "I'll be there on the next flight. Thanks for lett—"

"Allie, I'm so sorry," Luna said, breaking into tears. "Mama died this morning."

18

THE DEATH OF A THOUSAND CUTS

Everything Luna said after the words 'Mama died' washed over me like snippets from the local news. Shutting down wasn't all bad. Sometimes, emotional distance ensured my survival.

Mama must have known her time was measured because she was found with a note that contained instructions: A large packing box beside her nightstand was to be shipped to me upon her death. Mama requested that her attorney, Samuel Beauregard of Traxler, Malkoff, and Boyd, be notified of her passing so he could execute her will, which included her wish to be cremated. Additionally, any memorial service was to be postponed until I had 'vanquished my demon.'

My only demon was Toussaint.

I had fought the man for so long and so hard that I had often wondered what it would be like to finally kill him. I had assumed I would feel relief and a sense of pride, but when that moment came, all I felt was despair. Memories tormented me —childhood moments spent with a man who was like an older brother to me, and later recollections of him as my first love. Not only had Toussaint's death left me feeling empty, it had shattered Mama's heart. Her beloved bway was gone forever, and I was the reason why. Toussaint was her 'Dark Angel'. Mama had called him that since the day the charming, mischievous orphan arrived at her doorstep.

But *Manman* was more than our guardian; she was also the Hoodoo queen who had helped me battle Toussaint when he went rogue. The juxtaposition of those roles must have been agonizing for her. Once again, the blame fell squarely on my shoulders. I had needed her help to defeat him because my own powers weren't strong enough. Poor Mama. Helping me battle her Dark Angel all those years must have felt like a death by a thousand cuts.

My chest ached with guilt or grief. Maybe both.

I had let too much time pass without calling her or going home to visit. I'd been 'too busy.' There was only so much of me to go around, and biters never took a vacation. It struck me that I had only called Mama when I needed something—help with rootwork, an incantation, or advice. Sometimes, just to hear that she had faith in me. Not that she minded. Any excuse to talk to her Little Bird made her heart sing. The feeling was mutual, although now, I was sure my heart would never sing again.

A tearful Luna promised she would send me the box, as per Mama's final wishes. God only knew what was inside it. Under different circumstances, the irony would have been amusing. Even if I recognized the contents when I opened it, my chances of knowing what to do with it were slim to none.

I said that I'd take care of notifying Attorney Beauregard of Mama's death and ask him, since he was local, to handle the arrangements for the interment of her ashes at St. Roch Cemetery, Number Two, next to Johnse. There was no other place she would choose to be.

Just as we were about to hang up, I thought to ask about Mama's cause of death. While she was eighty and not in the best of health, her death, though unexpected, was not exactly shocking. According to Luna, the doctors said she had suffered a stroke due to uncontrolled hypertension. I could believe that, given the way she always cared for others but not herself. They attributed her demon sightings to some form of dementia, resulting from atherosclerotic changes in her brain.

But I knew better.

I had killed Toussaint six months earlier. Somehow, he had returned as a demon to torment me and to drive Mama to her grave. What the hell am I supposed to do now? I wondered. The only person who was strong enough to fight demons was dead.

I DRIFTED BACK to Rico's desk, tearless, and pondered the many ways I had let Mama down in life. Deep in conversation with Vinny, Rico barely glanced up when I arrived. He nodded absently toward the empty visitor chair and mumbled, "Have a seat. One of the unis took Ms. Money Socks home."

Seconds later, their conversation came to an awkward halt when they realized I was still standing.

Rico frowned. "Something wrong?"

"Mama's dead."

They gawked at me in silence. After a beat, Rico rose quietly and guided me to the open chair. "Sit down, babe," he whispered, squatting beside me and looking into my eyes. "I am so sorry. She was a remarkable woman. Everyone loved her."

Right, I thought. Everyone except the man who should have treasured her as much as I did. He killed her.

Rico's response had come from his heart. He hadn't known Mama well, but she'd welcomed him with open arms and had helped me save his life in New Orleans.

Vinny's eyes welled up as he swiped his hands through his

hair. "Nighthawk...Allie, I..." In lieu of finishing his thought, he reached across the back of my chair and pulled me to his shoulder.

I had yet to cry, and as long as anyone was near me, I wouldn't. I learned a long time ago that there's no crying in corpse whispering. Tears made me feel like a victim, and I had no time for weakness.

"How did she pass?" Vinny asked.

"A stroke, with some associated dementia."

"Probably from the stress of Toussaint's death, huh?"

Rico shot Vinny a disapproving look. I held no illusion that Toussaint's death wasn't at least a part of the equation. But I kept my thoughts to myself about the cause of Mama's alleged dementia. Experienced as they were at neutralizing deadheads, Rico and Vinny hadn't been involved in Voodoo, Hoodoo, and the spirit world for their entire lives like I had. Talk of Toussaint returning as a demon might have sent them screaming into the night—or think I needed a straitjacket.

Rico offered to drive me home, but I begged off. Vinny was there, along with Nonnie's car from his earlier escapade with Lucia. There was no reason to pull Rico away from his work just to gaze empathically at me, sharing in my sorrow.

I sensed he was disappointed that I hadn't taken him up on his offer, like maybe he saw this as an opportunity to demonstrate his unwavering love and devotion. It's not that I didn't appreciate the gesture, but our caseload overfloweth with a bimbo widow and beaucoup biters. Given the circumstances, one of us had to man up. Apparently, it was me. Besides, I figured a little space and time would do me good.

If I had looked a little deeper, I might have realized that I have absolutely no idea how to accept sympathy. But self-awareness is not in my wheelhouse. I'd be more likely to understand quantum physics than my own inner workings.

I gave Rico a discreet peck on the cheek when I followed

Vinny home on my bike and promised that I would call if I needed a shoulder to cry on. After we got back home, I disappeared into my bedroom while Vinny told Nonnie about Mama. This led to me being wrapped in another well-meaning but unwanted blanket of sympathy, after which I thanked them both for their concern, but begged them to just leave me be.

I shooed them off to The Blue Note and spent the evening drinking an unknown number of incredibly strong Jack Daniels slushies and crying my eyes out—alone. When early evening faded into night, I covered the birds in the kitchen, which was starting to look more like an aviary, and motioned Headbutt to climb into the bed beside me.

The last thing I remember is releasing my sorrow with a long, breathy sigh, closing my eyes, and hearing a distant, mocking laughter that was unmistakably Toussaint's.

19

———

SHELL OUT SOME
BUCKS, YOU CHEAP PUTZ

I woke up at ten the next morning, convinced that at some point during the night, an elephant had trampled my head and driven my eyeballs into my toes. The Avian Triumvirate and Headbutt, squabbling over the last of the dog treats, intensified the ache in my head. But it was Nonnie who drove the nail deep into my skull by broadcasting the bird's play-by-play at the top of her lungs. When I emerged from my bedroom and padded down the hallway to the bathroom, she stopped bellowing and raced from the kitchen to resume her motherly swaddling attempts.

I slammed the door in her face. Enough was enough.

After throwing on a clean pair of jeans and my "Zombies Hate Fast Food" t-shirt, I downed a cup of coffee and checked my phone. Three missed calls from Rico. He could wait another twenty minutes until I reached the precinct.

———

TEARING down I-71s and feeling the wind on my face cleared my head. I banished the memory of Toussaint's disembodied laughter and shifted my focus to the investigation of the mayor's murder, which had taken a back seat since the mini zom-poc at the precinct. I replayed every word of the ugly soiree in Cap's conference room with the bimbo widow, including the threats from her bulldog attorney. There was something about the freedom of the open road that made me think better—kept me sharp.

Mama always said idle hands were the devil's workshop. She'd spout that cliche when—

Mama's dead.

Ah, there it was, the reason for the hangover from hell and the pain in my heart. Even now, with my world collapsing around me, my brain refused to shut off. Staying focused on the job kept me from feeling, which was actually a good thing since Mama's favorite platitude wasn't the only memory that had come rushing back to me. I'd completely forgotten something that happened during the conference with the mayor's widow, and I couldn't wait to share it with Rico.

MY EXCITEMENT FIZZLED when Cap stopped me as I entered the 51st to offer his condolences. Strangely, his brief but sincere expression of sympathy hit me harder than the tidal wave of emotion expressed by everyone else, which seemed more focused on the giver's needs than the receiver's.

Cap's wife, Ingrid, had been killed years earlier in a late-night biter attack under an overpass after experiencing a blowout on the highway. Clearly, he remembered what it was like to stand in my shoes. I appreciated his restraint. But just when I thought our Hallmark moment was over, he made it awkward by following me through the bullpen toward Rico's desk. An uncomfortable silence settled in.

Eventually, I shot him a side-eye and asked, "Something else?"

"You two have caught another case," he mumbled.

Perfect. Just freaking perfect.

Cap and I strolled up to Rico's desk in unison and waited for him to tear his eyes away from his laptop.

"Nighthawk." Rico's voice carried a hint of surprise. "I didn't expect to see you here today."

"Yeah? Well, I'm not the sit-around-and-mope type. Besides, I might be on to something in the mayor's case."

Cap raised his brow. "Holding out on me, Nighthawk?"

I parked myself on the corner of Rico's desk and let my theory fly. "Remember our meeting in the conference room with that bimbo and her ambulance-chasing attorney?"

Cap's eyes glazed. "How could I forget?"

"When she got up to leave, her purse fell on the floor, and an appointment card fell out. I picked it up and handed it back to her. She has a four o'clock session today at The Giggling Goat Day Spa."

"And?" Cap asked.

"It's an appointment for Goat yoga and a mud bath."

Tumbleweeds drifted across the floor while I waited for a reaction.

"Don't you get it?" I asked.

Rico shrugged. "Enlighten us."

"Not that I buy into the whole holistic thing. I mean, nothing screams spiritual enlightenment like wasting rotters, right? But women talk. You pack some bougie bitches in a mud pit and they'll share everything, and I do mean everything. Throw in pygmy goats and who knows? We might find Jimmy Hoffa's body. See where I'm going with this?"

Zippo. Zilch. Nada. Crickets chirped. Time stood still.

"Oh, c'mon!" I cried. "Buy a freaking vowel!"

Cap frowned. "I'm all for mud wrestling. But what do you think Capshaw's widow is going to share with...the goats?"

"Maybe that she's coming into some money soon. Or planning a trip around the world. Or she's buying her boy toy a Rolex. Hell, I don't know! Maybe she bought a freaking lifetime leg-waxing package."

"Have you lost your mind?" Cap shook his head. "I'm not authorizing a mud bath for anyone. We've got bigger fish to fry. Last night, for the first time since the mass attack, third shift reported an increase in deadhead sightings. I want you two out there combing the usual hidey holes, checking for a hub where the damn things might be stockpiled, and figure out who's behind this. Wycowski's life depends on it."

As if either of us had forgotten. But as for me sharing who was behind the attack, our fearless leader wouldn't have liked my answer.

Cap strolled back toward his office after he gave us our new assignment. Once he cleared the corner, I pulled out my phone and said, "Hold on a minute, Partner. I need to call Mama's attorney first and tell him to make her final arrangements."

Rico busied himself with paperwork while he waited for me to finish. But no sooner had I ended that call than I made another one. Rico glanced at his watch, then at me, and then back to his watch.

Cheese-n-crackers. Wherever the biters are, they'll still be there in ten minutes. What's the rush?

I rolled my eyes. "Look, just because we have a new assignment doesn't mean somebody else can't go to goat yoga tonight."

Rico winced. "Nighthawk, who are you calling?"

"Vinny."

"He doesn't work for CPD, you can't—"

"Why not? His dumb ass got us into this mess in the first place. He needs to clean his own —Listen up," I said when

Vinny answered. "You want to set things right after the cluster-fuck you caused at the cemetery? Here's your chance."

After hearing my plan, the goat spa idea didn't sit well with him. In fact, he whined like a rusty hinge before flat out stating he didn't want to play the role of a bougie bitch.

"Not you, knucklehead. Phoebe! The widow hasn't seen either you or your girlfriend before. This is a perfect under-cover op."

Questions were one thing, but when Vinny asked who would be footing the bill for this hen party, I was done playing nice. "This is all your fault. Tell Phoebe what kind of info we need, shell out some bucks, and take her bony ass to that goat farm for a mud dip. Capiche?"

He grunted affirmatively and hung up. You'd think I had asked him to fly her to Paris. The cheap putz.

As Rico and I walked out of the precinct, I instantly questioned my judgment. Was Vinny smart enough to school Phoebe on the kind of proof we needed? And was Phoebe smooth enough to pull this off? What if she botched things up and the widow caught on? I was usually more on top of my game than this. But it had been a rough couple of days, and my thoughts were scattered. I told myself that if that's the worst mistake I'll ever make, I'll be lucky. But only if my guardian angel gets some backup. I'm pretty sure she drinks more than I do.

20

THE HUMAN TERRARIUM

Finding a stockpile of biters wouldn't be difficult. Deadheads hide in dark, abandoned buildings, under overpasses, or in any secluded area near their preferred food source: people. Most biters hunt at night because they are hard-wired that way, while others simply prefer the cover of darkness.

Not all rotters are created equal. Biters with earlier strains of the Z-Virus can't see in daylight. Others, suffering from more recent bio-engineered strains, don't have that limitation. Problem-solving and controlling the desire for flesh were the newest genetically modified traits added to the mix. Figuring out which biters were which could be a challenge.

Rico was unusually quiet as he wound his Mustang down I-75s toward one of the biggest biter havens in the city—the Over-the-Rhine (OTR) neighborhood, just north of downtown. I slouched in the passenger seat, half wanting to ask why the cat had his tongue, and the other half certain he was punishing me for rejecting his attempt to comfort me after Mama's death.

The emotional aspect of our relationship baffled me, just as it had when Ferris and I were involved. It's not like I had a lot of experience to draw on, but apparently, the few romances I'd had taught me nothing. Icky, prickly things like feelings had always been and always would be otherworldly to me.

Did men really want their partners to be needy and weak? That's not how I'm built. I'm self-sustaining...like a terrarium. If my sulking partner and I had a romantic future, he'd have to learn to love all of me, including my independence.

Rico pulled up curbside in front of the Hoffbauer Building and parked, then we grabbed some Maglites from the trunk. The ramshackle relic, covered by twenty years of overgrowth, had been scheduled for demolition for months, yet the eyesore remained a popular hangout for biters. We'd checked out the place before. It had an external entrance through a root cellar disguised by a state-of-the-art camouflage system—a pile of trash and biohazardous waste glued to its wooden doors. *Chez Zombi* couture at its finest.

We stepped into an ambush here last time, fought a battalion of biters, and narrowly escaped with our lives. The city came behind us and installed security measures to ensure the cellar remained rotter-free.

After fighting our way through the thicket of waist-high weeds, we located the entrance.

"Padlock," I said, pointing to a metal object several feet from the cellar doors. A split-second later, I nodded to a spot a few feet away. "And there's the chain." So much for the city's security measures.

A smell resembling burnt plastic tinged with ammonia wafted from the cellar as Rico flung back the doors. We drew our guns, switched on our Maglites, and descended the steps into darkness.

"Cincinnati Police Department," Rico hollered, moving his flashlight beam from side to side. "Anybody down here?"

I wrinkled my nose. "Lots of stink down here, but no *Eau de Deadhead.*"

"More like *Eau de Crack*."

Moving deeper into the cellar, I gravitated to a specific spot on the floor, and my heart sank like a stone. When Ferris went missing, we turned the city upside down trying to find him. Whispers at the 51st suggested he had gone rogue and was taking money from Toussaint. No way. Not Ferris.

That spot on the floor was where Rico and I discovered a pair of Oakleys I'd given Ferris, and beside them we found a manacle with dried blood on it. Our first solid clue that something horrible had happened to him.

Rico and I spun around as a crackhead, pipe in hand, bolted out the door behind us. Luckily for him, we weren't from the Drug Enforcement Unit. Crackhead: 1, Good Guys: 0. Biters: No Show. I couldn't decide if that was good or bad news. But the memory of the bloodied manacle would be another reason to lose sleep.

When we climbed the steps and Rico shuttered the cellar behind us, I tried a technique Barbara 'Babs' McMillen, an FBI psychologist turned profiler and former hotel roommate, taught me: I visualized the closed doors as a metaphor for shutting out that memory of Ferris. I hoped it would work, but taking advice from Babs, with her OCD and thermostat-control issues, seemed like a crapshoot at best.

The next stop on our biter tour was a dilapidated church on Freeman Avenue in the city's West End. Rico parked in the crumbling asphalt lot, and we climbed out to inspect the Gothic cathedral that provided sanctuary to some of the city's biter brigade. Once upon a time, the church had been the site of an epic battle between Vinny and Rowan Marlowe, a six-foot redheaded P.I. The prize? A rotter worth $180,000. The way it looked today, Rico and I would have another battle on our hands.

Disembodied moans and groans greeted us when we opened the massive wooden doors. Once we crossed the threshold, guns drawn, and the doors creaked shut behind us, a gaggle of problem-solving, speed-demon deadheads rushed us in the vestibule. The first one was on me faster than flies on zushi.

After a quick feint right, I ducked, swung left, and tried to raise my gun. The rotter powered past my arm and lunged, teeth-first, for my neck. I stopped, dropped, and rolled onto my back, squeezing off a round that nailed it center mass. A useless shot, except that it slowed the meatbag's momentum enough that my second shot drilled it right beneath the chin. Its head exploded like a blood-bag pinata, spraying bone and zushi from one end of the vestibule to the other.

Rico took cover behind a massive marble column and eliminated two more. A new group of freshies surged from the back pew and swarmed us. Rico and I began picking them off one by one. It was a solid plan, until they hit the vestibule floor, slipped on the zushi, and pinwheeled across the marble like meatbag missiles. Headshots in that chaos were nearly impossible, so we started drilling them as soon as they poured out of the pew.

By the end of the battle, we counted twelve permanently retired rotters, and we hadn't even ventured into the nave yet. Finding that many biters in one place wasn't a coincidence. This was somebody's stockpile.

A search of the nave didn't reveal any stragglers, so I headed to the cry room to look for more. After coming up empty, I figured the skirmish was over and headed back toward the entrance. About halfway to the vestibule, I noticed a confessional box.

"When's the last time you were in one of these puppies?" I asked, opening the door.

A biter bolted out like a scalded cat, knocked me down, and fell over my dumb ass. Rico picked her off in mid-air just as she was about to faceplant into my chest. I scrambled to my feet, screaming strings of curse words that had never been uttered before, and fired another round into her for no other reason than that she had scared the living shit out of me.

Freaking freshies.

The only room left to check was the sacristy. After opening the door and finding it clear, I mouthed a silent Hallelujah. The small room, filled with petrified animal poop, mold, and trash, looked like a dead end until we opened the vestiary door and discovered an antique dresser inside. The top drawer was stuck. After tugging on the handles and jiggling them several times, it flew open, revealing a rental agreement for a semi and a street map with the handwritten notation: 1329 Arlington.

Rico glanced over my shoulder. "Does that address mean something to you?"

"Yeah, but I'm not sure why." I pulled out my phone and Googled it. "Huh, no wonder. It's the Crosley Building. Harry Delk and I got suckered into an ambush there. We faced an entire horde and almost ended up a late-night snack."

"Arlington Street's in Camp Washington," Rico said, herding me out of the sacristy.

He called for a meat wagon as we strolled through the nave, picking our way through the bodies, blood, and unidentifiable biter bits. Out of habit, I left a Splatz card propped against the base of a bullet-riddled column. Why not? Somebody might buy the place and turn it into a goat yoga day spa someday. Jimmy at Splatz gave me a ten percent discount for every referral. In my line of work, that added up.

Lucky for me, Rico's go bag was in the trunk of his Mustang. It's a permanent fixture there because, as he likes to remind me, he is always prepared for both of us. He tossed me a towel, a spare set of my jeans, and a fresh t-shirt to change into.

"What do you think we'll find at The Crosley?" he asked as we put the church in the rearview window.

"God only knows," I said. "But how much worse could it be?"

***

Rico pulled onto the shoulder of the road above Hopple Street, switched off the ignition, and said, "Since we're here, we may as well check out the subway tunnel."

My stomach dropped.

The Mustang's interior transformed into a sweltering vacuum. My chest ached, and my lungs heaved. I swung open the passenger door and leaned out, gulping air, but no amount of oxygen could erase the memories tied to that subway station. It's where Toussaint murdered Doctors Christian and Ferris—and where I killed Toussaint.

Rico, who seemed oblivious to my predicament, bolted from the car and jogged across the street to the short retaining wall that separated the road from the ravine below. He leaned over the barrier as far as he dared to get a view of the tunnel entrance.

"I can't see the gate from here," he yelled. "We need to crawl down into the ravine."

I forced myself out of the passenger door and tottered a few steps away from the car. Everything disappeared—the sky, Rico, the road, and the concrete wall. They were replaced by the sight of Ferris' head exploding from the impact of Toussaint's bullet, pieces of his skull and white matter from his brain arcing outward in slow motion.

My legs trembled. My feet turned to clay. I shook my head to erase the vision but couldn't. After a blind stumble back to the car, I groped for the door. A soft mewling caught my ear. The mewling had come from me.

"Hey, you." Rico's voice sounded odd. "How's it going over there?"

"Umm, I..." Words failed me. The more I searched for them, the further away they seemed. "Something's..."

"You stay put, huh? I'll be right there."

The sound of his footsteps filled my ears. Then his arms wrapped around me, holding me upright as my knees buckled. I buried my face in his shoulder, panting and fighting the urge to vomit. The image of Ferris's shattering skull faded, and my vision returned to normal, except for the tears pooling in my eyes. I didn't dare blink. God forbid they spill.

Rico held me until my breathing steadied, then he lowered me into the passenger seat and crouched on the berm beside me.

"How we doing?" he asked softly.

I croaked some syllables that were supposed to form words but sounded like gibberish. After a long, deep breath, I tried again. "I can't. I can't go...down...there, Rico. Too many..."

He placed his finger below my jaw and lifted my head until our eyes met. "I've got this. Sit tight. I'm gonna shimmy down into that ravine and check the padlock on the gate. Make sure nobody's fucked with it. Be back before you know it."

I grabbed his arm. "No! You can't go alone. What if he's back? What if he's down there?"

"What if who's back?"

An awkward silence filled the air. I looked batty enough as it was. The answer would have made me sound certifiable.

"Just...just give me a minute," I murmured. "I'll go with you—"

"Not this time, Partner."

A rogue tear slid down my face. I swatted it like a bug. "You can't go alone. I can't lose you, too. Please don't go—"

"Look," he said, grabbing my phone from the Mustang's console and placing it in my hand. "I'll call you. We can talk the whole time I'm down there. If I run into trouble, you can climb down and rescue me." He kissed my forehead, stood upright, then tossed me a wink. "No sense in both of us getting dirty, rolling around in the mud. Unless you want to roll around in the mud with me. 'Cause that could be fun."

I forced a smile.

He pulled out his phone and called me as he walked across the road toward the tunnel.

I picked it up on the first ring. "Jesus, you're clingy."

We shared an awkward laugh, then he climbed over the wall and disappeared into the ravine. He chatted nonstop throughout the entire trip, his tone light and breezy, solely for my benefit. I should have been down there with him, but I was glad for the space. It gave me time to evaluate what happened.

I thought I had put Ferris's death behind me, but clearly, I hadn't. Revisiting the tunnel brought his murder back in living color, like a scene from a slasher flick. And how did I react? I lost my shit right there in the middle of the street. For a few terrifying moments, my senses crapped out, and reality took a vacation.

Before the last few days, I had never felt vulnerable in my life. The feeling sucked. I was a freaking corpse whisperer, damn it. Tougher than a two-dollar steak—arrogant, snarky, and headstrong. Earlier in the day, I'd been whining that Rico hadn't accepted me for the badass I was.

But when I dissolved into a basket case right in front of him, he hadn't even blinked. Since the day we met, he'd accepted everything I had thrown at him, the good, the bad, and the "classic Nighthawk." My partner didn't want me needy; he wanted to be needed. He didn't want me to be weak; he wanted to help me be strong. Maybe I was the one with the acceptance problem.

Or maybe I was losing my shit. I gave it fifty-fifty.

Rico hopped back over the retaining wall and trotted toward the car.

"Sealed up tight as a drum," he said, sliding behind the

wheel. "No dig marks in the surrounding ground, either. We can cross the tunnel off the list, and the Hudepohl Brewery, too. They demolished it a few months ago. If you're up for it, we can head to The Hoffbauer Building." He reached across the seat and took my hand. "But we need to talk along the way."

RICO DID MOST of the talking.

"There's no shame in being human, babe. You hadn't been back to the tunnel since that day, and you had a little...meltdown. I'm no expert, but that sounds like PTSD to me."

If he thought I would disagree, he was sadly mistaken.

"And the thing is," Rico added, "that doesn't go away on its own. Maybe you should call Babs."

"Aww, not Babs. Do I have to?"

"Better the devil you know than some poor, unsuspecting therapist who has never experienced...you."

True but hurtful. And I didn't want to break in another shrink.

"Fine," I mumbled. "I'll call her later, after we get back."

He rolled his eyes.

"I will. Swear to God."

"You didn't answer my question back there," Rico said, changing the subject as he headed toward the Crosley Building. "Who did you think was in the tunnel?"

I melted into the seat and stared out the window. "Pay no attention to the nutjob sitting beside you. She's delusional."

"You were talking about Toussaint, weren't you?"

"What if I was?"

"You know he's dead, babe. You killed him, right there in that tunnel."

Here we go. "But what if he's back...as a demon?"

Rico turned his eyes from the road to gawp at me. "Say that again?"

He didn't have to ask twice. It felt good to share all the things I'd been keeping from him, about my daydreams, memories, the waking visions that could have only been planted by Toussaint, and Mama's message about postponing her memorial until I was done battling my demon. Rico listened intently and remained silent through it all.

When I finished, he simply said, "I thought we were finished with that motherfucker."

I thought so too.

21

SHUFFLE, SHUFFLE, THUMP, THUMP

Fifteen minutes later, Rico parked curbside in front of The Crosley Building. I climbed out of the Mustang and stared at the façade of the crumbling ten-story colossus while he opened the trunk to grab a crowbar, a couple of Maglites, and extra ammo. Given the welcoming committee we'd had at the church, we weren't taking any chances.

A sign anchored to the side of the building said the property was undergoing renovation, but there wasn't a dumpster in sight, and the surrounding lot was still littered with broken glass, garbage, drywall, and rebar. The place reminded me of a concrete ghost town, even creepier and bigger than I remembered.

Rico shoved some magazines into his pants pocket, then tossed a couple to me along with one of the flashlights. My 9mm held ten in the mag, and one in the pipe, the same as Baby holstered at my ankle; Rico's Glock 34 held seventeen, plus one. God help us if we need more firepower than that, I thought while we reloaded.

The entrance had been boarded up since the last time I was there. Rico inserted his crowbar behind the plywood and gave it a tug. The board popped off easier than a Tupperware lid and clattered at his feet. The nails that had held it in place had been more for show than for security. Someone wanted to be able to come and go as they pleased.

Rico leaned his crowbar against the doorframe as we entered what looked like one of the large, open manufacturing zones of the facility. The farther in we walked, the more sunlight we lost from the doorway. Before long, the building was as black as an underground cavern. Beams from our Maglites pricked pinholes in the darkness.

Without tool cribs, tow motors, and machinery, the area we *could* see looked naked, nothing more than a wide-open expanse with a towering ceiling. Spiderwebs, caught in the beam of my flashlight, danced as I inched past them. With no electricity or air conditioning, the place must have been ninety degrees. My clothes clung to me like a second skin.

"Anybody home?" Rico called.

His voice echoed off the wide-open walls.

"Nobody but us…" Something whirred in my ear. "Did you hear that?" I asked.

"Hear what?"

I paused and listened again, but whatever I'd heard was gone. "Never mind," I said, feeling edgy. "Let's make this easy. You go right; I go left."

The echo of Rico's footsteps faded as I drew Hawkeye and ventured deeper into the darkness. If memory served me right, there were a few doors on my side, a couple that led to some small offices, and one that led to a stairwell.

Checking the offices didn't take long. Most of them were empty, unless you counted dead varmints, animal scat, and cobwebs.

I threw back the heavy metal door beneath the stairwell sign, shone my light up the steps, and caught a fleeting glimpse of something from the corner of my eye.

"Hello?" I called, hearing nothing but the echo of my voice.

The hair on the back of my neck stood up.

That was the second time since we arrived that my senses had played tricks on me. I wondered if my 'incident' at the tunnel had rattled me even more than I realized. I shone my light on the second-floor landing and climbed the stairs, hoping to pull myself together.

"He's up here," rasped a voice from the third floor.

I took the steps two at a time, flung back the door to the third-floor hallway, and lunged inside with my head on a swivel. The hem of a woman's skirt fluttered around the corner to my left. I sprinted down the hallway, following the beam of my flashlight. When I reached the end of the T-shaped hallway, a familiar voice from the right called, "This way, Little Bird!"

Mama?

I raced through a series of twisting hallways, reeling at the prospect of seeing her again. Hearing her footfalls and catching glimpses of her at the corners was proof that even in death, she had found a way back to help me battle Toussaint. Why was I surprised? If he could come back, crossing the void would be child's play for her.

A door creaked open ahead. I raised my flashlight and found Mama standing in the doorway, smiling, and gesturing for me to follow her. I reached the door on a dead run and sprinted into a large, rectangular room. But no one was there.

I froze in the darkness, bile rising in my throat, as a distant *shuffle, shuffle, thump, thump* caught my ear. *Shuffle, shuffle, thump, thump. Shuffle, shuffle, thump, thump.*

It hadn't been Mama who'd led me there.

The door slammed behind me. I shined my light straight ahead and sucked in a gasp as a wall of corpsicles shambled toward me shoulder-to-shoulder, their feet thudding against the concrete floor in a rhythmic *shuffle, shuffle, thump, thump.*

A few magazines wouldn't put a dent in a wall of deadheads. I spun and broke for the door, only to find it locked from the outside.

I was screwed to the max and had no one to blame but myself. Nobody should be dumb enough to get ambushed twice in the same building. If I lived through this, I would never hear the end of it. On the other hand, if I didn't come up with a plan soon, I wouldn't have to worry about the embarrassment.

A pair of industrial-length workbenches near the back of the room could form a makeshift barrier between me and the horde. I put my back into it, pushed with everything I had, and brought the ends of the benches together, reducing the possibility of being flanked. Then I moved behind them, wielding the flashlight in my right hand and Hawkeye in my left.

I took out the front-line rotters first. When they fell, they created a meatbag mound, causing the biters behind them to stumble and pile up on top of each other. It was a technique I perfected over the years that worked great until you ran out of ammo.

That wouldn't take long.

I had failed to consider that these were the overachieving, problem-solving rotters. They began to skirt the meatbag mound and shuffle toward the ends of the worktables to flank me. I swung Hawkeye toward the right end of the workbench, aimed, and fired, but nothing happened.

I was out of ammo.

After ejecting the empty mag, I reloaded, took a cleansing breath, leveled my gun, and began firing. Every shot counted. When Hawkeye ran out, I switched to Baby. Every squeeze of the trigger brought me one bullet closer to death. My last line of defense would be the seven-inch Ka-Bar knife in my belt sheath. I hoped it wouldn't come to that. Hand-to-horde combat is a terrible way to die.

Harry Delk's face popped into my mind as I fired my last

round. I wasn't surprised; we had fought deadheads side by side in this building under similar circumstances.

A little help right about now would be nice, Partner. I wasn't picky about which partner, Harry or Rico. Either would do.

The door burst open and crashed against the wall with a bang. Semi-automatic gunfire pierced the air. I ducked beneath the workbench, watching biters fall around me like matchsticks.

Rico bent down and tossed me another mag, so I slapped it in, jumped back up, and rejoined the fight. Once we mowed down the flanking biters, Rico moved beside me, shoulder to shoulder, behind the table. Firing in tandem, we shot the biters closest to us, then shot our way back through the horde until nothing was moving. After that, we stopped shooting for a beat and listened. The hair-raising *shuffle, shuffle, thump, thump* was gone.

"That's a lot of dead rotters," Rico said, scanning the room in the glow of his flashlight.

I holstered Baby, wiped zushi off my face, and smeared it on my pants. "Ha! Look at this room. Some contractor's going to have a cow." Cha-ching, I thought, pulling out another one of Jimmy's cards and laying it on the workbench. Two referrals in one day! Assuming either one panned out, Jimmy might let me parlay them into a twenty-five percent discount.

A shot rang out.

Rico grabbed my arm and yanked me down behind the workbench. We stared at each other and doused our flashlights, bewildered.

"Biters don't shoot guns...do they?" Rico whispered.

"Who the hell knows anymore?" I grumbled, pulling my nine milly again. "I'm putting in for hazardous duty pay. This job sucks."

22

AND THE OSCAR GOES TO...

"Now what?" I muttered.

Rico was the plan guy. I was hoping he'd have some strategic pearl of wisdom, but he was busy grimacing and holding his arm.

"We sit tight," he said, "I called in a 10-13 downstairs when I heard your gunfire. Backup should be here soon...ish."

I leaned in to check out his arm. "You hit?"

"Just a scratch."

I couldn't get a good look at his bicep in the dark, so I reached over and touched it. There was something wet on his sleeve. Was it his blood or chum from one of the crap-ton of rotters we'd put down? God only knew.

I lifted my head just enough to peek over the workbench, and another shot rang out. A splinter of wood from the top of the workbench zinged past my head. The first shot had taken us by surprise, but not the second.

"Up and to the right," Rico whispered.

With no windows in the room, Rico's 'up' suggested something like a platform or a stairwell. This shooter knew his stuff. I hadn't given him much to shoot at, and he almost nailed me.

"How can this guy see in the dark?" I asked.

"Night vision goggles."

We were pinned down, like ducks in a shooting gallery. Something needed to change. A fresh burst of semi-auto gunfire shredded the top of the workbench. Jesus, I thought, watching woodchips fly. When's backup going to arrive?

"Take off your clothes," I whispered.

"Excuse me?"

"And your shoes. Give 'em here."

Rico looked at me like I'd lost my mind.

"We need a diversion."

"Then you should take off your clothes."

"Rico, I swear. Just do—"

The clink of his belt buckle stopped me in mid-rant. He slid down his pants, then took off his shirt and shoes and tossed them at me with a harrumph. "This better be good."

I rolled up his shirt and shoved it into the lower part of one of his pant legs. Once it looked like a well-muscled calf, I shoved it into Rico's shoe and whispered, "At the count of three, I'm going to make a noise and push the fake leg out from the side of the workbench toward the door, like we're making a break for it. When our sniper takes his shot, you're gonna blind him with your flashlight beam and nail him."

"You've been watching *Reacher* again, haven't you?"

"You got a better idea?"

"I can't think without my clothes."

"On three. One, two, three..."

I racked my slide, producing an audible *click-thunk,* then inched the fake leg out from the side of the workbench. It worked like a charm—until the shoe did a 180 inside the pants leg and ended up facing backwards, like an inverted size-twelve Gumby foot.

Shit, shit, shitty, shit, shit.

"Oh, God! My foot! It's BROKEN," I screamed, in an Oscar-worthy performance.

The sniper fired. Rico popped up naked as a jaybird, centered him in the flashlight's beam, leveled his Glock, and drilled the bastard between his eyes.

A deathly quiet filled the room.

"Dude," I whispered, "I didn't know you were going commando."

We swept our lights from one end of the massive floor to the other, illuminating a score of dead rotters and one dead sniper. The shooter had been positioned on a catwalk, approximately ten feet up and twenty feet back from the workbench.

I whistled at Rico's impressive shot. "You're gonna make me call you Reacher now, aren't you?"

He must have heard me, but he didn't respond. Worried that he was wounded worse than he was letting on, I tried again.

"Well, maybe I'll save that for bedtime, huh?"

That remark was as charming as anything I'd ever said in my life, yet he didn't crack a smile.

"Just hand me my clothes," he snapped. "Now, before backup gets here."

I did as he asked and watched him scowl as he got dressed, mumbling something about 'fucking bullet holes in his pants.' When he finished, he called for the meatwagon to pick up the mountain of decommissioned deadheads.

"It's going to be a while," he said, massaging his temples. "They're still tied up on Freeman Avenue at the abandoned church."

"No doubt," I chuckled. "How's your arm?"

"I told you, it's just a scratch."

Rico's tone was flat, almost dismissive. What the hell is wrong now? I wondered. Interpreting his mood swings was going to take an instruction manual.

A parade of footsteps echoed from the first-floor stairwell, announcing the arrival of our backup. Rico picked his way through the mound of deadheads to the sniper's body, reached down, and slid the shooter's wallet out from his back pocket. Once he removed the sniper's ID, he held it in the beam of his flashlight.

"Mr. Carl Antenucci, from Atlantic City, New Jersey."

"Giordano country," I said, "What a coincidence."

The first of the backup officers bolted into the room, gawked at the carnage, and whistled. "Geezus, De Palma. You been busy."

"Ahh, the cavalry," Rico chided, swiping his bloody face with his even bloodier sleeve. "Do me a favor. Stick around 'til the meatwagon gets here. I gotta get cleaned up. Know anybody with a sandblaster?"

Without a single glance in my direction, Rico brushed past the officer into the hallway and started down the steps. I trotted after him.

"Hey, wait up."

He took a few more steps before stopping, but even then, he didn't bother to turn back and look at me.

Enough was enough.

"All right. Spill it," I said. "What's wrong?"

He shook his head and continued down the stairs.

"Talk to me, damn it!"

Rico stopped short and whirled around. "Why'd you run off on your own like that?"

"Like what? We agreed you'd go right and I'd go left. Remember?"

"This is a huge building, Nighthawk! You were two flights up—by yourself. The only way I found you was by following the gunfire."

I shrugged. "Maybe I should have waited for you, but—"

"What if I hadn't found you? You'd be dead, or worse, bitten. Who would save you then? Or Wycowski?"

"I get it, but—"

"And who would have to put you down if this strain doesn't respond to medicine? Don't ask me to do that, Allie. I can't."

"This is my job!" I barked, more loudly than I'd intended. "You've never complained about it before. And I'd never ask anyone to put me down. I'd eat my gun before I'd do that—to you or anyone else."

"Things are different now, damn it. I lov..." He took a breath and paused, sweeping his hands through his hair. "Why didn't you come get me? I'd have gone up there with you—"

"Mama spoke to me, Rico."

"Mama's dead."

I threw my hands in the air. "You think I don't know that! But it was her voice. And I saw her—hand to God. It was her. I *knew* it was her. But then she led me into..." I flung my arm toward the carnage on the third floor. "Toussaint was trying to isolate me. I realize that now. I'm sorry."

Weariness crept into Rico's voice. "You need to be smarter than that. For everyone's sake, Allie. I can't do this shit on my own."

RICO MIGHT HAVE BEEN PISSED at me, but I was thankful that I hadn't lost my nerve after my mini (okay, not so mini) meltdown at the tunnel. Part of me had been worried about that, though I hadn't mentioned it to him. Rico stayed quiet as he drove us back to my house. It was dinnertime, and we were exhausted. Resting my head against the seat, I closed my eyes to avoid overthinking his every expression. I didn't need Dr. Phil's insight to see that my partner was still upset. It probably didn't help that, for the second time in one day, we'd been scattered, smothered, and chunked in chum. Even the zushi-proof seat covers Nonnie had custom-sewn for the Mustang were soaked through.

As Rico pulled into the driveway, I opened the door to bail out, thinking it would spare him from having to lie about why he wouldn't be staying for dinner. But it was too late. Nonnie was outside throwing Headbutt's ball (and then chasing it for him since the only thing he chases are rotters).

She waddled up to the driver's side window and nearly swooned at the sight of the blood-drenched seat covers. When she recovered and said dinner would be ready in half an hour, Rico tried to beg off. Resorting to guilt, she said she had made his favorite. The odds were in her favor because everything she cooked was his favorite.

Before she let us into the house, Nonnie told us to leave our shoes on the porch. Then she had Rico take off the Mustang's seat covers and hose them down, along with our shoes and himself, while I went inside and took a shower.

After nearly falling asleep under the steady pulse of warm water, I dried off, got dressed, and carried my special biohazard laundry basket to the side porch for Rico to throw his seat covers into. Then I plopped into a chair at the kitchen table, head down and comatose, while Nonnie followed Rico to the bathroom and waited in the hallway so he could throw his blood-soaked clothes out the door and into her basket. I drifted off when she disappeared to the basement to start our laundry. My nap didn't last long.

"Looks what I found in basket near dryer!" she crowed as she trotted back into the kitchen, waving a pair of men's jeans and a Quantico t-shirt.

I had shoved them into the bottom of the old rattan basket months ago and forgotten about them. Seeing them now didn't hurt any less. They had belonged to Ferris.

"Mr. Rico must have lefts them here," she said. "Is very convenient, no?"

"No. I mean, yes. Sure," I mumbled, picturing Ferris running alongside me at Mirror Lake in his favorite Tee.

When the shower stopped, she took the clothes back to the bathroom for Rico to wear until his clothes dried. He wandered into the kitchen, barefoot, with the hem of the jeans grazing the floor and the waistline gapping.

He locked eyes with me and mumbled, "Are you, uh, okay with me wearing these?"

Nonnie laughed. "Is plenty goods for us, Mr. Rico. We not fancy-shmancies here."

"It's fine." I smiled, scooting a chair to him with my foot. "How's your arm?"

"All cleaned up. It's fine." He sat across from me, took my hand, and flashed a tired smile. "I'm sorry. Long day, eh?"

"Yeah. Me too. I should have—"

"Miss Allie," Nonnie interrupted, "Is something I needs to tells you. Don't be mads. Is about birdses."

I sucked in a breath. The last time an avian discussion started this way, I had bird eggs coming out my ass. "What about the birdses, eh, the birds?"

"Baby Gertie eats big picture window blind in living room."

Dollar signs danced through my head. "Eats as in swallowed or eats as in chewed?"

Nonnie frowned. "Is difference? Come see, Ms. Allie."

Rico and I tailed Nonnie into the living room and gasped. The left edge of the wooden window blind, from top to bottom, had been gnawed ragged.

Rico bit back a smile. "Is Gertie's daddy a termite?"

Nonnie wiped away a tear. "I pay, Ms. Allie. Just don't be means to baby. She getting big and needs strong beaks."

I counted to ten and tried breathing through my chakras or

whatever that shit was that Babs taught me. It didn't help. "How strong does her beak need to be, Nonnie? She eats seed!"

"Speaking of eating," Rico said, putting an arm around each of us and herding us back into the kitchen. "Something smells wonderful."

Freaking bootlicker.

"What's that?" I said, spying the massive daylily arrangement displayed on the coffee table that I had missed on my way into the room.

Nonnie dismissed it with a wave of her hand. "Flowers for you. Comes today."

"Are these from you?" I asked Rico, plucking out the card.

"No. Maybe Cap sent them."

When I opened the envelope and read the message, the card slipped from my fingers and fluttered to the floor. I stared at it in silence, as a rush of emotions washed over me.

"Well, who are they from?" Rico asked, scooping up the card and reading it aloud, "There's no one to protect you now. My condolences, Little Bird ~ Eternally, Toussaint."

23

—————

PHOEBE GETS HER FIZZ ON

Rico spewed a string of curse words, grabbed the flowers, and stormed into the kitchen. I cringed as the back door swung open and slammed against the wall, shattering the glass insert. Seconds later came the crash of the flower arrangement hitting the steel trash can at warp speed. Nonnie and I edged back into the kitchen just in time to see Rico reenter the house, red-faced and out of breath.

"Feel better?" I asked, eyeing the sea of broken glass on my floor.

Rico hung his head. "Why can't the bastard just die already?"

"Oh, he's dead. He's just a demon now."

"Either way, he's still an ass."

Nonnie, our resident kitchen witch, magically appeared with a broom and dustpan in hand, shooing us out of her way.

"No ma'am," Rico said, as he took them from her and started sweeping. "This is my mess."

I moved beside him and squeezed his shoulder. "Don't let him get to you. The tough-guy shooter, the flowers, and that cheesy message, they're all vintage Toussaint. He's still using the Giordano clan to do his dirty work. Nothing has changed."

I'd had years of practice sparring with my old nemesis, but my partner hadn't. Sometimes I forgot that after Rico's beat-down in New Orleans and the attack on Jade Chen, he had his own axe to grind with Toussaint. Plus, my romance with Rico made him overly protective of me, especially when it came to Toussaint. Rico had started to blurt something along those lines after I wandered off at the Crosley Building but then clammed up before he dug himself into a hole he couldn't crawl out of.

After Rico cleaned up the glass and boarded the broken window, the three of us sat down to a dinner of Pasta alla Norma, one of Nonnie's Sicilian dishes, made with rigatoni, eggplant, and ricotta salata. As if that weren't enough calories, she had made her secret-recipe cannoli for dessert. When nothing but crumbs remained, we pushed away from the table, exhausted and ready to explode. Nonnie took pity on us and told us to relax while she finished the dishes. She didn't have to say it twice.

We passed out on the couch during *Wheel of Fortune* and didn't wake up until Vinny and Phoebe burst in the kitchen door, chattering like magpies on meth.

Vinny whisper-shouted, "They're out cold."

Rico bolted upright from a dead sleep, knocking me face-first into the cushion. "You aren't built for stealth, are you, Vinny?"

"Well," I said, lying sideways on the couch and scanning my carpet for leftover goat poop. "How'd it go?"

"Goat yoga's the best!" Phoebe hiccoughed. "Dang, those little critters are so —hic— cute! And see how soft my skin is? It's like —hic—silk. You've got to try a mud bath, Allie."

For shit's sake. Mata Hari was hammered.

"No thanks," I snapped. "How'd it go *with the widow*? Remember her?"

"Oh, Cricket? She's fun! And feisty-ty too. We shared a —hic—a mud pit."

I darted a death glance at Vinny.

He wrapped his arm around Phoebe and whispered in her ear, "Tell them what she said about the mayor, hun."

"Oh, yeah. The mayor. Well, when I told her my boyfriend squaw...squawked about the —hic—cost—by the way, did you know this cost $500? That's aslot. She said her hubsand wasn't complaining about money—hic—anymore. And I asked wh-why, and she said because —hic—he's dead. She said, 'Screw him and his sl-lutty secretary, Be-Bethany.' Then we both laughed and drank more —hic—champagne. I like champagne. It fizzizzes."

I pinched the bridge of my nose. "Did she happen to mention whether she killed him?"

"No." Phoebe tilted her head like a Labrador. "Should I have —hic—asked that?"

Christ. At least she got a name.

Phoebe collapsed against Vinny's shoulder and started to snore. He swept her into his arms and trudged down the hall toward his bedroom.

"Hey," I called after him. "If she tosses her cookies, you're cleaning it up."

"I'll put my garbage can by the bed."

"Vinny?"

"Yeah, Nighthawk?"

"How'd you pay for all this?"

"The ACME credit card."

Son of a fucking bitch.

AFTER DREAMING of dollar signs all night, I woke up at 8:00 a.m. to a note from Rico saying he had gone home to get ready for work and would pick me up at nine. That gave me just enough time to growl at the sunshine filtering through the bird-eaten living room blinds on my way to the coffee pot and to check my email. The news wasn't good.

I had received an ECDC bulletin warning of a worldwide increase in biter attacks. Worse, post-mortem virology testing revealed that the new Z-virus strain wasn't fully neutralized by the existing antidote. At best, the antidote slowed 'total trans-mogrification' by ten days. Push comes to shove, I wasn't sure I'd even want that reprieve, if a one-way trip to Deadheadsville was on the other side. Ten days is a long time to dread the inevitable.

The notion reminded me that Rico didn't want to put me down if I was bitten. That he simply couldn't do it. I wasn't bluffing when I said I'd sooner eat a bullet than ask anyone to put me down. That's too much guilt to heap on any living soul, much less someone you love. Given what I did for a living, I had been incredibly lucky to have escaped being bitten. But it only takes once, and Wycowski's luck had run out.

How could I tell Rico that his mentor was doomed? Neither delivering the sad news to Wyco myself nor volunteering to put him down in the end would lessen his pain. I didn't know how to do that. But I *did* know that Toussaint had never created a virus without engineering its antidote. As my partner pulled into the driveway, I vowed that I would find that antidote before Wycowski turned—or I'd die trying.

24

MYSTERY, INTRIGUE, AND SEX

The update from the European CDC couldn't have come at a worse or better time, since Rico wanted to stop by the hospital to check on Wycowski. I'm not one to sugarcoat the truth, but even if I were, no amount of lipstick could pretty up that platypus. The man was dying. There'd be no escaping pain for Wyco or my partner.

As a dues-paying member of the 'keep it short and sweet' camp, I let Rico have the facts straight. The brooding silence that followed showed he was struggling. But then, it seemed like he'd been struggling with everything lately. I didn't have the time or patience to hold his hand every time his feelings kicked in. I had a demon on the run and an antidote to find.

Rico pulled into a parking spot at Christ Hospital and turned off the car. He stared out the windshield for a five-count, took a deep breath, then punched the shit out of the door panel.

Anger is good. I can work with anger. It beats brooding any day.

I offered to go inside with him, but he wanted to deliver the news to Wycowski alone. That was probably a good call, considering I was the face of his friend's illness —the tangible link to the disease that was eating him alive. As Rico closed the car door, I said to tell Wyco that I'd come back soon with the antidote in hand. A little hope never hurt anyone, right? If Rico heard, he didn't respond.

Alone and bored, I pulled out my phone to check my text messages:

Nonnie sent a picture showing that Gertie had progressed from eating the wooden blinds to gnawing the crap out of my baseboards. My response: Gertie needs to find a job to pay for replacement blinds and new baseboards.

Vinny asked if he could borrow the Lowrider, plus fifty bucks against his salary. My responses: No, and nice try. When did you go salaried?

Opie texted, asking me to call him. Apparently, he'd run into Burklander on the street, and the stuffed-shirt mentioned that copies of the Widow's lawsuit had gone out. It wasn't even 10:00 a.m., and the day was already chock-full-o'turds. When Opie said I needed to prepare for a mock deposition, a migraine bloomed behind my eyes.

"I haven't found anyone to rep you yet," he said. "Amazingly, no one wants to work for free."

"Why do I need to prepare?" I whined, massaging my temples. "They ask questions; I answer. How hard can it be?"

Opie's laughter pummeled my eardrums. "You need to provide simple, direct responses, stick to the facts, answer only what is asked, and not get argumentative. Nighthawk, the odds of you getting through a deposition without having a stroke are astronomical."

Well then, tell me how you really feel, asshat.

I flatly refused to meet in Opie's office. And holding the practice session in my kitchen, aka the aviary/ACME Central, would be like studying at the infield of the Kentucky Derby. I suggested The Blue Note with its small bar, ambient atmosphere, and unlimited supply of alcohol.

Since Rico hadn't returned yet and I still had time on my hands, I decided to check the dark web for zombie-related chatter. I expected to see snippets about increased biter attacks, and I found several. More troubling were the rumors of potential shelter-in-place warnings. If that measure were being considered, the ECDC would have notified me; in fact, I would likely have been involved in the preliminary discussions. Social media speculation would spike global panic. I wondered who started these rumors.

Philippe Boucher would know. But the cost for the answer would be high.

A mercenary corpse whisperer known for reliable intel, Philippe was a thirty-something charmer, mysterious and downright deadly, when the situation warranted. He plied his trade to the highest bidder, but underneath that capitalism lurked the heart of a whisperer who cared for humanity. More than once, he'd stuck his neck out for me. Possibly because he knew I was one of the good guys, or maybe because he wanted to sleep with me. Yeah, it was definitely the second one. I kept my text short and to the point.

Hey. It's me. Need your help.

Philippe's response arrived within seconds:

Bonjour, ma chèri! I have missed you. How may I be of assistance?

The ECDC says things are heating up. What are you hearing about the attacks? And who started the shelter-in-place rumors?

Not so fast. I adore you, but there is the matter of my fee.

With Philippe, everything came down to love or money. I thought for a moment before typing my reply.

I thought we had gotten past all that petty personal gain crap and were focused on saving the world.

The two are not mutually exclusive. But saving the world is

easier when I'm rich. Unless, of course, you have a trade in mind...

Oh, Dear God. I knew this was coming.

Sorry, Philippe, no time for fun and games. I'm under the gun. Really need your help.

Such a pity, *ma petite*. Fun and games sound delightful. As for assistance, my sources indicate the attacks have been concentrated in larger cities, where they are more noticeable. More bang for the buck, as you Americans say. This suggests that the activity is just getting started. I do not know who is behind the attacks or where the rumors originated. Now that our old nemesis Toussaint is gone, someone new must be on the rise. If I come into information that can help, I will share it, *ma chérie*. Are you sure you can't break free for one night if I fly in to see you?

Give it a break, Romeo.

Sorry, Philippe, as much as I enjoyed our dinner together, I am in a committed, committed sounded like a word Nonnie would use. *...I am dating,* dating sounded like Vinny and Phoebe making out in the Pinto. *Sorry, Philippe, as much as I enjoyed our dinner together, I'm seeing someone.*

The flurry of texts ground to a halt. I waited. And waited, then waited some more before Philippe's text popped.

Are you in love?

Rico jerked open the car door, and I fumbled my phone to the floor.

"How's Wyco?" I asked, sliding the phone closer with my foot and grabbing it.

"Like a man who knows he's dying and trying to cover. He did say that if he turns biter, he wants you to put him down, so he can haunt you 'til the end of time."

"How special."

"He also said he knows you'll move heaven and earth to find the antidote for him. But that if you can't, he knew the risks of police work, and would do it all over again, if he could."

"Wow," was all I could manage around the lump in my throat. Those were the words of a man saying goodbye. Not the words of the jackass who taped up a cartoon 'zombie wanted' poster when one of my rotters went AWOL. "Really?" I asked, after a moment's thought. "Wyco said that, huh?"

"Naw." Rico chuckled. "I made that part up. But if it makes you feel better, the haunt you 'til the end of time shit was all him." He started the car and backed out of his parking space. "What do you say we swing by City Hall and chat with the mayor's mistress/secretary, Bethany?"

"Eww! Mystery, intrigue, and sex," I said, pocketing my phone. "Count me in."

BETHANY BUZEK WAS CURRENTLY ASSIGNED as an executive assistant, working under the City Manager, Martin Gimball. Well, under his supervision, anyway. Give her time, I thought. From my sardonic perspective, lookers like Bethany often had a knack for climbing the ranks by lying flat on their backs.

Her thousand-watt smile flickered when Rico revealed that we were there to chat with her. She put her desk phone on DND and swept us down a hallway to a tiny, windowless conference room.

"I'd appreciate it if you made this quick," she said, glancing at her watch. "I have a luncheon with Risk Management in fifteen minutes."

Aren't we special?

Rico flashed an enigmatic smile. "We'll be as quick as we can. Some of our questions may seem overly personal but bear in mind this is a police investigation. We'll treat your answers with respect and as much confidentiality as possible."

Bethany nodded slowly.

"Ms. Buzek, were you aware that Mayor Capshaw was being investigated by the Ohio Special Investigations Unit for misappropriation of city funds?"

"Yes."

"Have you been interviewed by the OSIU regarding that investigation?"

"Yes," she said, fingering the collar of her suit jacket.

"Were you able to provide any relevant information?"

"No. If there was any funny business going on, I didn't know about it."

"I see." Rico changed course. "And did OSIU audit your work computer, personal computer, phone, and financial data?"

"They did. And they found nothing because I had nothing to hide."

"Ms. Buzek, were you having an inappropriate personal relationship with Mayor Capshaw?"

Bethany locked eyes with Rico. "Yes, I was."

"Why?" I blurted.

She gaped at me as if I were a new species of bug. "Excuse me?"

"C'mon, lady. The man weighed 350 pounds and looked like a beluga whale. What did you see in him?"

Her baby blues burned a hole through me. "Because he was nice. And connected, okay? He could get me places. In fact, the week before he died, he recommended me for my current job."

Rico nodded. "One more question, Ms. Buzek. Did you kill, or were you involved in the killing of Mayor Capshaw?"

"Certainly not! Now, if you've finished, I really must be going. New job and all. I wouldn't want to be late."

Rico rose to his feet. "Absolutely. If we need anything else—"

"You can request it from the OSIU. I've said all I'm going to say on this matter. I trust you can see your way out."

In one fluid motion, she rose from her chair and sauntered to the door, where she paused before glancing back over her shoulder. "You know, I wasn't the only one, Detective."

"Pardon?"

"The mayor's only side dish. He had plenty of them. He was a large man with...large appetites."

Rico tilted his head and smiled. "I don't suppose you know their names?"

"I have no idea who they were. But I paid the man's bills. He bought enough flowers to fill the Gardens of Versailles...and they weren't all coming to me." Bethany strutted down the hallway, leaving a toxic cloud of ambitchion in her wake.

"What do you think?" I asked. "Is she telling the truth?"

"Maybe. She sounded too bored to be lying." Rico's phone pinged. He pulled it from his pocket as we exited the City Manager's office and frowned at the message. "It's from Cap. Ronnie at Enzo's is trying to reach me. We need to swing by to see her."

Sex, lies, and bimbo number two. "I just dropped in to see her a few days ago, and she didn't have squat for me."

Rico shrugged. "Maybe she just misses my smiling face."

And your ass, and your shoulders, and your hips....

IT WAS close enough to lunchtime that just dropping by to find out what Ronnie wanted without ordering food would have been rude. At least, that's what Rico said as we walked into the bar. Bionic blondie raced across the worn hardwood floor and planted a kiss on his cheek. It would have landed on his mouth, but he had the decency to turn his head at the last second. Still draped over Rico, she side-eyed me and hooted, "Heya, Aileen! How 'bout some Fireball?"

The joke that never dies.

We sat at the bar, and after scanning the sticky laminated menus, ordered cheeseburgers. Ronnie caught Rico's eye and nodded down the hallway, across from the john—their usual super-secret decoder-ring meeting place. Only the cool kids were invited. Not me. Rico wandered off to chat with her, leaving me at the bar with the midday regulars, a swell bunch of guys, each of whom likely carried a minimum of three concealed weapons. Maybe it was the ambiance, or possibly the clientele, but the place was growing on me.

Once Operation Bimbo was completed and our burgers were gone, we resisted Ronnie's pleas to stay for a few. Rico tipped her fifty bucks, winked, and said he'd see her again. She blew him a kiss goodbye, and as the door swung closed behind us, I couldn't wait another minute.

"Well? Spill it. For fifty bucks, the intel must have been good."

"Worth every penny. The towheaded guy from the Winstel's video that you showed her stopped in for a few drinks yesterday. Ronnie said there was no mistaking his nose. His name is Charles Cain. He's fiftyish and wears a Special Forces ring on his right hand."

"Cain," I murmured, thinking aloud. "That's one of the names Vinny remembered from his kidnapping—"

"Which," Rico added, "establishes a connection between him and the Giordanos. According to Ronnie, after Cain left, the regulars said he was hiring indigents for some day-labor job. But talk on the street is that the guys he's hiring are going missing—as in never to be seen again."

We both let that scenario sit for a minute, mulling it over. And then a very ugly thought occurred to me.

"If you're breeding thousands of deadheads and trucking them into major cities to wreak havoc, along the way, you have to feed them...something."

"Or someone," we whispered in unison.

25

DID YOUR MOTHER DROP
YOU ON YOUR HEAD?

Having spent the morning away from the precinct, once we made our appearance, Rico beelined to his desk, leaving me to my own devices. I wandered into the breakroom for a cup of coffee and bumped into Cap's new secretary, whatever her name was. Who could remember? Our fearless leader's secretaries changed faster than Nonnie's hair color.

Rumors have circulated that I am responsible for the phenomenon of Cap's vanishing secretaries. That is entirely possible. The current dingbat cornered me by the cappuccino machine and mentioned that Cap had been looking for Rico and me.

Huzzah.

After glancing both ways out the breakroom door to ensure that Oh, Captain, My Captain was nowhere in sight, I headed to Rico's desk and found him glued to his laptop, reviewing official copies of the mayor's marriage certificate and Reverand Picken's officiant registration.

"So, they are legit," I mumbled, reading over his shoulder.

Rico shrugged. "We had to start somewhere. At least we can cross them off the list. The mayor's bank and credit card statements came in, too. Those will take some time to work through." Seconds later, his phone buzzed. He answered, nodded a couple of times, and said, "Be right there."

"Oh, yeah," I said as he hung up. "I almost forgot. Cap wants to see you."

"He wants to see *us*."

"Can't blame me for trying."

REPORTING to Cap's office felt like being called in to see Principal Durbin at Crescent City Academy. I might not always know why I was summoned, but the odds were, I wouldn't be happy when I left. As I entered Cap's office, the vein in his head was large enough to have its own gravitational field. And I hadn't even said a word.

Rico and I settled into our usual seats and waited while Cap put on his cheaters, rifled through the files on his desk, and pulled out three folders, respectively labeled: Eugene M. Capshaw Death Investigation, Zombie Attack on Precinct 51, and Cricket Capshaw v. The City of Cincinnati and Allie Nighthawk, et al.

Shit. Shit. Shitty, shit, shit.

"Updates, please," Cap said, picking up the Eugene Capshaw file. "Any headway in the mayor's death investigation?"

Rico called the ball. "The credit card and bank records came in, courtesy of OSIU, but the phone records are still outstanding. And I've requested subpoenas for his life insurance policy and his will. Both his marriage license and the officiant's license checked out, so they are off the table. We followed up on a lead concerning Bethany Buzek, his secretary at City Hall."

Cap raised a brow. "Really? Where'd that come from?"

I chimed in, hoping to bank a brownie point for the lawsuit portion of our conversation. "Actually, it came from the widow. She dropped an appointment card in the conference room the day she was here. I memorized the details before I handed it back to her, and then I orchestrated a little sting operation that worked like a charm. The widow let it slip *(to Vinny's drunk girlfriend)* that she knew her hubby was seeing his secretary." *Please don't ask for details. Please don't ask for details—*

Rico bailed me out. "Yeah. It seems our mayor was quite the hound dog. If he was murdered, I haven't ruled the secretary out, but she doesn't strike me as the killing type. She mentioned that Capshaw was seeing multiple women and had a habit of sending them flowers. The credit card statements might tell us more. His phone and text records should show up any day. We can always pull the security tapes and sign-in logs at the mayor's office to check out female visitors on or near the date of his death."

"Good." Cap nodded. "A solid start. Now, where do we stand with the attack on the precinct?"

Rico and I exchanged glances. Neither of us wanted to tell Cap that a demon from hell was responsible.

"We have a person of interest," Rico said, steering the discussion toward a more mainstream direction. "All those biters at the precinct needed a wrangler, right? Someone to handle the logistics and focus the attack. Nighthawk shared the video of her home invasion with Ronnie at Enzo's, hoping she might have seen the blonde guy around. A couple of days later, he showed up at the bar. Ronnie recognized him from the video and gave us a more detailed physical description. Our guy goes by the name Charles Cain. He has a broad, crooked nose and wears a Special Forces ring. He's been signing up homeless guys for day jobs—"

"And feeding them to the biters," I said, stealing Rico's thunder.

Cap's eyes grew wide. "My God. He's turning people into MREs."

"That's the word on the street." Rico scooted to the edge of his chair. "So, now we need to cast a net in the hidey-hole district to find this guy."

"Where are we on an antidote?" Cap asked.

Damn it. I always deliver the shit news. "According to Doc Sheridan at the European CDC, the current antidote only slows this strain of the virus by ten days at best. So, until we locate the antidote, Sheridan will have to try to reverse-engineer it from the virus."

"Jesus, Wycowski," Cap mumbled, swiping a hand across his bald head. The circles beneath his eyes spoke volumes. Everyone was worried about Wyco, and the clock was ticking.

"We'll find it," I said with more confidence than I felt. "Toussaint has never created a virus without producing the antidote, too."

"Wait a minute." Cap paused. "You say that like he's still alive and creating viruses. Toussaint's dead. He was diced into mincemeat in that subway tunnel."

Oops. Shit.

"What aren't you telling me?"

Rico darted me a quick glance.

"Nighthawk," Cap growled.

"Um...Well..."

Cap slammed the file closed. "I viewed the autopsy photos myself. If you tell me he's alive, I'm going to send you for a 5150."

"Psych eval," Rico whispered in my ear.

"Oh, no, Cap. Toussaint's dead. Dead as can be. But whoever is behind this would have created an antidote for their own safety, like Toussaint did."

"That makes sense."

"We'll get a jump on this," I said, eager to leave before I stuck my foot into my mouth again.

Cap pointed at me. "I almost forgot. Before you leave, Nighthawk, did you get your copy of the widow's lawsuit?"

"Not yet, but I heard they're on the way. My old attorney Tim Andrews can't represent me since he's with the DA's office now."

"Oh, that's right. So, you'll need to find someone else."

Not unless they work for free. "You bet," I said, rising from my chair and pulling my partner to his feet. "If that's all, Rico and I have a zombie wrangler and an antidote to hunt down."

Cap waved me back into my seat. "Not so fast. You are current on your liability insurance premiums. Right? Risk Management wants confirmation before the lawsuit proceedings begin."

"Hey, I'm flush. Remember? I got a fifty-percent cut of the bounty from Elite Trust for bringing in Ira Kleinfelder—that fossilized rotter Vinny took forever to catch."

"Yeah, sure. Okay." Cap eyed me like a hawk, searching for a tell of some kind. "I'll let Risk Management know. FYI, they'll probably ask for a copy of your proof-of-insurance."

"No problem. I'll let my new attorney handle it."

"And just so we're clear, Vinny is your employee. Not the city's. He has zero coverage or immunity bestowed by us."

"Crystal clear, Boss.'

"Good. Now stop wasting my time and get the hell out of my office. Every politician and media rep in the Tri-State is on me for either a resolution or a sound bite. Get me something quick."

Get him what? I wondered. Maalox? Trazodone? Paxil?

I could have used some.

Rico trailed me out into the hallway, closed Cap's door behind him, and whispered, "Nice save on the Toussaint issue.

When are you going to tell Cap we've got a demon on our hands?"

"He's not going to want to hear that."

Rico winced. "You didn't pay your liability premium, did you?"

"How could I? Ninety large doesn't spread as far as you'd think. By the time I paid Nonnie, Vinny, and me, covered my back taxes, bought a new roof, and reimbursed the Winstels for their stinky vine, I ran out of money. When shit goes south, everyone assumes it's my fault. Old man Templeman hosed me on the settlement for the explosion at the funeral home, and if I don't start paying off Combs BBQ soon, they'll slather me in sauce, shove an apple up my ass, and throw me on the smoker."

Rico sighed. "You still owe me for trashing my Mustang. Seriously. Stop using my car to mow down biters and impale them on wrought iron fences. Rotter goo wrecks the paint."

As if I'd had a choice.

There's a lot of history to unpack regarding my financial ruin, but the main takeaways include: I should never shoot bullets into formaldehyde bottles at a funeral home, because, Chemistry Class 101, it's explosive. Never battle a zombie horde inside a restaurant that serves the best BBQ in town. And never, ever borrow my partner's Mustang to meet a friend for lunch on a bright, beautiful day when nothing could possibly go wrong—because it's me we are talking about, and the flames from my dumpster-fire life burn eternal.

26

RISKY BUSINESS

Juggling our cases was making my head spin. I could only imagine Rico's frustration with his usual CPD backlog on top of that, but it couldn't be helped. Investigating the mayor's death had to wait while we searched for Charles Cain and the antidote for the new virus. Wyco's life depended on it.

In keeping with Cap's latest decree of 'bring me something,' we refined our search method, hoping to ferret out new biter nests. Broad daylight isn't exactly primetime for hunting dead-heads, but when you know what to look for, sometimes you get lucky.

Using a grid search approach, we would scour individual streets within the OTR area, exploring every nook and cranny. There were more than enough of possible nests to keep us busy.

Parts of the OTR had experienced a welcome transformation. Many of its streets bustled with shopping, dining, parks, and entertainment. But just a few blocks in one direction or the other, the scenery changed. Crack houses, abandoned buildings, and alleyways provided shelter not only for the homeless but also for criminals and deadheads. To the uneducated eye, newly-turned freshies looked like harmless drunks. The danger was far greater than the average person realized.

Rico parked on East McMicken. After we grabbed a couple of flashlights from the trunk, we hoofed it east, crossing Liberty, and cut through the heart of OTR, which let us explore north or south, depending on what caught our eye.

Most of the questionable types saw us approaching and wandered out of sight. Some turned their backs to block our view while they conducted their business. A couple of the more brazen dealers didn't even bother to hide their product. Not that it mattered. We weren't there for them anyway.

"Wonder what he's up to," Rico said, pointing to a guy about half a block away on 13th Street. The man, wearing a ratty jean jacket, strolled into a building with a sagging roof, plywood-covered windows, and an overgrown lot—all potential signs of abandonment.

"How'd he get inside?" I asked, shading my eyes against the sun. "The place looks boarded up."

As we moved closer, condemned notices posted on the building's crumbling brick exterior came into view. According to a weathered sign above the entrance, in its glory days, the building had housed the Filco Manufacturing Company. Someone had pried off the makeshift plywood door and leaned it against the building—presumably, Mr. Jean Jacket.

Rico rapped on the doorframe, announcing, "Cincinnati Police Department."

"Holy zushi," I said, wrinkling my nose as we crossed the threshold and walked inside. "That's a lot of corpsicle stink."

I expected the floor to be covered with newspapers, trash, and a jumble of used needles, but it was surprisingly clean and well-swept. The lobby was empty, except for a few folding chairs along the wall and what looked like the original receptionist's desk still in place. A small, lit banker's lamp sat on the edge of the desk. Curious, I thought. Why would an abandoned building have power?

A distant scream caught our ears.

We drew our guns and stopped to listen. A second shriek, louder and more frantic than the first, pierced the air, followed by a series of panicked, blood-curdling squeals filtering up from the floor vent. I knew that panic all too well. Someone was being devoured alive.

"Jesus," Rico muttered. "That came from beneath us. This place must have a basement."

A high-pitched whirring sound caught me by surprise. I spun, eyeing the walls and the ceiling. "What the hell was—"

The floor opened beneath us, plunging us into free fall.

MY TORSO TOOK the brunt of the drop. Lying motionless on a cold cement floor, I opened my eyes into tiny, narrow slits and listened. The panicked screams had stopped, but the cloying stench of decay was enough to make a maggot choke. I lay face down in a swirling pool of blood, guts, and other bodily fluids, stunned, with no clue where my gun and flashlight had ended up.

Where's Rico?

I slowly rolled onto my back and felt a stabbing pain in my ribcage. At least one broken rib, maybe more, I thought.

"Nighthawk?" Rico's whisper broke the silence. His phone screen flashed a few yards away, then quickly switched off.

I creep-crawled toward him in the darkness, wondering when some rando rotter would chomp down on one of my legs. Landing in the six-inch pool of zushi had been disgusting enough; wriggling through it in the darkness, worried about what I might bump into, was worse. As my eyes adjusted to the darkness, I saw Rico's outstretched hand pointing to the right.

"Keep it down," he whispered. "There's a scrum of dead-heads stuffing their faces. They're busy for the moment. But that won't last long."

A dozen or more biters were tearing apart and consuming the man who had walked into the building ahead of us. At least, I assumed it was him. The blood-soaked remnants of his jean jacket, floating in the chum, swirled around the legs of the rotters less than twenty yards away.

"You hurt?" Rico murmured.

"I've been better."

"Me too."

I stood up, fished out my phone, and cupped my hands around the light, checking Rico's face through the network of new cracks that spidered across the screen. He hadn't fared much better than I had, with his obviously battered cheekbone and split lip. His GQ looks had taken a massive but temporary hit.

"Shiiit!" I gave a muffled squeal and high-stepped through the bloody soup. A dismembered hand had risen from the zushi and grabbed my right ankle, squeezing it in a death-grip. I stomped on the hand with my opposite foot, driving my heel into its fingers. After a few solid whacks, the hand let loose, and with a surprisingly decent kick, I sent it tumbling end over end through the darkness. It landed near the rotters with a splash.

The wandering hand meant that the owner's brain was still functional. Its body parts were desperately trying to reunite with the rest of its body. The poor bastard.

And poor us. The splash had drawn the biters' attention.

The rotters lifted their heads from the mutilated corpse and froze as if they were unsure of what to do next. One of them sniffed at the air and pivoted slowly until it fixed us in its line of sight. The horde followed suit and began slogging toward us through the chum. In the dark, from that distance, there was no way to know for sure what kind of biters they were, but their stink and lumbering gait made it clear they were corpsicles. For our purposes, given our situation and the size of the horde, the slower the better.

But that didn't make sense. Why would anyone go through the trouble of building and stocking a feeding pit for corpsicles, the slowest and weakest of the zoms?

The answer hit hard: The basement-sized feeding trough was meant for an entire army of biters. So where were the rest of the deadheads? The really dangerous ones. I would have to worry about them another time. The corpsicles in front of us were more than enough to handle.

Hawkeye might have landed in the chum pond, but I still had Baby, my Glock 26, strapped to my ankle. And not a day went by that my Ka-Bar wasn't clipped to my belt. That was a start. But what were the odds that every shot would hit its mark? And Rico, who didn't carry an ankle gun, was fresh out of firepower. We needed some makeshift weapons. Hand-to-hand combat with a biter in the dark was risky business—like playing pin the tail on the deadhead blindfolded.

"Shuffle your feet," I said, pulling Baby from her holster. "Look for something sharp or extremely hard. The longer the better."

We were in the century-old basement of a factory. How hard could that be?

As slow as the corpsicles were, their original twenty-yard distance had lessened to ten yards. We retreated almost as far as we could without worrying about being pinned against a wall, then redoubled our efforts to find weapons. Rico stopped moving when a muffled clank came from the sludge.

"A length of copper pipe," he called. "This should—Watch out!"

I spun around and did a double-take. The bastards were trying to flank us!

My foot slipped on a chunk of zushi and skidded into something bulky. I reached into the chum pond and wrapped my hand around something long and cylindrical. One of the flashlights we'd dropped.

Would it still work after landing in the water?

Please work. Please work. Please work. I flipped the switch and prayed for the best.

The light flashed on, almost blinding me. After the dots faded, I saw the faces of three pusbags shuffling toward me from less than ten feet away—and there were too many behind them to count. I dusted the front row with three rounds from Baby, but now there were only seven bullets left in the mag, not counting the one in the chamber. I might need that for myself.

"Nighthawk!" Rico screamed.

I shuffled backwards to create some distance from the horde, then spun and centered my flashlight beam on him. He was about thirty feet away on the other side of the room, standing at the bottom of a stairway.

I had seven bullets left to get me there—and a five-foot cushion from the front of the horde.

The meatbags converged, cutting me off at the pass. Biters aren't that freaking smart. At least, they never were before. But even smart corpsicles are as slow as turtles stampeding through peanut butter.

After I feinted to my right, the mob shifted to follow me. Once they all headed in that direction, I pulled a reverse, swung hard to my left, and took off like a bat out of hell. The rotters on the outside of the mob saw me coming and swung with me, so I had to fire four more rounds. Things would have been fine if I hadn't slipped and faceplanted into Lake Zushi. A couple of biters at the front of the horde lunged at me. I rolled onto my back and drilled them between the eyes, then got to my feet and spent the last few yards playing slip-and-slide with a single bullet left, nestled in Baby's chamber.

By the time I hit the wooden stairs, the rotters were nipping at my heels.

Rico reached out and pulled me three steps up, snatched the flashlight from my hand, and pointed the beam at a spot ten feet away on the wall. "See that wire hanging there? Shoot it! And don't miss...the door at the top of the steps is locked."

"Oh, for the love of all that is holy! Why wouldn't it be?"

Rico swung his pipe at the biters, keeping them off the steps, while I lined up my shot and said a quick prayer to the gods of gunpowder. After taking a deep breath, I exhaled slowly and squeezed Baby's trigger. The electrical cord snapped in two, and the bottom half fell into the bloody pond.

The biters went up in a blaze of electrified glory, sizzling like Frankenzoms, flaming hair, arcing currents, and all. Once the fireworks display ended and the biters had turned extra crispy, I glanced at Rico.

"Is it safe to get back in there now?" I asked, nodding at the steaming roux. "I mean, did the circuit-thingy...trip?"

"Probably. But let's make sure." He climbed down to the last step, reached for the electrical box on the wall, and pulled the main.

"Oh, good. Didn't see that there," I mumbled, in a lame attempt to hide my ignorance of anything remotely electrical. Heaving a sigh, I shined the flashlight into the chum. "I guess now we get to hunt for our guns. Once we find them, we'll have to blast our way out since the door's locked."

"Yeah, about that..." Rico said, sliding his bruised jaw back and forth. "The door isn't locked. I just wanted to see if you could make the shot."

I climbed down the steps for a closer look at his injuries. "How's that feel?" I asked, gently palpating his face.

"Ow! Stop! That hurts!

"Good." I reached over, grabbed his nose, and mashed the bones back into place.

"Jesus!" he screamed, jerking away, and cradling his schnoz. "What's wrong with you!"

"The next time you feel like testing me, I'll do that to your nuts."

27

———————

GOD HELP ME, I'M GOING AWAY

Back at the Blue Note, Tiffany pulled the pencil from behind her ear, tapped it on a pad of fresh guest checks, and turned her apathetic gaze to me. "What'll it be? As if I didn't know."

"Double Jack, neat."

"No slushie, tonight? Must have been a day."

"You have no idea."

"Lord, what is that stink?" Tiffany jerked away, wrinkling her nose. "Like rotten hogs' feet in a gym bag."

I nodded toward Rico, as if I were sure it wasn't me. We'd done our best to shower off the stench, but corpsicle stench had a helluva half-life. Nonnie might make us sleep outside in a tent for a while.

Tiffany shifted upwind, tapped her orange talons on the bar, and shook her head at Rico. "Damn, Sugar, who mussed up that pretty face of yours? Never mind. I don't really care. Whatchu havin'?"

"Johnny Walker. Bring the bottle."

Our ride back from OTR had been, for lack of a better word, tense. We were both in pain and stank so badly that the traffic beside us rolled up their windows. Rico threw a hissy fit because the detailing job on his precious Mustang would cost at least half a G.

We went back to my place, where Nonnie hosed us down before she would even let me into my own house. After we stripped and threw our clothes in the biohazardous laundry basket (which was starting to disintegrate) we showered, and Rico called to have his car towed to the Shammy Whammy Detail shop.

By the time we accomplished all that, it was time to head to The Blue Note for my mock deposition—not that we wouldn't have ended up at the bar anyway. The only thing that could have salvaged that day was alcohol. And since Vinny had pretty much commandeered Nonnie's Pinto, our sole mode of transportation was my Lowrider—which was fine for now. But come winter, I'd call dibs on Nonnie's dirt-brown, wood-paneled wagon.

Vinny and Phoebe were already seated at the bar and deep in conversation when we arrived. Phoebe seemed to have recovered from her starring role in *Goats Gone Wild* with the Widow Capshaw from the night before. Vinny had a free day, so I took a shot and asked if he'd ever installed the four Ring cameras I wanted around the perimeter of my house. The sheepish grin on his face was my answer.

Phoebe swiveled her stool around and locked eyes with me as she sipped her first Pina Colada of the night. The girl was goofy and as ditzy as the day was long, but her stare was downright unsettling. She eventually grabbed my hand, zinged me with her energy, and spouted, "Beware of strangers bearing gifts."

Dear God, I thought. The chick's a freaking fortune cookie.

Rico stifled a smirk. "Greeks, Phoebe. Beware of Greeks bearing gifts."

"No. I'm pretty sure he's not Greek. He's blonde."

Rico and I exchanged glances.

I kept my tone light. "What else can you tell me about this guy, Phoebe?"

"Not much. But he's big trouble—for you and everyone around you."

Mental note taken.

Opie sauntered in and ordered a round of boilermakers in honor of Harry, whom I'd come to believe was permanently off solving whodunits in heaven. Once Tiffany brought our drinks, Opie whipped out his legal tablet and set the stage for my practice demo.

"I'm just doing this as a favor. If I can't find anyone to take your case, we might have to get you a Public Defender. Burklander will ask easy stuff to start with, your name, address, etc., to establish the record. Then he's going to ask more specific questions, relative to what happened that day in the cemetery —things that may get under your skin. He's going to do this on purpose, to rattle you. Your job is to remain calm—"

Rico's scotch shot out of his nose.

Opie sighed. "As I was saying, your job is to stay cool and stick to the facts. Keep your answers short and to the point. Be honest. Don't embellish. Don't volunteer information that isn't directly related to a question. Take your time answering. No need to rush. Better to take a moment and give the right answer than to misstate something."

I gulped what was left of my Jack. "And if anyone asks whether I have liability coverage, I just say yes."

Opie eyed me suspiciously.

"Answer truthfully," Opie said, doodling on his pad. "If you don't know an answer, it's okay to say so. If you fumble and try to wing it, you can create inconsistencies in your testimony. And if at any time you feel uncomfortable, you can always ask to consult with your counsel before answering a question. Easy-peasy. Got it?"

God help me, I'm going away. "Absolutely."

"Ready? Let's start with: What do you do for a living, Ms. Nighthawk?"

"I save the world."

Opie squirmed. "Maybe you could refine that a little, like, I perform zombie remediation services. I also work with the European Centre for Disease Prevention and Control, tracking the deadhead population and locating potential antidotes for various viral strains. Additionally, I use my God-given ability to raise the dead, assisting local and federal law enforcement in solving crimes."

"Got it," I said, wowed by his version of my job description, but knowing I would never remember it.

"Moving on," Opie said. "Question number two: Who pays you, Ms. Nighthawk?"

"Pfft. Nobody."

Vinny and Rico laughed out loud.

Opie closed his eyes and shook his head. "Work with me, Nighthawk. Try it again, without the pfft and the attitude."

I paused, giving the question more thought, then answered, "When I handle cases for the Cincinnati Police Department, I get paid by the city as a subcontractor. I also provide my services privately through my own company, American Corpse Management Executives, Inc."

Opie nodded. "At whose behest did you appear at Rose Hill Cemetery on Wednesday, June 13th of this year?"

"CPD, The Cincinnati Police Department, engaged me to raise the late Mayor Eugene Capshaw and ask about his involvement with, and or knowledge of, misappropriated city funds."

"Very good response. Short, honest, and to the point. Now, Ms. Nighthawk, what went wrong during that raising?"

"Not a damn thing. He awakened on cue."

Opie smiled. "You're getting the hang of this. Forcing the

attorney to ask specific questions is a smart move. Okay, Ms. Nighthawk, what prompted the late mayor to act erratically when risen?"

"There are four stages of zombification. Having been buried for less than two weeks, the mayor's corpse rose in what is commonly referred to as the flesh-eater stage. Flesh-eaters retain seventy-five percent of their pre-mortem reflexes and eat exclusively human or animal flesh and brains. Because the corpse is still somewhat agile, it can be highly unpredictable when awakened."

Opie tapped his legal pad and paused, pursing his lips. "I see. And what safety precautions did you take when raising the mayor?"

Damn it, Vinny. "We used duct tape."

"Is that a common means of restraint?"

"No."

"Why did you use duct tape?"

My lame-o assistant forgot... "The chains we typically use were in another vehicle."

Opie steepled his fingers beneath his chin. "So, you secured the mayor in an unsafe manner, which allowed him to break loose and run amok in the cemetery, forcing you to put him down in the interest of public safety."

"That wasn't a question."

"Pretend it was. Did your actions create a public danger, forcing you to put the mayor down by extreme means?"

"I'd like to confer with my attorney, please, if anyone can find him. Because the guy asking these questions is a dick."

Opie rolled his eyes. "Just answer."

"Yes. Okay, it was all my fault. Is that what you wanted to hear?"

"At least you're telling the truth. Last couple of questions. Ms. Nighthawk, do you carry liability insurance?"

My mind raced like a hamster in a wheel while I lifted my

boilermaker and took a painstakingly slow sip. "Yes," I finally blurted. "I purchased a liability insurance policy."

"And are you current on the premiums for that policy?"

The answer stuck in my throat like a pinecone. It was getting hard to focus. The brain bitch was laughing so hard, I thought she'd make me pee in my pants.

"Nighthawk!" Heads turned as Tiffany's voice boomed from behind the bar. "Phone call!"

God bless that crusty jailbird for stopping me from lying out of my ass.

I hopped off the barstool, tossed back the rest of my drink, and glared at Opie. "I get the picture. I just tell the truth and watch my counsel watching me get a new ass ripped. Oh, and then I pay them for that privilege."

Opie shrugged. "The paying part's new."

I strolled to the end of the bar, shaking my head, then took the phone from Tiffany and mouthed, "Who is it?"

"How the hell should I know? With everything else I got to do here, you think I'm your social secretary? Think again, runt."

"Damn, Stretch. Just when I thought I might tip you tonight." I raised the phone to my ear and barked, "Nighthawk."

"I hear you're looking for me."

"And you are...?"

"The owner of the rotters you fried today. Kudos on the quick thinking, by the way. I thought I had you. But that wasn't cool. You depleted my inventory."

"Ah, that would make you Charles Cain," I said, snapping my fingers to get Rico's attention. "Sorry about that. Well, not really."

"You know my name! I'm flattered."

"You'd be surprised what I know, Cain."

"Before this is over, we'll know all sorts of things about each other, Little Bird. I stopped by your house today and chatted with that lovely, blue-haired lady with the wild accent. Her rugelach is amazing! And those birds are a scream, but you really should put that dog of yours on a diet. I hear he's an excellent zombie hunter. Too bad. I'll have to do something about that."

My chest tightened. "Listen, asshole. If you ever come near my house again, or that blue-haired woman, or any of my pets or my neighbors, I will gut you like a fucking fish and throw you into your feeding pit alive."

Cain chuckled. "Hit a nerve, did I? Well, don't judge me too harshly...yet. I left a present for you at the house. Be seeing you soon, Aliyah Marie Nighthawk. Real soon."

How did he know my...

The line went dead.

28

NOW, IT'S PERSONAL

"Give me the key," Rico called as we sprinted out of The Blue Note. "You're too pissed to drive."

My first instinct was to argue. Nobody tells me what I can or can't do. But he was right. I tossed him my key and climbed onto the Harley behind him, my hands trembling with rage. "I swear to God, I'm going to tear out that fucker's heart and eat it for breakfast! He used my given name, Rico!"

"Settle down!" Rico snapped, giving the bike too much gas. He pulled a wheelie as we peeled out of the lot. "I've never seen you this mad. You'll give yourself a nosebleed." He throttled up but waited too long to change gears. The engine began to bog. When he finally shifted into third, the gears grinded like a garbage disposal.

I leaned forward and shouted into his ear. "Have you ever driven a motorcycle?"

"It's been a while. Let me concentrate."

I closed my eyes and prayed, Dear Lord, please don't let us die.

By the time we pulled into my driveway, I had swallowed my heart at least a dozen times. I hopped off the bike before

Rico even turned it off and ran to the kitchen door, certain I'd find it unlocked, with Nonnie and the menagerie butchered into a thousand pieces inside.

Relief washed over me when I turned the knob and saw that the house was locked up tight. Rico caught up to me as I slid the key into the lock.

"That bastard called me Little Bird," I said as we burst into the kitchen. "There were only two people in this world who called me that, and they're both dead."

Headbutt turned a bloodshot eye at us from his favorite spot on top of the air vent. The house was quiet. The dishes were done. Nothing seemed out of place.

"Nonnie!" Rico called out but got no response.

"The birds are covered. She's gone home for the night, "I said, wandering to the kitchen sink. I stared out the window into the darkness and sighed. "Maybe Cain was just yanking my chain about coming here today. Trying to get a rise out of me."

Rico walked up from behind and wrapped his arms around me. "He described Nonnie, babe—and Headbutt and the birds. And that parting threat about seeing you soon? I don't like it. I'm going next door to get Nonnie and bring her back here where I can keep an eye on both of you."

Again, with the protective mode. "I'm perfectly capable of—"

"No. I'm staying," he said, backing away. "She can sleep with you, and I'll take the couch. It's closer to the doors."

"Don't. She's probably asleep."

I turned to beg him to let it go, but he was already out the kitchen door.

"And where were you in all of this today?' I asked Headbutt. "What do you mean, letting a bad guy in here? You know better than that."

Headbutt whined and covered his head with his paws.

"Don't play cute with me, you overstuffed potato. I'll put you back out on the street where you came from."

It was an empty threat that sounded harsh even to me, so I grabbed his ball from the sink and rolled it down the hall for him. Until then, I hadn't realized dogs could look at a person with disdain. But I shouldn't have been surprised. To Headbutt, that ball represented control. By throwing it, I was telling him to chase it. He didn't like being told what to do any more than I did—something he never let me forget. That drooling, sour-faced basketball was my brother from another mother.

The doorknob jiggled. Headbutt's ears pricked, and I snickered at the thought of Rico locking himself out. How paranoid must he be to lock the door when he was walking thirty yards away?

As I reached to let him in, Headbutt padded in front of me and sniffed the threshold. "Oh, not you, too," I said, rolling my eyes as I threw open the door.

But Rico wasn't there.

Headbutt bolted past me, dug his teeth into a large dark blob lying on the porch, and shook it like a giant ragdoll.

The nauseating stench of decay enveloped me. There was no doubt about what Headbutt had in his mouth, but I couldn't bring myself to look at it. I'd seen enough zushi in one day to last me a month. Still, I turned on the porch light and acknowledged the blood-soaked lump because, for the second time that day, Cain made it personal by bringing the fight to my door.

"Leave it, Headbutt."

For once, my furry warrior obeyed me. He dropped the rotter and stepped back, glaring at me as if I'd taken away a slice of prime rib.

There before me lay an adult male corpsicle, snapping with what was left of its teeth. The rotter's arms and legs had been surgically removed. A Y-shaped incision ran from the top of each shoulder to the center of its chest, down through its abdomen to its pubic region. The skin flaps were peeled back and pinned for maximum exposure. Its entrails, still attached at one end, had been scooped out of its body cavity and flung across my porch like a giant loop of Italian sausage.

Tired of being denied, Headbutt grabbed the free end of its intestines and sprinted off the porch, unspooling them through the yard like a twenty-foot garden hose.

"Come back here," I yelled as Rico jogged across the lawn, with Nonnie trailing behind.

"What the hell?" he said, pulling his Glock. "I wasn't gone ten minutes. Where did this thing come from?"

I gave him two guesses, and the first one didn't count.

"Cain kept his promise. Look at this mess," I said, eyeing the neighbor's houses, hoping their lights wouldn't come on. All I needed was another HOA citation. At least this time, the floor show was on the far side, away from the prying eyes of the Winstels.

Rico raised his Glock, blasted a hole in the rotter's head, and barked, "Get Nonnie inside while I check the rest of the yard."

How discreet. Let's announce the gutted rotter to the world.

He should have let me kill the thing with my Ka-Bar. Gunshots drew attention. And he could take that cop tone he'd used with me and shove it all the way up, even if he was right. Cain could still be nearby, and Nonnie was vulnerable—at least until she started swinging a frying pan.

While Rico sprinted around the back of the house, Nonnie gasped her way to the porch, wearing her bathrobe and feeling pissed enough to spit nails, judging by her flailing hands and a string of Sicilian curses, most of which I didn't catch.

"*Stronzo,* Zumbas! *Something, something, something.* Middle of nights, middle of days, *something, something.* They no cares. *Vaffanculo, Zumbas!*"

After kicking at the ground and almost losing her balance, she waddled over and picked up the hose to spray off the porch.

"It's almost midnight," I said, taking it from her. "I'll call Splatz when we get inside. And you," I said, pointing at Headbutt, "Leave that stinky rotter alone and wipe your paws on the grass before you step one foot in the door."

Rico trotted around from the front and shook his head. "He's gone."

"Did you think he'd stick around to get caught? Why don't you go home? He won't be back tonight."

"You don't know that. And when he does come, you have no idea how many biters he'll bring with him."

"If I needed you to stay, I'd say so."

"No, you wouldn't."

"He stays!" Nonnie barked, stepping between us.

Outvoted in my own home. Damn. Something about that seemed wrong.

AN HOUR LATER, after I had, A: called Jimmy to order another pre-dawn cleanup and begged him to pull all the way up the driveway to avoid Winstel's video camera, B: bathed Headbutt and myself from head to toe, C: texted Vinny and threatened to kick him out if he didn't get my Ring cameras mounted, and D: covered the biter with an old tarp, lest one of my neighbors get up to pee in the middle of the night, look out their window, and see a disemboweled zombie on my porch... again, we were then ready to relax for the night.

I sank into my couch, closed my eyes, and convinced myself that most of my neighbors had stopped trying to catch a glimpse of the creepy Cadaver Diver in action. They were probably afraid of what they might see—except for the money-grubbing Winstels, who were probably hoping to capture

Rotters Gone Wild on their security camera. But not tonight; at least for now, Pitty Pat Lane was quiet.

Nonnie brewed some tea, while Rico kicked off his shoes and stretched out with his head resting in my lap. Headbutt, indignant from his unexpected bath, plopped on his floor vent, facing the wall, and pretended we weren't there. I'd nearly drifted off when Nonnie's voice tugged me back. Opening my eyes, I saw her standing in front of me, with a large shipping box at her feet.

"This comes for you today," she said, rolling her eyes. "I almost forgets with so much zushi. *Bah*, such messes! *Fokakta zumbas.*"

I took the box and frowned. "I wasn't expecting any deliveries."

For a moment, I wondered if it was another 'gift' from Cain, so I checked the return label: Luna Michon, 128 Rue de Triumph, New Orleans, Louisiana. *Oh, yeah. The package from Mama.*

Each reminder of her death was as painful as the last.

I scooted out from under Rico's head and leaned over the shipping box, peeled back the tape, and rummaged through the packing peanuts. There was a note from Mama inside that read, 'There is more to your destiny than you know.'

At the top of the box was an object wrapped in newspapers, about the size of an eight-by-twelve picture. I tore through the paper, moved it aside, and lifted a casting of a Voudon sigil from the box. It was beautiful, but for the life of me, I couldn't remember what it symbolized. It was molded in resin, with the design crafted in red and black. When I was a kid, it hung on a wall in Mama's greenhouse, where she taught me about spells and rootwork.

Toussaint was a much better student than me. He loved Hoodoo, the magical side of Vodou, with its herbs, oils, and powders. How many nights did he tutor me, poring over spells and rituals I didn't care about, just to keep Mama from losing her mind? Memories like that made it hard to understand how he and I had come to hate each other.

I reached back into the box and pulled out a velvet bag that was cinched at the top. After untying the knotted strings, I slipped my hand inside and took out a hand-tooled leather collar. Turning it over in my hands, I admired the inlaid replica of the same red and black sigil at its center, and the three channel-set stones on either side—one orange, one dark green, and one blue. Lying beside it in the bag was a wooden whistle, featuring the same channel-set stones. For the first time that evening, a tired smile crept across my face.

Gadyen's collar and dog whistle.

Fifty-five pounds of muscle, and my ride-or-die companion, the jet-black Xolo was as smart as they came. He loved us unconditionally and guarded us like a lion protects its pride. He lived a good, long life, and I was heartbroken when the time came to put him down. Mama loved him as much, if not more, than I did. I placed her gift back in the bag and cinched the strings tight, thinking that of all the treasures she might have sent, mementos from Gadyen symbolized the best of life in the Painted Lady.

My next foray into the box produced an old corncob pipe with a thin wooden mouthpiece.

"Huh," Rico said, raising his head for a better view. "There's a new vice for you to try."

"Mama never smoked a pipe, and she'd have tanned my hide if I did." I held it up and examined it, trying to jog some pipe-related memory loose, but couldn't. "Maybe she meant to send it to someone else." Tired as hell, I tucked the gifts back into the box. "I'll finish digging through this stuff another time," I said, shoving the big ass-carton aside. It might take me forever to get through everything inside of it.

"No. Is not where this goes," Nonnie tsked, then pushed the box down the hallway toward my bedroom.

"Perfect," I said, unable to stifle a yawn.

Rico shooed us off the couch so he could fall asleep for the night. What a helluva way to end a crazy day, I thought, as I shuffled off to bed with Nonnie in tow. Too bad clairvoyance wasn't one of my gifts, because the next day would bring even more surprises. And I fucking hate surprises. They're never for the good.

29

THE UNIVERSE DOESN'T PLAY NICE

The next morning came early, and I was in no mood for another mess.

"Oh, come on," I barked, staring at the top of the coffee table. "What the hell, Nonnie?"

Gertie, the two-legged termite with feathers and a crusty beak, perched on the living room drapery rod, ruffled and ready to rumble, throwing me a suspicious side eye.

"You'd better be afraid," I muttered, shaking my finger at her. "I hear fried parakeet is tasty."

Nonnie leaned against the kitchen archway, wiping her hands on a towel. "Now what wrongs?"

"Look!"

She peered over her cheaters at the mound of brown powder in my palm and asked, "What this is?"

"This is this!" I said, sweeping my hand toward the inch-by-quarter-inch crater in the top of my apothecary-style coffee table—an original Pottery Barn knock-off. "Gimme a break. It's not even real wood, Nonnie! What's Beakzilla's problem?"

"Shithead."

Nonnie and I spun in unison toward Gertie.

"Oh, sweet baby!" Nonnie gushed. "Is her first-est word!"

"And maybe her last."

Nonnie trundled over to the drapery rod and rescued the little pecker. "I buys her bigger cuttlebone. Keep her busy."

"Great. What about my table?"

"Give me," Nonnie snapped, dumping the bits of particle-board from my hand into hers. "I glues them back on."

"But it won't be the same color," I moaned. "Do we live in a dump?"

"Not me. I lives next door." Nonnie thought for a moment before adding, "I buys brown spray paint. New dump look same as old dump. Problems solved."

Sometimes, it was hard to argue with her logic.

"Where's Rico?" I asked, giving up and heading into the kitchen to pour a cup of coffee.

"He wents to work long time ago. Was still dark out."

Dear God. I flew to the window and craned my neck, searching for the Lowrider.

"Don't worries. He didn't takes your precious bike. He borrows my car."

Relief washed over me as I sat down at the kitchen table to sip my coffee and watch Nonnie fold what I assumed was last night's biohazard load.

"What's this?" I asked, spying a paper lying in the middle of the table.

"Is bill from Splatzes. They getting very spensive."

I skimmed the breakdown, looked at the total, and choked on a sip of coffee. "$5,000!" At the bottom of the receipt was a pre-printed note:

Dear Customer, like many companies in the service industry, we have had to increase our prices to keep pace with inflation. We apologize for the inconvenience and hope that someday the

economy will allow us to revert to our previous pricing structure. Thank you for your patronage.
Sincerely,
James A. Reardon, President and CEO, Splatz Biohazard Remediation Services

"My Ass!" I yelled, ripping the invoice to shreds.

I threw on some clothes, thought about how fast I'd been burning through them that week, and grabbed a spare set, then called Jimmy on the Harley's Bluetooth as I tore down the road to the precinct.

"Damn it, Jimmy! How dare you leave me a bill like that? I paid for that Mercedes Sprinter van you drive. You'd be broke if it weren't for me."

Jimmy responded, but all I heard was, "Yada, yada, yada. Blah, blah, blah."

"And another thing," I shouted. "Nobody reduces prices once they raise them. It isn't American. And what about my 25% rebate? I left your card at the abandoned church on Freeman Avenue just the other day."

Jimmy snorted. "That's for *signed* referrals, Nighthawk. You left my card at an abandoned dump—the operative word being abandoned. Who's going to sign with me?"

"How the hell should I know! Somebody owns the place, and it needs to be cleaned up. Don't blame me if they don't call. Maybe it's your stinking prices. I'm not paying this bill, Jimmy. Reduce it by half, or I'm taking my business to Infectious Wastes "R" Us."

"Fine," he said with an exasperated sigh. "Pay half and we're square—this time. Maybe you can do another commercial for me and bank some credit."

Because filming the last one had been such a delight.

"Fine. I'll send it in," *whenever.* "Just stop yanking my chain, okay? I don't have time for this shit. I'm busy saving the world. Goodbye."

"Holes in my freakin' table," I shouted as the wind buffeted my face. "Bills that make my head spin. It isn't even 10 a.m. What's next?"

I shouldn't have even thrown that question into the universe.

"The mayor's phone records came in," Rico said, as I plopped into his guest chair. "I thought since I'm still reviewing the credit card statement, you could start on those."

"Hard pass. I'd rather go hand-to-hand with a rotter than one-on-one with a spreadsheet."

"Lucky for you," Rico continued, "I found the mayor's favorite flower shop on his credit card statement and called Opie to try to rush a subpoena for their records. While we're waiting on that, we can hit the streets, looking for Cain."

Not a bad plan, I thought as we stepped out of the 51st. It was monumentally better than staring at a computer screen. Things were looking up. In hindsight, that should have been a clue.

Rico glanced at the sky. "Let's take the Pinto. It looks like rain, and I put a tank of gas in it this morning."

After grabbing my spare clothes from the Harley's saddle-bag, I climbed into Nonnie's shit-brown clunker and followed Rico's lead by rolling my window down because a Cincinnati summer without air conditioning can be lethal without airflow.

While my fearless partner headed toward OTR, the most promising place to run into Cain, I called Vinny to put an exclamation point on the text I'd sent him after our late-night attack at the house. Maybe it was the kind of day I was having, but Vinny had barely said hello when I ripped into him.

No. In retrospect, it wasn't the day. It was just because he was Vinny.

"Get off your butt and get it done," I scolded. "And fix that scratch on the Kapinski Mausoleum before Cap sees it's still dinged up. We're out looking for Cain today. If the cameras had been in place last night, I might know what kind of car he drives. But as it is, we're flying blind."

That was true, but it seemed like Cain had zeroed in on us. One way or the other, chances were good we'd run into each other. But Vinny didn't deserve to be let off the hook. Let him hang and feel bad a little longer. Maybe then he'd get the cameras mounted.

After hanging up, I settled back in my seat, looked into the sideview mirror, and frowned. "You know what I just said about not knowing what kind of car Cain drives? I'm guessing it's a late-model, beige Impala with Michigan plates."

"Oddly specific," Rico said, darting his eyes to the rearview mirror.

Cain closed the gap between us and rode our bumper. When Rico mashed the gas pedal, the Pinto bogged and began knocking like a rattle-trap bag of bones. If we'd have been driving the Mustang, Cain would have been eating our dust.

"What's his plan?" I asked, thinking we were about to get run off the road.

But Cain pulled into the next lane, matched our speed, and started pacing us. He reached for something on the passenger seat, then raised his hand, and brought a semi-auto to bear.

"Gun!" I screamed, ducking down.

Rico slammed on the brakes. A hail of bullets riddled the car; some thunking as they tore through the exterior, others pinging around the interior like pinballs. The Pinto spun out and squealed to a stop on the berm. Thick white smoke belched from the burning tires and poured through the windows.

"Son of a bitch!" Rico screamed, pounding his fist on the steering wheel.

I waved the smoke away from my face. "Did you get hit?"

"Yup. Twice."

I scrambled across the seat to check on him. He still hadn't healed from our fall into the biter pit. Today's wounds included a graze across his forehead that was pouring blood down his face, and a deeper gash through the fleshy part of his upper arm.

"Now I'm miffed, Nighthawk," Rico growled. "Really miffed."

I reached into the back seat for my clean t-shirt to wrap Rico's arm and winced. A bullet had skimmed the top of my shoulder. By the time Rico called the shooting in on his phone and we counted all our fingers and toes, Cain was long gone.

It was barely noon, and the day was already in the crapper. But the universe wasn't done with us yet.

30

KEN AND BARBIE TAKE A RIDE

Nonnie's '72 Pinto wagon, the little beater that could, limped back to the precinct in worse shape than the Plymouth in Stephen King's *Christine*. If the insurance company wouldn't declare it totaled, I would. But replacing it wasn't in the budget. Nonnie shouldn't have owned the car in the first place. She was an absolute menace on the road. And by not buying a replacement, she'd save money on insurance.

Yes! Saving money—that was the ticket. Coupons were Nonnie's love language. I made a mental note to share that tidbit with Rico because I sure as hell wasn't going to be the one to tell her that her car was toast. He had borrowed the car; ipso facto, he was the obvious choice to die.

With Rico's Mustang in the shop for detailing, our only transportation besides my Harley was a CPD pool car. Since the bike didn't provide protection against attack, the pool car won out. The last time we used one, we ended up with a prehistoric Taurus held together by superglue, duct tape, and rust. It dropped bumpers and door handles like a deadhead dropped body parts. The engine oil was as thick as cement, the wiper blades were down to metal, and the tires were bald. The car was a lawsuit waiting to happen. We called it the Torte Mobile.

After Rico requisitioned a car, Cap had one of the unis take us to Good Sam Hospital for the once-over and some stitches. Two hours later, with medical releases in hand, we returned to the 51st and waited until the pool car materialized. There was more than enough desk work to keep us busy, but there was a call I needed to make first—a call I dreaded. Rather than make it from Rico's desk, I wandered into the breakroom for some privacy. Ilse at the European CDC was less chatty than usual before putting me through to Dr. Sheridan.

"Doc, it's Allie. I was wondering if you've made any progress on the antidote testing yet. Our detective could use some good news."

Sheridan's voice sounded tired. "We just received Mr. Wycowski's blood two days ago. But early testing makes us... somewhat hopeful. That is not a guarantee; please do not accept it as such. We will know more later today. We're working around the clock. I know his time, and the time of many others, is measured."

"No one works harder than you, Doc." My throat tightened. "Not to add to your stress, but Olufemi Okoya passed away. So, all our hopes are with you now."

"Oh, no! The woman who made the tonic? Such a brilliant mind! Dr. Latka told me long ago that she raised you. Is that right?"

"From the age of fourteen."

"I am deeply sorry for your loss, Allie. I, too, have some bad news. The Z-virus has exploded in the Netherlands. A shelter-in-place warning was issued in Amsterdam two hours ago. The first of its kind anywhere."

My stomach bottomed out. I couldn't think of anything to say, except, "I'm sorry for bothering you, Doc. I'll send up some prayers for you and your crew. Let me know if there is anything I can do on this end."

My hand trembled as I shoved the phone into my pocket, thinking about how many people would turn or die before Toussaint and Cain were stopped. Would Wycowski be one of the dead? Was it wrong that my thoughts were with him rather than the thousands of other faceless, nameless victims I'd never meet?

I was so distracted that I almost bulldozed Cap on my way back to Rico's desk. I have no idea what expression was on my face, but it stopped Cap cold.

"You okay, Nighthawk? How's the shoulder?"

"It's nothing. How's Wyco?"

"Six days in and praying for a miracle."

Weren't we all?

"That leaves us four days," Cap said, locking eyes with me. "Any update on the antidote yet?"

"No. Sheridan is still testing. But he knows the clock, and they're working on it 24/7."

Four days before Wyco either turned or blew his brains out. Or worse yet, asked me to do the honors. We needed to force Cain's hand instead of letting him play cat and mouse with us. And even if we pushed him into a confrontation, he needed to have the antidote or the formula with him to be of any use. Without it, we only had Sheridan's research, and he didn't sound confident about meeting Wyco's 'drop-dead' date.

Such a short window with no guarantee of success and everyone waiting for me to pull a miracle out of my ass. I made it back to Rico's desk without having a panic attack, but I wasn't ready to rule one out.

Rico glanced up from his computer screen with a tired smile. "I called Ronnie at Enzo's. Told her there's a C-note for her if she can find out where Cain moved his biters after we busted the Filco Plant. Our pool car will be ready in an hour, and Opie emailed me the subpoena. I want to hand-deliver it—maybe speed up the process a bit. Care to take a shot at the phone records while we wait?"

I'd rather have a pap smear with a spork. "Sure."

"It's not as tedious as you think," Rico said, pulling out his laptop for me. "I sorted the calls a couple of ways but try starting with the most frequently called numbers and working your way down. See if anything pops."

He lost me after the word tedious.

Once I accepted that I was trapped, the process didn't seem too difficult. Although I'd never admit it, it felt like solving a puzzle—figuring out what each call or text was about and whether it was personal, professional, or anyone's guess. The text messages appeared mostly personal, like icky personal. Reading them made me feel like a Peeping Tom. The idea of someone digging through my own phone records made my skin crawl.

Rico dug into the credit card statements, searching for expenses that caught his eye, aside from flower deliveries, which we would follow up on soon enough. A text alert pinged on his phone, bringing him to his feet.

"The pool car's ready. Ready to serve that subpoena on the flower shop?"

Like he had to ask.

We bummed a ride from one of the patrol officers to the city garage. I waited for Rico near the cars while he stopped at the desk for the keys.

"Don't get your hopes up," he said, as we trekked past rows of shiny, late-model SUVs and freshly washed coupes. "Apparently, our car was confiscated in a felony DUI bust last week. The guy snickered when he handed me the key."

Seconds later, I understood why. There, sitting all alone in the last row of the garage, was a Pepto-Bismol pink, 1990 Cadillac Allanté convertible, with its top down.

"It's the freaking Barbie Mobile!" I screamed.

Rico paused in the middle of the aisle, with his hands on his hips, shaking his head.

"It could be worse," I said, trying to play it straight. "It isn't rusted. There's no duct tape anywhere. No trash inside, and it has two door handles. It's already better than the Torte Mobile."

"But it's a two-seater."

"Are we expecting company?"

"Fine. It's bright. Fucking. Pink." He opened the door and plopped into the driver's seat, sulking.

I climbed in and buckled up, willing to give him a minute to pull up his big boy pants, until he put on his sunglasses, slouched behind the wheel, and then drove out of the garage, looking like a twelve-year-old stealing his dad's car. What a weenie.

"Get a grip, Ken," I said. "No wonder Barbie dumped your ass."

TRILLION'S POSEY PATCH, with its sky-blue siding, brilliant hanging baskets, and ceramic garden frogs, looked like a welcoming place, the kind of shop that might be willing to expedite information to help the local police. But its owner, a fun-sized fossil named Elizabeth Menkie, was a silver-haired pain in the ass.

When I told her we were there to ask for a customer purchase list, she barely glanced up from watering the flowers and barked, "Absolutely not. My customer list is confidential."

"Perhaps you didn't hear me," I said, stepping closer. "We've got a subpoena."

"And I've got gout. What my customers buy and who they buy it for is nobody's business."

"Lady, I asked nicely. But now—"

Rico stepped in. "Actually, ma'am, Ms. Nighthawk is right. We do have a subpoena, which requires you to comply with our request." He handed her his card and the subpoena, pausing for her to look it over. "We're just trying to tie up some loose ends in a case involving Mayor Capshaw."

"Never heard of him." She shoved the subpoena back at Rico. "Now, go away."

"Are you sure, Ms. Menkie?" Rico flashed his million-watt smile. "Because we have a copy of his credit card statement, and he's bought *a lot* of flowers here."

"Fine. I'll email it when I get a chance."

"Or," I said, glaring at her, "You could print it now so we won't have to come back when you don't send it."

"Oh, whatever," she snapped. Heaving an exasperated sigh, she shoved her garden hose into my hand and headed into the shop. "Hold that. I'll be back once it prints."

"What the hell?" I gawked at the business end of the hose watering the pot above my head. "How long do I leave it here?"

Rico shrugged. "'Til it's wet."

I am the last person on the planet who should be trusted to water flowers. I've killed every plant I've ever owned. It's no secret. Ms. Menkie would find out soon enough. In the meantime, I devised my own watering system because it was hotter than blue blazes standing in the sun: I'd move the hose every minute, regardless of the pot size. What the hell did I care? My arm got tired from holding the hose above my head. Fifteen minutes went by. No report. No cranky, pocket-sized munchkin. I got to feeling hinky.

"Here, hold this," I said, trying to foist the hose on Rico. "I'll make sure the winged monkey hasn't flown back to Oz."

"I had the same idea," he said, brushing past me on his way into the shop, where Ms. Menkie met him with a six-inch printout stuffed inside a tattered cardboard box.

Rico raised his brows. "That's all for Mr. Capshaw?"

She nodded silently.

"That's a lot of flowers."

She dropped the box at Rico's feet and muttered, "Knock yourself out, chief." When she turned to me, her eyes flew wide. "Gimme that!" she yelled, snatching the hose from me. "Are you trying to drown the poor things?"

Jesus. The shit I put up with in this job.

"Nice caddy," she deadpanned, following us to the car.

I hopped into the passenger seat, counting to ten, praying I wouldn't rip her head off.

The trunk lid squealed as Rico lifted it and dropped the box inside. He smirked at the little troll, then climbed into the caddy and started the engine. "You have a nice day, ma'am."

She flipped him the bird. "Come back when you want to buy something!"

"Oh, don't worry," I yelled, as Rico pulled away. "We'll be back—with another subpoena for the money-laundering case we're working on."

"You can't prove a thing!" she screamed, stomping her foot.

Rico's eyes popped. "What money laundering case?"

"Lucky shot," I said, leaning back and closing my eyes. "Hey, you didn't hear her say we couldn't prove she was laundering money, did you? 'Cause that would make it sound like she *is* laundering money, which would mean a lot of paperwork. Do we —"

"I didn't hear anything, Nighthawk. And if I did, that's a whole different department. Let them deal with the old bat."

31

FAITH, HE SAYS

Rico shut down on our trip back to the 51st. The pressure was getting to him. His five o'clock shadow had morphed into a patchy beard, and his face, still bruised from our fall through the trap door at the Filco Plant, looked tired and gaunt. His tone was short. He seemed tense and overworked, and I was pretty sure he was still wearing yesterday's shirt. The guy who was my rock needed a rock of his own. Logic dictated that it should be me, but let's face it, when it comes to emotions, I'm more of a blackhole kind of girl. I'd have to try harder...for both of us.

Vinny's ringtone buzzed from my back pocket. For ten cents, I would have let the call go to voicemail. He was already on my shitlist, but only God knew what kind of trouble he could have gotten into.

"What?" I snapped.

"I just wanted to let you know the Ring cameras are up and working now. And I patched up the Kapinski Mausoleum. I screwed up, and I'm sorry."

"Thanks," I mumbled, wondering if I'd been too hard on him. "But now you've sucked all the fun out of being mad at you. The cameras are really important, especially with Nonnie at the house so much."

Gel Boy agreed, crossing his heart and hoping to die, but I hung up, thinking that some things never change. Since Rico was still stewing, I turned my thoughts back to how I could ease some of the pressure we were under and came up with an idea. After we got back to the precinct, I ran it past my partner in crime.

"Absolutely not." Rico shook his head at me like he was talking to a two-year-old. "You can't give evidence from an investigation to Nonnie to work on. There's this whole thing called the chain of custody. Maybe you've heard of it? We'd both get fired."

"Well, that would be impossible since only one of us is actually employed here."

"Oh, Allie, don't. Just...don't."

I knew better than to dredge up that old wound, but his telling me I could get fired was dangling some low-hanging fruit. Since day one, I'd begged to be taken on as a full-time employee of CPD, but they insisted on keeping me a subcontractor. That meant I had no benefits. Technically, the city couldn't fire me, but Rico's point was valid. CPD could cut ties with me if it had a reason to.

I leaned across his desk and whispered, "All I'm suggesting is that while you scan the flower shop records and load them onto a thumb drive, I'll *copy* the phone, bank, and credit card records onto a different drive. Then we give both drives to Nonnie and let her do her thing. What's the worst that can happen? If she comes across something, you can miraculously 'find' it on your computer. And if she doesn't, no harm, no foul. It's not like anyone else here has time to work on these records, with CPD's overtime freeze."

Rico steepled his fingers under his chin and gazed pensively into space. I'd gotten him thinking, and that was a start. So, I went in for round two.

"Look, we wouldn't be in this position if Vinny hadn't screwed up. And Nonnie's good at this stuff. Remember what she did with the Kleinfeld case?"

Nonnie's research had played a key role in recovering the $180,000 bounty from Elite Trust. For all her quirks, Nonnie "The Nose" had cultivated several sources for sniffing out information. One of them was her familial tie to the Vitale Crime family. Although she didn't discuss them much, she stayed in touch with the Vitales, and, lucky for us, she viewed Omertà as more of a suggestion than a rule.

But Nonnie also had an uncanny talent for digging up dirt on the 'Interwebs'. For someone who grew up decades before the computer age, with a little training, she'd taken to electronic surveillance like a teenage hacker.

"Fine," Rico said. "I'll scan and copy the flower shop records. That's going to take a bit. What you do while I'm gone, I'll have no way of knowing." He picked up the box, took a few steps, and then muttered over his shoulder, "There's a blank thumb drive in my middle drawer." After a few more steps, he turned to face me. "You should have said yes when the old bat offered to e-mail this report."

"Who knew it would be that big?"

Rico spun on his heel and trudged to the copier with the cardboard box tucked under his arm.

The data was still downloading on the flash drive when he got back. I waved him off, which might have looked odd if anyone had been watching. But it was after five, and the place was a ghost town. I watched the download creep along and pretended the thumb drive was Pac-Man gobbling dots.

A call came in from the ECDC in Sweden. I answered my phone, praying for good news, but the way things had been going, I wouldn't have bet on it.

Dr. Sheridan sounded drained, and for the first time I could recall, defeated. "The most recent test results on your officer's bloodwork came back. We were hopeful, but the current antidote, even with additional bioengineering on our end, did not cure the virus. Unfortunately, we have run out of time to manufacture, test, and deliver a cure for your officer. He will need to receive the actual antidote to survive...if one exists. I am so sorry."

I reached for the trash can, feeling like I was going to vomit. How would I tell Cap, Rico, and the others? A wave of dizziness swept over me.

"Allie, are you still on the line?"

'Yeah. Thanks, Doc. Stay on this, will you?"

"Of course. Have faith, my dear. The world needs us more than ever."

Faith, he says. It's going to take a lot more than just faith. Thoughts of Wyco flooded my mind—memories of the old codger at his best and worst, and of his bravery that day when he kept fighting after being bitten. I'd tunneled so deep into that rabbit hole I didn't hear Cap walk up from behind.

"Where's De Palma?"

"Geezus!" I jumped, quickly swiping a tear from my eye. "He's in the, ah...the head. Should be back any minute." I glanced at the screen just as the download finished and then stood up, blocking Cap's view of the monitor. "I'll tell him you're looking for him, sir."

"It's important," he said, plopping into Rico's visitor chair. "I'll wait."

Freaking awesome.

All I had to do was act like everything was fine until Rico made it back, so I could tell them the shitty news together. Within seconds, I let out a small sigh of relief. "Here he comes now." When Cap turned his head to look, I yanked the drive out of the computer and flashed Rico a weak smile. "Look who stopped by."

Rico dropped the box of records on his desk with a thud. "Hey, Cap. What's up?"

"Bad news, I'm afraid."

Plenty of that going around.

Cap shook his head with a sigh. "You've caught another case."

Rico sank into his chair, leaned back, and kicked his feet up on the desk. "No can do, Cap. I'm on overload as it is. Give it to somebody else."

"I know you're swamped, De Palma, but it doesn't make sense to give it to anybody else. Cricket Capshaw's been murdered.

32

NO ONE CAN MAKE
ME SIT ON MY ASS

"Oh, for the love of God," I said, slumping onto the corner of Rico's desk with a moan. "I hate when our chief suspect gets murdered. It throws the whole investigation off."

Rico's brow raised. "Damn, this case just got more interesting."

"Didn't it, though?" Cap grinned as he pulled his glasses from his pocket and slipped them on.

Perhaps I was still reeling from the dark news about Wyco, but their enthusiastic reaction to murder seemed downright disturbing. It must have been a cop thing. Give me deadheads any day. They're easy. You see 'em, you shoot 'em. End of story. It's dealing with manipulative suspects that makes crime-solving a headache.

Rico palmed me the flash drive containing Capshaw's flower shop records while Cap scanned the intake sheet and shared the highlights. "It seems Cricket's mother went to her house to pick her up around 10:00 a.m. for yoga class and found the body. She called it in at 10:05 and said Cricket's face was swollen, like she'd had an anaphylactic reaction. Her mom would know. She confirmed that Cricket has been allergic to nuts since birth, and they are her only known allergy."

I frowned. "So how does that turn into murder?"

"Funny you should ask," Cap said. "Cricket was found on her own kitchen floor. She'd never knowingly ingest nuts or come into contact with them or their byproducts. And if it *was* an accidental exposure, she had an Epi-Pen in a cabinet not ten feet away from her."

"No more mud baths for Cricket," I mumbled.

Cap threw me a long glance. "Doc Blanchard is finishing up the autopsy now, but he said her liver temp put the TOD around nine this morning. Histamine breaks down after death, so signs of anaphylaxis don't last long. He ran blood tests to check for allergies, but the results won't come back for a while. He's reviewing her medical records for mention of other allergies mom might not be aware of. Barring some unknown causative agent, we need to find the source of the nut exposure."

"Got it," Rico said.

Cap doled out his orders. "Check out the crime scene, confiscate the foodstuffs and oral hygiene products, like toothpaste, mouthwash, and medication — everything oral. Bring it all in so Doc Blanchard can do his thing. If the allergen doesn't turn up, we might need to dig deeper. And make sure the house stays cordoned off. We've been lucky so far, no newshounds poking around. Once the press picks up on this, the shit will really hit the fan."

Crap. The press! "What day is this?" I asked.

Cap frowned. "Monday. Why?"

"Our luck's about to end. Jade was due back from her honeymoon yesterday."

I wouldn't have known that except she picked up some

snake shed from me right before she and her new hubby left for Paris. Shed was the main ingredient in her tonic—the one that kept her from turning into a rotter. I ordered it from Mama. If it weren't for Jade needing snake shed and news about biter attacks, I'd never see her at all.

"Damn," Rico mumbled, rising to his feet. "I guess she had to come back sometime."

As he and Cap turned to leave, I blurted, "Wait! Dr. Sheridan called with the results of Wyco's latest blood test. Despite all their backdoor engineering, the antidote isn't working. They haven't given up, but even if they find something, it won't be soon enough to save Wyco. We're going to need to find the actual antidote—if there is one."

Cap lowered his head. "I was afraid of this. Damn overtime freeze. I feel like I'm robbing Peter to pay Paul. We need to find the antidote, and we need to solve the mayor's case because the press is breathing down City Hall's neck."

I'd never seen Cap look so defeated. Somebody had to do something.

"Well then," I said, hating what was about to come out of my mouth, "Maybe just this once, it's a good thing I'm not on the city payroll. They can't make me sit on my ass. I won't let Wyco down, or you either, sir."

"It's a funny thing," Rico said with a grin. "I feel an attack of sleep-work coming on."

Cap shook his head. "I can't ask you to do that. And I'll get my butt reamed if I let you."

"Then go home," Rico said. "One way or the other, we've got this. And what you don't know can't hurt you. Get some sleep," Rico said, waving Cap back toward his office. When our fearless leader was out of earshot, Rico spun to me and asked, "How the hell are we going to do this?"

"We're going to go collect that crap from Cricket's house,

bring it back to the morgue, and then hit the streets to look for Cain."

Rico ran his hands through his hair. "Who needs sleep anyway, right?"

"I do. I need sleep."

As far as I was concerned, once we found Wyco's antidote and solved the mayor's case, the top brass at City Hall had better come through with my full-time benefits, or they'd be waking up with corpsicles in their beds.

THE CAPSHAWS HAD LIVED in Hyde Park, where residences didn't have yards; they had grounds and groundskeepers, four-car garages, swimming pools, and tennis courts. Oddly, Rico's pink caddy looked right at home parked in front of the mayor's mansion. Some bubble-headed bleached-blonde out walking her Frenchie would give her eye-teeth for that Pepto-Bismol behemoth.

The red brick exterior of the mansion, cordoned off by crime scene tape, was tastefully decorated with evergreen shutters and brass coach lights. It fit the image of a conservative politician. But after crossing the threshold, I was convinced that we had quantum-leaped into the jungles of Borneo.

Faux animal prints covered the floors, drapes, and furniture. There were enough neon throw pillows and lava lamps to fill every Temu order from now until the end of time. Marble-top tables, gold-leaf mirrors, and overstuffed silk chaises rounded out a style I could only call Mid-Century Bimbo.

The kitchen, where Cricket's body was discovered, was bigger than the first floor of my house. According to the crime scene photo, she'd slumped to the floor in a seated position, with her back against the dishwasher. Death isn't a good look on anyone, and Cricket was no exception. She wouldn't have been pleased with the picture. I imagined her demanding a retake and stifled a smile.

Officer Pickens, who had been waiting for us to arrive, showed Rico the Epi-Pen still in the cupboard. Rico photographed the syringe in situ and handed the officer an evidence box to pack up the dry goods.

While Rico checked the first-floor powder rooms for medication, I pulled the fat-free yogurt, fruits, and veggies out of the mostly barren refrigerator/freezer and packed them into plastic-lined totes, wondering where she'd kept her ice cream. Surely, the woman had ice cream. After filling several totes in the kitchen, I followed Rico upstairs to the master bath, where he photographed and fingerprinted a pharmaceutical jackpot of pill bottles, inhalers, lotions, and creams, and then packed them into plastic-lined totes.

After taking one last look around to make sure we hadn't missed anything, we loaded the bins into every available space of the caddy and the officer's cruiser, headed back to the morgue, and dropped them off. The excursion to the mayor's house and the morgue had taken roughly three hours. It was nine o'clock, and the sun was setting.

Time to hunt for Cain.

In retrospect, calling Nonnie to let her know I wouldn't make it home was a mistake. Her voice went super-sonic and warbled like a loon. "Oh, Miss Allie. Is terribles. Terribles! I don't know what to do with that naughty golem. He causes so much troubles."

We only had one golem. Its name was Headbutt.

"What did he do now?" I asked, stifling a yawn. "Pee on Sid Winstel's feet?"

"No! He mates with their schnoodle, Princess."

"Well, shit." *That took an unexpected turn.*

"Mr. Winstel very angry! Says he sues you for ruining his Princess."

"Tell him to suck an egg, Nonnie. Never mind, I'll tell him myself when I get home."

I hung up, thinking that maybe I should have seen this coming, but how was I supposed to know the stupid Winstels hadn't fixed their dog? Jumping that hairball was the biggest insult Headbutt could lob at them. Kudos to my Bully for originality, but frankly, I was a little surprised. I never saw Headbutt going for neurotic, floofy-haired bitches. I figured him to be more of a full-figured curvalicious mutt.

Wow. Just when you think you know a dog.

RAIN WAS STARTING to spit as we left the 51st to track down Cain. While Rico futzed with the cloth top of the caddy, I second-guessed our method of intercepting Toussaint's right-hand man. We'd had no trouble finding him so far. Or was he finding us with a little help from his demon boss? I put my money on the latter.

Cain was nothing more than a human familiar to run interference while Toussaint worked his plan. Other than messing with my mind, I wasn't sure what that plan was. But as I sat beneath the dark, clouded sky, feeling rain spatter my skin, the answer dawned on me: I was the only thing that stood between Toussaint and world domination through his manipulation of the Z-Virus. Turning my mind into mush would remove me from the mix.

Game over.

"I've been thinking," I said after Rico fastened the last of the caddy's cloth top hooks and slid behind the wheel. "We're letting Cain run us in circles when we should be chasing Toussaint."

"Fair enough," Rico said, swiping rain from his face. "But how do you chase a demon?"

"We don't," I said. "We bring him to us."

I directed Rico to the place where, once, not long ago, Toussaint had broken me so badly, I swore that I'd never raise the dead again.

33

LET'S DANCE

Thunder rolled in the distance. The rain, which had started as sprinkles, was now coming down in sheets. As we parked in front of Spring Grove Cemetery, I knew that my hunch would pay off. It had to. Toussaint could never pass up the opportunity to relive the worst moment of my life.

Gloat while you can, I thought, because this time I'm ready.

The memory of that moment, which happened before Rico and I became partners, was as fresh as if it had happened yesterday. It was a night like this one, wet, wild, and windy.

A group of us—cops, DAs, and regulars at The Blue Note— had gathered at the bar for an impromptu wake in honor of Harry Delk. A biter complaint came into dispatch around midnight. Cap's second in command phoned me, reminding me that I was on biter call. Hell, when wasn't I? I told him I'd been at the wake and tried to beg off, but he wasn't having it.

I shot down the expressway feeling uneasy. A late-night biter call from a cemetery sounded hinky. Who would have been there to see it? Maybe it had shown up on a security feed. When I arrived, the Pinkerton guard, eager to steer clear of biter business, waved me through the cemetery gate and never looked back.

Rico and I weren't that lucky this time. As the storm centered over us, we had to get into the cemetery the hard way —clambering over the perimeter wall. To his credit, Rico didn't hesitate, never tried to change my mind, or question why we were there. He knew the story.

Four years ago, in section twenty of this very cemetery, Toussaint had raised my father from the dead out of spite just to watch me fire a 9mm round through his brain so he wouldn't wander the Earth until the end of time.

That was the depth of Toussaint's evil.

Anger burned inside me as we sprinted around Geyser Lake. In an effort to find Cain and the antidote, Toussaint had forced me to resurrect that memory like a bodiless corpse. He'd drawn me back to this place to bait me for a showdown.

So be it, I thought. Let's dance.

Thunder rolled as rain puddled at our feet. The wind began to howl, so I sucked in a breath and yelled above the roar, "I'm here, you bastard. Show yourself!"

Lightning flashed electric blue and struck a nearby tree, knocking Rico and me to the ground.

"Are you okay?" he shouted, flat on his back, shielding his eyes from the rain.

I stumbled to my feet, stunned, and scared shitless because my vision had begun to flicker like a silent movie. Within seconds, the night grew quiet, and the relentless rain stopped. Thunderheads parted and scudded across the sky, revealing a brilliant full moon and the silhouette of a crooked woman hunched on top of the nearest rise. As I stepped closer, I realized she was calling to me, but for some reason, her words carried away on the breeze.

What is she doing out on a night like this?

I trudged through the tombstones to the base of the hill and looked up, noticing the wet mud caked in her hair and the muted reds and yellows that had settled into her cheeks. God help me, I gasped at the sight. The woman was Mama Femi. She cackled and reached for me with her bony, gnarled fingers. I spun away, blinded by my own tears, and ran, nearly falling into an open grave.

Bracing myself at the edge of the hole, I turned to face my father, dressed as he had been when I put him down four years earlier, in the tattered remnants of his burial clothes. The few remaining patches of his rotting skin glistened in the moonlight, wet against his fish-belly white skull. He rasped a brittle laugh through lips permanently fixed in a snarl. "There's daddy's little girl," he croaked.

"Get out of my head," I screamed. "This isn't real. None of this is real! You couldn't possibly have Mama. She was so much stronger than you. And we both know my dad is out of your reach now."

"You want real?" asked a disembodied voice. "I'll give you real."

A bolt of pain shot through my ribcage. I doubled over, struggling to catch my breath. He'd reached across the void and attacked me. *How much more of this can I stand?*

Mama's silhouette faded. A vision of Nonnie and Vinny, ugly, terrifying, and earthshakingly real, took its place. They were chained side-by-side in a pit, surrounded by a throng of corpsicles, shambling toward them.

Nonnie sobbed and begged for mercy, as tears streamed down her face. Vinny jutted his chin and told Toussaint to kiss his ass in a voice that refused to waiver. The demon had gone from planting bullshit in my brain to attacking the people closest to me.

The battle needed to end here and now.

"Enough," I screamed, pulling Hawkeye. "Stop fucking with

the people I love—people that you don't give a rat's ass about. Come for me. Now! Do it!"

Toussaint materialized. His voice shook and his eyes filled with rage. "The people *you* love? What about my wife? When you left me, she was the one who picked up the pieces. She brought me happiness. And you killed her to spite me!"

The wound I had inflicted on Toussaint that would never die.

I shook my head. "She was infected with the Z-virus! You chained her up and fed her—fed her healthy, living people because you couldn't bear to let her go. Putting her down was an act of mercy, and you know it!"

"You lie!" screamed the demon. "But you're right about one thing. Your friends mean nothing to me, and they will die tonight."

I planted my feet and leveled Hawkeye. "Call off those biters or I shoot."

"You have nothing to bargain with. Do you really think your bullets can stop me?"

Tears burned my cheeks. "Maybe not. But I need the satisfaction of pulling the trigger with you in my sights."

"Allie! Allie, you don't want to do this. Allie...Alli—"

The instant I fired Hawkeye, everything went black.

"ALLIE, WAKE UP!"

I clawed through the darkness and sprang to my feet, wild-eyed. *Where am I? What's happening?* Crouched, with outstretched arms, I spun from side to side like a trapped animal, searching for escape.

Rico lunged and grabbed my arms, holding me in check. "It's okay. Settle down. I've got you."

While his grip was firm and his eyes showed concern, he was calm. Instinct told me I was safe...for the moment.

"What happened?" I instantly regretted speaking. My face throbbed.

"You don't remember?"

"Clearly not," I mumbled, fingering my jaw.

"Sorry. I had to clock you when you fired at me."

"I did wha—are you okay?"

"I'm fine. Have a seat," he said, guiding me back to the ground.

After a beat, sitting crossed-legged and breathing deep, a blur of images swirled through my mind. Thunder and lightning. My father and his open grave. Toussaint and Mama. Nonnie and Vinny. *Oh my God! Nonnie and Vinny!*

"Where's my phone?" I yelled, patting my pockets but coming up empty. "I think Nonnie and Vinny might be dead!" Tears welled in my eyes as I searched the ground around me. "Damn it! Where is it? I need to call them!"

"Here," Rico murmured, handing me the lost phone. "It was lying next to you in the grass."

"What time is it?" I asked, dialing Nonnie.

"Midnight, give or take. Why?"

"She's probably asleep."

After seven rings, when she hadn't picked up, I dialed Vinny. He didn't answer, either. I dropped the phone into my lap, covered my face, and let the tears I'd been blinking back fall.

Rico knelt beside me, grim-faced. "Let me try something," he said, pulling out his phone. He made a call and waited for a moment, then sighed in relief. "Nonnie, hi. Everything okay there?"

"Where is she?" I barked.

"At your house," Rico mouthed. "Hold on, Nonnie, Allie wants to talk to you."

After I grabbed Rico's phone, she explained that she'd fallen asleep on my couch, waiting for me to come home. Vinny and Phoebe, who had gone out to dinner, returned about an hour ago and were watching TV with her in my living room.

I sighed in relief. "Tell Gel-Boy to answer his phone when I call. And tell him to lock up tight and keep his gun handy. Everybody stays put at my house tonight. I'll explain when I get there."

I hung up, thankful that the vision of their deaths was just another of Toussaint's lies. Or...was it? I wondered. *Maybe their deaths are still to come. Or maybe they really are dead, and all of this is in my head. How can I be certain what's real and what's an illusion? How can I ever be sure again?*

Maniacal laughter echoed off the tombstones and mausoleums, filling the air around me and sending chills down my spine. I slipped my hand into Rico's and whispered, "Please, tell me you heard that?"

There was a weariness in his eyes I had never seen before. "Heard what, babe?"

I sprinted toward the gate, wondering if Rico thought Toussaint had broken me. I wasn't sure he hadn't. After my partner and I scrambled to the top of the retaining wall to leave the cemetery behind, I looked back and saw a huge black hound with glowing red eyes staring at me from atop a stone burial ledger. An ominous howl followed me as I slipped over the wall and landed on my feet outside the cemetery grounds. I had a feeling that hellhound and I would meet again.

34

DOWN AND TROUBLED

The moment we got back in the car, Rico let loose. "Was that your plan?" He pulled away from the curb, feigning interest in the traffic but clearly couldn't bring himself to look at me. "You asked me to take you to the cemetery to confront Toussaint, so I did. We're not there five minutes when a freak storm rolls in. We get knocked on our asses by a lightning bolt. You leap back up, wild-eyed, fall into some kind of trance, freak out at things I can't see, then pull your gun and shoot at me. Was that what you had in mind?"

His recap sounded almost funny, but the frustration in his voice was clear. He wanted to help me, and to his way of thinking, that meant concocting a strategy. That's how he did things, but he knew better than to ask about *my* plan.

Plans never go according to Hoyle. I end up pulling a Hail Mary play out of my ass to save the day. So I skip the planning stage and go straight to the Hail Mary. That's always worked best for me...until tonight.

Tonight was a disaster. I owed him an explanation, so I did my best to give it to him, even if it sounded incredibly stupid coming out.

"I thought that if I called Toussaint out at the cemetery, he'd engage with me directly instead of distracting us with Cain. But I didn't consider his... demoness. His powers are stronger than before."

"Okay," Rico said, with an encouraging nod. "Then where do we go from here?"

"I have no freaking idea."

Rico went silent and focused on the traffic, leaving me to stew in my misery. I had no clue how to fight Toussaint, and for the first time in my life, I was genuinely afraid of him—of the way he manipulated my thoughts and actions. With every attack, he grew stronger, and I grew weaker. For God's sake, I'd pulled a gun and fired it at my partner. The man I loved. How could I let that happen?

It was one thing to put myself in danger, but Nonnie and Vinny were also in Toussaint's crosshairs. What would Vinny's father, Leo, say? How could I keep my promise to protect his son when I couldn't even protect myself?

With Mama gone, Nonnie was the only mother figure left in my life. If Toussaint killed her, how could I go on knowing that I was the reason? And then there was Wycowski, a thirty-year veteran of the Cincinnati Police force. Unless I found the antidote, he would die an agonizing death, all because he defended the precinct in an attack that was meant to cripple me. Cap had lost his wife to a biter years ago. What would he think if I didn't measure up? What would Mama think?

I was failing the people who mattered to me. As for anyone else, how could I possibly save the world from a necromancing demon when his powers were light-years ahead of mine? In a matter of days, I'd become a shadow of my former badass self. As we pulled into my driveway, it occurred to me that I would become a punchline for every late-night talk show host around, not to mention the star of every rotter meme to hit social media. At least, for a little while—until people started dying in droves—all because of me.

AS I STORMED through the backdoor and raced from room to room, checking the windows and locks, Nonnie, Vinny, Phoebe, and Rico looked on in silence. Rico sat on the couch while I gathered boxes of 9mm mags from the basement, along with a shotgun, some shells, and an assortment of knives, and then passed them out like party favors. It should have dawned on me that weapons were less than useless against a demon, but I hadn't been thinking clearly all night.

By fortifying my house, at least I was doing *something* other than wringing my hands and gnashing my teeth. Once my arsenal was in place, I sat next to Rico and shared the news about the supernatural events at Spring Grove Cemetery with Nonnie, Vinny, and Luna. Their reactions weren't comforting.

"Gotta watch those demons," Luna whispered. "They can come home with you. I saw that on *Ghost Adventures*."

Nonnie gasped and crossed herself twice. "You didn't brings the *dybbuk* back with you, dids you?"

"So, Rico," Vinny asked, casually, "did *you* see Toussaint?"

My partner looked at me like he needed permission to answer. "No," he finally said. "But Allie did, and she wouldn't lie."

Vinny's question pissed me off. It suggested that the credibility of my story depended on Rico's corroboration. But Rico's response was a worse betrayal. His half-hearted attempt to defend me with 'she wouldn't lie' should have been followed by a clear statement of his unwavering support. But then, how could either of them have faith in me, if I didn't believe in myself?

My last official act of the evening was to dig the flash drives containing Eugene Capshaw's transactional data out of my pocket and flip them to Nonnie. I asked her to work her magic. Hopefully, she would find some juicy tidbit to help us solve the case.

I huffed into the kitchen, announcing that I would be spending the rest of the night in my room—alone. My self-doubts were more than enough to handle, without adding theirs to the mix. In the past, a moment like that might have prompted me to call Mama. Her patience and wisdom had made her the rock in many of my storms. Less than a week had passed since her death, and I already missed her more than words could say.

Instead of pouring a Jack Daniel's slushie, I grabbed the whole bottle of Jack, called Headbutt to join me, and shuffled down the hall to my room. Snippets of the conversation about Nonnie's sleeping arrangements for the night drifted into my ears. Should Vinny and Rico share Vinny's room? Or Phoebe and Nonnie? Or should Nonnie sleep in Vinny's room alone? Or should Vinny and Phoebe bunk on the floor, with Rico taking the couch? Oy, vey. Let them figure it out, I thought, with a chuckle. What was left of the night was reserved for Mama and me.

I followed Headbutt into my room with my bottle of Jack and closed the door. Once Headbutt jumped onto my bed and circled a few times to find the perfect spot, I joined him, and laid down, pulling Mama's carton of treasures alongside me on the floor. After a hefty swig of Jack, I opened the box and pulled out Gadyen's collar. Strangely, running the thick, hand-tooled leather through my fingers made me feel close to him. How many years ago did he die? I wondered.

Scooting closer to the headboard, I leaned back against a pile of pillows, closed my eyes, and pictured Gadyen with his black, hairless skin, sitting tall, ears peaked, head held high. People said he was odd-looking, but the word that came to my mind was regal. Gadyen's smiles were few and far between. He was too busy watching over his family in the Painted Lady, but Mama said he saved his smiles for me.

After another sip of Jack and a long, tired yawn, I put the collar away and shoved the box into the corner, then turned off the light, and snuggled up to Headbutt.

As I closed my eyes, a memory surfaced that reminded me how much Gadyen had meant to me. Mama and I had been working in the greenhouse when she asked me to weed the vegetable garden. The Xolo followed me out the door closer than my own shadow and plopped into the grass beside me.

The day was scorching and humid, like New Orleans always is during summer. I was barefoot, wearing a yellow sundress, kneeling between rows of green beans, and pulling out weeds by their roots. I forgot Gadyen was there until he lunged and bit my arm, pulling me away so hard that his teeth broke my skin. He dove back into the beans, then charged out seconds later with a copperhead in his teeth, cracking it back and forth on the ground like a whip.

Mama flew out of the greenhouse, following the sound of my screams. By the time she reached the garden, the snake was dead, less than six feet from my foot. But Gadyen, with two deep puncture wounds on his front left leg, lay panting in the grass.

I sobbed so hard that I hyperventilated, convinced our dog would die because he'd been protecting me. But Mama, the parish's best rootworker, tore off her hem, tied it like a tourniquet above the bite, and coaxed Gadyen back to the greenhouse, where she cleaned his wound and lanced it to make it bleed. When I gasped at the sight of her taking a knife to his leg, Mama explained that bleeding made some of the poison run out.

I studied her every move as she measured and compounded a cure no one would find at a vet's office. For the first couple of hours, she fed him a blend of echinacea tincture water and spread it on his wounds, too. Then she made him a poultice of slippery elm bark powder, activated charcoal, bentonite clay, apple pectin, and turmeric powder to draw out the venom.

Since the dressing needed to be changed during the night, I insisted that Mama let me sleep in the greenhouse beside him and watch over him the way he had watched over me. By the next morning, Gadyen was out of danger, and he and I were attached at the hip.

As I drifted off to sleep, I remembered Mama telling me Gadyen was more special than I knew, and that a day would come when he would protect me yet again.

"That hasn't happened yet, Mama," I murmured into my pillow. "I guess no one is perfect. Not even you."

35

WHO NEEDS A PLAYBOOK?

Rico stopped me on my way to the kitchen in the morning with a kiss. "Good news," he said, sipping his coffee. "Jade left me a voicemail last night. One of her sources said that a guy Cain tried to 'hire' got the heebie-jeebies walking into Cain's new place and stood him up. She left me the address."

"It didn't take long for her to get back to work, did it?" My tone had a bit of a tone. "Now that we know where to find him, we can force his hand. We just need to come up with a pla—no, not a plan," I said, grasping for the right terminology. "A spontaneous on-the-spot improvisation."

Rico's coffee almost shot out of his nose. "With all the four-letter words that spew from your mouth, you draw the line at plan?"

I plopped into my chair at the table and handed out the gang's new marching orders, starting with Vinny. "Hang out here today with Nonnie and Phoebe. Keep your gun and a couple of extra mags on you. Nobody leaves. Got it?"

"Sure," he mumbled, scrolling through Facebook on his phone. "After I hit the gym, okay?"

"No, Mr. Potato Head, it is not okay. This isn't a game. If Cain shows up, you need to be ready. Next up, Nonnie," I said to the short-order cook hunched over my stove. "Get a jump on the data from those flash drives. I'm looking for odd credit card transactions, banking anomalies, repeat flower deliveries, suspicious texts, calls to strange area codes, anything that stands out. Capiche?"

"Rogers that," she said, waving her spatula over her shoulder.

"And Phoebe," I hesitated, temporarily at a loss, "burn some sage or something."

"That's a great idea!" She reached across the table and patted my hand. "The aura around you is as black as tar. That's usually a sign of grief, emotional pain, or that you're going through a hard time."

My stare burned a hole through her head.

"Or maybe not," she mumbled, lowering her gaze to her bacon. After a pause, she added, "Oh, by the way, Mama hit me up last night after you went to bed. She called you her Little Bird and said you needed to start listening and paying attention. She's been trying to talk to you, but you're never quiet long enough to hear her."

Rico and I exchanged glances.

"But you know me," Phoebe said with a shrug. "Prolly got my wires crossed."

Prolly not. "Meeting adjourned. Time to leave," I said, motioning Rico to the door.

Nonnie gave him a peck on his cheek as he walked by, then grabbed her skillet and held it high, promising that no zumbas or bad mens were getting in on her watch.

Thank God that blue-hair was deadly with a skillet. We didn't dare give her a gun.

WE HADN'T BEEN in the precinct long enough to grab coffee before Cap summoned us to his office.

"Doc Blanchard got Cricket Capshaw's medical records this morning. He wants to chat."

Rico and I scooted the ratty visitor chairs around Cap's desk while he made the call and put the city's medical examiner on speakerphone.

"I didn't find anything unusual," Doc said. "But the records from her attending confirm that peanuts were her only known allergy."

"Who is her doc?" Rico asked.

"Hang on." Doc's hunt-and-peck typing echoed through the speaker. "Dr. Richard Blasnick."

"Why is that name familiar?" I asked.

"It is, isn't it?" After a few more keystrokes, Doc added, "Well, now. It seems Blasnick was also the attending physician for Mayor Eugene Capshaw."

"Ah," Rico said, shifting to the edge of his seat. "The same doctor who signed off on Capshaw's cause of death so he wouldn't be autopsied?"

"Give that man a cigar," Blanchard said. "It's not unusual for a husband and wife to share the same doctor but considering that both spouses died under murky circumstances in quick succession, the odds are awfully slim."

Rico nodded. "I'm going to call Blasnick in for an interview. Rattle his cage a bit. See if this is the world's biggest coincidence or if there's something more to it."

"Solid plan," Doc said. "You can bet I'll be examining the foodstuffs and meds with a fine-tooth comb."

Cap ended the call, then excused himself to get a cup of coffee. On his way out the door, he asked us to hang around. I died a little inside, knowing he was going to ask for an update from last night. The time had come to level with him about

Toussaint's involvement from beyond the grave. That conversation would be one for the books.

After Cap disappeared, Rico looked up Blasnick's number and gave him a call. The receptionist said the doctor was busy and tried to take a message, but when my partner wanted something, the bulldog in him bared its teeth. "Tell Dr. Blasnick this is an official call from CPD. He needs to pick up."

While we waited for the doctor to answer, Rico leaned back, balancing his chair on two legs, and pressed the speaker button on his phone. Blasnick took his sweet time, but just when I was thinking he was dodging us, he came on the line. When Rico explained the reason for his call, Blasnick's tone fell flat. "I wish I could help, Detective, but I'm booked solid today."

Rico pushed harder. "I'm going to level with you, Doc. The deaths of the mayor and his wife are becoming a PR nightmare for City Hall. We won't keep you long. If you can't come in, we'll come to you—at your office with your patients—though I doubt that would be your preference."

"Fine," he said, in a decidedly not fine tone. "I'll give you one hour, between twelve and one."

After expressing our eternal gratitude and giving him the address, Rico hung up with a cynical, "This ought to be interesting."

When Cap returned with his coffee and sank into his squeaky, worn-out chair, Rico shared the news that Blasnick would be coming in for an interview."

"Excellent." Cap nodded in approval. "If he's hiding something, get it out of him."

"Will do," Rico said. "I'll check with my CIs too, sir. See what else I can dig up on Blasnick."

"Good. Now, let's switch gears. Where are we with Cain?"

Rico smiled. "We've got a bead on him, sir. After we busted the old Filco Plant, we knew he'd have to move the biters. One of Jade Chen's sources came up with an address for the new holding pen. We'll move on Cain tonight, after dark—less chance of him seeing us coming."

I threw in my two cents, intentionally opening the biggest can of worms in the history of wormdom. "We need to get our hands on the antidote, right? These new biters might follow commands and be trained not to attack their handlers, but they're still biters. Cain must have the antidote in case something goes wrong. I would. If we find him, we find the antidote for Wyco. Which is great, but Cain's not at the top of the food chain."

Cap waited for me to continue, but I froze.

How do I explain that Toussaint came back from the dead as a demon without sounding like a lunatic? I really should have practiced this.

"Well," Cap snapped, "who should we be looking for?" He leaned forward, waiting to be enlightened.

After discarding a handful of ways to ease into it, I blurted, "Just...hear me out and keep an open mind."

Cap grunted.

"Remember the city-wide influx of biters?" I said. "And the siege at the precinct when Wycowski was bitten? How I zoned out and stopped shooting in the middle of the firefight? Toussaint Le Clerc was behind all of it. He does this mind control thing. It's totally insane. I've nev—"

"Nighthawk, stop." Cap shook his head. "We already had this conversation. You killed him, remember?"

"Yes, sir, I did. But he came back as a..." I glanced at Rico, eyes pleading for support, but he was staring at Cap, waiting for him to break out the butterfly net. *Thanks for the help, Partner.* I cleared my throat and started again. "He came back as a demon, sir."

Cap flicked his eyes at Rico.

"It's true," Rico said. "We figure Cain is like Renfield, Dracula's human helper."

Speechless for the first time I could remember, Cap opened his desk drawer, pulled out a bottle of Crown, and took a hefty swig. Then he held the bottle out to Rico and me, but Rico waved it off.

Damn it.

After a second swig, Cap put the bottle away and wiped his mouth on the back of his sleeve. "Assuming I believe all this," he said, "and trust me, I don't, what's your play? How do you plan to bring in a...demon?"

Like I have a clue. "Still working on that, sir."

"Well, then," he said. "Get to it. Do...whatever it takes." He showed us the door with a sweep of his hand, muttering, "First zombies, now demons." As we left his office and started down the hallway, his voice followed us. "What's next? Witches? Vampires?"

Hell if I know, I thought. My playbook went out the window days ago.

RICO and I spent the rest of the morning prepping for Blasnick's interview. Prior to the doctor's arrival, Rico made sure to crank up the heat in interview room one. It had to be nearly eighty degrees in there. Just the way he wanted it.

Blasnick arrived grumpy, with a boulder-sized chip on his shoulder. Rico set a bottle of Aquafina in front of him, then started with the softball questions, trying to put him at ease. But the doctor tapped his watch and said, "Let's get on with this, shall we? I have patients to see." He loosened his tie and clasped his hands on top of the table, looking thoroughly bored.

The arrogant prick.

Rico flashed his killer smile. "Sure thing, Doc. We noticed

you were the attending physician for both Eugene and Crickett Capshaw."

"That's correct." When Rico didn't respond, Blasnick added, "Why do you ask?"

The thought bubble over my head exploded from my mouth. "Well, they died so close together that it just seems a bit...unusual."

"Not at all," Blasnick said, sipping his water. "Eugene had been in poor health for some time."

Rico nodded. "You signed off on his death certificate, right? Let's see," he said, flipping through the file. "Yes, here it is. Natural causes. And what about Crickett?"

"What about her?"

"She was significantly younger than Eugene, and she died—"

"Of allergy-induced anaphylaxis. She had a peanut allergy, Detective. It's in her medical records. Where are we going with this?"

Rico narrowed his eyes. "I don't recall mentioning how she died."

"You didn't," Blasnick snapped. "Crickett's mother, Sarah Winston, called me. I treat her as well. She found Crickett's body, with signs of facial swelling, consistent with anaphylaxis."

"In any event, it looks like our ME, Dr. Blanchard, agrees with your assessment of Crickett's cause of death."

"Thank heavens," Blasick deadpanned, pushing back from the table. "This is absurd. I'm afraid we're—"

Rico rose from his chair, wearing a wry smile. "Just one more question, Doctor. Were you and Crickett having an affair?"

The brain bitch had a stroke.

"Excuse me?" Blasnick's jaw dropped. "How...how dare you? I am a happily married man. You have no right to... to..."

Rico shrugged. "I'm sorry to ask that question, Doctor, but it comes with the territory. You understand. Not everyone has a great marriage. You've been very cooperative. No offense," he said, reaching across the table to shake hands. "Have a good day."

Blasnick hesitated before grasping Rico's hand. "Goodbye, Detective. Best of luck with your investigation."

"Let me show you out," Rico said, opening the door. "Oh, one more thing. Were you aware that the mayor was under investigation for misappropriation of city funds?"

"Certainly. It was all over the papers. But I don't put much stock in the press these days. They're a pack of hungry jackals, all vying for a bite of the same bone."

Ain't that the truth.

Rico nodded. "I don't suppose he mentioned coming into any money?"

"I was his doctor, Detective, not his confessor.' Blasnick grabbed his bottle of Aquafina and headed for the door. "You should really have your AC looked at. It's beastly in here."

I hung back in the bullpen, watching Rico escort him to the street entrance, praying he would toss his water bottle into the trash can near the door. He didn't. We had planned to compare his fingerprints and DNA to the trace evidence lifted from Crickett's medicine bottles.

Blasnick: One; CPD: Zero.

We could try again to obtain Blasnick's samples. All we needed for testing was some of his trash, but the results would take forever to come back, and Cap's neck was on the line. We were running out of time and options. If we didn't close this case soon, Cap would become the face of the city's PR nightmare. It occurred to me, as I watched Rico trudging back from the precinct doors, that there was only one way to get the proof we needed quickly.

"Come with me," I said, grabbing Rico's arm and pulling him down the hallway. "We need to talk to Cap."

"Again? We just came from there."

"I've got an idea."

"Will he take it better than the Toussaint is a demon thing? 'Cause that almost gave him a stroke."

"Even odds," I said, rapping on Cap's door.

"YOU WANT TO WHAT?" Cap stared at me like I'd lost my mind.

"Raise Crickett Capshaw."

"The woman who sued you, and the city, after you raised her husband despite an injunction order, let him escape and run wild through the cemetery, and then blew off his head?"

"We've covered all this before, sir."

"Duly noted. The answer is no, Nighthawk. Now, go away. You're giving me a migraine."

"Just hear me out," I said. "That Epi-Pen was less than ten feet away from her, sir. I'm sure her mother wants to know the circumstances surrounding her death."

Cap sighed. "We should wait for the trace evidence to come back."

"You know how long those backlogs are. That'll take forever! And you still won't resolve the missing funds issue or whether the Mayor was murdered. If I raise Crickett, we might be able to wrap everything up at once."

"The mother won't go for it."

"Let me try," Rico said. "I'll call her in and see what I can do. If she agrees, we can handle the raising in the morgue before Crickett's interred. That way, Allie can control the situation, and Crickett's mother can still arrange for an open casket if she wants."

Cap snorted. "I can hear Blanchard screaming from here."

The snort was fair. I'd raised a few corpses in the morgue, and the process never went smoothly. Blanchard would have a cow, a horse, and a pig.

Cap closed his eyes and pinched the bridge of his nose. "If the mother agrees to the raising, you'll still need to loop in Legal on behalf of the city. And Nighthawk, you make sure your counsel signs off for you, too."

What counsel? Who would have thought that raising the dead would be quicker than handling the paperwork?

Me. That's who.

Attorneys get paid to cut through red tape. Rico and I had more important things to do—like investigating murders and catching Cain. For the rest of the afternoon, while Rico waded through desk work and posted Blasnick's interview notes, I borrowed the Caddy to run a vital errand. With any luck, by midnight, Operation Catch Cain would be in the bag.

36

THE HONEYMOON IS OVER

Rico and I headed for Lower Price Hill around 11:00 p.m., under a full Strawberry Moon. As stunning as it was, clouds would have provided better cover. Jade's tip led us to an abandoned building on Exeter Way, about a ten-minute drive west of Cincinnati's OTR district.

The three-story Italianate eyesore, nestled in an acre of scrub brush, had been vacant for over a decade. The foreboding red brick monster with boarded-up windows would be the perfect haven for rotters, and fingers crossed, a handler like Cain who needed privacy.

Rico parked the Caddy around the nearest corner on a quiet, dimly lit side street. The element of surprise was crucial, and it was a hot, muggy June night. People might be sleeping with their windows open, so we needed to keep the noise down.

After easing out of the Barbie-mobile, we pulled on coveralls over our street clothes (because Nonnie was tired of our zushi-filled laundry) and turned toward our target. A loud thump came from inside the trunk.

"Not yet," I growled, smacking the trunk lid.

The thumping stopped. After a quick glance around to

ensure no porch lights had flickered on, Rico grabbed his bolt cutters and a pair of FLIR night-vision binoculars from the backseat. We moved on, creeping through a jumble of backyards and overgrown lots toward Cain's newest stronghold, followed by the distant sound of renewed thumping.

A chain link fence surrounded the property about forty yards away, give or take. From that distance, the house was as dark and silent as a tomb. An oversized storage shed, covered in weeds, sat at the back of the property near the fence.

After we closed the gap, Rico pulled out his bolt cutters and snapped a body-shaped outline in the chain-link mesh. Then he pulled the loose fencing aside, made a hole, and we crawled underneath it onto the property.

Location secured.

Rico boosted me onto the roof of the storage shed, where I peered into one of the few intact windows of the house using police-issued FLIR night-vision binoculars. The flickering of a TV lit the interior just enough for me to identify Cain as he passed by the window. I ducked, heart pounding, and waited, wondering if I had been made. But no lights came on, and no one looked outside.

Target acquired. Phase one of Operation Catch Cain was complete.

After I hopped down from the storage shed, we ducked back under the loose fence and retraced our steps to the car. Everything was quiet, except for the incessant hum of insects on the warm summer night. A patch of clouds drifted in front of the moon, and the light waned.

The perfect time for phase two to commence.

I grabbed my custom ten-foot dog catcher's pole from the backseat of the car, then stuck the key into the trunk lock and gave it a twist. A flurry of thumps and growls rose to greet me. Apparently, Fred, the 'vital errand' I had run earlier in the day, wanted out. A coordinated two-man process followed, wherein

Rico raised the lid, and I used the dog-catcher's pole to lasso my secret weapon: Fred the Freshie.

While Rico had been busy catching up on desk work, I had been out searching for an old-fashioned, run-of-the-mill rotter that ate anything it stumbled across and couldn't follow a command, no matter how many brains you threw at it—an early edition biter that Cain couldn't control.

The idea was to smuggle Fred onto the property and make enough noise that Cain would think one of his biters had escaped. He'd race outside to capture it, and by the time he realized the 'ringer' rotter wasn't one of his, we'd be all over him.

I grabbed the dog pole and trudged backwards away from the car, pulling a very pissed-off biter out of the trunk. The harder I yanked, the louder Fred growled. Between the thumps, growls, and moans, we were lucky the whole neighborhood wasn't hunting us with lanterns and pitchforks.

"Hey, Partner," I said once Fred safely cleared the trunk. "Grab that road atlas from the cargo net, roll it tight, and shove it down Fred's throat."

"Who's Fred?"

"The zombie."

"Shove it *where*?"

"Here. Hold this," I said, handing Rico the pole. Once he had a firm grip on it, I let go, darted to the trunk, reached for the atlas, and rolled it as tight as I could. "Open wide for the airplane," I said, cramming the atlas into Fred's mouth.

"Well, isn't this good timing?" whispered a voice.

I spun and found Jade Chen hovering on the far side of the Caddy.

"Damn it, get out of here, Jade!" I yelled, not caring who heard. "This is dangerous."

"Not a chance, sister. My tip, my story." Jade motioned her cameraman out from the darkness. "Pull in tight, Rip. I want a shot of that wad sticking out of the rotter's mouth. Eww, the ACL's not gonna like that. Hi, Hot Stuff," she said, blowing Rico a kiss. "Missed you at the wedding. Nice Caddy. Didn't figure you for pink, though."

Rico flashed a tired smile. "Welcome back. But Nighthawk's right. We're in the middle of an op. You need to leave."

"Listen," she said, squaring off with her hands on her hips. "You wouldn't even be here without my help. Rip and I are here for the duration. Let it roll, big guy."

Jade's long-time Cameraman, Rip Saccha, got some great action shots of Fred, thrashing and straining against the pole. I wasn't worried. It was custom-made of Titanium. No way that sucker would snap. And it didn't. However, the locking device that secured the noose had the tensile strength of a lo mein noodle.

After a faint *pop*, the pole snapped back empty, and Fred the Freshie was in the wind.

"Stay here!" Rico yelled, pointing to Jade and Rip, as we took off after the damn thing.

I kicked myself as we chased it through the tangle of back-yards and thorny overgrowth. After careful consideration, I'd chosen a freshie for the job because it needed to be fast enough to reach Cain before he figured out what was going on.

Freaking freshies.

Fred headed straight for the house, as if that broken-down behemoth was a mothership calling its young. And after all the work Rico did, cutting through the chain-link, the stupid rotter bypassed the hole and ran along the entire fence line toward the front of the house.

We changed course and sprinted diagonally, hoping to intersect it, but we just made it to the front yard when the damn zom triggered an IED and exploded in a crimson cloud of zushi.

Rico and I hit the ground, covered our heads, and lay there waiting for the shower of mud, rocks, and biter bits to stop.

"Don't move!" Rico yelled as the last of the debris fell. "There might be more devices. I'm calling Bomb Squad."

So much for the element of surprise. Cain and the antidote would be long gone by the time we could safely move again.

And of course, I had to pee.

"So, we just lay here or what?" I asked, brushing dirt off my face.

Rico didn't answer, but he was talking to someone; hopefully, Bomb Squad. The Channel 10 news van raced down the street, slammed on its brakes, and slid in along the curb. Jade and Rip burst from the van like a tactical team on a mission.

"Stop!" Rico screamed, lying on the ground and waving his arms. "Don't come into the yard. It's booby trapped. Go home, Jade. There's nothing you can do here."

"Except get blown up," I yelled.

The news floosy flashed her porcelain caps. "Why would I leave? You're stuck there until someone tells you it's safe to move. I can ask anything I want. Rip will film from beside the van, and I'll run the interview here at the curb."

Interview?

Jade nodded to Rip. "On one. Three, two, one. Good morning, Cincinnati! This is Mrs. Jade Chen-Hendrix, for ABC News Affiliate Channel 10, fresh from my ten-day honeymoon in Figi. We are on location in Price Hill, covering what appears to have been an explosion mere moments ago. Detective De Palma of the Cincinnati Police Department, what can you confirm?"

Rico lifted his head, swiped mud from his face, and glared at the camera. "There *was* an explosion mere moments ago."

"Do you know who or what triggered that explosion?"

"Yes."

Silence reigned.

Jade narrowed her eyes. "Can you elaborate on that for us?"

"I can. But I won't."

Jade stomped her size-six Louboutin pump. "I'm sure our viewers—"

"As you know, Ms. Chen, it's police policy not to comment on ongoing investigations."

"It's *Mrs.* Chen-Hendrix...with a hyphen." She turned to me and scowled. "Also here this evening is world-renowned zombie hunter and corpse whisperer, Allie Nighthawk. Ms. Nighthawk—

"Go away and let me blow up in peace, Mrs...Chenen-whatever."

She hadn't called me a cadaver-diver, but I'd squashed her like a bug anyway. Old habits die hard.

The bomb squad's arrival, along with a parade of patrol cars, EMTs, and fire engines, put an end to the interview. The Channel 10 news van was immediately banished from sight on the far side of a yellow police tape. That thought struck me funny at first, until I considered why. We could have been, and might still be, obliterated. I winced, wondering for the first time if Nonnie might be waiting up for us and catch Jade's snippet on a Channel 10 news update.

A tall, forty-something balding guy decked out in protective gear climbed out of the bomb squad van, strolled to the curb's edge, and nodded at Rico. "Who'd you piss off, dude?"

"Miller, good to see you. His name is Charles Cain—a Special Forces alum if you believe the ring on his finger. Not sure if he's still inside or not."

"He's not, or I wouldn't be standing here talking to you. We sent up a drone and had a look around. There's no heat signature inside. Who's this?" Miller asked, eying me."

"Allie Nighthawk, meet Randy Miller, head of ordinance detection and control. Randy, Allie."

I stuck my hand up from the ground and waved.

"Nice to meet you," he said. "Don't worry. We'll get you out there. But if you hear me say oops, kiss your ass goodbye."

The smile on his face, as cool as a Bahama breeze, was meant to reassure, but it never reached his steely eyes. Randy radiated fearlessness, confidence, and guile. He struck me as someone who was very skilled at his job—and someone I never wanted to play poker with.

Miller's drones, equipped with ground-penetrating radar, thermal sensors, magnetometers, and AI computer vision, found two more IEDs in the yard, one of which was just a few yards from Rico's right foot. After Miller guided us to the sidewalk, he sent Boom Boom, their explosive ordinance robot, into the yard to disarm the devices. Unfortunately, drone searches inside the house were a no-go. Indoor airflow was limited, and there were too many tight spaces and high-density metal objects to negotiate.

Standing on the sidewalk with all my limbs intact, I was as surprised as anyone to see we were still alive. A double Jack sounded like the perfect celebration. But the night wasn't over yet. We had a horde of rotters to neutralize, and Cain was MIA...again.

37

AN ENDLESS GAME
OF WHACK-A-MOLE

Once the drones confirmed the presence of ambient-temperature movement inside the house (geek speak for a pack shuffling rotters), our options were to either blow it up, when it was possibly filled with explosives, or clear the biters and then bring Miller's squad in to do their thing.

Blowing it up got nixed because Jade Chen, who already knew about the biters, was sitting in the Channel 10 news van parked just beyond the yellow police tape, waiting for her headline. Nobody wanted to deal with that PR nightmare, so we would be going in.

Thanks, Jade, you noxious cloud of Aqua Net.

Rico shot through the lock on the front door and kicked it open wide. We stepped back from the porch and began picking off the endless parade of biters as they shambled outside. The three-story house had a full basement. Which biters were shuffling out from which floor was anyone's guess.

When the line of deadheads ended, Rico and I stepped inside, our shoes sinking into the blood-soaked carpet as we moved from room to room, clearing the first floor. We took positions at the stairwells, holding off stragglers from the upper levels while Boom Boom did its thing.

Once the bomb squad declared the floor cleared with no devices found, we held a quick meeting. It seemed unlikely that Cain had enough time to arm more devices, and if he had, he'd have probably rigged the first floor to blow. Rico and I searched the other levels, slicing the pie from left to right at the end of each stairway, astounded by the carnage in front of us.

The stink of blood filled my nose. Half-eaten bodies—not zombies—dead human bodies and pieces of dead humans littered the floors like naked, discarded chicken bones. Blood and zushi painted the walls and ceilings as if someone had taken a chainsaw to the bodies, severing the flesh, bones, and sinew.

More than likely, these people had been alive when they were dismembered. I knew that because Doc Blanchard once remarked that arterial spray only comes from victims with a beating heart. Trying to match up these scraps, limbs, and pieces of limbs to torsos and their respective heads would be a gruesome job. I didn't envy Doc.

To keep the site from becoming a bigger circus than it already was, Rico called in a couple of unmarked semis to haul away both the human and rotter remains. Around 5 a.m., as I watched Miller's Bomb Squad and the parade of emergency vehicles pull away, I wondered how many transient and down-on-their-luck folks had accepted Cain's unimaginable offer of 'day' labor.

The thought sent chills up my spine.

How many more might end up this way if we don't stop him? Catching Cain had become an endless game of Whack-a-Mole. We'd stop him in one place, only to see him pop up in another. It was hard catching someone who, thanks to the help of a certain demon, was always one step ahead of us.

Where did that leave Wyco, or any of the worldwide victims

of the new virus? People like Wycowski, bitten early on, were down to two plus days before turning, and we were no closer to finding the antidote than when this whole mess started.

How long could they hang on to hope? And how long could I keep going, with their lives hanging over my head?

HEADBUTT OPENED a single bloodshot eye as Rico and I kicked off our zushi-covered shoes, shed our blood-soaked coveralls, and crept through my back door just before sunrise. While Rico took a quick shower, I gave my bully buddy a treat and silently thanked Nonnie for having covered the Avian Triumvirate's cage. Lately, between Baby Hyrum's screeching and Gertie's wood chewing, I was ready to boot them both to the nearest tree.

After pouring myself a generous double, I plopped on the couch, took a sip of warm, smooth Jack, and closed my eyes. Just for a minute, I thought, to relax before my shower. Maybe it was the IED explosion or the horrific things I'd seen in that house, but the shadow of Toussaint loomed over me. An occupational hazard, given the life I lived. My thoughts drifted back to a time when the watchful eyes of Mama and Gadyen had always made me feel safe.

GADYEN RESTED at my feet on the steps of Mama's restaurant late one hot summer night after closing. Moonlight glinted off the gemstones in his leather collar.

"They're beautiful," I murmured, nudging the collar to make them sparkle.

Mama, seated beside me, smiled. "And rich in meaning, too. These," she said, fingering one of the brilliant blue stones, "are

Lapis Lazuli. They signify strength and wisdom to see beyond the veil. The bright orange ones in the middle are Carnelian, for loyalty. And the Bloodstones, the dark green ones with red flecks, are for courage."

"Gadyen has all those qualities," I said, scratching behind his ears.

"Oh, and more, Child. In fact, the name Gadyen means Guardian in Creole. Someday," she said with a heavy sigh, "many years from now, after I am gone, you will need him, and he will come to you."

"Mama," I scoffed gently, "Dogs don't live that long."

"Gadyen isn't like other dogs." She cupped my face in one of her strong, gentle hands. "Do you remember what I taught you about Papa Legba?"

Ugh. Pop quiz. I can never keep the lwa straight. "The old man with a corncob pipe and the hat who walks with a cane?"

"The very one. He is the gatekeeper between the spirit and human worlds. Papa Lega protects and loves dogs, as he does us. It is his nature. Your Gadyen was one of Papa's favorites."

"Then why doesn't he live with Papa?" I should have phrased my question better. Gadyen was flesh and blood. Papa Legba was a spirit who could take human form, but I had never seen him. It was hard to understand how they could exist on the same plane.

"Papa wanted you to have him, Child. Gadyen is and will always be your protector."

The memory made me smile.

The pipe and sigil from Mama's box had been tributes to Papa Legba. There were so many moments with Mama and Gadyen that I'd forgotten over the years. It would have been nice to see you tonight, boy, I thought as I drifted off to sleep.

Then again, maybe Gadyen had been with me after all. I was still alive.

38

DON'T EVEN TELL ME THE ODDS

"Where's Rico?" I asked, squinting at the clock on the stove. It was nine o'clock in the morning.

Nonnie, laying bacon in the skillet, answered without turning around. "He left for office. Said to lets you sleep. Go take shower," she said, nodding toward the hallway. "You needs it."

The stink of blood was still in my nose. I'd taken the coveralls off outside, but my hair and skin reeked of it.

As I hit the shower, a foggy memory hovered just beyond reach. Something about Mama and me and Gadyen. The more I tried to recall it, the more it slipped away. I threw on a clean pair of jeans and the "Zumba Hunter's Rock" t-shirt Nonnie had given me and then started thinking about what we needed to do that day. First on the list was trying to convince Crickett's mom to let me raise her daughter.

I shoveled a spoonful of scrambled eggs onto a slice of bread and headed for the door. "Thanks for breakfast, Nonnie. Stay on those records, okay?"

The chief cook/computer wiz blocked my exit. "Wait! Yesterday, I founds a delivery address in flower shop records.

This lady, Gloria Fiori, she gets flowerses every week. The card always says samer thing, 'XXX ooo, Gene.'"

"Nice catch!" I said, kissing Nonnie's cheek. "Have Vinny check it out today, okay? And keep looking."

When I headed out the door, as a last-minute nod to Nonnie and her sensitive ears, I rolled my Lowrider down the driveway before hopping on and speeding toward the precinct. If Vinny hit the jackpot with the lead on the Fiori woman, I'd pass the info to Rico to stumble upon himself. But I soon realized my partner had come into a lead of his own.

RICO INTERCEPTED me as I beelined to the breakroom for my first cup of coffee. "Guess what I found in my text messages this morning."

"It's too early for games," I said, refusing to break stride. "Just give it to me straight."

"One of my CIs has scoop on Blasnick."

"Really? What's the story?"

"I'm on my way to meet him now. Wanna come?"

No way I was getting stuck there, combing through Capshaw's records by myself. "Fine, but we're stopping for coffee. Let's see if we can chat with Crickett's mother, Sarah... something, while we're out."

"Sarah Winston, and way ahead of you," Rico said. "She's expecting us before noon."

"Well, aren't you Mister Efficient?" I said, as I followed him out the door.

Rico rolled his eyes. "It's funny what you can accomplish when you get to work before the crack of ten."

Jimmy Z, Rico's informant, seated at the counter of Dunkin' Donuts, was sipping his double latte and working his crossword. The short, bald bookie looked more like somebody's grandpa.

Rico ordered us coffee and a dozen mixed, then nodded Jimmy toward one of the tables. "Whatcha got for me?" Rico asked as we joined him.

"Whatchu got for *me*?" Jimmy asked. "And I ain't talkin' donuts."

Rico slid a C-note across the table. It disappeared faster than Jimmy's cruller. "Blasnick likes to play the ponies. He don't book with me," Jimmy explained, "Or you and me, we wouldn't be conversatin'. But word on the street is, he's into Benny C. big time."

"How big?" Rico asked.

"100K, so I hear."

I nearly spit out my coffee.

"We about done here?" Jimmy said, fidgeting. "I got to see a man about a horse."

Given his line of work, I wondered if he meant that literally.

"Then I'll leave you to it. Thanks, Jimmy." Rico reached for the donut box as we rose to leave, but Jimmy beat him to it.

"Don't go cheap on me now, De Palma. Nice to meet you, young lady," he said, with a wink.

"Back at you, Mr...Z."

Jimmy Z...Benny C. Did no one in the underworld use a last name?

After Jimmy drove away in his Ford F-150, we slid back into the Caddy, and Rico whistled. "100K sounds like motive to me."

People have killed for less.

As we headed for Crickett's mother's house, it occurred to me that getting what we wanted from Jimmy hadn't taken much, just a hundred bucks and a box of glazed. Convincing Sarah Winston to let me raise her daughter would take significantly more—the promise of getting to the bottom of her daughter's death. Any information Crickett might provide about Capshaw's death or the misappropriation of city funds wouldn't mean a damn thing to Sarah Winston.

Was Crickett's death accidental? Or was Blasnick involved? Would Crickett even know? What were the odds on any of these outcomes? I bet Jimmy Z. could tell me, but I was probably better off not knowing.

CRICKETT CAPSHAW AND HER MOTHER, Sarah, had lived on opposite sides of the tracks. Sarah's tiny yellow-frame bungalow on the east side of town didn't have a garden, a pool, or even a garage, but it was squeaky-clean and smelled of lemons. Pictures of Crickett hung on every wall. Sarah had yet to say a word, but I knew she had loved her daughter. As we exchanged introductions, I wondered what had happened in Crickett's short life that had taken her from a high school diploma to a rap sheet. It was as if Sarah had read my mind.

"My girl was the prettiest thing. And good as gold, too, until she discovered boys...well, a boy," Sarah said, correcting herself, "with bags of coke and lots of money. All that flash must have been hard to pass up for a girl used to wearing thrift shop clothes."

Sarah picked up a pack of Marlboro Reds and tamped one out. "When the boy got tired of her, the money dried up and so did the coke. That's when Crickett got a job. Called herself an escort. Eugene Capshaw thought she hung the moon. Made an...honest woman of her."

The word honest had stuck in her throat.

Sarah's candor stuck in my heart.

She coughed out a plume of smoke. "Bastard was thirty-five

years older than she was. I couldn't stand the thought of him touching her, but he got her off the street, so..."

An awkward silence hung in the air.

"The Princeton Vikings," Rico said, pointing to a picture on the wall. Crickett wore a scarlet and gray cheerleading uniform. "I went there, too. Quite a few years ahead of your daughter."

Sarah pursed her lips. "What can I help you with, Detective?"

"We need a little help getting to the bottom of Crickett's death."

"From me?"

"In a way," Rico said, glancing at me.

Sarah seemed like a brass-tacks kind of woman, so I laid it out straight. "Mrs. Winston, do you think it's strange your daughter didn't grab her Epi-Pen?"

"Strange? It's fucking impossible."

"That's what I thought you'd say. What if I could ask your daughter why she didn't grab that pen?"

Sarah narrowed her eyes. "You want to raise my daughter."

"Yes, ma'am."

Sara sat on the couch and snuffed out her smoke. "Then maybe it's time I ask just what happened to my son-in-law Eugene at Rose Hill Cemetery."

The subject was bound to come up, even though I prayed it wouldn't.

"Fair enough," I said, having no idea what was going to come out of my mouth. "When I raise a ~~corpse~~ person in a cemetery, after they've been interred for a while, the person's response is unpredictable. The Mayor awakened in an agitated state. He broke through the ~~duct tape~~ security bonds we used and...*shit, shit, shit* ~~bolted, escaped~~...and—"

"Hightailed it across the cemetery like a big, fat razorback hog?"

"Yes, ma'am. The mayor attacked my associate and tried to bite him, so I had to shoot him in the head to stop him."

Sarah locked eyes with me. "And is that how you intend to lay my daughter to rest when you're done talking with her? You gonna blow her head off, too?"

"Oh, God, no!" I said, scrambled beside her on the couch. "I want to talk to your daughter while she is still at the ME's office, before she's interred. And when the conversation is over, I have a way to very quietly and discreetly disconnect her brainstem ~~with a knife~~. She won't feel a thing. And if you want to, you can still have an open casket viewing."

Sara looked away. "And she'll tell you how she died?"

"If she knows, yes ma'am."

"And if she don't know?"

"Then she doesn't know. But she doesn't have the capacity to lie. I'd like to ask her about the mayor's death and the missing funds, too."

"I got no problem with that."

After a beat, I asked, "And if Crickett had a hand in Eugene's death?"

"I'd like to believe she didn't. But in the last years of her life, I barely knew her anymore. If she was involved, she'll answer to God for it. Not me."

Sarah rose and stood before me, staring into my soul. "You swear before God, if I let you raise Crickett, you won't blow her brains out?"

Dear God, please, please don't make me a liar. "I swear."

"Then let's do this. I'll sign whatever I need to." She turned her eyes to Rico. "Crickett always had an Epi-Pen handy, and she knew how to use it. Used it more times than I could keep track of. You mark my words, Detective, Crickett was murdered. I want her killer brought to justice."

We thanked her for her time, told her that we had to take

her verbal consent back to the office, and that we'd be back in touch with her soon.

Sarah walked us to the door, and then lingered in the threshold, eyeballing me before she let me pass. "I expect you to keep your promise, Ms. Nighthawk. Don't make me regret this."

Amen, sister.

"Scary lady," Rico muttered as we climbed back into the Caddy.

"Tough lady," I countered.

There was a difference. Sarah Winston's pain ran deep. I respected her, and I'd do whatever it took to make Crickett's raising go smoothly. My thoughts must have appeared in an air bubble over my head.

"I know she pushed you into a corner," Rico said as he drove back to the office. "But how are you going to make sure Crickett's raising comes off without a hitch?"

"I don't have the first clue," I said. "But it won't involve duct tape."

39

I KNOW BETTER THAN
TO ANNOY MYSELF

I called Opie from the passenger seat to tell him Sarah was on board with raising Crickett. That was our desired outcome going in, but my conversation with Sarah weighed on me. She'd pressured me into promising something I shouldn't have. Raising Crickett would be easy. What happened next was anyone's guess. For Sarah's sake, I hoped that I could avoid resolving it with a gun.

Opie was slow to answer my call. I'd been keeping him pretty busy, for someone who didn't represent me.

"Nighthawk," he finally blurted. "Sorry, I had a defense attorney on the other line."

"My condolences," I said, tapping the speakerphone icon so Rico could listen in. "What's going to happen to Crickett's lawsuit, now that she's passed?"

"Ask your attorney. Oh, that's right. You don't have one."

"I'm hoping this will all go away before I need one."

"Well, Burklander won't drop the suit yet. As the only surviving relative, Sarah Winston could claim rights to a potential damages award."

She could definitely use the money. But Sarah seemed more

grounded than her daughter, like the kind of person who might view the suit as nothing more than a money grab.

"Speaking of Crickett's mother," I said, "Rico and I got her verbal approval today for the raising."

"No shit." Opie sounded stunned. "How'd you manage that, after the clusterfuck with the mayor?"

"I had to promise not to blow Crickett's head off."

"Nighthawk, on what planet could you promise that with a straight face? Have you ever raised someone and *not* blown their head off?"

"Fuck off, Opie. It's not as easy as it looks. And yes, I have."

Just not usually.

The game starts with someone saying, "I know! Let's have Nighthawk raise the corpse!" Like I'm going to wave a wand over its ass and presto change-o solve the case. But when things go south, and there's running and screaming, and floor-to-ceiling zushi, whose ass gets raked over the coals? Mine, that's whose.

I stared out the passenger window, annoyed at myself, because this time, the suggestion to raise the corpse had come from me. "Just can the jokes," I said, "and let me worry about the raising. By the way, Sarah Winston is also fine with you inquiring into the mayor's death and the missing funds."

"Great!" Opie paused. "You didn't mention anything about Crickett's lawsuit, did you? That conversation has to involve her counsel."

"Christ, Tim," Rico blurted. "Give us a little credit."

"Let's stay on topic," I barked. "Opie, can you coordinate with Legal and have them draft some kind of release for Sarah to sign, so we can get this done pronto? Everybody and their brother is leaning on Cap. He needs some breathing room."

"Sure, if you stop calling me Opie."

"Fine," I snapped. "Tell me when it's ready, Tim."

I mashed the end call button with my thumb, pissed that

there is no way to slam the receiver on a cell phone. When you need to vent, nothing compares to a good old-fashioned phone slam.

THE SMELL of Ricardo's Pizza, wafting through the 51st, told my stomach it was lunchtime. Rico and I snagged a couple of slices each as we trudged through the bullpen and headed for his desk. The sight of a pink message sheet taped to his laptop made the hair on the back of my neck stand on end.

Rico yanked the note off with a sigh. "We've been summoned."

Eighty-three steps and one and a half slices of a Ricardo's Cheese-n-ator later, we assumed our usual flogging positions in Cap's raggedy red visitor chairs. Our Fearless Leader hadn't shown up yet, so we crammed in the last of our pizza. Cap showed up mid-bite.

"Don't let me interrupt your lunch," he said. "In fact, kick back and watch this little treat from the noon news I taped for you."

The news.

Little Allie's balls shriveled inside.

Cap settled in, pressed play, and kept his eyes on us.

"Good afternoon, Cincinnati! This is Jade Chen-Hendrix, with the mid-day report, coming to you live from Channel 10, the station that digs deeper for news than any other—deeper than even the Cadaver Diver herself, Allie Nighthawk."

And we were back to normal.

Rico slouched and hid his face while Jade's report continued.

"Channel 10 first aired this story this morning, but due to the serious potential impact on the city's residents, it bears repeating. Overnight, CPD, with the assistance of Allie

Nighthawk, raided a house in the Price Hill area and uncovered a huge cache of zombies allegedly amassed by one Charles Cain, a retired member of the military's Special Forces unit. A single explosion occurred, presumably from an IED intentionally planted on the property. No lives were lost. One zombie was blown to smithereens. The exact nature and scope of Cain's plot are still under investigation, but if history repeats itself, we could experience a significant spike in zombie activity. We at Channel 10 will keep you updated as warranted. In the meantime, lock your windows and doors. Avoid going out alone after dark and steer clear of lonely, isolated areas. Your safety and that of your loved ones may depend on it. Remember, you heard it here first, from Jade Chen-Hendrix, on Cincinnati's own Channel 10."

Cap turned off the TV and waited for our response. The clock ticked. The air conditioner hummed. He waited a little longer. I could have held out forever, but when things got awkward, Rico folded like a crappy lawn chair.

"We didn't tell Jade anything, Cap. In fact, she's the one who gave us the tip."

Cap scowled at us over the top of his cheaters. "And then she tailed you."

"Yeah," I muttered, avoiding his gaze. "But when Rico and I got pinned down in the yard, the unis moved the news van out of sight—which was great because at least she didn't report on all the biters we mowed down once they shambled outside." *Not yet anyway. It's only a matter of time until even Jade puts that together.*

Cap pursed his lips. "Let me get this straight. I'm supposed to tell City Council we're lucky she didn't witness part of an operation that she shouldn't even have known existed?"

"Exactly!"

Rico changed the subject. "Sarah Winston said she'll sign off on Crickett's raising and that she'll allow questions related to the mayor's death and the missing funds. Tim Andrews is working with Legal to draft a release for her to sign ASAP."

"That's a start," Cap mumbled. "Anything else?

"Yeah, one of my CIs says Blasnick is in to his bookie for 100Gs."

"No shit." Cap smiled for the first time since we walked into the room. "I'm liking Blasnick for Crickett's death more and more."

Rico grinned. "Me, too. But we need more than warm fuzzies for a warrant."

"We'll get there. What's next on your agenda?"

"I thought we'd nose around the Price Hill site, see if we missed something Cain might have left behind."

"Like an antidote?"

"Yeah...hopefully," Rico murmured.

A heavy pause settled over the room.

"How much time does Wyco have?" Cap asked.

"A couple of days," I said, "more or less. Less to be safe."

"Then get on with it."

Cap nodded toward the door and turned his attention to a file on his desk, the official sign that the meeting was over and our presence was no longer required.

"Way to get us out of the doghouse," I whispered as we cleared Cap's desk and headed into the hallway.

Soulja Boy's 'Pretty Boy Swag' blared from my phone as we reached the bullpen.

"It's Vinny," I said, "meet you at the car."

Rico nodded, keys in hand, and continued toward the entrance.

"Wasssup, Gel Boy?"

"Give me something hard next time. That took like fifteen minutes."

"What did you find?"

"That Gloria lady who got all the flowers is the mayor's

mother. From what I see online, she was widowed and then remarried. That's why her name's different."

Crap. "Tell Nonnie to keep looking, okay? Anything unusual, I want to know."

"Hey, listen. Phoebe's having a cow. She says you're in danger—"

An explosion slammed me to the ground. Glass and debris sliced through the air like a barrage of jagged knives. The lights went out; everything fell silent. When I woke up, my ears were ringing. I was lying on my back, covered in debris. A lot of it so mangled that I had no idea what it had been or where it had come from. Except for one piece—a tiny, twisted hunk of bubblegum pink metal just beyond my fingertips.

Oh, my God, Rico!

40

THE LOW SLUNG, WRINKLED POTATO

"Allie!"

Rico's voice filtered through the chaos.

"Over here!" I called, struggling to my feet. Clouds of drywall dust billowed through the remnants of the bullpen. After picking my way through a sea of broken glass, I climbed over a toppled desk, slack-jawed and batting away the dust.

As I searched through the haze for Rico, a soft voice called, "Allie, help me."

The outstretched arm of Vera Armstrong, the dispatcher, reached out from beneath an overturned workstation.

"Are you hurt?" I asked.

"I don't think so. Just stuck."

"Hang on."

I grabbed the side of the workstation and heaved, surprised at how easily it moved. Rico, who had walked up beside me unseen, was pushing the top of the unit. Together, we shoved the cubicle upright.

A rush of emotions welled inside me. Anger, sadness, and relief, I felt them all. But mostly, I felt connected to my partner more in that moment than I had ever known was possible.

Rico bent down and carefully lifted Vera to her feet. She threw herself into his arms with an anguished sob. He held her while she cried, his eyes fixed on me, filled with the same ambivalent mix of emotions that I felt. But the thin set of his mouth made me think anger overshadowed the others.

Sirens wailing in the distance grew closer. Cap joined the employees of the 51st as they sifted through the rubble, extracting people and counting heads. Miraculously, there were only minor injuries and no one died. The front of the building near the entrance took the brunt of the impact. Cap's office, the break area, and meeting rooms in the rear of the structure escaped unscathed.

A swath of charred concrete where the Caddy had been parked moments earlier was the bullseye that marked the site of the explosion. The Barbie Mobile was history.

"You never liked that pink piece of shit anyway," I muttered, fishing my cell phone from my pants pocket to take pictures of the damage to the building.

As I angled my phone to snap a pic, a text message pinged. After reading it a few times, I shrugged and handed it to Rico. "Look at this."

Back off, or next time they'll be picking up your body parts.

Rico heaved a heavy sigh. "Giordano must be tired of us raiding his rotter repositories."

"He ought to be," I said. "We're costing him a pretty penny."

It didn't take long to type my pithy reply. FUCK OFF.

"LOOK WHO'S HERE," Rico said, pointing toward Vinny climbing over a pile of debris near the entrance.

That's right, I thought. We were talking on the phone when this happened.

"Nighthawk!" Vinny rushed forward and swept me off my feet in a bear hug. "I thought you were dead."

"Me too. Hey, ease up. You're crushing me."

His eyes drank in the shattered windows and the chaos of the bullpen. "Giordano?"

I nodded. "How'd you get past the police tape?"

"I slipped in while they were putting up the rope. Things are getting dicey. Good thing I got those Ring cameras up."

Rico clapped his shoulder. "Better late than never, dude."

My thoughts drifted to Vinny's comments just before the explosion. Phoebe had warned him I was in danger. As much as I loved mocking her psychic abilities, she'd come too close to home more than once.

While shaking shards of glass from my hair, I motioned Rico aside for a private chat. "I was on the phone with Gel Boy when the bomb went off. He checked out Nonnie's lead about the floral deliveries. It was a bust. The flowers were for Capshaw's mother."

Rigo shrugged. "Cross another clue off the list."

I glanced up to see that Cap's eyes had zeroed in on Vinny from across the room. Fearless Leader was on his way over.

"Thanks for coming, Vinny, but you need to go," I said, tugging on his sleeve.

"Rodger that," he said, trudging back toward the entrance. He gave Cap a quick nod as they passed.

There wasn't a chance in hell Vinny's presence would pass unmentioned.

"What was he doing here?" Cap asked when he reached my side.

"We were on the phone when the bomb went off. He was just checking on me."

"No civilians in or out," he snapped. "I'm posting uniforms around the perimeter until the building is boarded and secured. Let me guess," he said, turning to Rico. "This is Giordano's handiwork."

"The one and only."

"Then get his ass. The FBI and ATF have jurisdiction over this, but you've got the inside track. Stay on it. Just don't get in their way."

"Will do," Rico said. "As soon as I requisition a new pool car. The one I had is in a million, tiny pieces."

"Hold on. I've got this." Cap whipped out his phone and made a call. "I need a car delivered to the 51st, pronto. Yeah, that's right. The one that just got bombed. And no pink fucking Cadillac this time. Understood?"

EVEN WITH CAP PULLING STRINGS, pronto at the motor pool took two hours, but the black government-issued SUV theygave us was primo. By six o'clock, we were cruising to my house in style with wood-grain paneling, leather seats, and Sirius XM radio.

As much as I wanted to catch Cain and hang him from the precinct's roof by his cajónes, even God took a rest on the seventh day. We'd been burning the candle at both ends for too long. It was time for a good meal and a night of dreamless, demon-free sleep. Toussaint and his Renfield wannabe, Cain, weren't going anywhere. And when the time came for us to face off, I'd need all my wits about me.

In honor of our survival, Nonnie cobbled together a feast for our crazy, chosen *fagmiglia*. When Rico and I walked into the house, Vinny, Phoebe, Dallas, and Nonnie were gathered around the table, waiting to dig in. The aroma of roasted garlic, onions, olive oil, and tomatoes teased my nose. I doubted that even heaven smelled that good.

Dinner conversation centered around Dallas's upcoming seventy-first birthday. Nonnie and Dallas had been spending a lot of time together. It was good to see them happy. And party planning, any kind of planning, was right up her alley.

Nonnie clapped her hands to stop the crosstalk at the table and assign our jobs. "We will haves party at The Blue Notes. Everyone joins in. Allie tends bar so Dallas cans relax. And Rico, you dos the decorations."

Rico and I exchanged glances.

"Vinny and Phoebe, you helps transport foods. So much foods."

A knock came at the back door. My heart jumped as Nonnie got up to answer it. Apparently, Rico's had as well.

"I'll get it," he said, darting a glance to me.

Nonnie looked out the window. "Bah! Is only Mr. Winstel," she said, shooing Rico back into his seat.

"Mrs. Nusbaum," Sid Winstel barked as she opened the door. "I'd like to speak to Allie."

I bit off a piece of my garlic knot. "We're having dinner, Sid. Maybe later." *When hell freezes over.*

"Now, Nighthawk. Excuse me," Sid said as he pushed past Nonnie into the kitchen.

Rico scooted his chair back, but I shook him off.

"That's far enough," I said, climbing to my feet. "What's your problem?"

"That slobbering brute of yours raped my Schnoodle."

"Nonnie told me. What would you like me to do?"

"Do? There's nothing you can do. Princess is a designer dog. We invested in her for breeding. And your...ogre ruined her!"

I glanced at my low-slung, wrinkled potato bellyflopped across the air vent and jutted my chin. "Maybe your ho-bag yapadoodle wanted it. Ever think of that, Sid? Waving her high-priced hormones at my ogr—my Headbutt. He was a virgin, you know." *Not likely.* "What do you have to say about that?"

Sid's mouth fell. "This isn't over—"

"Bye-byes, now," Nonnie said, slipping a garlic knot into his hand, then guiding him back to the threshold, and giving him a gentle nudge outside. "Always nice to sees you, Mr. Winstel."

I strolled to the door, slammed it in his face, and then twisted the lock behind him.

"Allie Cat," Dallas chuckled, "You've got the social skills of a turnip."

Ugh. He was the only person on earth who could get away with calling me Allie Cat, and just because something might be true does not mean that it should be said.

After we scraped the last bit of cannoli from our plates and finished the dishes, I repeatedly reassured Rico I could handle things overnight. The Ring cameras were up, and besides, Vinny would be here. My partner put up a fight but eventually left for a good night's sleep at his place. As an added precaution, Dallas volunteered to take Nonnie home with him. Vinny settled down on the couch for an all-night session of Counter-Strike 2.

Just what the doctor ordered, a quiet evening.

I shuffled down the hallway, wanting nothing more than to sink into a hot bubble bath, when Phoebe grabbed me by the arm, pulled me into my room, and shut the door.

"Girlfriend," she whispered. "This is going to blow your mind!"

41

THE MAGNIFICENT, LONELY GIFT

"Phoebe, I raise the dead for a living. Nothing blows my mind. Go tell Vinny."

"Not on your life, sister." Phoebe locked the door. "Mama Femi is dialed into my brain like a freaking earworm. Pull that carton over here," she said.

"Why?"

"Because what I'm gonna say won't make any sense without the things inside it." "It's just Mama's stuff from New Orleans."

Phoebe stomped her foot. "Mama says she knows what it is. She's the one who put it in the damn box. Stop arguing and bring it here."

"Mama didn't say damn."

"No, I added that. The two of you are killing me."

"Fine," I said, diving off the bed and shoving the box over in front of her. "Now what?"

Phoebe shifted her weight from foot to foot, gesturing, and opening her mouth like she wanted to say something, but nothing came out.

"Oh, for God's sake," I said. "Am I going to need a time machine to hear this?"

"Just bear with me. Okay? And remember, no matter what happens, I'm just the messenger. Open the box and pull out the collar, and…"

"And?"

"Put it on."

"Put the dog collar on *me*."

Phoebe nodded, and I rolled my eyes.

"Mama says stop rolling your eyes like a sassy pants or she'll have me take a ladle to your behind. Is she talking about…a soup ladle, Allie? Don't make me do that. Just put the damn thing on."

Mama had taken a ladle to my backside more than once when I was a kid. No way Phoebe would have known that. My doubts about her psychic ability had all but flown out the window. When I picked up the collar and snapped it around my neck, a tingle surged though my fingers, similar to the sensation that runs through my hands when I raise a corpse, only stronger.

Phoebe and I exchanged glances.

"Now, pull the other pieces you already opened out of the box," Phoebe said.

One by one, I pulled out the sigil, the corncob pipe, and the dog whistle, and laid them on the bed.

Phoebe nodded. "Mama says to remember your lessons about the Vodoun lwa."

I gave her a blank stare. "Any particular one?"

"Aliya Marie Nighthawk!" Phoebe's blazing eyes and seething tone were Mama's made over. "Think about it. Which lwa loves dogs and smokes a corncob pipe?"

"Papa Legba," I mumbled.

"Correct. Now, pick up that whistle and blow it."

Making Mama wait was never a good idea, but I hesitated anyway, wondering how Headbutt would react. Would he be confused? What if he—

"Blow it NOW!"

For better or worse, I snatched the whistle from the bedspread and brought it to my mouth.

When the whistle passed the collar around my neck, Phoebe squealed, "Look they're glowing!"

The inlaid stones in both pieces twinkled in unison.

All right, Mama. You win.

I blew the whistle and waited—but not for long. The room grew hot and sticky. Phoebe and I stared at each other wide eyed, as the air around us began to ebb and flow in translucent waves. A dark mist leapt from the waves, writhing and twisting, and morphing and stretching as the mass took shape.

The air stilled; the temperature cooled, and I stood breathless at the sight of the most regal-looking dog I had ever seen, with furless skin so black it shone indigo blue. Intelligent, almond-shaped eyes, black as midnight, gazed into mine, twinkling like they always had when I was a child. While I couldn't begin to explain the magick behind it, my puppy had risen after twelve years in the grave.

His long, tall ears pricked toward me, and his thin, tapered tail whipped back and forth.

When his mouth curved in a wide smile, I laughed and took a knee. Gadyen hurled himself into my arms and whined softly as he rolled onto his back. His skin was soft and warm. His heart thrummed beneath my fingers as he waggled against me and licked my face. He woofed softly, and I put my finger to my mouth.

"Hush," I whispered, shaking my head. "What am I going to do with you? Holy Hannah, how am I going to explain you?"

Phoebe, who hadn't spoken since Gadyen appeared, found her voice. "Did *you* do this?" she whispered.

"No," I murmured. "I loved him too much to bring him back."

Anything or anyone I raised could never stay. No matter how much I loved them.

Phoebe reached for my hand. "Mama says Gadyen is your protector in death as he was in life. He's mortal now, which means he can be injured, suffer, or even die. It takes a lot of energy for him to cross the veil. He can remain in his physical form for an hour at most. If you don't send him back to the other side, he'll return on his own. When you need him, blow the whistle once, and he'll come to you. Blow it twice, and he'll assume his spirit form to protect you against demons. When it's time to lay him back to rest, blow it three times."

"What about Nonnie and Rico? Or Vinny, Headbutt, and the birds?" I asked. "Can they sense Gadyen?"

Phoebe paused and tilted her head, as if listening. "When he's in his physical form, yes, they can. But Mama says he's vulnerable now, and others' awareness of his existence could jeopardize you both."

"Does that mean you're in danger?" I asked.

"God, you're right." Phoebe's voice held a mix of fear and awe. "But Mama chose me for a reason. I can't walk away, especially now. You might need me."

I shook my head at her, thinking she was either very brave or very stupid. Maybe both, but she was loyal.

Phoebe raised a finger, signaling me to wait. "Mama says when Gadyen is in his spirit form, other sensitives like me may sense his presence, too. It's best to keep him separate from the living, for both your sakes."

Wow. What a magnificent, lonely gift Mama had given me.

Vinny's voice drifted in from the living room. "What are you girls doing back there?"

"Just girl stuff. Hair and nails," Phoebe called back.

Hair and nails?

"Really?" Vinny asked. "Nighthawk's getting her nails done?"

Clearly, his clairvoyant girlfriend was the worst liar in the history of liars.

An idea came to mind. "Phoebe, can you let Headbutt bunk with you and Vinny tonight? I want to visit with Gadyen. His scent on my sheets might send Headbutt into a hissy fit."

"No problem." She smiled and crouched in front of Gadyen, looking deep into his eyes. After a few seconds of non-verbal chit-chat, my gorgeous Xolo stretched forward and licked her hand.

"What did you say to him?" I asked.

"I told him that I'm your friend."

"And?"

"He said that makes me his friend too."

"You heard Mama," I said giving her a solemn look. "Not a word of this to anyone, Phoebe. Swear it."

"I know you think I'm a flake, Allie. But I meant it. And here," she said, handing me a small flask of holy water. "Mama wanted you to have this. See, we've both got your back."

"Cross your heart and hope to die?"

"Stick a needle in my eye," she said, easing open the door to leave.

"Phoebe," I whispered. "You aren't a flake. I was wr...wrong. I'm sorry."

God that hurt.

"No duh," she said, slipping out and shutting the door behind her.

Nothing like having my apology—one of the rare few that have ever crossed my lips—stuffed into a Walmart bag like a half-eaten burrito and chucked into a dumpster. Since she was involved up to her eyeballs and risking life and limb for me, I let the slight pass.

"Hey, boy," I murmured, plopping onto the bed. "Hop up here next to me, until you have to go."

He leapt up beside me with such ease that it looked like he

might take flight. God, how I used to love this dog—how I still loved this dog. And how he loved me.

"Do you know how special you are?" I murmured, scratching behind his ears. "You were one of Papa Legba's favorites until he gave you to me. Guess we're glued at the hip until the end, huh, fella?"

Gadyen circled a few times, before he laid down and stretched, looking at up at me like I was the sun and the moon and the stars. I wrapped him in my arms and buried my face against him, breathing in his scent, saddened that our visit would be so short. My last waking thought was that maybe together we could beat Toussaint. But I never got to share that with Gadyen. When I awoke, he had returned across the void, where he would wait patiently for me to summon him again, for the biggest fight of our lives.

The wait wouldn't be long.

42

EVERYONE'S A COMEDIAN

After my shower the next morning, I came out of the bathroom and caught Headbutt sniffing around my bedroom. He let out a woof and shot me the mother of all stink eyes. Withering under his glare, I tried to pet him, but he turned his back and marched to his floor vent in the kitchen. No question about it. As far as Headbutt was concerned, the Xolo was out of the bag, with less-than-optimal results.

I sipped my coffee at the kitchen table pondering the mystery of Gadyen. Nonnie sat across from me, mumbling words with lots of consonants while pouring over Mayor Capshaw's records on her laptop. When Phoebe shuffled in, our eyes met but quickly disengaged. There was nothing like secrets to make life awkward. Moments later, Vinny joined us dressed in a suit and tie.

The hair on the back of my neck raised. "Where are you off to?"

"Nowhere." He sat at the table, stared into the side of the stainless-steel toaster, and adjusted the knot in his tie. "I'm filming some promotional videos for ACME. Testimonials and stuff. We can post them on social media and YouTube."

"Good call. Lots of deadheads there. How'd you come up with that idea?"

"Jimmy from Splatz." Vinny laughed. "He showed me the testimonial you did for him."

"Ah, yes. The one he wrote for me."

I grabbed my keys and headed for the door but stopped in my tracks when Nonnie let out a whoop.

"I founds it! Is important," she screamed slamming her hand on the table. "Come! Come sees!"

We gathered around her chair, eyes glued to the split screen on her laptop. "Sees this," she said, highlighting an out-of-state number in the mayor's phone records. "Number is for Danforths Security Vaults in Louisville, Kentuckys. Now sees this!" She underlined a $500 charge on one of Capshaw's credit cards from the vault company. "And now this." She pointed to the home screen of Danforth Security Vaults website and clicked their pricing tab. The annual fee for a large bank box was $500 on the nose.

"Holy shit!" I said, sinking into my chair with a smile. "This could be huge." I wrote the details on a sheet of paper to give to Rico the minute I hit the office. "Nonnie, you are the best!" I bussed her cheek and ran to the door, thinking about how lucky I was to have the most dedicated, computer-savvy, clean-freak, sensational Italian chef as ACME's office manager.

I hovered in the doorway and phoned Opie to give him the good news. Since the DA and the OSIU were working the misappropriated funds case, they'd want in on this. He agreed to meet us at Cap's office to review the proof.

"Nonnie, remind me to give you a raise someday," I said as I shot out the door, headed to the 51st. Maybe with Vinny's videos and a little luck, all three of us could get raises. Anything was possible. But I'd settle for snacks that weren't dog biscuits.

ONCE I MADE it past the yellow crime scene tape and into the precinct, I navigated the remaining piles of detritus and made a beeline to Rico's desk.

"Look at this," I whispered, showing him the details I'd jotted down. "I think Nonnie's on to something."

Rico pulled up the information on his laptop and grinned. "It's the best lead we've had yet. But we still need a warrant to get the evidence."

"Opie's on his way over."

I'd been so excited about Nonnie's news that I'd shoved Gadyen's existence into the back of my brain. It sucked to have such mind-bending news and not be able to share it with anyone other than Phoebe. But at least my partner and I could make Cap's day.

Rico downloaded the data onto a flash drive while I grabbed some coffee from the breakroom. We were so lucky no one got hurt, I thought, as I glanced out of the kitchenette at the aftermath of the explosion. Toussaint, Cain, and Giordano would pay for this, if it was the last thing I did. By the time I returned to Rico's desk, we'd been summoned to our Fearless Leader's office.

"Did you tell him about the vault?" I whispered, as we threaded through dusty the bullpen.

"No. It's about the bombing."

Cap's secretary of the week wasn't at her desk, so Rico rapped lightly on his door.

"Come in. Have a seat." Cap swiveled his computer monitor around. "Does this guy look familiar?"

He showed us the precinct's time-stamped security tape from shortly before the explosion. A man wearing a dark hoodie pulled tight around his face edged into frame. He bent over, careful not to show a full-face view, deposited something beneath the pink Caddy, then quickly walked away. The grainy video wasn't conclusive, but the subject fit Cain's general build.

Rico shrugged. "That looks like Giordano's guy, Cain."

"It looks like half the male population of Cincinnati," Cap said. "The FBI and ATF will have guys here within the hour. The more men involved in the search, the sooner we can start narrowing the field."

The light in his eyes was gone. He looked exhausted, nearly beaten. It tugged at my heart.

Rico slid his laptop data across Cap's desk. "Take a look, sir. I think we may have stumbled onto something big in the mayor's case."

Cap put on his cheaters and studied the data linking Capshaw to the out-of-state vault company. When he finished, a half-smile crept across his face. "This is some good work, De Palma."

"I...have to agree with you, sir." Rico's cheeks flushed.

Nonnie's face had surely flitted through his mind.

A rap on the doorway caused us to turn our heads. Cap's secretary, apparently back from her walkabout, popped her head inside. "Excuse me, Captain. Tim Andrews is here from the DA's office."

I scooted to the edge of my chair. "I called him, since he needed to see this too."

Cap's brow raised. "Wow, he got here quick.'

Rico and I exchanged glances.

"Send him in," Cap said. As the secretary walked away, Cap swiped a hand across his bald head. A win would take one case off his already crowded agenda. It wasn't much, but it was something.

"Tim," Cap said, rising to his feet and shaking hands with Opie.

"Good to see you, sir. I hear we have a first-class lead on the Mayor's misappropriated funds case."

While Cap, Rico, and Opie poured over the evidence, my thoughts returned to Wyco. He would die soon without that antidote. I didn't want that on my conscience. We needed one more shot at bringing him in.

"This is good stuff," Opie finally said. "Not enough to act on but email it to me. I'll share it with the Ohio Special Investigations Unit."

Rico handed him the flash drive. "Way ahead of you."

"I've got some news of my own," Opie added. "Depending on how it turns out, it might be help us put several cases to bed. Legal said Sarah Winston signed off on the release to raise Crickett Capshaw. Nighthawk, since you haven't retained counsel yet, there's a copy for you to sign, too."

Opie slapped the copy down in front of me. "It's pretty straight forward. It says you'll do everything humanly possible to avoid the use of disfiguring measures in putting Crickett down after the raising. That gives you some wiggle room if you need it. But you don't have to sign the form now if you want to hire your own counsel to review it first. That's your right."

Wiggle room notwithstanding, I had told Sarah I wouldn't blow her daughter's head off, and nothing any attorney could tell me would absolve me of that promise. I took a deep breath, signed the form, and handed it back.

"Additionally," Opie said, "We have permission to inquire about everything—her murder, the mayor's murder, and the missing funds case. Sarah wanted it done quickly, so she can inter Crickett sooner rather than later. Sooner is great for us too since her testimony can be included as circumstantial evidence in support of any search warrant requests. I'll call Doc Blanchard to see if we can set it up for this afternoon at the morgue. Let's shoot for two. That gives him time to move things around to avoid any accidental cross-contamination."

An image of a scarlet-faced Doc Blanchard, mouth open in a perpetual, silent scream passed before my eyes. I tried to banish it, but Blanchard's shrieks were so deeply embedded in my brain that nothing could erase them.

Cap grinned. "I'm sure Nighthawk would be willing to call Doc for you.'

"No, sir," I said, looking at Cap like he had lost his mind. "I think the request needs to come from the DA's office, since it's a joint task force investigation."

Opie, heading for the door, turned and fixed his eyes on me. "I'll let you know if the time changes; otherwise, be at the morgue by two. And no, worries. I'll let Doc know that City Council anticipates his full cooperation—and that Nighthawk will do everything humanly possible to avoid turning his morgue into the backdrop of a slasher movie."

Hilarious, Opie.

When things go sideways, raising the dead is like opening Pandora's box and then having to shove all the bad shit back inside. Dear God, I prayed as our meeting ended, I don't ask for much. But for once, can the bad shit just stay in the box?

43

WE'RE GOING TO BE DANCING SOON

We didn't have much time before the raising, but we intended to make it count. "What was the name of that place on Republic Street where Giordano's men took Vinny when they kidnapped him?"

Rico and I fell in step with each other as we left the precinct and headed for the car. "Something Tire,' he said. "Yeah, Troy Brothers' Tire. Maybe we should shake that tree and see if a Cain falls out."

Great minds think alike.

Enroute to OTR, my thoughts turned to Dallas's upcoming birthday. "What kind of decorations are you thinking for Dallas's party?"

Rico snorted. "A few empty beer bottles and a couple of shot glasses."

"Nonnie put you in charge, pal. Better be careful. You won't be her favorite anymore."

"Got any ideas?"

"Buy a pack of balloons and call it a day."

"Works for me," he said, merging onto the expressway.

I looked out the window and yawned. "It's a good thing we're into zombies because we suck at party planning."

Twenty minutes later, we arrived at Troy Brothers' Tire, a greasy, rundown hole in the wall with wired glass windows and a bullet hole in the door. A little seedy for a typical, respectable-looking mob front, which made it the perfect place.

We parked the SUV on the street and nosed around a bit on our way to the entrance. Worn-out tires with shitty tread and missing valve stems lined the outer walls of the building, but no new tires. And the place was quiet, way too quiet for a tire store. No pneumatic air guns, no music, no chatter, not even a mechanic.

A bell above the door jingled as we entered, announcing our arrival. Maybe ten Mississippis later, a muscle-bound guy in a suit came out from a room marked 'office' and closed the door behind him.

He placed his hands shoulder-width apart on the counter and eyed us. "Something I can help you with?"

"Hi there!" Rico's tone was light, but his smile was taut. "What if I said I wanted to buy a set of tires? I didn't see any new ones out there."

The guy's eyes grew dark. "I'd ask why an SUV with the sticker still on the window and government-issued plates needs new tires."

"Noticed that, did you?"

The suit nodded.

"Okay. New question," Rico said, pulling his badge. "What can you tell me about the bombing at the 51st precinct yesterday?"

A smaller guy came out of the office. When he closed the door behind him and sauntered to the counter, his suit coat bulged. This dude was packing.

"Hey, Paulie," the beefy guy said, "you know anything about a bombing yesterday?"

"I might have heard something about that on the news. What city was that in again?"

These mobbed-up, full-of-shit, game-playing suits were wasting my time.

"Where's Cain?" I asked, rounding the counter.

"Not so fast, honey." The big guy blocked me hard. "No warrant, no search."

Rico shook his head. "Sorry. Exigent circumstances. Stand aside."

The suits didn't move.

"What's so, ah, exigent you need back there?" the smaller guy asked.

"An antidote," I said.

"There's no antidote back there."

Rico brushed past them and opened the door. The stark white room held a small metal desk, a telephone, two chairs, a TV, and a closed-circuit monitor hanging in the corner, with views of the garage and lobby. Rico rummaged through the desk drawers and found a stack of blank invoices, envelopes, and a pen. He checked above the acoustic ceiling tiles. No Cain. No antidote. Nada.

A breeze wafted into the room, making the aluminum blinds clink together. The window was open and the screen lay on the floor. Cain had been there and taken off when we showed up.

The goons glanced at each other and shrugged.

Rico fixed them in a steely glare. "You should get that fixed. You wouldn't want any scumbags in here."

We'd been so close, damn it. It hurt to think Cain might have had the antidote on him.

I couldn't contain myself as we walked back to the lobby. "Tell Cain we'll dance soon, and to be sure to bring the antidote. Just him and me. Winner takes all." As we headed for the front door, I snatched a free hide-a-key box from a display rack.

Little suit slammed his hand on the counter. "Those are for the customers!"

"Tell Cain to come and get it," I snapped.

The heat of their stare followed us as we crossed the street to the SUV.

Rico climbed in and smacked the dashboard. "Fucking Cain. I knew he was in there."

Damn straight he was, hiding like a little bitch. But not for long. Mama had chosen this time to send Gadyen to me for a reason. We needed to be ready. Things would be coming to a head soon.

I could feel it.

"What were you thinking?" Cap yelled.

Rico's face blazed. "That Wyco is hours away from being put down like a dog unless he gets the antidote."

"And exigent circumstances was your ticket into that office?"

"Yes," Rico muttered from his shitty red visitor chair.

Cap threw up his hands. "You've been a detective for how many years? Explain how exigent circumstances applied to your situation at the tire store." He didn't give Rico a chance to answer. "Was there blood coming out from under the office door?"

"No."

"Was there a person in need of medical assistance?"

"Other than Wyco, no!" Rico snarled.

"What made you think the antidote was back there?"

"My gut."

"Well, as good as your gut is, it isn't enough."

"Cap, wait," I said. "I'm the one who moved behind the counter. They got nasty and—"

"Of course, they did. It's their shop, and you had no business back there. But this isn't on you. It's on Rico."

"Cain was there, damn it," Rico said. "He crawled out the window while those asshats stalled us in the lobby."

"You know this for a fact?"

"Why else would they work so hard to keep us from looking at an empty room? And why would the window screen be out, lying inside on the floor?"

Cap took a long, deep breath, wiped his face with his hands, and then checked his watch. "It's time to head to the morgue for Crickett's raising. I'll chat with Legal afterward. Maybe they can smooth things over with Giordano's counsel. He doesn't want a lawsuit; he wants to stop you from busting their chops with bullshit excuses."

Yeah, I thought, and Rico wants Wyco to live. Sometimes, none of us gets what we want.

THE RIDE to the morgue was quiet like several we'd shared lately, but this time I got the sense Rico was angry with himself, not me. That's as far as insight took me. I was impressed with myself for getting that far. Rather trying to be clever or beat around the bush, I tried a page out of Bab's playbook.

"Talk to me."

Rico's eyes didn't veer from traffic. He kept his hands at ten and two and stared straight ahead. Dear God. He was playing the silent game.

"I want to help," I said, "But I don't know how."

"Cap was right."

"That's it? That's all you have to say?"

"I consider you to be my equal, Nighthawk. But Cap's right. None of this falls on you. I'm the one with the badge. I rolled the dice, hoping we'd find the antidote. We didn't." He shrugged. "Tell you something else. If I had it to do all over again, needing to find that antidote? I wouldn't change a thing. Wyco's life is worth more than my badge."

I don't pretend to understand why, but my eyes welled up. Maybe it was his sincerity, or his willingness to sacrifice for the sake of someone else. Or maybe it was simply because he was the most decent, honorable man I'd ever known.

Kind of makes you feel like a shit heel, doesn't it? chided the brain bitch.

I could sit beside Rico and spout platitudes about what a great guy he was, but I wouldn't trust him with the biggest secret of my life—a fifty-five-pound Xolo who wanted to protect me just as much as he did.

Mama said that word of his existence could jeopardize us both. Rico would never hurt anyone I loved.

So why couldn't I bring myself to tell him?

44

A RUN FOR MY MONEY

Rico and I arrived at the morgue just before two and found Doc, Cap, and Opie waiting on us.

"Did you remember the chips?" Rico whispered as we walked through the door.

I was a zombie hunter, damn it. Of course, I remembered the chips.

Freshies like Crickett, once I raised her, eat anything from paper to mailboxes. But junk food gets them every time, and Lay's barbeque potato chips top the list. Scientists say the fat in processed foods activates a biter's taste for flesh. I say Lay's just taste good.

Doc folded his arms across his chest and shot me a death stare. Sometimes I wondered if, over time, my annoying presence had caused his brow to permanently furrow.

The autopsy suite was cold at 65° but not as cold as the walk-in. Subway-tile walls joined seamless resin-floors, both designed for easy sanitizing. Other than a single wrapped tray of sterile tools, a few plastic-covered machines, and the autopsy table holding Crickett Capshaw's body, the room was empty. Doc had outdone himself. Somehow, he'd managed to pile all the biters from the church on Freeman Avenue and the human body parts from the house on Exeter in his walk-in. Only God could think of a way for me to contaminate anything, and I wasn't about to ask Him.

Crickett, having only been dead for a few days, had been kept in cold storage. Under the fluorescent lights, she looked lifelike, as if she were sleeping and could open her eyes at any minute and wonder how she'd gotten here—until I filled her in.

Not that anyone ever asks but telling people they're dead sucks.

If all went smoothly when we finished questioning Crickett, I would lay her to rest by sticking my knife into her apricot, better known as the medulla oblongata. Once her brainstem bisected, she could never return as a card-carrying member of the zom-dead.

I repeat, *if.*

To increase those chances, I'd packed a pair of restraint straps in my knapsack. But Crickett's autopsy table had its own set of straps, one secured across her thighs and the other high across the top of her shoulders.

"Can we tilt the table up about 30° and slide the top strap down to her biceps?" I asked.

Doc frowned. "What's wrong with the strap placement?"

"I need more room to angle my Ka-Bar."

Doc harrumphed but made the adjustments.

"We can only do this once," I said, staring at the crisp white sheet covering Crickett. "Do you have your questions ready?"

Opie handed me a yellow legal sheet filled from top to bottom.

"That's a lot of questions," I said.

"Well, she's got information on three cases, so..."

It wasn't asking the questions that bothered me. It was keeping her controlled long enough to answer them all. But it didn't serve anyone to put Crickett through this and come away with less information than she could provide. It helped knowing her biter brain would lack the capacity to lie, so whatever she said would be the truth as she knew it.

Opie backed away from the table, joining Cap and Rico along the wall.

"Remember, no matter what happens," I said. "No guns unless I say so."

They each gave a solemn nod.

Since I'm left-handed, Doc planted himself beside me on the right side of the table—no doubt to oversee my actions in case things went pear-shaped.

The room went silent. I closed my eyes and channeled the mysterious God-given power that allows me to raise the dead. My fingers tingled and burned. The prickling sensation traveled into my palms, filling them with electric heat. I gathered my thoughts, then placed my hands over Crickett's body and felt the discharge of energy flowing from my essence into hers. A soft hum vibrated within me as millions of electrons arced through the air in tiny tendrils.

"Crickett Capshaw, in the name of God, I command you to rise!"

Nothing happened at first, but then, of all the things she could have done, she twitched. I should have known. Anyone as bitchy as she was in life was bound to give me a run for my money in death. We were in for a wild ride, but there was no backing out now.

I bent down and whispered in her ear, "Crickett Capshaw, rise."

A soft moan escaped her lips, but that was the extent of her cooperation.

Cruella the Corpse needed some motivation. I placed my hands on her chest and yelled. "Awaken!"

Crickett's eyes snapped open, wild and unfocused. She struggled against the restraints, but they held. This was the part about raising that I hated the most, watching the fear and confusion after I ripped the dead from their rest—no matter who they were or what I'd thought of them in life.

Crickett rocked from side to side beneath her restraints a few more times but then appeared to settle down and peer around the room. After taking it all in, she gazed up at me with a mixture of anger and resentment.

"Yoouuu," she whispered, dragging out the word in the same highbrow tone she'd used in life. The tone that was intended to make people feel lower than pond scum.

Back atcha, toots. "Crickett, do you know where you are?"

She started to shake her head but then stopped and glanced around again. "Am...Am I...dead?"

"Yes. I'm very sorry," I said truthfully, in spite her attitude. "You have passed on."

She looked more curious than afraid.

"Why am I...here?"

"We need to ask you some questions."

She nodded slowly.

"Crickett, how did your husband Eugene die?"

"Rich...murdered...him."

"Rich who?"

"Richard Blasnick."

A collective chatter rose behind me.

"And why did Rich murder Eugene?"

"For stolen...money, so we...could be...together."

So they were having an affair.

"What stolen money, Crickett?"

She rocked and shimmed, trying to break free of the straps.

"$300,000 Gene stole...from the city."

"Where is that money now?"

"Danforth...Safe deposit box...Louisville."

The whispers behind me sounded almost giddy.

"How did Rich murder Eugene?"

Crickett writhed beneath the straps. I was making her recall unpleasant things; besides, this Q and A session was entirely too long. She'd go batshit soon, if we weren't careful.

"He gave Gene a potassium...shot...said it was ...Vitamin B."

This question wouldn't sit well. "Do you remember how you died?"

Crickett grimaced and struggled beneath the restraints. "Richard!"

"What did Richard do?"

"Put peanut dust in...my blood pressure...pill."

"Why did he kill you?"

Crickett stared up at me and snarled. "Double crossed."

"Why?"

"Money...gambling debts...stole deposit box...key."

I turned to Opie with a silent shrug, and he gave me a thumbs up. We got everything out of her but the kitchen sink. It was time to let her go.

With all Crickett's rocking and writhing, she'd shimmied her body far enough down the table that the upper safety strap had worked its way to her neck. Her arms were free, and the displaced upper strap was too loose to keep her head in place. A bad combination—one that, despite my promise to Sarah, might make a clean ending for Crickett impossible.

I tried to hold her arms down, but freshies have incredible strength. I'd get one arm pinned and the other would pop loose. She wiggled and writhed, scooting further and further down the table, snapping her jaws at me. Her teeth came within a hair's breadth of my arm.

"Hold her!" I yelled, pulling my Ka-Bar.

Before anyone could move, Crickett dug her heels into the table and scooted even further down. Her head cleared the upper strap. She bolted upright, grabbed my knife hand and swiped the blade across my right forearm. The Ka-Bar fell from my left hand and clattered away on the floor.

Rico pulled his Glock and repositioned for a clear shot, but waited for me to give the word, while Cap scrambled after the knife. With one final push, Crickett slid out from beneath the bottom strap, dropped to the floor, and sprang to her feet, hissing like a feral cat.

"Don't shoot!" I yelled. "Doc, walk up behind me and hand me a scalpel."

Crickett snarled, as I took three steps back to create some space between us. I reached behind me and Doc slipped the blade into my hand.

"Opie," I called. "Toss me the chips from my knapsack."

"The *what?*"

"Just open the chip bag and hand it to me."

A dumbfounded Opie did as I asked. When Crickett's eyes zeroed in on the chips, it gave me the distraction I needed.

"Come and get 'em," I said, leaning forward, waving the bag in front of her face. "Bet your scrawny ass hasn't had a carb in ten years. Eat up, girl."

She reached out and wrapped her fingers around the chips but didn't take them from me. We stayed that way, locked in a tableau, eyes connected, hands, separated by inches, grasping different ends of a plastic bag, until she twitched a hideously dark smile.

Time froze as her features began to melt and morph, changing colors and shapes, until they settled into a face I hadn't expected to see. The sculpted cheekbones, ebony skin, and mesmeric smile took my breath away. Almond-shaped green eyes bored into mine, forming words inside my head.

"*Bonswa*, Little Bird. What's this—another corpse you've risen? Tsk, tsk. The dead belong to me. This battle of ours is exhausting. What say we end it?"

My telepathic response came quickly. "Name the place and time."

"Ault Park, at midnight. Your soul for my horde. Winner takes all. Weren't those the stakes you set for Cain?"

Toussaint laughed and then faded away, leaving me shaken. Crickett's facial features slowly settled back into place. Both of us were still holding the bag of chips. How long had Toussaint possession of her lasted?

I yanked my hand back as if the bag were infested and watched her shoved the chips into her mouth. She was oblivious to me but only for the moment.

My lungs ached. *Breathe...you just need to breathe.* My hands began to shake. I was losing my edge. *Get a grip.* Willing my hands to be still, I inched behind her and jabbed the scalpel into the base of her skull, then caught her in my arms, and carefully laid her on the morgue floor, with her body intact. A tiny one-inch wound marred the back of her neck where no one would see it.

I'd kept my promise to Sarah. But at what cost?

I swore right then and there, that not a single living soul would ever know what I had seen—or what I thought I'd seen. The uncertainty of it all was madness.

Get the fuck out of my head, you bastard!

"Nice work," Cap said, handing me back my knife. "You just solved three crimes and got City Council off my back. All we need now are search warrants on Blasnick."

Opie nodded. "I know a judge down in Louisville, a bass-fishing buddy of mine.

Between the physical evidence and Crickett's testimony, I'll coordinate with the OSI and have search warrants by lunchtime tomorrow." He looked at his watch. "I gotta run. I've got a three-thirty back at the office. Catch you all later," he said as he headed toward the door. But he stopped at the threshold, turned around, and left me with the only compliment he'd ever given me. "Well done, Nighthawk."

Rico eyed me. "You okay? You seem...off."

"It's nothing." My response sounded short, but I managed a thin smile and redirected his attention toward a couple of blood droplets on the floor. "Look, I didn't even trash the place."

"The day is young," Doc muttered, slapping a bandage on my lacerated forearm.

When Doc was finished, Rico pulled me aside for a private conversation. "A text came in while you were dealing with Crickett. The FBI and ATF investigators flew into CVG around one. Cap wants me to keep an eye on things, and those guys work until they drop. It's looking like an all-nighter."

I squeezed his hand discreetly. "No problem. I need some rest anyway. After a good night's sleep, I'll be good as new."

Rico stared into my eyes. "You were amazing. Call me if you need me."

The greatest guy in the world walked out of that morgue, and I felt sick inside. Rico loved me enough to die for me, but I had deliberately not told him about Toussaint's possession of Crickett during the raising. Why? It wasn't a matter of trust. Through thick and thin, no one had earned my trust more.

I loved my partner enough to die for him too—and far too much to put him in the crosshairs of a demon. The only way to protect Rico was to keep him in the dark about my midnight battle with Toussaint. But Mama Femi, my lifelong source of courage and protection, was dead. Who was left in my corner?

Mama's voice whispered from beyond. *Gadyen, Little Bird. Gadyen will always be in your corner.*

I hoped my beloved black Xolo was up to the task.

45

UNFINISHED BUSINESS

Nothing settled me like a ride on my Harley. The blue sky above and the hum of tires on the asphalt lulled me into a peace even Toussaint couldn't desecrate. Within that peace lay clarity. If this was my last day on Earth, I had unfinished business to address. Visiting my parents seemed like a good place to start.

Memories of my last visit to the cemetery surfaced. But on a cerulean day like this, without a cloud in the sky, what had happened that night seemed surreal. The memory of being thralled into nearly killing Rico made me even more certain that keeping him away from Toussaint was the right choice.

But was keeping him away really keeping him safe? Little Allie asked.

Who knew how far Toussaint's reach extended? Since the bastard had a track record of killing people I loved, keeping Rico out of sight and out of mind seemed the wiser choice.

Sitting in the fresh-mown grass between their graves, I imagined a telepathic conversation between us. I apologized for the ugliness of my last visit, which likely scared them half to death (in our imagined conversations, they were always very much alive.) After I shared the news about Mama's death, my mom laughed and assured me that her dearest friend was with her now. Talking about Rico felt awkward. He was the first 'boy' I'd ever mentioned to them, so that made sense.

They quieted at news of my upcoming showdown with Toussaint. Maybe they knew the outcome and didn't want to burden me. I thought I heard Mama shouting, trying to get through to me, but it drifted away in the void. I said my good-byes and told them I'd bring Phoebe next time…if there was a next time and then headed for my house.

Pulling into the driveway, it occurred to me that one-way conversations with dead people were easy to manipulate. The only sentiments were mine. Nonnie, on the other hand, was an emoting bundle of gelatinous goo who should be avoided until absolutely necessary. I reached for the backdoor knob, determined to skulk inside, quiet as a Ninja.

"Miss Allie!" Nonnie boomed, throwing open the door before I even touched it. "Whys you homes so early? Ares you sick?" She lay the back of her hand against my forehead. "You don'ts feel hots."

"I'm just tired," I said, sliding past her into the house. "Oh, Rico's stuck at work, so he won't be here for dinner. Why don't you take off with Dallas for the evening?"

She eyed me suspiciously. "What wrongs with you?"

There was no fooling Nonnie the Nose.

I gave her a wan smile. "A raising today didn't go so easy. I just want some sleep. Have a good night."

Silently thanking her for being the best Sicilian grandmother anyone ever had, I kissed her cheek a little longer than usual and then called Headbutt to follow me down the hallway to my bedroom. Shutting the door behind us, I swiped a tear from my eye before it fell. Damn it. Face-to-face goodbyes were not my style. Whatever else I had to say to Nonni or anyone else would be in written form.

Thankfully, Nonnie took my suggestion to heart. Within an hour, she knocked on my door and said, "Dallas and I goings to movies. Vinny goings to Blue Note to helps Tiffany. Will you cover birdses tonight?"

"Sure thing," I called through the door.

Moments later, when she drove off down the street, her Pinto wagon backfired loud enough to wake the dead. I returned to the kitchen, poured myself a doozey of a double Jack and diet and grabbed an unopened bag of Doritos. The best last meal I could imagine.

I pulled some stationery and envelopes from a box of Nonnie's ACME office supplies, plopped on my bed with Headbutt, and wrote letters to everyone in my life, Cap, Vinny, Phoebe, Wyco (in case a miracle happened,) and of course, Nonnie and Rico. The next time I looked up, the notes were finished, and it was dark outside.

Headbutt wanted a potty break and the birds needed to be covered. I walked outside with Headbutt to take a long, deep breath, hoping to catch the scent of Nonnie's roses. Turning around, I caught Evelyn Winstel staring at me from her deck. She sent a friendly wave that caught me off guard.

"Hi," she called. "I know Sid's being an ass about this, but I can't wait for these little mutant puppies. Can you imagine what they'll look like?"

Mutant puppies? My inclination was to return the wave with my middle finger, but I needed some good karma, so I waggled them all instead.

"No worries," I said, letting Headbutt scoot through the door ahead of me. "Sid's always an ass."

Evelyn chuckled. "I'll make sure he gets you a copy of the survey. Your fence was actually in our yard, but I told him to just rebuild it in place when the pool's finished."

Ha! After all these years, who knew? "Thanks, Evelyn," I said. "That'd be great."

The Avian Triumvirate harangued me for their nighttime treats when I stepped back into the kitchen, so I spent a few minutes cuddling them and asking them nicely not to literally eat me out of house and home.

They were probably stunned by all the affection.

I loaded my guns, gathered extra ammo, made sure my knife was in its sheath, and my boot blade was in tucked in place, and then remembered to put Phoebe's holy water in my jacket. After setting my alarm for eleven, I cuddled up beside Headbutt for a nap.

The next thing I knew, the alarm went off and Phoebe was standing at the foot of my bed in the darkness, staring at me.

"Something I can do for you, Pheebs?" I asked, squinting at her through one peeled, sleepy eye.

She didn't answer, so I turned on the light. She didn't even blink, just stood still as death, staring at me, as if she were lost in a fog.

I waved my hand in front of her face. "What's up, Phoebe?"

"It's in the fountain," she murmured, and then did an about-face, wandered out my door and down the hall to Vinny's room where she disappeared inside and closed the door.

That's odd, I thought. Vinny never mentioned she sleepwalks.

I splashed some water on my face, then snapped Gadyen's collar around my neck, and glanced at my reflection in the bathroom mirror. The collar looked natural there, almost like an extension of me.

After shoving Gadyen's whistle into my jacket pocket, I sat at the kitchen table and lit it a candle. Then I poured two cups of black coffee, a glass of rum, and grabbed some of Nonnie's hard candy as an afterthought. After placing everything on the tablecloth in front of me, along with Papa Legba's sigil and corncob pipe, I bowed my head and prayed as Mama had shown me years ago.

"Papa Legba, please open the gate between the human and the spirit worlds. Hear my plea. Accept these offerings and protect Gadyen and me tonight as we battle Toussaint Le Clerc. Please keep us from all harm. We are grateful for your righteous protection."

After my prayer service ended, I sipped one of the cups of coffee and mentally cataloged everyone and everything that held meaning in my life. After kissing Headbutt one last time, I hid the letters I'd written beneath my pillow, grabbed my jacket, and headed for Ault Park to pick a fight with a demon.

46

TAKING OUT THE TRASH

I roared down the expressway, deep in thought, letting the warm midnight wind wash over me. My mind was clear. I was laser-focused and thinking three moves ahead. Strategy was key.

Battles with Toussaint were never easy. The bastard salivated over the thought of destroying me, but for shits and giggles, he might let Cain have first crack at me.

Toussaint's minion was 6'0" and weighed a buck ninety. Ronnie at the bar had described him as a fifty-something ex-special-ops grunt. If that was true, he was bigger, stronger, and better trained than me.

On the other hand, I was half his age, so I should move faster and have quicker reflexes. Motivation and fear were in my favor, too. I'd come loaded for bear with Hawkeye and Baby, my ankle piece, extra ammo, a Ka-Bar knife, and a smaller boot blade. No doubt, Cain would be equally well armed. A betting man would put his money on Cain. Anyone who knew me would know better.

Toussaint 2.0 was another unknown in the equation. The powers he'd had in life were not the powers he would wield tonight. How much stronger was he now that he was a demon? That was anyone's guess. But if I lived to fight another day, I'd be thrilled to put a check in the 'W' column.

The abilities of Gadyen, my ace in the hole, were equally mysterious. The four-legged guardian sent by Mama should help level the playing field. But an instruction manual for my spirit-dog might have been helpful.

With all the uncertainties, this battle would be the mother of all crap shoots. By the time I arrived at Ault Park, the ambiguity was driving me crazy.

I killed the lights on the Lowrider, cut the ignition, and coasted to the curb on Observatory Avenue. Stashing my bike in the bushes seemed wise. A guy like Cain might have a scumbag or two on hand to complicate a hasty exit by cutting my gas line.

The wrought-iron gates at the entrance of the park were roughly ten feet tall and easy enough to scale. Once inside, I ducked off the entrance road into a copse of trees, looked up at the brilliant full moon, and realized that Toussaint hadn't mentioned the precise location of the battle.

The park was over two hundred and forty acres, filled with gardens, trails, and scenic views. The necromancer could be anywhere, but instinct pulled me toward the pavilion, the largest, most elegant structure in the park. The century-old, two-story pavilion featured a cascading waterfall nestled between twin stone stairways. The opulence alone would appeal to Toussaint. But more importantly, from a practical perspective, the pavilion was backlit against the night sky, making it visible from the asphalt loop throughout the park.

I switched on my flashlight and crept through the woods, feeling familiar, subtle changes inside me. Sweat raced down my back. My breathing grew shallow.

Settle down, I muttered, fighting the adrenaline. *Not yet. Just a little longer.*

A gruff voice broke the stillness. "Nighthawk, you came."

The hair on the back of my neck rose up.

Cain, thirty yards away, posed like a statue at the base of the pavilion, hands on his hips, head high. That body language alone told me that he had no fear of me.

Underestimate me at your own peril, dude.

No matter how strong Cain was, he was human. Using Gadyen to fight him would reveal my secret weapon too soon. The spirit Xolo needed to stay under wraps until my battle with Toussaint.

I drew Hawkeye, strode out from the tree line into the meadow in front of the pavilion, and closed the distance between Cain and me, with slow, measured steps. From the corner of my eye, I spotted his goons pacing me on either side.

My adrenaline surged.

Racing heart, check. Dry mouth, check, check. I visualized the placement of my weapons. All present and ready to rock. *Your breathing's too shallow. Focus.* Inhaling long and slow through my nose, I held each breath for a four-count and then exhaled. *Stop trembling.* I forced my quivering hands into fists.

Cain leaned against the balustrade of the pavilion staircase, now twenty feet way, looking as cool as a Mango Mai Tai. "Ooh-wee!" he cried. "Look at those hands shake. I thought Toussaint said you were tough."

"Tough enough."

The words had sounded stronger in my head.

"Listen to you, all piss and vinegar," Cain said. He laid a glass vial on the ledge of the fountain and threw me a wink. "You want this antidote? You're gonna have to fight for it."

"Count me in," I said, raising Hawkeye.

"Not so fast. We got rules, see. This here's a hand-to-hand fight. Toss your weapons."

"Not in this lifetime."

"Have it your way." Cain nodded to one of his goons.

The guy lunged and wrapped me from behind in a choke hold. It would have been impossible to get a clean shot off at that angle without hitting my own head or blowing out my eardrum. I dropped Hawkeye, grabbed hold of the guy's arms and leaned into him, then kicked up my legs and flung myself to the ground. He tumbled over the top of me. I scrambled away and rolled to my feet, with four nine millys bearing down on me.

"Toss your weapons, now," Cain snapped. "Including the one at your ankle and that pig sticker clipped to your belt."

So much for being loaded for bear. I kicked my weapons beside the stone stairway. Far enough to comply but not too far.

Cain circled to his left and fixed me in a stare that was as cold as death. "Now, isn't this nice? The two of us, fighting mano-a-mano. That reminds me, where is the partner of yours anyway?"

"Be glad he's not here," I said, syncing my movements with his. "Rico's still miffed about the landmine incident. Besides, if he were here to kick your ass, it'd ruin all my fun."

"You sure got a mouth on you. A pretty one at that."

Cain led with a jab. I blocked the brunt of it with my forearm. Then he sidestepped and swept me. I landed with a thud, biting my tongue. The coppery taste of blood filled my mouth. *Pretty quick for his age.*

Cain darted in and out, then launched a right hook. I ducked and countered with a shot to his ribs.

His gasp told me it was a decent shot.

He circled and shook it off, then bounced back and hurled a haymaker. I sidestepped and nailed his nose with a left cross, feeling the cartilage give beneath my fist. Blood poured down his face.

Cain's eyes blazed.

That's two punches in a row. Two more than he expected.

Even so, I'd given him my best, and I'd only succeeded in pissing him off.

We traded blow for blow and block for block until his snap kick drilled my shin.

I sprawled on the pavement, clenching my teeth. *Get up! Get up!* My breath came in spurts. I struggled to my feet and stared him down.

Cain laughed. "I stand corrected. You are a hellcat."

I circled slowly, trying to walk it off. He had seventy pounds on me. If he nailed me like that again, I might not get back up.

Fight dirty. Eyes, knees, throat, groin, anything to—

Cain spun in with an elbow, grazing my chin. He snatched my hair in a death grip. I grabbed his hand, turned in, and pile-drove my knee into his groin. His knees buckled. He doubled over and grabbed his crotch. "You little bitch!" He back peddled, sucking air, buying time to recover.

Control the fight.

I laughed out loud, mocking him, then lowered my guard and drew him in. He fired off a left hook. I blocked it with my left elbow and cracked his mouth with my right. His head flew back. Bits of tobacco-stained teeth littered the ground. He stumbled, stunned, and grabbed his bloodied face. I kicked him in the gut and doubled him over for the second time, then drove him to his knees with an elbow to the back of his head.

Cain let out a war cry and dropped me with a double-leg takedown, slamming my head to the pavement in front of the fountain.

Fireworks burst behind my eyes. He crawled on top of me, wrapped his hands around my neck and squeezed it like a vise. My vision started to fade.

Relax. Don't panic.

I shimmied my leg out from under him, reached inside my boot, and groped for my backup blade.

Target acquired.

"This is for Wyco, you son-of-a-bitch!" I buried the knife in Cain's heart.

"You fucking whore!" he muttered, then slowly closed his eyes, and went limp.

I rolled him off me and lay on the pavement, panting. The applause of a single pair of hands caught my ears.

"Well done! Well done! I thought he had you for a minute."

Despite my exhaustion, the adrenaline dump started all over again. Toussaint Le Clerc had arrived.

"Get lost," the necromancer said, waving off Cain's goon squad. "Your employer has been...liquidated."

Breathe. Four-count hold, release. Think.

I rolled to my feet and brushed myself off, furtively searching my jacket pocket for Gadyen's whistle—and found nothing. A second attempt ended the same. I shook my pants legs and sleeves, then scanned the ground around my feet. Nada.

"Problem?" asked Toussaint.

"No," I shrugged. *More like a catastrophe.*

After mentally retracing my steps, I was sure that I'd put the whistle in my right jacket pocket. The extra ammo was still in the opposite pocket where I remembered putting it. *What the hell?*

"Ahem." Toussaint tapped his foot. "I'm not interrupting anything, am I?"

Stall. Keep looking.

For the first time that night, I looked long and hard at the demon. He appeared normal, human even—solid, and three-dimensional. Nothing like what I'd expected. After Gadyen's spectacular transformation in my bedroom, he had looked normal too. Call me picky, but I found that disappointing and very anticlimactic. A return from the spirit world deserved bells and whistles.

I eyed Toussaint defiantly. "Shouldn't you be ten feet tall with red skin, blazing eyes, and horns?"

"Like this?" he asked.

In the blink of an eye, the bastard was everything I had described, but with insanely long arms that tapered into Grinch-like fingers tipped with gnarly black nails.

"Perfect," I deadpanned and returned my eyes to the ground. Cain and I had been fighting right there, in front of the steps of the pavilion near the fountain. Where could the whistle have gone?

The fountain! Phoebe's vision—she'd said, "It's in the fountain."

Oblivious to my epiphany, the demon tried to impress me by opening his jaws to impossible proportions and showing me the flames of hell. He extended one of his nasty claws to me with a sneer. "Come join me. It'll be hot, like old times."

"No thanks," I mumbled, backpedaling toward the illuminated waterfall. The whistle lay on the third step of the fountain not twenty feet away. The antidote, sitting on the stone ledge where Cain had left it, tempted me like Eve's apple.

All in good time. Annihilate the demon first.

I dashed for the fountain, leapt into the water, and grabbed the whistle off the step, then scampered back to the concrete walkway at the base.

Toussaint craned his neck and peered curiously at my hand. "New toy?"

"An old one," I said, wiping the whistle dry on my sleeve. *Blow it once and Gadyen will come to you. Blow it twice and he will assume spirit form to protect you against demons.* I raised the whistle to my lips and blew once. Its inlaid stones began to twinkle, and so did the stones in my collar.

"Nice light show. Shall we get on with it?" Toussaint snapped.

A luminous mist rose in the air. The particles swirled slowly at first, then faster, shooting outward and then rushing back together, over and over, until they assembled into the form of Gadyen. The Xolo sat tall at my feet, dark-skinned, regal-looking, head high, and ears peaked.

Toussaint's eyes narrowed. "Well, now. Who have we here?"

Gadyen locked eyes with him.

"Drawing a blank?" I asked.

Toussaint cocked his head. "Looks a bit like that mutt Mama gave you as a child. What was its name?"

"Gadyen," I said, blowing the whistle a second time. "He was one of Papa Legba's favorites. Remember? Legba gave him to Mama to protect me."

Toussaint sneered. "The mongrel's a bit dead for that now, isn't he?"

Gadyen growled and sprang into spirit mode, massive, more than three times his size and terrifying with huge, bared teeth and four-inch claws.

"I never did like that dog," the demon muttered.

"Yeah?" I said, pulling the flask of holy water from my jacket. "He never liked you either." I shook the flask at the demon. The blessed water sizzled when the droplets hit his skin, but overall, the results weren't what I'd hoped for. I'd have needed to drown him in it to disable him.

"Oh, you wicked little bitch!" he laughed, wincing. "Good for you. Didn't know you had it in you."

Toussaint raised a spindly claw from his side and jabbed it at me, hurling an electric-blue ball of energy toward my head. I snapped up my arm to block his attack and prepared to kiss my mortal ass goodbye. A martial arts block couldn't possibly ward off a magickal assault.

Yet, somehow, it did.

The stream of energy Toussaint heaved at me had bounced off my forearm and boomeranged back to him at twice its original speed. The incoming barrage burned a softball-sized hole through his scaley midsection. The charred edges of the void crackled, and the stink of singed demon hide filled the air.

Toussaint staggered back a few steps and joined me as we gaped at his hole in utter disbelief.

Hell, yeah! I thought. How did I do that? And how do I do it again?

The reasonable answer was that the combined powers of Gadyen and me were enough to knock a demon on its ass. As cool as that sounded, the theory unraveled when a pissed-off Toussaint regained his composure and morphed into a ten-foot-tall flaming torch. The walking bonfire came straight at me and spewed a stream of fire.

At the last second, I dove to my right. The flames seared my left calf as they shot past me. *Oh, shit, shit, shit. This hurts.* Tears welled in my eyes. I rolled clear, patting my leg to make sure nothing was still smoldering. From the corner of my eye, I saw Rico running toward me, yelling my name.

How can that be? He doesn't know I'm here. I closed my eyes to block out the chaos, and the answer came to me.

It isn't real. It's one of Toussaint's tricks.

Gadyen leapt into the flames and sank his jaws into Toussaint, pulling him away from me. The demon grappled with the Xolo, who appeared to be impervious to fire. In a flurry of movement, Toussaint wrapped his arms around my dog, lifted him up, threw him aside, then spun to me with a wicked grin, and said, "It's no trick, dear. Your man is standing right behind you."

I spun around, but Rico was gone. When I spun back, Toussaint had returned to his human form. He snapped his fingers with a laugh and created a containment square around Gadyen.

The fucking bastard had tricked me again.

Stop letting him into your head.

I crab crawled backward away from Toussaint as he sauntered over, planted his legs on either side of me, and looked down with hatred blazing in his eyes. "You weren't there when Mama died, but I was, Little Bird. She asked for you. I told her that you'd finally given up and joined me on the dark side— that you knew she was checking out and didn't care enough to say goodbye. That you said she was a demented, two-dollar-Hoodoo queen who just needed to die."

"You lie!" I leapt to my feet and grabbed him, then pulled my boot knife and went for his throat. The moment my hands touched him, his energy arced, infusing me with more power than any human could absorb. I sailed through the air and landed twenty feet away, gasping for air.

The fight wasn't going the way I'd planned.

Gadyen was imprisoned, while I was hallucinating and struggling to stay alive. Something had to change.

Maybe, I thought. Just maybe.

I scrambled back to my feet and stumbled into the fountain, drawing Toussaint with me. Gadyen, who'd been having a fit in his invisible cage, settled down. It was almost as if he knew what I had in mind—not that the demon was worried. He had plans of his own.

"What's that?" Toussaint said, holding his hand to his ear. "Is that a horde of biters I hear?"

Are you fucking kidding me? What next?

"You're such a loser," I snapped, plopping down into the water. "After all this. Your...big-ass hole," I said, pointing to his torso, "the flaming torch thing, and that blue energy ball. You're just going to run off like a scared, second-rate imp and let your deadheads finish the fight? You should be embarrassed."

Toussaint tilted his head and paused. "Perhaps you're right. Finishing you off myself would be a bit of poetic justice, wouldn't it? Besides, if I leave you to the deadheads, God knows how many you'll take out before they destroy you. You've killed off far too many as it is."

The fire returned to his eyes. He dismissed the approaching deadheads and then morphed into the massive, red-eyed hellhound I'd seen at Spring Grove Cemetery. A low growl hummed in his throat. For every stride forward he took, I climbed one step higher in the fountain. When all four of his gigantic paws were in the fountain, I pulled the blessed flask from my pocket and screwed off the cap.

Here goes nothing, I thought, staring down the beast. "What are the odds this holy water will consecrate the entire fountain?"

The hellhound's red eyes widened.

"Let's find out," I said, launching myself through the air and dumping the entire bottle into the fountain. Landing squarely on his back, I knocked the demon flat and immersed his entire body in the sacred water.

Toussaint let out a long, torturous scream as his leathery hide began to sizzle and stink. Gadyen's invisible fence instantly collapsed. My courageous Xolo bounded into the fountain and jumped on Toussaint to keep him submerged.

When the demon's flesh was more holes than hide, Gadyen leapt out of the fountain and into my arms, giving me a lifetime's worth of kisses. His skin looked a little singed, but nothing a spirit dog couldn't recover from. He sat quietly in my lap for a bit, and we cuddled like we used to when I was a kid. But we both knew his time here was short and he needed to return across the void until I needed him again. As sad as it made me, I blew his whistle three times.

"You think you could take out the trash for me?" I asked, nodding to the crumpled husk of Toussaint floating in the fountain. Gadyen jumped back into the water, grabbed him by the scruff of his neck, and then loped across the park, where they disappeared into the misty moonlight on their way to the gates of Hell.

I lay back on the grass, breathing in the night air, thinking about Mama, knowing Toussaint had lied about being at her side when she died but still feeling the sting of the horrible things he'd said. A voice caught me by surprise.

"Nighthawk, is that you?"

Rico jogged to my side, dropped to his knee, and kissed me. "Where the hell have you been? You had me worried sick."

"Just...getting rid of a little trash."

"Damn it, Allie. You came after Cain alone."

"He won't bother us again," I said, nodding to his corpse. "Although we might run into some biters wandering around."

"What about Toussaint?"

"How did you know I was here?" I asked, avoiding his question.

"When I got home and you weren't there, I knocked on Vinny's door. Phoebe said she had a dream you might be here. Crazy, huh? I think she might really be a psychic."

"You know," I said, kissing him long and hard, "I think so, too."

47

THERE'S ALWAYS
MORE TO THE STORY

Someone (Dallas) had the great idea of turning his birthday party into fifty-cent wing night. A customer-oriented sales promotion, he called it. A royal pain in my ass was closer to the truth. The bar was standing room only and the jukebox was so loud the fillings in my teeth rattled. Those of us on the employee replacement roster struggled with our assignments.

Nonnie poured pasta into the wing sauce. I broke a tray of glasses behind the bar and Tiffany Swarosvski lost a talon on someone's chili. When the customers began to grouse, Dallas slipped back into the kitchen to lend a hand, and I begged Vinny to bail me out behind the bar. Phoebe played Jack of all trades—everything from barback to restroom upkeep to washing dishes. Rico's plan to decorate The Blue Note with his empty beer bottles and dirty shot glasses was a rousing success. Lucky for him, Nonnie was too busy to notice.

Cap and Opie huddled at the corner of the bar where Harry used to sit. My ghostly partner had been absent since I watched him walk into the light, but it would be great if, from time to time, he could visit and hang with his gang from the 51st. Even Doc Blanchard, minus his perpetual frown, dropped by for a drink or two. Why not? Everyone connected to the mayor's cases was due a little R&R.

Vinny and I worked side by side, filling drink orders. When we finally had time to take a breath, he leaned in and shouted over the music, "I got to thinking about the Headbutt/Princess paternity fiasco, so I checked out the Ring camera videos. Get this—Headbutt didn't trespass onto the Winstel's property and attack their little Princess. She tunneled out beneath the fence, sashayed into our yard, and did everything but slide down a stripper pole in front of Headbutt."

"Yes!" I shouted, giving Vinny a high five. "Wait till Sid gets a load of that video."

"Yeah, he's a trip. But the puppies will be cute, huh?"

Don't say it, Vinny. Don't say it.

"Nonnie wants to keep one, you know."

Damn it. I said don't say that. "Bite your tongue, Vinny."

That was just what I needed, another mouth to feed. On the flip side, the Avian Triumvirate might slow its bid for dominance if another walking hairball took up residence. Call it a balance of power.

Just as the crowd began to thin, Wycowski sauntered in the door, drawing a standing O from the gang. I joined in and added a two-finger whistle. The prehistoric gumshoe, tougher than rawhide and too mean to die, was the last of his breed. The kind of guy you'd never count out...until you had to.

The longer I had chased the antidote he needed, the more elusive it became, and Wyco's time ticked from days down to hours. Once I wrapped my fingers around the vial, every second of the drive from Ault Park to Christ Hospital had seemed like an eternity.

Had Wyco's life expectancy dwindled from hours down to minutes, or from minutes to seconds, by the time the antidote was administered? Who could say? The old fart may think he knows how close he came to meeting his Maker, but he'll never know that my Ka-Bar was hidden beneath my t-shirt in case I arrived too late to save him.

In honor of his appearance, I took a break to join the gang on the other side of the bar. Cap, who had reasons of his own to celebrate, was working on his third beer. He looked more relaxed than I had seen him in a long while, as if a weight had been lifted from his shoulders. With the zombie attacks over and the mayor-connected cases were winding down, City Hall might finally get off his back.

"Do you think he's gone now?" Cap asked. He was referring to Toussaint. The demon necromancer had been a thorn in his side since I worked my first case with CPD and would continue to be as long as Cincinnati was my home.

I swirled my glass of Jack and smiled. "So you believe me, about him being a demon?"

"Cain and the Giordano's don't have the smarts to manufacture viruses without somebody's help. Toussaint's been the only game in town since day one. Who else could it be?"

"Eternity is on his side, Cap. He's biding his time now, trolling for some new version of Cain to do his bidding. There will always be another Cain...and another attack." I took a sip and paused. "Maybe it's time I move on."

Cap raised his brow. "Why? What would that solve?"

"Cincinnati isn't exactly the biter capital of the world. The only reason Toussaint targets this town is because I'm here. If I leave, he'll follow me, and he'll stop ramping up the city's biter population."

"Look at the big picture," Cap said, tipping his beer. "At least if you're here, you know where he'll strike. And the sooner you derail his attacks, the better off everyone will be."

I was glad Cap felt that way. Leaving the city would be hard. Cincinnati and its people, especially Rico, were part of me.

After glancing around to make sure no one was looking, Cap leaned into the group and kept his voice low. "Since we helped OSIU with the misappropriated funds case, they've agreed to keep an eye on Blasnick for the next couple of days until we're ready to charge him with Crickett's murder. Wouldn't want him bugging out before we have the evidence to back up her testimony from beyond the grave."

Doc Blanchard grabbed a handful of bar nuts. "I put a stat order on her lab work, and it came back today. Her blood pressure pills were positive for trace amounts of peanut dust. I'll let you know when the DNA results from the pill bottle come back. Sorry, I can't help you much with the mayor's murder. It's too late to test his remains for potassium poisoning."

Thank God. The thought of exhuming his body again made my eye twitch.

"I'm not giving up just yet," Opie said, setting his glass of Guinness on the bar. "Normally we wouldn't charge Blasnick for the Mayor's murder without physical evidence, but since the missing funds case, Crickett's poisoning, and the Mayor's murder are all connected, I think we may have an argument. Either way, Blasnick will be going away for a long time."

High fives traveled around our little corner of the bar.

"Oh," Opie said, taking a sip of his ale, "I almost forgot. OSIU processed the search and seizure warrant for the safe deposit box at Danforth Vault today. I sent one of the assistant DAs to Louisville to check it out. She said the box contained $300,000 on the nose. The money is on its way back, and an arrest warrant will be issued in the morning."

"Son of a bitch." Cap laughed. "No wonder they was so willing to babysit Blasnick for us. Now that the money turned up, they need eyes on him anyway until we can get him for the murder."

While Rico ordered another round, Opie pulled me aside. "Word to the wise. Eric Burklander is dropping Crickett Capshaws' mental anguish suit against you and the city. He could have let it play out, but given her role in her husband's murder, she wasn't exactly a credible claimant. And her mother, Sarah, didn't want any part of a recovery. So, congratulations. You're officially off the hook."

That was the best news of the night. Rico got so excited, he leaned over and kissed me in front of God and everybody.

"I didn't see that," Cap said, shielding his eyes as he climbed off his barstool to leave. "And I don't want to see it ever again. But it's about damn time!"

Huh. Rico and I mustn't have been as discreet as we thought.

Not too much later, the bar ran out of chicken wings and the crowd dwindled to nothing. Since it was Dallas's birthday, I told him that Tiffany and I would close up shop. My old jailhouse buddy issued a loud harrumph and tapped one of her flaming red claws on the bar.

"Speak for yourself, sister."

"Give it up, girlfriend," I said, risking bodily injury by punching her shoulder. "You ain't going nowhere."

Her eyes burned holes through me as she disappeared into the kitchen with a tray of dirty dishes. A hinky feeling snaked up my spine. Within seconds, the muffled sound of the back-door opening and closing reached my ears. Son of a biscuit eater! She was a proven flight risk, and I'd let her out of my sight. It wasn't that bad, I thought, walking into the kitchen to fill the sink.

Washing dishes gave me some time to consider everything that happened at the park with Cain and Toussaint. Cain was the easy part of that equation. He was dead. In a him-or-me scenario, I was willing to bet on me—even though he was an ex-special forces grunt. I wouldn't lose a minute's sleep over killing him, either. He was the bastard who picked the fight, I just ended it.

Toussaint 2.0, on the other hand, had proven his necromancy powers hadn't died with his human body. As a demon, he created a new reality from which there would be no escape. I could never again be just a corpse whisperer; from now on, I'd have to be a demon hunter too.

Let the games begin, I thought. At least I'd have Gadyen by my side.

On that sobering note, I gave up on the dishes and emerged from the kitchen, weary but accepting that my role in the world had changed. Dallas and Nonnie, looking happy but exhausted, decided to call it a night. Vinny announced that he and Phoebe, the last customers of the evening, were leaving too. Gel Boy had struck gold when he reeled that girl in.

Phoebe and I had shared an incredible secret and a unique bond over Gadyen. I owed her, and not just for her silence. Without her psychic vision on the night I battled Toussaint, I likely wouldn't have been around to celebrate Dallas's birthday. I strolled up beside her as she and Vinny walked to the door, and whispered in her ear, "Thanks for...you know."

"Whatever are you talking about?" she said with a wink.

I hovered in the doorway, as they disappeared arm-in-arm into the night, wishing that I hadn't kept Gadyen's existence a secret from Rico, and that I had told him I was going to Ault Park to battle it out with Toussaint. Instead, I'd lied to myself, saying that I didn't want him there because he might get hurt. What did he know about fighting demons? But the truth was that with all of Toussaint's mind games and the self-doubt they created, I was worried Rico wouldn't believe that Gadyen was real.

It sucked to admit I hadn't trust the man I loved. He deserved better.

Rico had grown since the day we met, when he labeled my ability to raise the dead 'freaky Voodoo shit.' I'd grown a little myself, too. Earlier in the day, I called Babs to chat, because despite popular opinion (mine), I'm not as invincible as I thought.

I hadn't told Rico about that call either.

"Help me with the dishes?" I asked, trying to ignore the guilt that pricked like a straight pin to the heart.

"I'd do anything for you," Rico said, wrapping his arms around me and kissing my neck. "Even dishes."

What are you waiting for? the brain bitch shouted. *No more secrets, no more half-truths, no more lies of omission. This is the guy. The ONE. Show him that you love him! Do the one thing he knows is hard for you. Trust him.*

"I, ah...I did run into Toussaint at Ault Park. We kind of had it out. I'm sorry I didn't tell you that night. It's a whole big thing. Can we talk about it later?"

Rico looked a little wounded at first but then chuckled. "I was pretty sure there was more to that story."

"Oh, and I talked to Babs today," I said, soaping up a beer mug and praying I wasn't about to make the biggest mistakes of my life. "She's coming in town next week to chat about my episode at the tunnel."

Rico leaned over and kissed my head. "Look at you, all sharing and stuff. I'm proud of you, babe."

I hope you still feel that way in a couple of minutes. "Yeah? I'm proud of you, too. The way you believed me when I told you Toussaint came back from the dead."

Rico nodded. "That was, ah...That was tough to wrap my head around."

"Completely understandable," I said, gazing into his beautiful brown eyes. "Now, from one to ten, using that same tough-to-wrap-your-head-around scale, "where would you rank a supernatural demon-fighting dog?

ACKNOWLEDGMENTS

Lisa Morton, without your encouragement and guidance, I never would have wandered down the path of novel writing. Thank you for your generosity and time.

Christiana Miller, you took a chance on Allie Nighthawk, and you have been my friend and ally ever since. May fate be as kind to you as you have been to me.

Bryan Prince, Valerie Williams, Tom Deady, Mike Deady, Larry Hinkle, Terry Emery, and Ken Godfrey you guys elevate my writing without fail. Thanks for the love.

Greg Laird, you were my jack-of-all-trades. Thanks for answering your phone.

Ashley Logan, you have been my faithful Creole interpreter throughout the series. Thanks for hanging with me and helping my characters come to life.

Scott Burdick, you are my go-to weapons dude. Thanks for stepping into your dad's shoes. You rock!

ABOUT THE AUTHOR

H.R. Boldwood, an Imadjinn Award finalist, is the author of the Corpse Whisperer series, urban fantasy, mystery/thriller novels, and countless short stories. In another incarnation, Boldwood is a Pushcart Prize nominee and winner of the Thomas More College Bilbo Award for Creative Writing. Boldwood's characters are often disreputable and not to be trusted. They are kicked to the publication curb at every conceivable opportunity. This author takes no responsibility for the dastardly and sometimes criminal acts committed by this ragtag group of miscreants.

Boldwood's works are available in Kindle and in print wherever quality books are sold.

Sign up for H.R.'s Rotter Blotter Newsletter at: https://hrboldwood.substack.com/.

To contact H.R. or to learn more about her work, visit:
www.hrboldwood.com
hrboldwood@gmail.com

ALSO BY H.R. BOLDWOOD

A small press bound by the belief that every voice matters.

Sign up for our newsletter to learn about new releases and more.
https://oliver-heberbooks.com/subscribe/

Follow us on social media:

facebook.com/oliverheberbooks

instagram.com/oliverheberbooks

amazon.com/oliverheberbooks

youtube.com/@OliverHeberBooksPublisher

9 798900 430874